THE BRUTUS LIE

A COLD WAR NOVEL

JOHN J. GOBBELL

Severn River Publishing
www.SevernRiverBooks.com

This is a work of fiction. Names, characters, businesses, places, events and incidents are either the products of the author's imagination or used in a fictitious manner. Any resemblance to actual persons, living or dead, or actual events is purely coincidental.

ISBN: 978-1-64875-530-9 (Paperback)

ALSO BY JOHN J. GOBBELL

The Todd Ingram Series

The Last Lieutenant

A Code For Tomorrow

When Duty Whispers Low

The Neptune Strategy

Edge of Valor

Dead Man Launch

Somewhere in the South Pacific

Other Books

A Call to Colors

The Brutus Lie

Never miss a new release! Sign up to receive exclusive updates from author John J. Gobbell.

severnriverbooks.com/authors/john-gobbell

To Janine

PREFACE

Technical liberties in this book are based on available systems. For example, fuel cells have been used for electrical power sources on U.S. spacecraft for many years. Now, these air independent propulsion systems (AIP) are becoming operational on foreign submarines, the German Navy's being the most notable. The hydrogen peroxide fuel cell system is being evaluated by the U.S. Navy as an alternative for submarine and unmanned underwater vehicle propulsion.

Benefits gained by the United States via Ivy Bells, a 1980s U.S. naval submarine intelligence operation in the Sea of Okhotsk, were lost through the traitor Ronald Pelton who was an analyst for the National Security Agency. The submarine base in Petropavlovsk, on the Pacific side of Siberia's Kamchatka Peninsula, and the Baikonur Cosmodrome in the south central Kazakhstan are actual Russian bases – see chart..

Scenes in Sweden and Libya are portrayals of real episodes, the latter being the most prominent. In particular, the incident in the Eastern Mediterranean is a dramatization of events that took place with disturbing regularity between U.S. and ex-Soviet warships worldwide. The two navys gathered around the table in the early 1970s realizing life and property had been risked needlessly. The Incidents at Sea Agreement (IncSea) adopted in 1972, put aside the nonsense of taunting one another's ships and saving face under convoluted interpretations of nautical rules of the road: one laborious step toward ending a fifty year cold war. Unfortunately, we now see these hideous incidents re-occuring between men-of-war of these competing navys. Once again, tensions are escalated. Who knows where it will end?

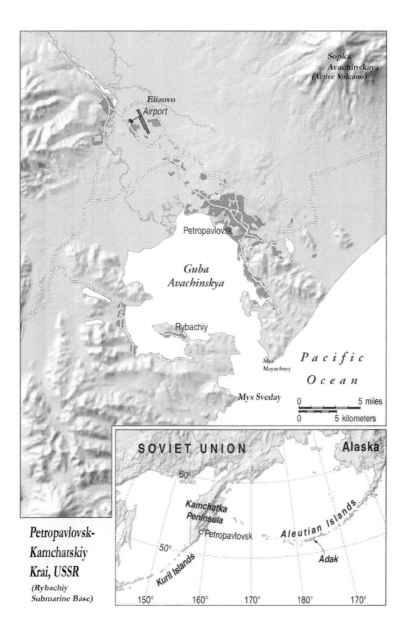

Sopka
Avachinskaya
(Active Volcano)

Elizovo
Airport

Petropavlovsk

Guba
Avachinskya

Rybachiy

Mys
Mayachnyy

P a c i f i c

O c e a n

Mys Sveday

0   5 miles

0   5 kilometers

Petropavlovsk-
Kamchatskiy
Krai, USSR

(Rybachiy
Submarine Base)

SOVIET UNION   Alaska

60

Kamchatka
Peninsula
    Petropavlovsk   *Aleutian Islands*

50°   Adak

Kuril Islands

150°   160°   170°   180°   170°

CAST OF CHARACTERS

AMERICANS

Brad Lofton -- (Ernst Lubeck) Former SEAL, naval architect. On loan as Program manager to Dr. Felix RBenkin of NSC to build the minisubmarine *X-3*, nicknamed, *Brutus*.

Lieutenant Commander Lester T. Thatcher, USN -- *X-3* skipper.

Bonnie Duffield -- Sales staff at Butler Engineering.

Howard Butler -- Bonnie's father, President Butler Engineering.

Walter Kirby, M.D. -- Former-SEAL, Lofton's friend, orthopedic surgeon.

Dr. Felix Renkin -- Director of Congressional Liaison, codenamed National Security Council. In charge *X-3* project; Lofton's temporary boss. Codenamed MAXIMUM EBB

Ted Carrington – Former CIA, Renkin's assistant and body guard.

SOVIETS

Lieutenant Colonel Anton Dobrynyn -- (Manfried Lubeck) Member of elite *Spetsnaz*, attached to the *Voyenno Morskoy Flot*, The Soviet Navy. Educated as naval architect.

Master Sergeant, Josef Ullanov -- Dobrynyn's *Spetsnaz* adjutant.

Captain Second Rank Vladimir Zuleyev -- Skipper Soviet (NATO desig. Whiskey Class) Submarine *PL 673* on Karlskrona, Sweden recon mission.

Captain Third Rank Pyotr Kapultichev -- PL 673'S *zampolit*, political officer.

Captain Second Rank Yuri Borodine -- "Cultural Attache," Soviet Embassy, Washington D.C., undercover agent for Red Banner Pacific Fleet Intelligence, Fifth Division. Codenamed SPILLOVER

Dr. Gregor Sadka -- Psychopharmacologist attached to the KGB with the rank of colonel.

OTHER

Katsunori Nagamatsu -- Posing as mate aboard Japanese pelagic fishing vessel, *Kunashiri Maru*; Codenamed PARALLAX in reality, is a CIA agent responsible for extracting PITCHFORK.

CAPTOR Mine. enCAPsulated TORpedo. Laid as a mine by air or submarine. A mark 46 homing torpedo swims from its capsule when a programmed target is detected and attacks.

PITCHFORK -- Soviet signals officer in Petropavlovsk on the Kamchatka Peninsula. Wants to defect to the U.S..

IVY BELLS -- U.S. submarine covert operation on Sea of Okhotsk seabed listening to Soviet cable traffic from Kamchatka Peninsula to the Siberian mainland.

JET STREAM -- Soviet disinformation project to counter IVY BELLS.

Sow a thought, and you reap an act;
Sow an act, and you reap a habit;
Sow a habit, and you reap a character
Sow a character, and you reap
destiny.

- Anonymous

PROLOGUE

Berlin, 1951

Wrecked buildings, now reduced to neatly piled rubble, stood as mountainous graveyard sentries to terrible days past and lay ready for legions of trucks to haul away in the spring. Here and there new buildings rose sporadically, gleaming in an otherwise decayed landscape. Two weeks ago, they repaired the leaky six-inch water main on Kreuzberg Strasse and the overturned, burnedout trolley car had been dragged away from the front of Anna Lubeck's two-room flat.

Anna pushed her perambulator and pulled her scarf tighter. No matter how much she withdrew herself, the wind still found fissures to spin through her army greatcoat and graze her flesh.

Her twin babies were well bundled beneath olive-drab U.S. Army blankets, their bodies tiny motionless mounds. Only condensation, occasionally escaping from small airways Anna had made, showed they were breathing. But Anna could tell if something was wrong. When one cried, the other would join in, making the clamor unbearable until Anna took care of whatever was wrong. And when one was silent, the other would stir. Their names were Ernst and Manfried, named after her father and older brother, who were killed on the Eastern Front, and today the babies were running temperatures. Anna was afraid they had measles and hoped Steiger, the pharmacist, had what they needed.

The perambulator's wheels squeaked as she walked in the uncommonly dry, subzero temperature, each step an effort. The wind swirled dust from the rubble, coating her with a gray, hoary cast. Anna wished the water main were still broken, for then stagnant pools and slush would help soak up the grime and carry it off. Checking the sky, she prayed for snow. Darker clouds roiled to the northwest. Maybe they would bring enough moisture to hold down the grit.

She was surprised to see the three-quarter ton lorry rumble past and stop in a small whirlwind before a new building. She'd been used to these lorries in the old days, a constant reminder of the Allied bombing and the last, grisly Russian artillery barrage in 1945 before they took Berlin. Then, Anna had lived in the subway for three weeks while death rained above, the same death that stole her mother. Anna fought starvation for three months until finally the four powers occupied the city.

From the corner of her eye Anna saw two British soldiers jump from the lorry. Three other soldiers, two Americans and a Soviet, climbed out the back and dropped the tailgate. Anna paid no attention as the three catcalled to her while they set up their apparatus and stamped their feet on the hard ground. Soldiers had been kind to her years ago but now, at twenty-two, she was no longer a spindly child begging for food. The handouts weren't gratuitous. Now there was a price Anna didn't always want to pay.

"Brew up and get on with the bloody job," the British Sergeant spoke sharply to his men.

Anna longed for the warmth of the fire they were sure to build; she'd watched them before; she knew them. Two weeks ago, the British had set up their equipment a block away and the same two Americans and the Soviet had been along. They'd made real coffee. She remembered smelling and seeing it percolate when she walked by. Maybe they would make it again. She could have all she wanted, she knew.

If.

Anna was slender, with long ebony hair, high broad cheekbones, and an inviting smile when she chose to deliver it, especially when she tilted her head. Customers, mostly enlisted men always argued over her as she swayed through the Gasthaus serving beer. Some of them liked her smile, others her eyes, engaging and intelligent. Anna had used both as her customers boomed their songs and pounded their tankards; she would brush her hip against the one or two she favored for the evening. Later, in the upstairs hallway, a bargain would be struck and Anna would submit to yet another soldier's will while the party roared in the basement.

Anna's bargains became more profitable one evening when a client revealed himself as a Russian NKVD agent. If she passed along what she heard, he told her, she could feed and clothe herself properly. Her earnings doubled when the Russians took the room next door, setting up cameras and microphones. It was a good arrangement, especially when a young naval ensign came into the Gasthaus. His withdrawn, understated bearing struck Anna as something that would be of interest to her Russian contact. When, without protest, the thin American allowed bellowing sergeants and privates to shove him into a corner, Anna knew the man had potential. He sat alone at his table. Anna delivered her steins, then found time to linger before him: Finally he mustered his courage, posed the question in fluent, formal German, and they went upstairs.

He told her his name was Felix and he returned the next day. As they rested between their lovemaking, she learned he was a London-based courier whose route took him through Berlin every week or so. He'd spoken loud enough so the microphones picked up every word.

He seemed intelligent and he was considerate, unlike those animals in the Gasthaus basement. Ten days later she allowed him to come to her flat, where she gave him carefree evenings over the next six weeks. The NKVD didn't like it, but when she skipped her period and discussed that with her control, the man looked pleased.

Two weeks later the American almost broke her door down. The NKVD had shown him sixteen grainy pictures of himself and, far more incriminating, played wire recordings, which they threatened to turn over to his commanding officer. They might also send a packet of photos to his parents in Ohio. The American gave in and did as they asked and were bound to ask again: He turned over his courier pouches for photographing. And they'd said he had made Anna pregnant. Was this true? Felix demanded. When Anna nodded he walked out, shaking his head.

Two weeks later, Anna's control told her Felix had arranged a transfer to Japan. Wasn't that typical of Americans, the NKVD man had asked, that Felix didn't love her and hadn't given a second thought about fathering her child? And that he liked the idea of making NKVD money, for they had promised him money as well, as much as she did?

Anna returned to waiting on tables at the Gasthaus, and gave birth to identical twin boys in that terrible winter of 1950, a year after the blockade. But she no longer wanted to work for the NKVD, making do with her wages and tips. Now she was applying for a job in the new hospital commissary, where the pay would be a little better and the hours more reasonable. The hospital even provided a workers' nursery.

Anna edged past as the soldiers dispersed around the new building. They were good, she knew, part of a crack British team; their lorry said simply *Bomb Disposal.* The two Americans and the Soviet occasionally worked with them, some sort of exchange agreement, she'd heard. She avoided their eyes as they grinned at her. And having Ernst and Manfried along helped. Otherwise, the soldiers would have been more demanding. Or insulting.

She sniffed. A wonderful aroma. The American *had* brought coffee. She shook her head, trying to forget it, and wondered which of the limeys she'd taken on long ago. The sergeant, Phipps, she thought, as she wrapped tighter and pushed the perambulator.

She was moving faster down Kreuzberg Strasse. Wind shoved her around the corner to Steiger's Apotheker.

"I think the boys have measles," she mumbled to the bespectacled, thin-haired man behind the counter. One of the twins, Manfried, gave a small cough. His timing was perfect.

The druggist was unmoved; his lips were pressed together, his hand firmly clutched the medicine as he watched her push two coins across the counter.

She hesitated and raised her brow.

The druggist kept his hand out.

Anna fumbled in her purse. "No eggs for two weeks," she said.

Steiger's hand stayed out.

Anna forced a smile, "No milk for my babies, either."

Steiger's hand was steadfast, his elbow locked.

Anna sighed, then nudged the rest of the coins toward Steiger's expectant claw. She had no time to argue. Ernst and Manfried needed the medicine.

She stepped outside. Steiger's thermometer, a luxury, registered five below and the bitter Nordic wind made it colder. She tightened her scarf, hunched her shoulders, and pushed the carriage around the corner to a gale like blast. Shivering, she bent as Ernst's blanket lifted and tucked it tightly. The wind tore at her; she pushed hard. Two blocks of this. Each winter she thought she would get used to it but she never did stop hating it.

Ahead, she saw two fires, inviting orangered beacons about thirty meters apart. She walked to the nearest one at the lorry's tailgate. The wind lessened behind it, and she eased the perambulator over the curb. With nods, the two Americans made room for her as they beat their arms against their chests. A five gallon can, holes punched in the side, sand, kerosene; it felt wonderful. She pushed the perambulator close to the blaze and held out her hands, knowing Ernst and Manfried would be warmed, too.

The American corporal next to her was bareheaded and wearing headphones. He raised a steaming mug to his lips and gulped. Seeing Anna's eyes fixed on his mug, he asked in awkward German, "Coffee ma'am?"

Anna saw his gold wedding band and relaxed, "*Bitte.*"

An American sergeant stood next to the Soviet. She pretended not to understand when he said, "She's a whore, Lofton. Give her a pound of coffee and you can have all you want for a whole year."

"Rattick, You sonofabitch." The corporal nodded to the next fire. "Go over there and get her a cup of coffee."

"I ain't carrying for no kraut whore. And we can't leave anyway."

"Hell, they just said they were done."

The Soviet, wearing a heavy coat and fur cap, stooped and poked a finger in Manfried's blanket. Before she could stop him she heard Manfried goo and cackle. The Soviet had found his cheek. Manfried laughed when his cheek was tickled. Ernst, too.

The Soviet looked up with a broad grin. "*Da*? *Da*?" His eyebrows shot up.

Anna smiled thinly. The Soviet went back to tickling Manfried.

The sergeant shook his head. "Ain't gonna move 'til they say to unplug."

"All right. Damnit." The corporal turned. "Ma'am, it's our coffee and you're welcome to it. But you'll have to go get it. Here." He reached in the truck, handed her a mug and pointed.

Anna looked down to the perambulator. The Soviet had both twins cackling.

The corporal called Lofton followed her glance. "Uh, Kunitsa's OK for an NKVD type. Don't worry. We'll watch 'em." He stooped and pushed a forefinger in Ernst's blanket. The baby giggled and the corporal grinned.

It's not far, she told herself. They're warm behind this lorry, warmer than what remained at home, ten lumps of coal, a few bits of wood would make them.

"*Danke*." Anna walked out from behind the lorry. The wind ripped at her as she headed for the next fire. The percolator sat on top, beckoning.

Phipps and Wadleigh ignored her approach. They knelt near the curb, Wadleigh carefully scooped dirt from a three foot crater.

She didn't think they would notice when she poured. They were so intent, consumed, they weren't looking up.

Reaching for the pot, she glanced from the corner of her eye. Phipps, with headphones dangling around his neck, bent on his knees fumbling in a tool box. Wadleigh had shifted to all fours and peered in the crater.

Phipps muttered, "...strange one, it might be a mod nine..."

Wadleigh caught her eyes when he reached in the crater. "Get away, Anna."

"*Nein, ein Minute, bitte. Ich--*"

"Now, Anna."

She stepped back.

"Shit! Harry! It *is* a mod nine! The damned tail fuse just kicked over. Tell Lofton to--"

The ground lifted. Anna felt a roaring, then heat and ripping and tumbling. Then, nothing.

PART I

You don't learn to hold your own in the world by standing on guard, but by attacking, and getting well hammered yourself.

—George Bernard Shaw

CHAPTER 1

With the matte black hull awash, algae laden water swept over *Brutus,* making the deck slippery. Lofton stood, his hand on the hatch, and watched *Brutus* glow softly in the occasional phosphorescence. A wavelet swirled over his foot. It glowed, too. He peered down into the red lighted interior. It beckoned. His conning station, the deep, form fitting pilot's seat, the glass cockpit, like an F-14. Food, hot showers, clean sheets, the embracing security tempted him.

Brutus. Ironic name.

One of his yard technicians, an overweight, pockmarked ex-boatswain's mate, had called the sixty-five foot minisubmarine *Brutus* because of its stubby torpedo shape. They all laughed about it. *Brutus* was a he-submarine, not a she-submarine. The name stuck and so did *Brutus*'s gender.

But *Brutus* would die if Lofton didn't refuel.

Hurry.

Lofton stooped and closed the hatch. He could barely see the anechoic skin as he checked his digital watch: 2137:42. He was committed now. *Brutus* would dive in fifteen seconds.

Lofton sat straddling his sanctuary. He glanced at the moonless sky. Stars glistened off the oily south swell. The water bit him, colder than he would have thought in this late end of California's summer, but the project, overwork, and lack of sleep had dropped his weight to 180, accentuating the chill. Lofton's long face was gaunt; he looked like a runner, with telltale splotches under quick, grayblue eyes. Taller than most at six feet two, five months ago he would have mildly chastised his overweight 195 pounds. Now, it was no longer necessary.

A wave lapped forward and surged around his legs. Maybe sharks are out tonight. Maybe the pinger won't activate and bring *Brutus* back.

A prolonged hiss, water gurgled around him. Lofton took a final check of his scuba gear. The dark shape trembled, then surged forward a few feet and poised, undecided. Lofton mentally rechecked the sequence. Too late to change any screwups now. Either *Brutus* was programmed correctly or the sub would end up standing on its nose in two hundred feet of water. Wouldn't the Catalina tourists like that?

Brutus dropped beneath Lofton's buttocks. A ground swell caught him and raised him off the hull. He took a breath and pushed himself down for a final check. His feet found the sinking mini-sub. Legs spread wide apart, he checked *Brutus*'s level; zero inclination as far as he could tell. Good, no screwups in the program. Three urgent strokes brought him to the surface. He caught his breath and looked at his watch: 2138:26.

He couldn't get back to *Brutus* now if he wanted. It would take the automatic surface blow program fifteen minutes to set up and activate. He pictured servos and valves clunking as they reordered themselves for the next sequence. Time to get on with it.

The Avalon Casino, his beacon, twinkled brightly before him. Automatically he took three cross bearings; the Casino, Long Point, Abalone Point. He had to fix a rough position in his mind in case the GPS crapped out. If it did, he would find *Brutus* somehow.

Satisfied, he kicked toward Descanso Beach, five hundred yards away. It should have been an easy swim. He'd done things like this as a kid, but now he had all this damn gear, clothes, foulies, underwear, money, ID, even a sleeping bag. He hoped it wouldn't get wet as he nudged the half-sunken rubber sealed bag along.

Avalon's September evening light loom glistened, inviting him across the water and ashore. The ground swell was less pronounced. The distance looked the same, but he checked the bearings and found he was much closer. Voices now, laughter, and yes, The Invisibles' rock music blasted from the Casino and caromed off the hillside.

The Avalon Harbor moorings were jammed, as were the twin rows at Descanso and Hamilton Beach. Bobbing shapes rose before him, gleaming brass and white glistening hulls. Boat cabins beckoned as soft, yellowish lights filtered through warm curtains. The larger vessels would have coordinated interiors. They'd be open and airy, much different from the functional, cramped home he'd ditched below, a sixty-five-foot aluminum powerhouse with a hundred times their potency.

His teeth chattered as he nudged his gear along. A trawler wallowed ten feet ahead of him, darkened, occupants either asleep or ashore, partying. He only needed the mooring for a few minutes. A number stood out on the bobbing white can: W37.

A diesel engine roared, a yellow mass shot between the buoys two moorings away, turned sharply, and headed straight for him. The searchlight blinded him. He kicked hard, cursing. He'd forgotten about the crazy water taxi drivers around here. Five feet.

"Hey, look out." The hull swerved, not slowing. The bow wave rolled over him and pushed him into the buoy. He knocked his head and frantically grasped his bundle.

"Whoosat?"

"Some drunk."

"Jesus, don't people ever learn? Hey, Suzy!"

Laughter.

Lofton held on to W37's heaving chain as the wake dispersed. Even the trawler above him, a forty-footer, bobbed and strained on its bowline.

He waited three minutes to catch his breath and let the water settle down. Time to get moving, his watch read 2157:06.

He tied the bundle to the anchor chain by its pendant. Then his weight belt came off, followed by his wet suit, fins, mask and snorkel. He looped a line securely around his scuba gear and attached it to the weight belt, letting it all slide down the anchor chain. If someone glanced down through the crystal clear water tomorrow it should look like another medium size rock in the sand thirty feet below. He only needed a few days.

The other end of the line was secured to the top link of the buoy's anchor chain, a double bowline just to make sure.

Odd to be paddling around in just his swimsuit. He felt strange, free, almost like a tourist. The water was warmer in here as he untied the bundle from the anchor chain and pushed for the beach.

A hair dryer whirred aboard the trawler. Soft light glowed from the aft cabin.

"...Damnit, Linda, how long are you going to run that thing? The auxiliary's almost out of gas--"

"--Fred, you know I can't sleep on damp hair and if you want me nice for the Robbins' tomorrow, you'll just have to be patient...."

He slowly kicked for the inner row of moorings, nudging his bundle along.

"...this was your idea. A working vacation and he hasn't offered you a damn thing on the office building. Not even an option...."

"...bitch..."

He swam between two sailboats moored on the inner row, twenty five footers, both dark. He checked the can numbers just to be sure: W-19, W-20. An imaginary perpendicular from the beach through those two buoys would lead him to W-37 and his gear.

He stopped at the aft end of W19, untied his canvas deck shoes from a loop on the bundle, and put them on. The beach, he remembered, was rocky, no sand, and he had to be quick.

It was quiet. Now! Push! Powerful strokes, a wave surged, his knee banged a rock and pain jingled up his spine. Keep going. He could stand, it wasn't deep. One last look around the beach; empty. Music cascaded from the Casino off his left shoulder. Everybody else was either in town having fun or on their boats. For a long moment, until he shook it off, he was seized by a bleak emptiness. I am alone, he thought. There is no one who can help me.

Kneedeep, he hoisted his bundle and ran up the small rocky beach through a sandy playground and into some low bushes beyond. Waiting, he caught his breath. Then slowly, methodically, he undid the rubber waterproof material from his gear bag. That would go into a trash can later as he moved into town.

Lofton put on a teeshirt, smoothed his hair, grabbed a deep breath, and stepped from the bushes. Soon he found the asphalt pedestrian walkway that wound past the Casino and into Avalon.

He felt better. He was safe for the moment, safe among the weekend Avalon throng. Renkin wouldn't find him here, and *Brutus* rested in fortytwo fathoms, 252 feet down on a sandy bottom, nuzzled among rocks, sleeping, yet waiting.

The night air cloaked him. Almost seventyfive degrees, and the asphalt path still radiated the day's sun. He would dry off soon. Then, a quick public shower in town would put him right. Dress like the rest of the tourists, find a gin mill and he could find his ride to the mainland. He had to hurry. It wouldn't be long before Renkin's net reached him even here.

Music thundered as he walked past the brightly lit Casino. Screaming, clapping inside; ripping, throbbing amplifiers and synthesizers. A poster announced, "The Invisibles Saturday Night Only." Mingling with the occasional strollers and lovers, he tried not to walk too fast. Avalon lay two hundred yards down the palmlined promenade.

After his shower, Lofton felt better. He changed into a clean set of Levis and teeshirt; no socks. He fit the part of a weekend tourist, but his canvas topsiders still squished. The nighttime throng on Avalon's main drag, Crescent Avenue, embraced him, made him feel safe and comfortable. A group disembarked from the glass-bottom boat and caught up to him. He was, for the time being, one of them as they strolled along, looking in shop windows, buying ice cream.

Crescent Avenue bulged with overcrowded, raucous bars. Too much noise and confusion, a younger crowd. Chances were, he calculated, his target sailboat skipper would seek a milder form of relaxation.

Lofton rounded the corner and walked up Sumner Avenue. A sign read *Gig and Galley*. He edged into a dim, nautical decor. Ships' lanterns, overhead nets, and dilapidated boat models surrounded the room. He needed a group of three to five people, a boat crew on the town. He ordered a beer, a Carlsberg Elephant dark, and listened to two men next to him.

"...so I changed to fifteen pound test and it seemed to work. But I should have..."

Fishermen. No help there. He moved down the bar. Another group; three men, a woman, and a young boy about ten.

"...Let's try Two Harbors tomorrow. They say water skiing is good around Cherry Cove. You can buy beer right there at the..."

Next group scuba divers he sighed and moved on.

A short, stocky man, no more than five feet, seven stepped on his foot.

"Oh, sorry."

Lofton smiled back and silently nodded. The man turned to two of his friends and resumed conversation. They looked in their early fifties and all three wore pale blue polo shirts trimmed in thin white stripes. Over the pockets was the name *True Blue*. Contrasting white sailing shorts completed the arrangement.

Bingo. He sipped his beer, smiled, and tried to catch their eyes as they talked.

The short man glanced at him, then continued, "...I think we should get a jib top, you know, a double headsail rig, for these long reaches to Long Point. Did ya see Terry? He popped one up right away as soon as he rolled out of the Long Beach breakwater."

"Yeah, but Terry's been racing for twenty years, he knows how to trim."

"We can't let that get us down, we're faster, we rate about the same, we should be able to beat him."

"I know, Howard. But Tom and I can't do everything."

Lofton took a sip of his beer and dove in.

"Excuse me, I couldn't help overhearing. You're shorthanded?"

Dumb. If I were them, I'd walk away.

Conversation stopped. All three turned to measure him. Their eyes darted over him.

Now or never. He extended his hand to the short man. "Hi. I'm Matt Thompson."

The man looked at him, chewed a cigar stub, not moving. His eyes squinted, mulling it over. Somehow his short, white, frizzy hair made him look young, compensating for his height. Finally, his hand shot out. "Howard Butler." The grip was firm.

The others followed.

"Tom Downs."

"Virgil Hollenbeck."

Lofton continued. "I'm sorry. The reason I asked is that I had to work today so I couldn't race over with the fleet. I took the water taxi and was supposed to meet..." he made up another name and hoped it worked, "...*Seventh Heaven*, but I just found out she didn't make it. Apparently she didn't even leave the dock, a broken spreader or something."

They seemed to relax. Butler asked, "*Seventh Heaven*? What kind of boat is she?"

Here comes the hard part. "A J35. She's new, this was supposed to be her first race."

Butler smiled. "And now you're stuck here. Too bad. Yeah, we could use a hand. What do you do?"

"Mast, bow. I don't mind grinding either." It would be what they wanted to hear.

Hollenbeck asked quickly, "You mean you can do spinnaker work?"

"Oh, yeah," he decided to add a little spice. "Bloopers, chickenchutes, half ounce, you name it."

Downs and Hollenbeck smiled to each another. Butler chomped his cigar, rubbed his chin, and turned to the others. They gave small nods. He looked back. "We've got an Ericson 35 and we're shorthanded. Trouble is, we're too old to go up to the bow," he chuckled, "and set a chute and take it down properly. When the wind kicks up, we're the first to go out of control--"

"--and then into death rolls, Mr. Helmsman." Downs elbowed Butler with a smile.

"Awright, awright," Butler growled back and took a long sip of his drink. "But we have a good time. Do you think you could fit in?"

"Yeah, I could help you out. Is it just the three of you?"

"And my daughter," Butler smiled. "She's the best sailor of all of us. But she's back on the boat now. Doesn't like the raucous nightlife. Actually, she's trying to be polite and let us old farts have our fling. Yeah, you can come along. We'll even feed you lunch. Do you have a place to stay, Matt?"

"Over at the hotel, but thanks," he lied. He didn't want to get into an all-night drinking bout in the cramped confines of a thirty-five-foot sailboat. He took a long pull and finished his beer. "Where are you?"

Butler stuck out his chest and pointed to the name on the pocket. "You'll find *True Blue* at White's Landing. First gun at Long Point is at noon so we'd like to shove off at eleven. Is that OK?"

"OK." Lofton smiled. "It sounds like fun. I'll grab a water taxi and see you at eleven." He yawned. "Would like to hit the sack. Big day tomorrow and I appreciate the ride. Hope I can do a good job." He shook hands again and walked out.

He needed rest, solitude, and he hoped it wouldn't take long to find a place to stay. He had to think, figure out how to find JP-5 for *Brutus* before Renkin found him.

Lofton tried two hotels. Both were full; tourists jammed the Island this time of year. At the third, the Catalina Mariner, the bored clerk shook his head even before Lofton could speak. Lofton eyed the man, then pulled out his wallet and silently pushed two one hundred dollar bills toward the clerk's right hand. A twenty-dollar bill slid toward his left. The clerk smiled, pocketed the bill with his left, and gave him fifteen dollars change with his right.

Lofton wordlessly scrawled "Matt Thompson" on the hotel register, took his key, and went upstairs.The clerk had given him the bridal suite. The bed squeaked, but Lofton fell immediately asleep and woke three hours later. Thatcher. He had been dreaming of Thatcher. That was why he was sitting up. He breathed deeply and blinked at the ceiling. Sweat ran down his arms, his chest. In his mind's eye Thatcher still lay there. Bloody. Dead. It seemed like a nightmare--it was a night-mare. How could it all have happened? Could he have stopped it?

With a sigh Lofton got up and padded into the bathroom, carefully washing his face and then his dripping chest.

This kind of thinking wouldn't help him. He could go over everything again in the morning, but what he must have now was sleep. He weaved back into the bedroom and sat on the bed, staring blankly out the window for a long time. Finally, he lay down and waited for sleep.

When he woke again it was morning. Sunlight was streaming past the blinds. In the streets below, people were laughing. He heard a dog barking and the television murmured in the room next to him. His Casio read six-forty-five. Time to get moving. He stood in the shower for twenty minutes, maybe his last for a long time, and shaved again. It felt strange to have a clean face. Two days ago he'd had a neatly trimmed full beard, streaked with gray, which matched his short, sideparted hair. Now he felt naked, his cheeks and chin tingled with the new sensation.

He dressed carefully and repacked his gear bag. Before he zipped it shut he checked two crucial pieces of equipment. One was his GPS receiver, an olive-drab box the size of a cigarette pack. He clicked on the power and the small red light flashed. Lofton waited while the box warmed up. The twotiered display read all zeros. He punched the Lat/Long button. The digital display read:

33° 20'.18 N
118° 20'.01 W

OK, that looked reasonable. He didn't have a chart but the numbers on the display seemed to be close to the latitude and longitude coordinates of the Catalina Mariner. Now for the other. The big one. Did this thing remember where *Brutus* lay? He entered a coordinates code, then punched the small keyboard with his old Navy serial number: 714208. The display flashed, a two-second wait, a small yellow light blinked on. He pushed Lat/Long. Then:

33° 21'.14 N
118° 19'.17 W

Good, the Global Positioning System memory checked with his memory. He could find *Brutus*. He tucked the GPS receiver back in the sleeping bag. The hardened ABS case clunked against another small black box. His pinger. This would awaken *Brutus* and bring him to within thirty feet of the surface. Both boxes were critical. He zipped his seabag shut, took one last look around the room, and went down into the morning.

Find a newspaper, then eat.

Mabel's Diner was next to the Gig and Galley. The windows were streaked, the vinyl booths were greasy, fly specks adorned bare light bulbs.

The bacon, eggs, toast, orange juice, and coffee were excellent, his first solid meal in days.

When he opened the *L.A. Times* there was nothing. No screaming headlines. He quickly scanned parts one and two. Zilch. He sat back. They hadn't reported it. Why? He checked the front page again. It was the final edition, something should have been there.

Lofton's stomach knotted and what remained of his enjoyable breakfast froze as it dawned on him why *Brutus* hadn't made the *Times*. Renkin had hushed it. The carillon above Avalon struck eight but Lofton didn't hear it.

He left the diner, heading for the pier, staring unseeing at the bay. A Sunday crowd, many in swimsuits, babbled about him.

Renkin. Only last Wednesday evening he had actually admired the guy. He had been glad to see him, almost, when he'd looked up from his computer keyboard to see Renkin rocking on his heels in the doorway to Lofton's office. Renkin had just flown in from Washington and was in his usual getup: brown herringbone suit, gray bow tie and patent leather loafers, shiny, as if he'd just had them polished. Except for his bald sunspotted head and gray flecks in his thin moustache, he could have passed for fortyone instead of the sixty he was.

Lofton had checked his cursor, paused the program, then turned in his chair. "There're just a couple of things, Lofton..." Renkin was saying.

"Shoot." Lofton sat waiting and watched light bounce off Renkin's glasses.

"I'd like to see the most accurate updates on Thatcher's SDV launch coordinates. Also, the council is demanding a review on the full production *X-3* feasibility study by Tuesday, along with more information on its payload compatibility analysis."

Lofton groaned under his breath. He *would* miss Kirby's party. Not that it was all that important but....

"I had been planning to leave for a party. But O.K.. That'll take a while. We can't figure it out--I checked today. Whole blocks of data are missing from those programs which is really strange since the equipment is already aboard *Brutus* and should be available now. And the velocity prediction table is screwed up. We can't--"

"--What's missing?"

"Weight distribution and trim forecasts for the SDV post launch phase. We do have the prelaunch stuff, but then there's some minor things, ah, like throughhull pressure tolerances for the umbilical system, Oring compatibility--let's see--temperature and corrosion predictions, lubrication routines--"

Renkin walked in. "I think we borrowed some, if not all of that, Brad. That's one reason I flew in today; to combine what we have and centralize the database here in San Diego with you."

"OK, when do I see it?" Lofton leaned back in his chair, puzzled, then rubbed his eyes. His promotion to director of the *X-3* program had taken its toll. He'd been working twelve to fourteen hours a day, seven days a week, and over the past two weeks during *Brutus*'s first mission, he'd worked even harder. Last night he hadn't gone to sleep. *Brutus* had returned at three in the morning, fifteen hours ago; no fanfare, no grinning faces, no thumbs up. Thatcher had simply popped the hatch, climbed out, and nodded to the openmouthed maintenance team; then he went upstairs, ate two Big Macs and fell asleep on a cot. He was still asleep now as far as Lofton knew. Everybody else had gone home dead tired after inspecting and preparing *Brutus* for the next mission, which was supposed to be soon. Lofton had had to remain for Renkin's surprise visit, otherwise Kirby's party would have been a good break from what was becoming a very demanding job.

Renkin turned and called down the hall, "Carrington! Could I have my briefcase, please?" He waited.

Carrington appeared with Renkin's thick cordovan leather attache' case. His dark gray suit and wing-tipped shoes complemented a six foot four inch, 220 pound frame of thirtysix years. Carrington was constantly at Renkin's side, serving him, seeing that he kept to his daily workout routine. He handed the attache' case to Renkin, then eyed Lofton. "How you doing, Brad?"

"Fine, Ted." Lofton had given a tired grin to the blond, thinlipped man. "How's the spook biz?" They'd crossed paths once or twice when Carrington was in the CIA and Lofton was a SEAL.

"It's great, Brad, you should have stayed in." Carrington looked at Renkin, who nodded toward Lofton's desk. He set the briefcase down, dialed the combinations, unsnapped the locks and stepped back.

Renkin opened the briefcase, "Right, Carrington. You know, there's a fish place around the corner I saw as we drove in. Could you run over and pick up some takeout dinners for us? Orange Roughy, if they have it."

"Yes, sir."

Renkin looked at Lofton, "You, too, Brad?"

Lofton shook his head.

Carrington paused for a moment, then said, "Back in a jiffy." He walked out.

Renkin reached into his briefcase. "Here's the disk pack, which should have most of your data. But I understand you have to integrate it with the actual mission data from the vehicle itself."

"That's right. And we haven't pulled any of the disks out of *Brutus* yet, on your orders."

"Didn't Thatcher bring anything out?"

"I don't think so. He just climbed out. Looked like he hadn't slept for days. I asked him if he was OK. He just stared at me and said, 'tired,' then went upstairs to the cot in the lounge."

Renkin turned and examined Lofton's chalkboard. Finally he said, "A violation of regulations."

"Pardon?"

"I said Lieutenant Commander Thatcher has violated regulations. I'll have to speak to his commanding officer."

"Felix, the guy was trashed. He looked like he'd been dragged through a knothole. Hell, he's still asleep upstairs in his poopie suit. He probably still has his keys on him."

Renkin tapped his palm with his fist. "A definite breach of security. He should have put the keys in the safe here in your office before anything else." He looked at Lofton, who shook his head. Renkin continued slowly, "And you have a duplicate set, don't you?"

Lofton nodded. He was well aware of Renkin and his moods. The man was exacting, everything according to procedure, the book. He could feel it coming.

"--why didn't you--"

"--Look, Felix." Lofton stood up. He was tired, he'd had enough of this crap. He should have left an hour ago, but he had volunteered to stay when

Renkin's secretary called from Washington and said the director of congressional liaison for the National Security Council was airborne and due at 5:45, local time. "Thatcher's your man. I have no control over what he does. My team and I are only responsible for turning *Brutus* around and getting him ready for your next operation. That's all we civilians are getting paid for, and what you or Thatcher or the NSC does with *Brutus* is none of our concern."

Renkin held the stare; his glasses shot sparks about Lofton's small office. "I see, Mr. Lofton. Well, here is what we're going to do. Get your keys and we'll go to *Brutus* right now and retrieve the file. Then I'll have a word with Lieutenant Commander Thatcher after his beauty rest. He's been asleep for--how long? Twelve or thirteen hours? Let's go, please."

Lofton blinked, then turned to his safe, dialed the combination and grabbed a set of keys; one a standard notched type, the other a magnetic card. He closed the safe and looked up, "OK, after you."

They walked down the hall of the fifty year old, three story clapboard building. It was a typical preWorld War II government issue, most recently a tuna cannery until the NSC took it over. Their footsteps clicked on linoleum hallways. Lofton took the lead down a flight of stairs, through an extensive machine shop toward a thick double doorway.

Renkin sniffed, "This place smells oily. You sure that there aren't any unnecessary fire hazards?"

Lofton unlocked the right door and shoved it aside. It rattled on large overhead rollers. "JP5. Some of it spilled when we started refueling, so we had to stop. The fuel truck's pump malfunctioned. It'll be fixed tomorrow."

He stood and let Renkin pass. Then he followed him into the large, dark chamber. Water dripped, echoed. Waves lapped among the evening sounds of San Diego Harbor outside, the chug of a tour boat, a jet took off from nearby Lindbergh Field. And they felt, rather than saw, the presence of something occupying the darkness immediately before them.

"Lights," ordered Renkin as he walked into the gloom, his hands behind his back.

"Be careful, don't fall in." Lofton fumbled for the wall panel.

Renkin stopped abruptly. "Why don't you have anyone here? There should be a twentyfour-hour guard."

"Doesn't seem necessary, Felix. With all of your security people outside, why have 'em in here? Besides, you said the fewer eyes, the better. Here." He found a bank of large switches. The chamber lit up in a series of loud clicks as Lofton flipped the toggles. Then he stepped alongside Renkin as the assistant director examined his charge.

"The X-3," murmured Renkin, looking up at the bow. The long, dull black shape hung suspended over water from two large slings. Renkin reached up and touched Brutus's blunt nose. "Have you finished refueling?"

"Just about; sixty one bladders, over sixty-one hundred gallons of 70 percent hydrogen peroxide. That's what took so much time today. Once the JP5 is aboard tomorrow he'll be almost ready to go again."

Renkin nodded, then turned to Lofton, "Brad, are you happy with this assignment?"

Lofton twitched at the change of pace. "It's been interesting duty, Felix, but basically I was finished six months ago when we launched Brutus. Now it's a nobrainer for me. Clean the bilges; run the power plant; fill 'em up with H_2 O_2 and JP5; check the charcoal filters; make sure the carbon monoxide monitor is working. No, I don't mean to sound ungrateful, but my career is at stake. I should be working on designing attack submarines. The SSN-21 program is going full bore now and I'm missing out on the action. And with the defense cuts, it's about the only program where I can get ahead."

Renkin looked down, then, "Yes, I don't mean to be ungrateful either. You're the best, especially with your SEAL background. That's why I asked for you. Tell you what, let me talk to Thatcher and Captain Summers; we'll discuss a replacement and see if we can spring you loose in the next few months."

Lofton started to reply when Renkin did it again, "Tell me, Brad, how many times have you been aboard Brutus?"

"Hundreds, I guess. I practically live on him when he's in port, especially now."

"No, I mean at sea. How many times have you been to sea with Brutus?"

.   .   .

"Whenever you guys let me, and that's only been twice, both times with Thatcher and Carrington. We had to trace a persistent power surge in the BQR37 and I had to be aboard under actual conditions."

"BQR37?"

"Yeah, it's a miniaturized BQR20 like they have in the big boats for shortrange rapid scanning; you know, mines, steel nets and SDVs."

"Do you think you could operate this vehicle?"

Lofton looked up to the long torpedo-shaped *X-3*. "Yeah, I think so. *Brutus* is user-friendly, all automated. Just punch the keyboard for what you want and everything's done automatically. One joystick, five CRTs and a keyboard take care of hundreds of switches, servos and valves; except, I don't know what you want this sewer pipe to do. So, I guess all I can say is that I could maneuver *Brutus* from point A to point B, and that's about it. Why?"

"Just curious. We don't have a backup pilot, you know."

"What about Carrington? I thought Thatcher had checked him out in *Brutus*."

Renkin looked down. "...yes, unfortunately Carrington's duties have become rather complex. And, quite frankly, I need him around. He's my administrative assistant for council liaison and on the NSC's payroll. No, we need another good primary pilot."

Toeing a wooden plank, Renkin said in a flat tone, "What do you say, Brad? You could work directly for me."

"You mean on the NSC's payroll?"

"Well, yes."

Lofton smiled, "No thanks, Felix. I got out of the spook business years ago when I bailed out of the SEALS. I'm happy pushing pencils now, not midget submarines."

"Actually, you were almost dismissed because you struck a superior officer, an Army colonel. Isn't that right?"

Lofton felt his face burn. "It was a long time ago." He eyed Renkin, "Do you want to get those disks now?"

Renkin's look pierced Lofton. "Yes, let's go."

"O.K." Lofton mounted the scaffolding that curved around *Brutus*'s topside and jumped easily to the submarine. He sat on the lip of the small

open hatchway and his feet automatically found the rungs that led to darkness below. Renkin knelt beside him.

Lofton muttered, "Power's shut down inside. Better let me go in first and
fire up the auxiliary load." *Brutus* swayed slightly in his slings from their
motion. Renkin reached out and fumbled for the wooden platform. "You--
you go, just unlock the disk cabinet and hand them to me."

"OK, it'll take me a couple of minutes to get powered up so I can see
what I'm doing."

"I'll wait here, but please be quick." Renkin looked down past *Brutus* to
the black water below.

"On my way." Lofton slid through the hatchway into total darkness. His
feet touched bottom. He reached around the ladder for a redlensed battle
lantern, found the switch and flipped it on. *Brutus*'s control room sprang
into an eerie hemoglobin likeness. Objects ran together as he tried to focus:
the pilot's chair, a joystick, the panels, and the darkened CRTs, asleep like
Thatcher up on the third floor. He looked forward toward the open hatch to
the diver's chamber but it was black in there. Piping, valves, electrical
conduits ran over and around him in dizzying patterns.

He moved forward. It was difficult to stand straight and he slouched
into the pilot's console on the port side of the narrow passageway. He
reached overhead to check the battery levels: One, two, three, five, and six
were in the yellow; number four showed barely green. He tried the auxiliary power master toggle switch. Nothing. No load from the outside. He
shook his head. Tiredly, he remembered that they'd disconnected all the
auxiliary umbilicals today when they'd bunkered up with hydrogen
peroxide. The cumbersome thousand pound bladders and their hoisting,
grappling machinery had taken precedence over the shoreside
connections.

"What's wrong down there?" Renkin barked.

"Nothing, they just shut everything down for the night. They even
pulled the power cables and auxiliary ventilation ducts. I guess I'll have to
use ship's power."

"Just hurry," Renkin's voice faded.

Brutus jiggled slightly in his slings, Lofton smiled as Renkin retreated to
the platform. Lofton knew *Brutus* made the assistant director feel claustro-

phobic. Renkin had only seen the *X-3* once before and had been quite emphatic in declining an invitation to inspect the interior.

Lofton kicked in the number-four battery, then turned to another panel and brought up the interior lights. They were incandescent, yet soft and indirect, allowing one's eyes to comfortably rest on the control panel, the glass cockpit with its CRTs, the keyboard, the LED switches, and the allpowerful joystick.

Lofton knelt to the HP 9060 computer cabinet and inserted the two keys. Then he flipped four thumbscrews and the side panel slid away. Renkin's disk nestled toward the back. He reached up and punched the main power button, then hit "cartridge eject." Nothing. Damn! He'd forgotten about the panel interlocks. He knew it would take forever to look up interlock override. Thatcher's manual lay carelessly piled among other manuals and soiled clothing on the starboard side bunk, directly across from the pilot's chair.

Duct tape.

He crouched and snaked aft past the ladder and past the small galley to the tool cabinet. Plenty of tools, spare parts, more operating and maintenance manuals, but no duct tape. He sighed and went up the ladder.

Renkin stood on the platform. "Got it?"

"Not yet. I need some duct tape to get through the cabinet interlocks. Hold on for a minute, I'll go down to the machine shop and get some."

"Brad, I haven't got all night."

"Be right back." Lofton jumped down to the platform, headed toward the machine shop and checked his watch. Kirby's party would start soon and he was going to be stuck here all night. He flipped on the machine shop main lights, opened a supply cupboard and rummaged for the damn duct tape.

"Hi, Brad."

Lofton jumped and turned, "Les, you're awake. How do you feel?" Thatcher's thick, dark stubble matched his blue coveralls. His hair was mussed and red creases crosshatched the right side of his oval face where he'd slept. But he seemed normal again; quietly powerful, quick intelligent eyes, thick moustache, and bulky body. Thatcher always had a hard time squeezing through *Brutus*'s hatch. Except when he'd returned last night.

Then, he was gaunt, drained. No sleep for fortyeight hours, navigating through the offshore SOSUS network, could do that to you.

"Better now." Thatcher yawned. "Hungry as hell, though. What do you cheapskates have to eat around here?"

"Yeah, hold on for a bit. I'll nuke some chili for both of us. But I have to get *Brutus*'s computer disks for Renkin first."

"What? He's here, already?"

Lofton nodded his head toward the hangar.

Thatcher jammed his fists on his hips and stared through the door. Then softly, "That little sonofabitch! When I blow the lid on him they're going to nail his ass, but good."

"What?" Lofton watched Thatcher move toward the hangar. He shook his head, then went back to his search for duct tape. Next cabinet, then another. He finally found it.

Their voices were loud when he returned to the hangar. He couldn't see them, they were behind the partition in the small office. He walked down the platform, rose up the scaffold, moved toward the hatch and stopped, listening.

"I said, I'm not going to tell you, you little bastard."

Lieutenant Commander Lester T. Thatcher yelling? Yelling at Felix Lloyd Renkin, Ph.D., one of the most powerful men on the National Security Council, one of the finest strategic minds in the United States, and certainly one who could have Thatcher's head and see him in Leavenworth if he so chose?

Lofton lowered himself through the hatch.

"...you said it was only a towing exercise, you mealy bastard, you didn't say they were live CAPTOR mines."

"Let's go upstairs," Renkin said evenly.

Lofton found the bottom rung but kept his head out of the hatch.

"Come on, Commander, not here," he heard Renkin say more quietly.

"Yes, here," Thatcher shot back, "and to the press, to the chief of naval operations, to the President; everybody and anybody."

"Where's Lofton?"

"Back in the machine shop, looking for duct tape so he can bypass the cabinet interlocks and pull your precious incriminating disks for you. Except, you won't get them."

Silence.

Thatcher started in again. "I don't believe it. I didn't figure it out until I was almost all the way back; I didn't have enough fuel to return and retrieve the damn things."

"You're jumping to conclusions."

"Like hell." Feet shuffled, Thatcher's voice roared. "I taped the acoustic signature you had programmed into those CAPTOR mines. Just one acoustic signature each. And guess what? Not for an enemy ship; one CAPTOR's now at six hundred feet, programmed for some nondescript Japanese trawler and the other's--for crissake--alongside and it's programmed for the USS *Harry S. Truman*! And I got buddies on that old boomer. Why the hell do you and your jerkhead spook friends want to take them out?"

What? The *Truman*? Lofton rose higher in the hatch, his hands braced on *Brutus*'s sleek topside. A Japanese trawler and the *Truman*? He knew that ship, too. She was one of the original Polaris nuclear-powered submarines. They'd dismantled her missile systems and filled her missile tubes with cement a few years back and converted her to an auxiliary submarine. Now she carried a dry dock shelter, a large pressure chamber on her back for underwater launch and recovery of swimmer delivery vehicles, SDVs, for SEAL recon of hostile coastal and harbor installations, and other covert missions. Lofton thought about that. He still had a few buddies in the SEALS.

"That's enough, Commander Thatcher. As of now, you're relieved. You will return to your--"

"--No, Dr. Renkin, you're the one who's relieved. You're washed up. As of now, you should be picking up that telephone and calling a lawyer."

Lofton felt cold, a chill ran through his arms and to his chest. The hell with the disks, call the cops, find out what's going on. Sit these two guys down and sort this thing out. The *Truman*? To be hit by a Mark 46 torpedo launched by a CAPTOR mine? Impossible! As he lifted his knees out of the hatch he saw Thatcher walk slowly from behind the office partition.

Before he could stand he saw a hand flash from behind the partition.

The long, thin screwdriver, eighteen inches at least, penetrated Thatcher's back and popped out through the front of his poopie suit. Two hands grasped the handle and pushed harder, the screwdriver went into the hilt.

Thatcher stumbled, gurgled, then fell to one knee. He reached behind futilely trying to grab the screwdriver handle, his face white, jaw working. No words came as he dropped to both knees.

His hands fumbled at the shaft of the screwdriver in front, trying to push it back through. Red froth bubbled around Thatcher's lips, blood smeared his spasming hands.

Lofton stood. "Stop, for crissake! What're you doing?" he yelled, then jumped to the platform.

Thatcher's hands wiggled at the screwdriver shaft. Renkin appeared behind him and raised a wooden mallet.

"Stop! No!" Lofton sobbed and ran toward the pair.

Renkin swung and the mallet hit Thatcher's skull with a dull thud. Blood spurted and Thatcher fell forward on his chest, his arms splayed before him. The screwdriver handle rose as his chest found the floor.

Lofton drew up before a twitching Thatcher, then looked at Renkin, who pushed his glasses on his nose.

Renkin stepped back and raised the mallet. "Carrington!" he yelled. "Carrington!" It was a long scream this time.

Lofton had no desire to tangle with Renkin's batman now. He moved in. Renkin cocked the mallet and swung. Lofton caught his wrist easily, then spun Renkin around and twisted his wrist up his back, hard.

"Owwww."

"Drop the mallet now or it's broken."

The mallet thudded to the floor. Lofton spun Renkin again, then hit him full in the face. He crashed over a stool and fell in a heap. His feet protruded from under a drafting table.

Silence. Water lapped below *Brutus*. Lofton heard his own ragged breathing, then the sounds of San Diego Harbor, and willed himself to control. He took a deep breath, then turned around. Thatcher's body lay where it had fallen, his two bloody hands like inert claws.

CHAPTER 2

The water taxi howled on its fifteen-minute ride to White's Landing over clear, flat blue water that glistened under a warm, cloudless morning. Lofton scanned the dry bluffs rising steeply from the ocean and angling into hills and peaks covered with scrub oak and dry grass. Boulders stood out in places, especially in the craggy canyons. A herd of mountain goats grazed next to a fifty-foot cliff.

Ahead, two silvery fish glided over the wavelets, airborne for a few seconds, disappearing as others rose to take their places. As the taxi whirred along, the sharp mountains drew inland and the coastline yielded to one of Catalina's few beaches.

Moonstone Cove nestled under small cliffs, dark, glistening rocks giving onto the ivory sands of White's Landing, where a pier jutted out to receive small boats. Sail and power boats lolled at their moorings, occupants stretched on their decks, sunning themselves, diving, reading.

Lofton pointed toward *True Blue* at the far end of the cove, almost to Hen Rock. The taxi driver nodded and worked his craft alongside other boats, dropping passengers and embarking new ones for the return trip. Finally, they swept alongside *True Blue* and the driver expertly slewed the taxi's stern. The transmission clunked and the engine blared in reverse.

Lofton reached for *True Blue*'s toe rail. A hand grabbed his arm and pulled him into the cockpit as the water taxi shot out from under him.

"Hi, Matt, here...let me take your seabag."

Lofton stood and looked down into Howard Butler's clear blue eyes and relaxed grin. Butler looked fit, maybe they hadn't been drinking all night.

"Morning. You guys sleep well?"

"Like babies, eight hours. We're just cleaning up from breakfast. Come on down and have some coffee."

Lofton spotted a familiar outline as he followed Butler down the hatch. His head twirled, surprised.

They weren't coming. he thought Walt said they wouldn't do it. But there was *Bandit* moored three buoys away. Fortunately, her sleek seventy-foot profile was partially masked by the spars and hulls of two smaller boats. Lofton caught a glimpse of her skipper as he hurried after Butler. Walt Kirby was perched on the stern pulpit in his ridiculous dayglo green knee length trunks.

"Here," Butler was saying, "you remember Tom and Virg from last night, and this is my daughter, Bonnie."

A woman sat in the corner of the small dinette. She had thick, straight, sandy hair, blue shorts, white sleeveless blouse; her bare tan legs were drawn up, she held a large book--it looked like a text. He took another quick glance: about thirty, he guessed, full lips, yet delicate.

"Hello, thanks for helping out." She flashed thick glasses which masked an inviting yet unintentional vulnerability. Then she went back to her book.

"Bonnie, come on, it's almost time to--"

"The meeting *is* tomorrow, isn't it?" Bonnie raised her glasses and brushed hair from her green eyes.

They were wide apart, Lofton decided. What had they called it in his optics class--interpupillary distance--a sign of intelligence? Hold it. Not now. He was here to get back to the mainland.

Butler grinned at him. "Let's go topside. We've got work to do, especial-ly," he winked, "if we're disturbing people here."

On the deck, Butler began wiggling levers on the steering pedestal and cranking his engine. The other two cast off the bow and stern lines and in a few moments they powered easily toward Long Point.

Home, Lofton thought.

So many times. All this sailing, yet he'd taken it for granted. If he closed his eyes he knew he could imagine himself back on *Bandit* or on *Triad, Feather's Farthing, Due Diligence, Gaucho,* or any of the other boats he'd raced over the years.

He listened to *True Blue's* engine mutter with an irregular gurgle. The exhaust overboard gate valve didn't tap its rhythmic pattern, maybe over-heating.

"...What do you do, Mr. Thompson?"

"I'm sorry?" Bonnie had come topside and had taken the seat opposite in the cockpit.

"Naval architect." It slipped out, he would have to be careful.

"What kind of naval architect?" She had big, green eyes. She pulled up her knees and reclasped her hands around her legs, a single gold wedding band flashed.

"Tankers, barges, freighters. I did a dredge once." He waved a hand. "But it's mostly conversion stuff. Put a bulkhead in here, a kingpost there. 'We'd like a hot tub for the captain please, now, what does that do to the righting moment?'" He hoped it was what she wanted to hear.

He looked at her wedding ring again, "Mrs...."

"Duffield. My name's Duffield."

"What sort of work are you in?"

She peered at him, her head on her knees. "I work for my dad. Butler Engineering. We manufacture a premium line of aircraft pumps." She nodded down toward the cabin, "That's what my book was all about. We make a presentation to Pratt & Whitney tomorrow. We're bidding on a series of fuel pumps for the PW 4000 engine." Bonnie's head dropped back to her knees, taking him in.

"Hey, that's great. It sounds like a big--"

Clattering and flapping sounds interrupted as Downs hoisted the mainsail.

Lofton stood, "Maybe I better help out."

Her eyes bored in. "Have you ever sailed on an Ericson 35 before, Matt?"

"No."

Butler stared at him.

"How about racing, Matt? Have you ever raced before?" Bonnie wrapped her arms tighter around her legs.

"Uh, yeah, enough to help you pop a chute and get you to Long Beach ahead of some other boats." He glanced at Butler again. "Look, maybe I should go up there."

"Okay." Bonnie stood up. "I'm going back to work."

Several classes, sixty or more boats, milled below Long Point while the race committee waited for wind. Butler stood at his wheel and chomped an unlit cigar while *True Blue* bobbed in circles. It gave her crew time to sort out the Ericson's running gear.

A mile to the west, sunlight glittered off wavelet patches. Wind was headed toward them.

Lofton jumped inside the cabin. Bonnie ignored him as he made sure the spinnaker turtle was packed correctly. Bam! Lofton heard the report from the committee boat's shotgun. *True Blue* would start soon with the PHRF A fleet.

Lofton went topside to the mast and helped Downs snake up *True Blue*'s jib. Bonnie quietly followed, sat in the cockpit, and worked both the jib and main sheets for a light air start.

An hour passed. Butler had guided a drifting *True Blue* to a decent start and Lofton sat on the leeward rail with the grinning, beer-drinking Downs and Hollenbeck. He checked his watch: 1248. The wind was filling in, but not fast enough to get him where he had to be. He watched small particles in the rich turquoise Catalina waters glide past. I wish life was this easy, he thought. Better to sit here, cook on top the cabin, and drift all day than face what's waiting.

A zephyr ruffled the back of his neck. "There's another one, Howard. Keep working it," he coaxed softly. "We have weigh on, maybe a knot or so." Lofton had conned Butler to the front of the fleet by eking the most from small wind gusts.

Butler eased in helm and growled. "Fine with me. As long as we stay ahead of Terry, we're in fat city."

"Howard, I think fat city will get fatter. See that?" He pointed to port.

"What?"

"That...that dark patch of water. The westerly is filling in. And there, you can almost see Palos Verdes now; the smog is blowing inland. I'd say we'll get a nice breeze in the next five minutes or so. How 'bout I hook up the chute?"

"Fine with me." Butler spat tobacco juice over the side.

Lofton reached into the cabin, grabbed the spinnaker turtle, and padded to the foredeck.

He'd just finished securing the spinnaker to the bow pulpit when he felt it; the breeze tingled hair on the back of his neck, his collar, his arms.

"As advertised." Butler grinned from behind his wheel.

Lofton said, "We'll hoist in a couple of minutes."

"How are we going to do this?" Hollenbeck muttered as he stumbled aft to the cockpit.

Downs followed with a groan.

Lofton checked to port. Whitecaps began to roll--popcorn--a good westerly; they'd be romping in a few minutes. He was a blur as he attached spinnaker gear. Downs and Hollenbeck gaped at him. Hollenbeck managed a nod, put his beer on the seat and fumbled at a winch.

Lofton winked at them. "Virg, when I ask for it, pull the afterguy back a couple of feet. Tom, you set the topping lift--

yeah, that one--and snug the foreguy once we're set."

"OK."

"And Bonnie, you're on the main?"

"Got it."

Then, "Ready when you are, Howard."

Butler raised a fist in the air and looked back. "Ya hoo! So long, Terry. Look at that, we've even got *those* bastards beat." He jabbed his cigar butt to port, "Go for it, Matt!"

Lofton looked around. *Bandit* paralleled them one hundred yards to weather. He'd been busy on the foredeck and he hadn't noticed the seventy-foot sloop had muffed her spinnaker set and *True Blue* had caught up. The pink, gray and black paneled chute was knotted tightly around the other boat's headstay as her cursing crew tried to save it.

Kirby, useless at the wheel, looked aft toward overtaking boats. Finally, his head jerked to Lofton.

Lofton whipped around, hand-over-handed his halyard and to-blocked the chute in five seconds.

"OK, Virg, afterguy back. Pole up, Tom." Lofton sidestepped aft to the cockpit with his back to *Bandit* and grabbed the spinnaker sheet. He pulled, the winch spun, its pawls clicked loudly. The spinnaker flapped and snapped loudly as Lofton tailed more sheet.

"Ease the guy forward a bit, Virg, that's it. Bonnie, main in a little and give us some vang."

The chute filled with a loud pop. *True Blue* heeled and joined the breeze. Lofton ran forward once more and tripped the jib halyard. The headsail flapped and clattered to the foredeck. Then he sprang to the cockpit and trimmed the spinnaker sheet.

Butler laughed.

"More foreguy, Tom. How's it look, Howard?" he asked.

"Outstanding! Six point two knots and," Butler looked aft, "Terry's back there in the crap. Caught him with his pants down. So long, you sonofabitch. Ya hoo!"

"Ya hoo," echoed Hollenbeck and Downs. They crawled forward, bunched the jib, made pillows, and lay back, their beers once again in hand as *True Blue* sizzled before a quartering sea.

Bonnie looked up at the mainsail and pulled in more vang, intent on her trim; she did it nicely, Lofton noted. He glanced over to *Bandit*. The maxi could almost match *True Blue*'s speed under mainsail alone. The top of her spinnaker puffed around the headstay while her cursing crew worked the knot loose from the lower half. They would have it properly set in a few minutes, he reckoned. Kirby looked over and studied *True Blue*. Lofton turned his back, eased the main a bit and yanked the foreguy.

"Ya hoo!" yelled Butler.

A twentytwo knot breeze sent a slewing, deathrolling *True Blue* through the finish line for an undisputed first place. Butler whooped, threw both fists in the air then yanked Bonnie behind the wheel and hugged her. Yelping, she returned to her mainsheet. Downs and Hollenbeck took her place and thumped their cigar chomping skipper on his back.

Their cheers and cackles were quickly stifled when Lofton pointed to the beach six hundred yards dead ahead.

They all looked to him. How to douse the overpowered chute and save the boiling, pounding machine from floundering? Bonnie had her hands full with the mainsheet. Downs' eyes suddenly became fixed on the cabin sole. Hollenbeck said, "Oh, oh."

Butler leaned into his helm, looking more grim as he worked to keep *True Blue* from broaching. Lofton knew that Downs and Hollenbeck had no idea how to recover all raging 1,250 square feet of the red, white, and blue triradial cut spinnaker.

He ran to the mast, tripping the halyard and dousing the chute in the water. Instantly, the spinnaker became a giant sea anchor, and *True Blue* groaned to a stop two hundred yards from the surf line. It took Lofton, Bonnie, Hollenbeck, and Downs five minutes to snake the water gorged mess over the stern pulpit and dump it in the cockpit.

Twenty minutes later, they docked in the Long Beach Marina. From habit, Lofton stayed to help fold sails and stow gear. But he worked quickly, almost rudely. Too many people could recognize him. An undaunted Butler, like a high school sophomore winning his first mile relay, waved when Terry Anderson docked his boat, four slips away. Anderson looked at Lofton and shouted, "Who's the ringer?"

Butler pointed to his watch, his bellow echoed over the Marina. "Fifteen minutes, Terry. Stop for a beer somewhere?"

Butler dropped a canvas gear bag in *True Blue*'s cockpit and strutted toward Anderson's boat with a grinning Downs and Hollenbeck in tow.

Lofton ducked below and shoved sail bags in the forepeak while Bonnie wrestled with the soaked spinnaker topside.

"Damnit, Howard!" she yelled. "Will you get back here and help me with this?"

Butler, Hollenbeck, and Downs ignored her. The threesome waved beer cans and cigars and poured victorious whoops over a thinly smiling Anderson as he knelt on the dock to fold sails with his crew.

Bonnie gave up and tried to shove the slithering sail into its turtle.

Lofton climbed through the hatch and said, "Everything is stowed down below." He watched her struggle with the spinnaker for a moment. "Why not wash and dry it?"

"How?" She stood back, her hands on her hips.

"Make a bathtub. Just plug the drains, leave the chute on the sole, and fill the cockpit with three or four inches of fresh water. Then you raise it upside down. Here, I'll help you."

"All right," she muttered.

Lofton, working fast, spread the saturated spinnaker over the cockpit deck, ducttaped the drains and began flooding the chute with fresh water from a dockside hose. He said softly, "Sorry it got wet, Bonnie. Had to dump it in the water to stop the boat." He checked his watch.

"It's OK. It's long overdue for a wash, anyway. Look, you're in a hurry. I can finish up here."

"I'll raise the chute before I go." He smiled.

"Okay."

Lofton connected the spinnaker, hoisted it, cleated the halyard, and dashed below for his seabag. He vaulted off *True Blue*, eased past Bonnie, and had barely made the gangway when a small patch of wind uncurled the free clew. Suddenly, the spinnaker shuddered. The halyard shackle spun. With a loud snapping flutter, the chute unfurled and flagged out behind *True Blue*. A cloudburst shed thickly on Bonnie and she ran shrieking to the safety of the main dock.

He turned to see Bonnie whip water off her hands. She took off her glasses and riveted Lofton with a quick glance. Her eyes. She didn't look at him or through him. Bonnie looked into him. Deeply.He walked back and stopped before her.

Bonnie clutched her glasses with both hands. Her hair was soaked, rivulets ran down her cheeks and chin and dripped onto her drenched windbreaker. Her lips were pressed tightly as she wiped thick lenses with a wet handkerchief.

Suddenly it wasn't funny to Lofton. Somehow, not with this woman.

"Bonnie, I..."

She nodded slightly.

"I'm sorry, I thought you knew," he lied. He paused as she smeared at her glasses, her head down. "That was awful, I should have told you to move forward. I'm really sorry."

Bonnie Duffield raised her green eyes, squinted to a decent focus, and offered her right hand. He took it.

"Thank you for your help, Mr. Thompson. My father got his first place. He's happy. So am I. And I hope you are, too." A thin smile, water dripped inside her collar. *True Blue*'s spinnaker flapped lightly overhead as it dried. Bonnie dropped Lofton's hand, walked back to *True Blue*, and disappeared down the main hatch.

Lofton stopped at Anderson's boat and said his thanks and goodbyes to Butler and his friends.

Butler stuck his cigar in his mouth, then pulled his wallet out of his back pocket, "Here's my card. Let me know if you want to ride with us again, Matt."

Lofton pocketed the card, shook hands again and walked up gangway twelve toward the parking lot. He turned for one last glance at *True Blue*.

Bonnie Duffield stood in the aft cockpit shaking the spinnaker to help it dry. She looked quickly at Lofton, then up to her sail, pulling the luff tapes in rapid jerks.

He almost stopped, but the thoughts flashed: *Brutus,* Petropavlovsk. He walked quickly up the gangway ramp.

As Lofton checked his watch and started walking the sun dropped toward downtown. He'd left his Audi in the opposite corner of the Long Beach Marina, at least a half mile away.

He was relieved that his mind felt clear. He checked through the next step in his plans. *Brutus* had to be provisioned. Three weeks' foodstuff should do that. The difficult part would be finding jet fuel.

He turned the bend at the quay wall, passing strollers and handinhand couples enjoying the sunset. Two kids in kneelength surfing trunks whooshed by on skateboards. One jostled Lofton's seabag as they pushed on and looked back with pubescent laughs.The parking lot was emptying. Weekenders headed home for a quiet Sunday evening in front of their VCRs. Then to work tomorrow, and the freeways, and the gridlock. How he wished he had that luxury.

But, in one sense he was free now. Renkin had impeccable credentials as a deputy director on the national security council with access to the Defense Intelligence Agency, the Office of Naval Intelligence, the Central Intelligence Agency, the FBI, Interpol, and all their damned innumerable clandestine offshoots, but he still couldn't use the regular Navy. That would make it too public. And, if the regular Navy wasn't notified, then Lofton had the world's oceans to hide in, the Pacific at least, until he decided what to do.

Lofton had seen Renkin's decrypted dispatches and had figured most of it. Ivy Bells, the lat/long coordinates, Petropavlovsk, the *Truman*'s route, dates and times. Code names leaped from Renkin's files: PARALLAX and PITCHFORK. He had to contact them.

Lofton spotted his Audi's nose four hundred feet ahead, where three days ago he'd tucked it behind a dumpster two rows from the quay wall. Lofton crossed the first row and wove into the second. A car started, drew up behind him, and stopped. Lofton stepped aside to let it pass, then turned andKirby! Lofton's mouth opened when he saw Kirby's scowl behind the wheel of his black Mercedes 560 SEC. Kirby beckoned with his left hand. The Mercedes's window glided down.

"Brad, get in," he called softly.

"Walt, I can't."

"Now, damnit. Move!" Kirby's voice was a hoarse whisper through clenched teeth.

Lofton checked his Audi, shrugged, walked around the Mercedes, and got in. He shut the door with, "Walt, look--"

"In a minute," Kirby turned in his seat and began backing down the long row. "Fine friends you have."

"What?"

"In a minute. Shut up." He slowly backed against the oneway traffic, barely missing two girls in a Volkswagen Rabbit convertible. He found the aisle, stopped, then pulled out onto Marina Drive.

"What was that all about?" Lofton asked, looking back.

A grim, silent Kirby dogleged right on Pacific Coast Highway and headed south. "Where's your beard?" he demanded.

"I shaved it off. Is *that* why you grabbed me?"

Kirby growled, "A great stunt you pulled today, you bastard. I thought it was a joke. Maybe it was. Was that why you dropped out of the race?"

"Walt, I had to."

"Shut up. So I decided to go, anyway. 'Screw Lofton,' I said. 'If he doesn't want to steer his own boat with his partner, then that's his problem.'"

"But--"

"Hell, I know how to drive that boat. I've done it before, if you'll remember. So, I slap together a crew and take off. We have a good time going over Saturday, we get a bullet--" "Congratulations."

"--then comin' back today I spot my good buddy Lofton on this Ericson 35 nuzzling up to some goodlooking poontang. 'Ah, so that's what this is about,' I say to myself, 'Brad's got this dynamite new broad stashed away he's not telling Nancy and me about. He just wants to dip his wick quietly.'"

"No, that's not what happened."

"Shut up. So, *Bandit* goes crazy on the way back, we have a lousy spinnaker set and who goes toolin' by in his little thirtyfive-foot boat? The punch artist of the West Coast. At least that's what I thought until I found your car and waited for you."

Lofton ran his hands over his brow. Something was in Kirby's tone.

Kirby continued softly, "I was waiting for you to walk to your car. I parked about ten stalls down. I was going to, hell, I don't know, roar down the aisle, try and scare you, flip you the finger, have a beer, whatever.

"Then I see this car pull up, a white Ford sedan with--and get this--U.S. government plates. One guy gets out, does a recon, then the other gets out, they're both in dark suits and ties."

Kirby banged the steering wheel. "I still don't believe this. One guy is standing lookout; the other guy runs to your car, and the door is popped open in thirty seconds."

"What? It was locked."

"Yeah. Next thing I know your hood is up and the guy is installing a small bundle, half the size of a shoe box, with wires dangling from it."

"My God!"

"Yeah, your God. That bundle is now under your hood and those guys are still parked in the hotel lot across the street, watching, waiting for you to go 'poof.'" Kirby snapped his fingers.

Lofton felt his stomach tighten, his head swirled. Renkin. They'd found him, they knew how. Cover the subject's familiar habitats and friends. It must have been an enormous and expensive operation, in so short a time. "Did they see you?"

"I don't think so. I was pretty far away and hiding just like they were, except for a different reason. Now, you and I have seen five-pound bundles like that before, old buddy. Right?

"And, something else, how'd you get to Catalina in the first place? I know you weren't on the Ericson 35 Saturday 'cause we saw 'em come in and grab their mooring last night. Nobody could miss that knockout broad. And you weren't aboard. In short, what the hell is going on?"

"It's involved."

Kirby gave him a sour look. "Brad, this is serious. Talk."

"I think I'm hungry."

"I'll heat up a pizza at my place. Then you talk."

Kirby fell silent as they crossed over the Santa Ana River bridge into Newport Beach. Dusk settled, deep ambers swept over the Mercedes's rich leather, hood ornament reflections gleamed and jinked like--Renkin's glasses. Lofton glanced at his friend. He wore Levi's, one of their red *Bandit* polo shirts, and topsiders. The last of the sunset glinted off his natural olive skin, now deeply tanned from the weekend. Kirby had had the same butch haircut since they met in SEAL training in 1971. Kirby's lopsided smile, with those impossibly white teeth, had softened some of the edges in BUDS, Basic Underwater Demolition School. But one of the more hardened, ghoulish instructors took personal offense when Kirby failed to crack. He made Kirby camouflage his teeth, along with the rest of his face. Too much of a giveaway at night, he said. He made him put some black crap on his teeth, but only once. A barroom fight with the man nullified any further requirements.

And now, Doctor Walter Kirby, successful Newport Beach orthopedic surgeon, boat partner, and close friend, could be contaminated, permanently, if Lofton told him what had happened.

Kirby drove up to the guard gate on Bayshore Drive and was waved in. Three minutes later he eased the Mercedes into his driveway. The garage door yawned open to his signal. They pulled in beside a jeep Cherokee and stopped. The garage door descended behind them with a dull thud.

Kirby lived alone in a smallish single-story Cape Cod style waterfront house, vintage 1936. He'd renovated it with new wiring, plumbing, and a security system. The kitchen, undersized by modern standards, looked as old as the house but had been modernized with welldisguised hitech features.

Kirby popped a frozen pizza into the oven and opened two bottles of beer: a Corona for himself and a Carlsberg Dark Elephant for Lofton. Then he sat with Lofton in the breakfast nook, laying the back of his hand on the table and motioning with his fingers.

Lofton's mind spun. What could he say? "Spook stuff. I can't tell you much."

Kirby rolled his eyes, "My ass. You can't talk about it? I'm really proud of you. History will record Brad Lofton as the most patriotic sonofabitch who ever went up with five pounds of C4."

They locked eyes. Lofton sighed, "Walt, you saved my life back there. I Know you're trying to help, it's the buddy system, just like our SEAL days. Except for one thing. These guys don't screw around. They don't wear uniforms. Hell, you saw two of them; this time we're not just doing a recon of some Cuban Coast Guard station. Those guys are stalking me on my home turf and maybe now, you."

He glanced out the window and his voice dropped a notch, "I don't want you hurt, Walt, or Nancy either, for that matter. That's why I tried to sneak into Long Beach today. I didn't want anybody to see me."

Silence. Kirby swigged his beer then sat back and waited, his mouth set. Lofton mulled it over. How much could he really tell Kirby? How far should he drag him into this? That his own life was in serious danger was evident. Somehow he would have to deal with it. If Renkin caught him, they would squeeze it out, he knew, torture or chemicals, one way or the other. They would make him betray anybody he had been in contact with. Walt could die, too.

Brutus. That damned sixty-five-foot floating turd. Why had they chosen him to do their damned spook dirty work? He could have been back in Connecticut working on real submarines. Instead, he was stuck with this seventy-three ton "black project" that had been taken over by Renkin and his boys at the NSC.

Revolutionary, the Navy had said. Jenson Industries was happy to furlough Lofton from the SSN-688 attack class modifications he was working on to take over and prove the *X-3* concept. They slapped his back and roared their congratulations. Do it! Go to San Diego, get the project moving, and launch that damned prototype. Think of the prestige, Brad, climb the corporate ladder.

Lofton bit: hook, line and periscope.

He knew many navies had tried long-range minisubmarine programs. The results were limited. The British had crippled the giant German battleship *Tirpitz* in a Norwegian fjord in World War II, but minisubs required a mother submarine for delivery, which burdened valuable assets for limited objectives. After the war, the Allied nations experimented with new power plants to extend the minisub's range and wean them from larger boats. The U.S. Navy built the *X-1*, which employed a reciprocating Walther cycle engine. Using hydrogen peroxide, the engine had great promise for extended underwater operations, since the fuel carried its own oxygen and the *X-1* was not required to surface to feed its power plant with air. They called it an air independent system (AIP).

But the *X-1* blew up dockside. People were killed. The fuel was too caustic and too difficult to keep in a pure state. If foreign matter came in contact with the hydrogen peroxide, usually during fueling or handling, it would react--violently. The *X-1* was converted to a diesel electric boat, which eventually became a useless hulk and was decommissioned. The Navy was concerned with global operations and large carrier groups, not little submarines with limited capabilities that exploded all the time. They gave up.

But the Navy did inherit the bathyscaphe *Trieste* and designated it the *X-2*. She was a success and a propaganda coup, and dove to over 35,000 feet in the deepest part of the world's oceans, the Marianas Trench, in the late 1950s. But strategic planners called the *Trieste* an underwater elevator. She was only a research vehicle, not a minisubmarine suitable for long-range tactical missions. Then, in the 1970s, the Navy resumed interest in covert reconnaissance activities. They developed small self-propelled swimmer delivery vehicles, SDVs, for their SEALs. SDVs were housed in special chambers aboard mother submarines for transport to foreign shores where a small group of SEALS would exit for reconnaissance and espionage.

Once again, "mother submarines": valuable assets and personnel were tied up. Proposal requests were issued for new concepts. MIT responded with a technology that had been in use on space vehicles for years: fuel cells. They proposed a design in which one fuel cell could generate an astounding forty-two kilovolts. Six fuel cells linked to a single DC motor and supporting, say, six batteries could drive a fifty-to seventy-foot submersible at twenty-five to thirty knot sustained speeds depending on desired efficiency, for well over 20,000 miles. With a shrouded, five bladed screw, it could have a dash speed of thirty-five knots, which meant batteries would be drained after two hours.

No matter. Twenty-five knots sustained was plenty. Such a vehicle, MIT researchers said, would be extremely quiet, no large grinding pumps, no generators, very little rotating machinery to throw off a sound signature, and compared to nukes, a much, much, lower heat signature. Very stealthy.

The Navy R&D staff sat up...what if?

Yes, what if such a submersible, let's call it the X-3, were mass produced in the sixty foot range with a ten-foot beam, an aluminum hull, an anechoic sound deadening skin in a streamlined, "torpedo" shape? They considered the advantages. Aluminum was elastic, submarines could cycle time and time again from great depths, well over twenty-five hundred feet, without sacrificing watertight integrity. And aluminum was nonmagnetic, it would help degauss the boat. The anechoic skin would help absorb sonar waves, and the streamlined shape, one without any topside protrusions, including a conning tower, would insure optimum hull speed.

"But," the Navy asked, "what about the fuel cell? What would it burn?"

"Hydrogen peroxide and JP-5," MIT said.

"What? Mix that stuff and jet fuel? Everybody will blow up! We've been there. So have the Brits and the Germans. No thank you."

But the MIT concept prevailed over the old guard. Safe methods had been devised for handling hydrogen peroxide. The main improvement would be in materials; polyfluorinated containers, tubes, and flow control equipment were recommended. Six thousand gallons of the 70 percent solution would be packed in thousand pound Teflon bladders. Sixty bladders would partially surround a four-by-twenty foot access tunnel that ran from the X-3's control room aft to the motor room. Hydrogen peroxide was heavier than water, so that would absorb the lower portion of the fuel area for stability purposes. The upper half would provide tankage for thirty-six hundred gallons of JP-5, which was lighter than water. From there, the fuels would be processed through a reformer, which had decomposers, separators, diffusers, and catalytic plates. Finally, the reformed fuels would be burned in a chamber at only three or four hundred degrees, in the presence of a cathode and an anode, which generated the electricity. An amazing by-product was pure water, tons of it, enough for unlimited cooking, laundry, and hot showers, and excess still had to be pumped over the side.

The interior configuration became a battleground over which engineering group offered the most "elegant solution". Just after his assignment to the program, Lofton insisted on ergonomics, and the X-3 became a ship-fitter's nightmare. Taking a cue from NAVAIR, Lofton designed the interior configuration to resemble a fighter plane. The only piece of equipment normal for a ship was a muted Chelsea clock over the galley table. One conning station did it all, with a "glass cockpit," four seven-inch CRTs surrounding a large multifunctioned CRT, taking the place of the innumerable of dials and gauges seen in a submarine. In a deep leather chair on the port side, the pilot had instant access to all readouts and, using foot pedals, joystick, and throttle, could control all aspects of the X-3's movement. A periscope housing above the pilot snapped into place giving him conventional surface views with TV enhancement for the rest of the crew. The electronic equipment and its software was astounding, downsized from the X-3's big sisters. It provided battle management, communication, navigation, seakeeping, power plant, air scrubbing, fuel control, underway repair, and maintenance and artificial intelligence programs. All on five screens.

The prototype X-3 would carry forty-eight limpet mines in racks below the main deckplates. The SEALS would exit through a large escape trunk in the bow to sow them. Future designs were projected for ninety-six limpets so the SEALS could really go out and play.

The worst problem for the X-3 was the same as for her grown sisters: crew endurance. Food, air, power: no problem. But what do three or four people do for twenty thousand miles without seeing the light of day? Lofton had done his best just before he went to the Coast to supervise the prototype buildup. He designed an efficient galley that doubled as a lounge, the shower/toilet was shifted to the divers' trunk forward, and two pilot berths were added to starboard across from the control station. Two watch-standers would be up at all times.

What of the mission? Strategic planners put their heads together. They went to their desks, their drafting tables, computers, data banks, yeomen, commanding officers, vendors.

Recommendations were drawn, redrawn, deep-sixed, then redrafted. The *X-3*, they decided, was not just a hotrod to be used by a bunch of glory-hungry, twenty-four-year old, grinning SEALS. Why not a Battle of Britain scenario? The Spitfires going after the Heinkels? Yes. Add torpedo tubes to the next mod and the *X-3A* could go after boomer and attack submarines for a fraction of the cost. Tactical and strategic possibilities became intriguing with a twenty- thousand-mile range and thirty-five knot dash speeds. Throw in low active and passive signature profiles and the carrier group admirals took notice and put their shoulders to the concept.

Finally, they went to their budgets and Capitol Hill. But euphoria over *glasnost* had penetrated the closed doors of exhaustive Armed Services Committee meetings. And it wasn't a "guns or butter" decision this time. New democracies in Eastern Europe and Central America, pointing out that the U.S. had deliberately set the stage for their freedom, were asking for large amounts of aid to prime their economic engines. Accordingly, the committee pared the Navy's request to one experimental boat, not the anticipated production run of thirty.

The Navy countered that, unlike the Army or Air Force, their global seakeeping mission hadn't changed measurably, *glasnost* notwithstanding. They argued the Soviets still had one of the most powerful navies in the world, were modernizing their fleet, discarding old equipment, and were proceeding with new aircraft carrier and nuclear missile submarine programs, the latter having improved capabilities to devastate any city on earth. The admirals added that demands on them were actually increasing with the limited and virulent conventional wars and terrorist campaigns that popped up from time to time. And that the *X-3* would be of great value in that category too. "Besides," they offered, "one *X-3* is a quarter the cost of an F-16".

The Committee, referring to the new foreign aid as the Marshall Plan--

Act II, replied, "One boat is all you get for the time being. You're lucky we didn't cancel the whole *X-3* program."

Jenson Industries had transferred Lofton to San Diego after the hearings, just as prototype construction was to begin in a secret waterfront pen, a converted tuna cannery. By then, the project had been transferred to the National Security Council. The Navy didn't know why and without thinking, heaved a sigh of relief; civilians no longer asked deep, penetrating questions that required complicated technological responses. The *X-3* became a black program funded by money of the same color. Now, a prototype, maybe two, could be successfully completed with all the gadgets, *perestroika* be damned.

Kirby was silent, waiting. Lofton felt his stare. Kirby wanted answers.

Lofton bit a thumbnail. How much could he tell Kirby? *Brutus?* Renkin? Thatcher? Catalina? Should he tell him about Petropavlovsk? Should he--

"You gonna keep suckin' your thumb, Brad?"

"Walt...you...people can get killed."

"So I noticed. C-4 does a good job when packed by those kind folks who work at Langley. And those guys back there looked like Virginia country gentlemen. Now, give."

"Not the CIA, Walt."

"My mistake. Those guys are on location from Disney Studios." Kirby sighed heavily.

Lofton's shoulders sagged. "OK. It started with a spook project called Ivy Bells..."

CHAPTER 3

Leningrad, 1959

They came for Manfried in the late afternoon. He heard their voices in the corridor as they spoke to Olga Horoshkin.

"...Theo's been gone for several days," she said.

"...we're here to clean out his shit..."

Their voices trailed. But Manfried heard Olga gasp, "No!"

A grunt. Then, "Where?"

"They're assigned to that room. The boy is in there now. Manfried."

A second voice growled, "This is the German whore's kid with the American brother? The one Slick Theo adopted?"

Manfried put aside his book and jumped up. What about Theo? What was wrong? He squeezed his eyes closed and tried to remember what Theo had last said. His absences were more prolonged but Theo was finally learning the ropes. They were making progress. Wasn't there food for them now? They didn't have to stand in the lines anymore.

Two weeks ago, he'd reached over and tousled Manfried's hair after a late evening meal. His eyes glittered as he tossed off his vodka, saying, "They are finally sending me to the other side, Manfried. Soon, we'll have our own apartment instead of this..." he waved an arm, "this communal pigsty."

Later that night, Theo moaned in his sleep, calling for Katya and their daughter, Katarina. They'd been lost to the Germans in 1943 during the 880 day great siege of Leningrad. Then, in 1951, a Berlin-stationed Theo Kunitsa adopted one of two orphaned twin boys. Their mother had been killed by an Allied bomb while it was being defused. The father was unknown.

Feet shuffled toward the door while Olga babbled something about a pension. Would she be eligible even though they weren't married? After all, hadn't she helped with the boy?

Manfried stepped to the center of Kunitsa's gray one-room redoubt. It was nestled in a common set of three rooms and a closet-sized kitchen. Two other families lived there and they were still at work. Only a widowed forty-six year-old Olga and Manfried remained.

Two giant, fire-hydrant-shaped men thumped in; they stood, their eyes darted around the room. Olga squeezed in behind with glistening eyes. One of the men spotted Kunitsa's cardboard suitcase. He threw it on the bedroll and said, "You're leaving, Fritz. Pack."

"What?" Manfried managed.

"Now, Fritz. You're going to Melekhov. Tonight."

"Nooooo!"

A thumb and forefinger vised his ear and sent him to a clothing pile at the foot of his bedroll. Manfried's ear burned as he bent to his things. There wasn't much; a blanket, two pair of Kunitsa's old socks, a heavy woolen shirt and a tattered army greatcoat. He made sure his math and English books were tucked in the blanket folds. One of the fire hydrants held out a paper sack; the other sniffed as he dumped Kunitsa's two medals and new green KGB shoulderboards inside. They clinked once and disappeared. When they weren't looking, Manfried grabbed three potatoes and crammed them among his things. Olga winked at him while the remaining food, the rest of the potatoes and a half-dozen cans, disappeared with Kunitsa's medals. The sack was stuffed in one of the fire hydrant's overcoats.

One man's name was Andrei. He seemed wider than the other. His knee-length overcoat snagged on drawers as he turned and piled Kunitsa's uniforms and clothes in the middle of the floor. Then he peered in drawers.

The other stooped to pry up floorboards. Satisfied, he trudged down the hall to check the toilet tank.

It didn't take long to secure Kunitsa's things. Andrei quickly bagged everything and tied string around it. The room was empty now except for Manfried's suitcase and two thick brown paper-wrapped bundles. The few furniture pieces would remain for the next tenants.

Manfried chewed his thumbnail. Finally, he stammered, "What happened? Where's my father?"

"Shut up, Fritz," Andrei shouted, his thick lips formed a cavern. He jammed his fists on his hips. "Where's your brother?"

"I don't have a brother."

"He's in America, isn't he?"

"I don't have a bro--"

"And if you want to know, Americans, their CIA, shot Kunitsa. Hell, your real father is one of them, too. An American."

The man had kicked him, he was sure. But when Manfried was able to focus again on Andrei's belt the man stood in the same position. Above him. Towering. He hadn't moved.

"Nothing in the tank." The other man walked in. "Its dry. Hasn't been flushed in weeks. Whew! I had to piss out the back window."

Andrei stooped. He found the youngster's cloudy eyes and growled, "It's time you found out. Americans killed Theo. And both your father and brother are Americans. How do you feel about that, Fritz?"

Manfried tried to square his shoulders. "My name is Manfried Kunitsa".

Andrei's thick hands pressed on his knees. He rose. "Not any longer, Fritz. Sergeant Theodore Pavel Kunitsa ceased existing three days ago. You don't either. You're to Melekhov Hall. They'll figure out what to call you."

Kunitsa, dead. Melekhov! Manfried caught the other man's glance, to see if he would cry. He choked it back.

The men took a last check. Andrei said, "I think we have it all." He rumbled, "Good-bye, Theo."

The other said softly, "Yes, good-bye, you dumb bastard." He slowly shook his head. "Slick Theo. Hero of Berlin. All he did was shine paper-clips and count prisoners. He always wanted to be a hero. Instead, he screws up a wet job in Zurich. They knew that would happen. They shouldn't have let him try to be a hero."

They pushed Manfried out the door, through the corridor and into the main hallway. Static, then a low squealing seeped under one of the doors as they crowded down the hall.

"What the hell?" Andrei blurted. "Nobody in this building has a radio permit that I know of."

"Later, Andrei. We'll check it later."

Manfried shook away Olga's hand and took the steps with her stride for stride.

Americans. Kunitsa had taken him to an American movie once. They showed it in a cellar down the street. Men drank and roared at the gangsters. One wore a white suit, wide-brimmed hat, and two-toned shoes. The other gangster, a cigarette dangling from his lips, fired a submachine gun from waist level. The first gangster's chest splattered with dark splotches as he jinked and whirled back into an alley.

Americans. Their submachine guns were inferior to the PPD models Soviets had used in the Great Patriotic War. Both had drum-type magazines, but the PPD was superior. Kunitsa had told him. He'd smuggled one home and taught himself to field strip it blindfolded. Then he taught Manfried.

His foot caught a step but he kept up with Olga. The other two trudged behind. Silent.

Yes. The PPD was better.

Americans.

CHAPTER 4

Lofton slouched on his elbows, drained. Telling Kirby had brought it all back. The *X-3* project. His escape in *Brutus*. The run to Catalina. And Thatcher. Lofton could still see Thatcher's bloody lips. The screwdriver-- trying to push it back through Thatcher's chest. Renkin swinging the mallet, crushing Thatcher's skull.

The oven bleeped. Lofton lowered his head to his hands while Kirby retrieved the pizza.

Finally he said dully, "I think I've said too much."

"Here. You have to eat."

"I've lost my appetite."

"I'm not surprised. Talking about it can do that. When was the last time you had a solid meal?"

A sandwich on *True Blue*, breakfast at Mabel's this morning, Lofton couldn't remember before that.

Kirby looked at him, then made a face, "No wonder your appetite is gone. That dark beer tastes like goat piss. Why do you drink it?"

"I like it. You know that."

The pizza tasted good. Lofton munched, drinking the Chianti Kirby silently produced. Next, a tall salad with oil and vinegar was shoved in front of him.

As he ate, Lofton scanned the Sunday evening lights gleaming on a now-empty Newport Bay; they jiggled on the water quietly, mournfully. The weekend was gone. The houses around him and across the bay on Lido Isle were quiet and sedate, as if someone had turned down a master rheostat. Next Friday would be a different story, life would be back to full swing. But he would be gone.

Lofton sat back and looked at the dock in front of Kirby's house. His twenty-foot Skipjack, *Them Bones,* was tied across from the gaping space where *Bandit* usually moored. "When are you bringing *Bandit* back from Long Beach?"

"Probably Tuesday or Wednesday. O'Connell will bring her down." He stood over Lofton, "Coffee?"

Lofton leaned back in the chair, folded his hands on his stomach, and nodded.

Kirby produced two coffees and sat with a paper and pad. He started to write, then looked up. "OK. You say Felix Renkin is a spy?"

Lofton nodded.

"And that he killed this guy Thatcher?"

"Yes."

"Why?"

"I ran Renkin's disks. I'm convinced Thatcher's right. Those CAPTORs are programmed specifically for the acoustic signature of the *Truman* and the Japanese trawler he spoke of. And, according to the stuff I saw in Renkin's briefcase, the *Truman*'s exit route takes her directly over those two mines."

Kirby knitted his brow.

Lofton nodded. "Come on, Walt. CAPTOR. Encapsulated torpedo. It's like they stick a Mark 46 torpedo in a big bottle or flask and sow it like a mine. You can program it to search for a wide variety of ship sounds or magnetic signatures. Once the right signal goes off on the CAPTOR's detection gear the end pops off, the torpedo swims out and heads for the target. And it has a nasty little ninetyfive pound charge that is bad enough for a trawler but devastating to a submarine, especially at depth."

Kirby wrote "CAPTOR--Mk. 46" on his pad and looked up.

Lofton rubbed his eyes. "Renkin had told me that *Brutus*'s first operation was to be a towing exercise for SDVs. A spook launch was supposed to hook them up off Coronado Roads. I realize now that Thatcher knew he was towing CAPTORs, presumably to see if *X-3*'s could lay them successfully. I don't know where he got them but I'm convinced he thought it was just that: a towing exercise. He didn't expect them to drop off when they did; they were released automatically. I don't know how. Thatcher hung around for a while trying to figure out what to do, but then he had to come home 'cause his fuel was running out. I think that's when he figured out the CAPTOR's program. He had Renkin's floppy disks on board and had time during the voyage back to play with the computer and decipher Renkin's instructions."

Kirby shook his head slowly, his pencil twirled. "So Renkin kills Thatcher, the *X-3*'s pilot, because he knew too much?"

"Yeah."

Kirby looked at his notes and flipped the pencil on the pad. "Brad, for crying out loud! How is anyone supposed to believe this? I mean, Felix Renkin is a powerful man. He's served under three presidents."

"Damnit. Don't you think I know that? Until last Wednesday, I thought the guy walked on water. But I saw him do it and I read the stuff in his briefcase. Ivy Bells. That must be it. He's selling Ivy Bells and probably a bunch of other stuff."

"Maybe it's something to do with *glasnost*. The Cold War is over, you know."

"Not in this operation. Someone out there, besides Felix Renkin is still playing for keeps."

Kirby tore off a clean sheet of paper. "OK. Let's get to that. What the hell is Ivy Bells?"

"One of Renkin's folders is labeled Ivy Bells. There're only a few memos so I'm piecing it together. Best thing that I can come up with is that Ivy Bells is a listening operation in the Sea of Okhotsk between the Kamchatka Peninsula and the mainland of Soviet Siberia."

"The Sea of `O.'"

"Right. Kamchatka is damned long and rugged, eight hundred to a thousand miles. There're no highways or railroads to the mainland. Seems like Ivan has to run land lines between the Kamchatka Peninsula and the Siberian mainland."

"Induction?"

Lofton raised an eyebrow and nodded. "You're way ahead of me. That's what it sounds like. Apparently our submarines have been sneaking in there for a long time listening to Soviet telephone traffic over those cables via some sort of induction device."

Kirby smiled.

"Yeah. You got it. Petropavlovsk. Our guys have apparently been listening to Ivan's juicy stuff for a long time from the Okhotsk seabed."

"But why now?" Kirby's smile faded. "I thought we were in some sort of military stand-down."

"Yes and no. Yes with offensive and some strategic weaponry. No on the intelligence side, especially passive intelligence. Apparently, both sides don't entirely trust the other's press clippings."

Kirby waved a hand. "But why? Look at Eastern Europe. Look at--"

"--I know, Walt. I know." Lofton shook his head. "I wish I knew all the answers. Maybe there are a few diehards on both sides."

Kirby grunted and went back to his doodling. As a SEAL he had learned of Petropavlovsk's strategic importance. It was a major Soviet seaport on Kamchatka's eastern or Pacific side toward the tip. Starting as a whaling village in the eighteenth century, Petropavlovsk boasted dry docks, shipyards, lumber mills, fish canneries, and a population of well over two hundred thousand. The juicy part Lofton referred to was that Petropavlovsk had become a major naval base. Twenty-five percent of the Soviet Pacific Fleet was homeported there, including all their Pacific-based missile submarines. And the U.S. Navy had been monitoring their cable traffic.

Lofton eyed Kirby's pad. "That's right. Ivy Bells sounds like a neat, tight little operation and guess who runs it?"

Kirby penciled out "FELIX RENKIN - NSC."

"Right again. That's one of the reasons they took over the X-3 program. They want to use mini-subs for listening instead of big ones. The cost-benefit tradeoff is enormous. Makes the NSC happy and the Navy gets their regular subs back."

"Makes sense." Kirby paused. "Except you say Renkin has told the Russians about it. That means..."

"I know. It scares the hell out of me. The Russians know we're in there. It's shallow. They could blow 'em up or something."

"International waters."

"Doesn't matter. They're experts at saying `so sorry.' At the very least, the operation is compromised. And so is the *Truman*. She's there right now." Lofton's voice drifted. "She's an old boomer, almost thirty years old. Her missile systems have been disassembled. She has an SDV chamber on her back, they call her an auxiliary submarine now." Lofton nodded to himself. "That would be an easy job for her."

He looked at Kirby. "Walt, her exit route is through the Kuril Straits, and those damn mines are on the Pacific side of the Straits, right along the *Truman*'s track."

He tapped a finger on the table. "Those guys won't have a chance. There are two of those mines; one is programmed for the *Truman*, and another for--"

"All right." Kirby scrawled on the pad. "Let's get this right. Why does Renkin want to sink the *Truman*?"

"I found a CIA top secret memo addressed to Renkin in his briefcase. There's a Russian signals officer in Petropavlovsk who wants to defect. His code name is PITCHFORK, and from Renkin's scribblings, it seems that PITCHFORK knows about Ivy Bells. That means this guy can spill every-thing about Renkin if he comes to the U.S.. And since it's a CIA operation, not NSC, Renkin has no control over the defection or what the guy says when he's debriefed.

"There's another asset in the memo called PARALLAX. I think his name is Katsunori Nagamatsu and he is PITCHFORK's CIA control. PARALLAX works aboard a Japanese fishing trawler, the *Kunashiri Maru*, which calls regularly at Petropavlovsk. That's how they intend to extract the defector. PITCHFORK sneaks aboard and the ship sails for Japan."

Lofton leaned forward, his eyes glimmering, "PITCHFORK could provide enough evidence to expose Renkin, Walt. That would clear me, too. The thing is, Renkin can't afford to have that happen. That's why he had those CAPTORs laid. He wants both ships sunk at the Kuril rendezvous. He doesn't know which one PITCHFORK will be aboard."

Kirby's pencil twirled furiously. "So he doesn't mind sinking two ships and killing all those people just to make sure the guy doesn't reach the U.S."

Lofton nodded. "Another CIA memo in Renkin's file said the *Kunashiri Maru* is supposed to drop a load of fish in Petropavlovsk on the twentieth. Then she leaves on the twenty-third. If I can get out of here within the next day or so, I can make it. That's what I'm thinking of doing, Walt. Going to Petropavlovsk and grabbing this guy PITCHFORK off the *Kunashiri Maru*. If I can bring him back here, then I have a case against Renkin. I also would have time to swing south to the Kuril Straits and disarm those two CAPTORs before the *Truman* exits."

"Why not just disarm the CAPTORs and let the two ships rendezvous?"

"Yeah. I thought of that. The trouble is, Renkin is very resourceful. I'd like to grab PITCHFORK before he gets lost in all those covert channels and safe houses. One of Renkin's boys could get to him and kill him before he has a chance to talk about this operation. Lofton shook his head. "I can't see a better way, Walt. PITCHFORK is the key to exposing Renkin. He's the key to getting me off the hook. And I can save a lot of lives besides, if I disarm the mines, too."

"How the hell would you do it?"

"Phase one is the easy part. Lie on the bottom near the trawler, exit *Brutus* and board her. The specs on the *Kunashiri Maru* are in the folder. She isn't very big; only five hundred tons or so, 175 feet long. So it shouldn't be too hard. I can leg up an anchor chain or crawl up a piling if it's moored alongside a dock."

Kirby snorted. "Just like the old days."

"It gets sticky in phase two. I have to sort out Katsunori Nagamatsu from the crew. Then phase three, is an even harder job; get Nagamatsu to talk, sign a statement and get him to lead me to PITCHFORK." Lofton cracked his knuckles. "I'll beat it out of him if I have to."

Kirby shook his head.

"All right. I'll persuade Nagamatsu and his buddy, PITCHFORK, that they've been set up. I'll show them a marginal note on one of the CIA memos. It's in Renkin's handwriting: ` *Terminate both assets @ Captor site.*'

"When they see that, Nagamatsu and PITCHFORK can't ignore the fact that they have been set up. That Renkin wants them killed by a Mark 46 torpedo which was manufactured and sown by the same benevolent government that feeds their Swiss bank accounts."

Kirby snorted, walked into the kitchen, clanked his coffee service, and returned with the pot. "You don't have a good plan."

"Maybe not, but I'm running out of time. My biggest problem is that I need to refuel *Brutus* right away. I have a full load of hydrogen peroxide but the damn thing's almost out of JP-5. If I don't bring him up, he dies right there. I have him on a low auxiliary load but he'll only keep for a couple more days."

Lofton eyed Kirby. "If *Brutus* dies I not only lose the submarine, but Renkin's stuff and the computer disks are still on board. They would be gone as well. Problem is, Renkin knows what's on my mind, since I have his briefcase. He also knows I need JP-5, so he'll do everything he can to keep me from getting it and doing something rash like taking a quick trip across the Pacific."

Lofton paused. "So, old buddy, I need you to help me find some JP-5. Quickly and quietly."

"Brad, I dunno. This is all happening so fast."

"You did say there's C-4 planted under my hood?"

"I did."

"So maybe we can work it from both ends. Say I shoot over to Petropavlovsk, make the pickup, and disarm the CAPTORs. In the meantime you figure out a way to go through channels and stop Renkin from this end."

"God, who would believe we're talking about Felix Renkin this way?"

Lofton said, "One of us should make it. If we don't a lot of people will be dead."

"Like Thatcher," Kirby said softly.

"Like Thatcher." They stared at the lights on the water. Thatcher. Lofton waved off a refill.

Kirby poured coffee for himself. "Let's go over it again. You really saw Felix Renkin kill Thatcher."

"Yes."

"And then you decked Renkin?"

"Yes."

"Are you sure Thatcher was dead?"

"Yes."

"What did you do then?"

Silence. Lofton put his head in his hands.

"Brad, what did you do after you knocked out this Renkin guy?"

"I tied up Renkin and called the cops."

"Hell, why didn't you say so? What happened next?"

"They were there in five minutes."

"Good. And then?"

Lofton looked at Kirby through spread fingers. "You wouldn't believe it. Carrington's guards wouldn't let 'em through the gate. I watched through a window. A ten-foot chain-link fence with barbed wire surrounds the place and they just wouldn't let the cops through the gate. I watched 'em haggle. Carrington drives up and joins the discussion, then I see him flipping out IDs." Lofton snapped his fingers. "The cops take off just like that. The next thing I know, Carrington is heading for the building without his orange roughy and the phone line goes dead while I'm trying to call the Shore Patrol."

Kirby nodded. "I think I remember this guy Carrington. Ted Carrington? You said he was CIA? About six three, six four, blond curly hair?"

"Yeah."

"He's pretty good. Isn't he the guy we had to take ashore that night in Beirut?"

"Uhhuh."

"And then we extracted him two nights later. Yeah, I remember. We knew he had some big-time scalps in his belt, but he wasn't talking much, just a few words to put us down. A real wetjob man in more than one sense of the expression." Kirby looked at Lofton. "Did you remember your BUDS training?"

Lofton said, "I did. He wasn't quite ready, didn't know what to expect. I stood behind the lobby door and chopped him on the back of the neck. He went down without a sound. Then I tied him up and took his .38 and all his money. He had plenty, too, over thirtytwo hundred bucks."

"Beautiful."

"Then I went back and took Renkin's money. Twelve bucks." Lofton smirked. "There was nothing else on him, no ID, no nothing."

"OK. Look. Why did you steal the sub? Why didn't you just jump in the bay?"

"To what? There was a two-knot current running and these guys have boats all over the place. But the real reason was that I was curious to see what was on Thatcher's computer.

"It was fairly simple. I locked the doors, then ran to my office and grabbed my seabag which I had packed for the *Bandit* trip this weekend. I threw that aboard, along with my diving gear. I punched the hoist button and *Brutus* plopped in the water. But then, Walt, I remembered Renkin's briefcase. I went back to the office and grabbed that, too."

Lofton unwound. "I opened the outer doors, jumped on *Brutus*, and backed out of there on battery, right to the middle of the channel."

"I thought you said the batteries were weak when Thatcher brought the submarine back."

"Right. So I submerged and sat on the bottom for a half hour while I let the fuel cells and the rest of *Brutus*'s systems wind up. Plus, I needed time to think."

Kirby shook his head. "I can see why the whole world is looking for you now. No wonder those guys planted C-4."

"Not the whole world. I checked the *L.A. Times* this morning. Nothing was there about *Brutus* or Thatcher. Have you seen anything in the past couple of days?"

"No," said Kirby.

"I don't think Renkin can afford to tell the Navy. For that matter, I don't think he can tell anyone outside his own shop. But still, his world is nonconventional, covert, weird alliances. It's one I don't understand."

Lofton sipped his coffee. "There might have been a better choice. But all I could think of was Les Thatcher lying there with a screwdriver in his back, and something he said about CAPTOR mines programmed to take out the *Truman* and a Japanese trawler."

"So you took your submarine to Catalina."

"Right." Lofton watched a late evening cruise boat meander down Newport Bay. He got up, walked to the windows and came back.

"But I took a side trip first. Almost got killed."

"What?"

"Well, I sat there on the bottom and I thought. Walt, I couldn't believe it. Last Wednesday evening, I was punching on my PC and working late like any other slob. Hell, the screen was still lit up when I left. Then, a half hour later, I'm sitting on the bottom of San Diego Bay and a guy's dead.

"I got *Brutus* moving and experimented a little with him to make sure I could operate the damn thing. Then I headed in and parked him under the *Star of India.*"

"What?" Kirby remembered the nineteenth century bark, now a maritime museum moored at San Diego's Embarcadero.

"Safe place, steel hull overhead, plenty of depth. Who would have thought to look for me there?"

"No one. Unless someone decided to drop a sonobuoy over the side."

Lofton gave a shallow smile, "No sonobuoys aboard the *Star of India.* I exited from the divers' trunk, surfaced, and climbed up the pier pilings and hid for a few minutes in my swim trunks and shirt. Then I walked to the hotel across the street and checked in.

"Boy, did that girl look me up and down! Thought I was some reconstituted drunk."

"Stupid."

"Uhhuh. Next morning I bought some clothes in the gift shop and then called you."

"That's why you sounded so weird."

"Yeah, except I thought you were going to cancel the Catalina trip. That's what I was trying to get you to do."

"Didn't work."

"Walt, I ran some of those disks while I was in *Brutus.* After that, my mind wasn't working right. I had this crazy plan, and everything fell apart. I had to get out of San Diego. I had to provision *Brutus,* and I knew San Diego would become too hot."

"Hot isn't the word for it. Why didn't you--?"

"I decided on Long Beach. Luckily my car wasn't at the old tuna factory.

I'd had it lubed that day at a garage two blocks up the street. So I picked it up, drove to Long Beach, and hid it in that stall where you found it. Then I took a bus back. I don't think I was followed, at least it didn't seem like it."

"You sure?"

Lofton sipped his coffee, "No, especially now after those guys you saw with the C4. But they'd have grabbed me if they'd seen me, don't you think?"

Kirby shrugged.

"When I got back to San Diego I took a cab out to the sub base on Point Loma to check on the *Truman*. I wanted to make sure."

Kirby rolled his eyes and slapped a palm to his cheek.

"I know, I know, it was stupid. But, what would you rather do? Try to stop the sub here or out there?"

Kirby nodded.

"I wanted to know if this wasn't an exercise or some hideous spook screwup. My ID got me on the base but I didn't get past the OD's office. I didn't have to. All I had to do was look out the window. The *Truman* wasn't there. I talked submarines with the OD for a while and he finally let on she had been gone for some time. And I got the guy to tell me when she returns. He checked his schedule and said the first of October. She's due for an extended overhaul alongside the tender. Walt, that means she really is on station now. In the Sea of Okhotsk!"

"But you're not positive."

"As positive as I am that Thatcher's dead."

"All right. Let's say the *Truman* really is on station. What did you do next?"

"I got out of there. I found another cab, went downtown, and, what do you know? I was about two hundred feet from the hotel when I saw Carrington and Renkin walking out of the lobby."

He watched Kirby. "Yeah, now you're getting the idea. Thatcher's dead, no cops have been called, no Navy search. The *Truman* is sitting out there and doesn't know a bomb is on her doorstep. Renkin and his people are all over San Diego and probably the whole West Coast now, looking for me. If I try the FBI or anybody else, the *Truman* will have been blown up by the time my story is verified. If she's warned, fine. But I still need to gas *Brutus* and pick up those guys in Petropavlovsk to prove my case against Renkin. And I want to get them before somebody else does."

"OK, OK. What happened when you took off for Catalina?"

"Yeah, I detoured around the hotel, snuck down to a pier, jumped in the water and swam back to the *Star of India*. Then, like you and I learned, I held my nose and dove to *Brutus*'s escape trunk. I had left a diving tank stashed in there and used it while the trunk emptied.

"Then I powered him up and picked my way out of San Diego Harbor, and if you don't think that was hairy! It was one in the morning and I steered out by periscope. Trying to pick up the nav lights from all the shore lights was a nightmare, especially with the periscope only a foot or so above the water. One time, I think I was abeam of Shelter Island, I was taking fixes all around and feeling pretty good about myself when I looked ahead. I see a green light and a red light and they're getting wider apart and higher, and the lights are on the wrong side of the channel. Damn! It was a destroyer. Almost ran over me. I got *Brutus* down and listened to that thing howl over me, it sounded like a freight train. After that I was able to clear the harbor, that was Friday night. I spent the next day getting used to *Brutus* and then put into Avalon Saturday--last night."

"OK." Kirby folded his arms; his face became clinical. "Brad, I understand what you're saying. But I still believe you shouldn't take this on. Are you sure there isn't somebody who can help?"

Lofton shook his head, "Who? Not with Renkin and his NSC connections. Besides, there isn't time, not with the *Truman* sitting out there."

Kirby propped an elbow and laid his cheek in his palm. "I'm in overload. Let's sleep on this. Maybe tomorrow we can figure out something else."

"O.K.. But I really do I think I'm out of options. I need three weeks' provisions and thirtysix hundred gallons of JP5. The food is easy, but how the hell do I get JP5?"

Kirby looked at him. "You're crazy." He grinned.

"I don't think Thatcher was crazy."

Silence.

"JP5, Walt, how do I get JP5?"

"I dunno. My Mercedes must have at least twentythree gallons of ninetytwo octane. How do I know?" He looked at his watch. "Damn! Eleven thirty. This sounds menial but I have patients to see tomorrow, a knee arthroscopy at ten. Tell you what, after I do the surgery I'll turn my schedule over to another guy in my building for the rest of the week. Then we'll figure out what to do about JP5 and the rest of this crap, including whether or not you really have to go to Kamchatka--OK?"

Lofton nodded.

"Where is *Brutus* now?"

Lofton waved a hand, "Sleeping in fortytwo fathoms of water off Hamilton Cove parked among some rocks. He's nearly invisible and on a very low hotel load."

"What load?"

"Auxiliary load. There's not much time."

"Scratch ten million," Kirby yawned. Then, "That's a tough dive down to two hundred fifty plus feet. You sure you're up to that at your advanced age?"

Lofton rolled his eyes.

"Seriously, that's what I'm talking about, Brad. This deal is too--"

"No," said Lofton. "No, Walt. I don't do two-hundred-fifty foot dives anymore. It's pitch black down there and I'm scared of the dark and the creepycrawlies. No, I have a pinger."

"Pinger?"

"Yeah, like a miniature sonar signal. It puts a bleep into the water. I've got *Brutus* programmed to rise to thirty feet and a small light goes on. I stashed my scuba near an inshore mooring so I can swim right to him." Lofton looked down. "I...I was about to install a new system next week. *Brutus* shoots a bluegreen laser. The beeper receiver detects it and gives the swimmer a digital compass vector. That way others can't see the light from shore or nearby boats, or even searching aircraft. But now..."

"Climb aboard, step into hot showers and eat hot chow. A beeper, huh?"

"Yeah. It's a hand-held job. Here, I'll show you." Lofton picked his seabag off the dining room floor and unzipped it. He dug around, produced the beeper, and gave it to Kirby. He dug around some more. "Damnit!"

"What's wrong?"

Lofton stood, emptied his seabag on the dining room table and swept his hands through his clothes. "Damnit!"

Silence.

"My GPS is gone."

"Do you need it that badly?"

"Yeah, the beeper has good range, but I don't want to spend all night swimming around looking for *Brutus* thirty feet under water. I want to be as close to him as I can. There are too many people around Avalon. Somebody could see that damned light.

"I want to be inside within a minute. The light will go off as soon as I shut the outer hatch."

"Well, think. When was the last time you saw your GPS?"

"Avalon, this morning. I checked my bag before I zipped it up."

"Then what?"

"Then I...we...that's it, that must be it! *True Blue*. The boat was doing death rolls. Howard Butler had a hard time steering the last few miles. We almost crashed a couple of times with gybebroaches. All of our stuff spilled to the deck inside the main cabin. The girl, Bonnie, went below to get my foul weather jacket. I was next to Butler helping him on the wheel. She left my bag unzipped, 'cause that's how I found it when we docked. The damn GPS must have fallen out when we were rolling and mixed with all their stuff. Damn! Even the bilge cover had popped off. It's probably lying in *True Blue*'s bilge right now."

Kirby yawned again and stood. "I'm really out of gas. Wait and get it tomorrow. Let's hit the sack."

"Yes--no--let me think." Lofton rubbed his temples, then, "I save time if I recover the GPS tonight. Besides, I don't want to break into the boat in broad daylight. If I find it, fine, otherwise I'll call tomorrow to see if they have it."

Lofton stood and pulled on his jacket. "I'll be back soon. Hit the hay so you'll be fresh for your surgery tomorrow."

"All right, take the jeep in case someone saw us in the Mercedes, and be careful. Don't even think about going near your Audi."

"--maybe I ought to drive by and see if it's still in one piece."

"No way. Enter from the Marina's east end. It's too early to think about your car. Besides, having two people detailed to watch it on a twenty-four-hour basis eats up a lot of man hours. That's six, maybe eight less guys who could be actively on your tail. And make sure the gangway is clear before you break into that boat. You remember how to do it, don't you?"

"Right."

Kirby's jeep glided into the empty marina parking lot. Lofton drew up to gangway twelve, stopped, switched off the engine, then ratcheted the emergency brake. He looked up and down the aisles, empty except for a red Chrysler LeBaron convertible two stalls down and a derelict Alfa Romeo on blocks three hundred feet away; nothing else. He sat for five minutes watching. A few boats glowed with anticondensation lights. At least, he hoped, there were no live aboards nearby. The harbor was quiet, the water flat, barely lapping, viscous and oily looking. He picked out *True Blue*'s white mast poking skyward among hundreds of others in the late Sunday night marina.

OK.

He sighed, opened the door, got out and walked to the gangway and listened and watched. The ramp sign read "No visitors after sunset." Lofton walked down the ramp, his light steps sounded like thunderclaps.

Sleeping boats seemed to leer at him as he padded along the gangway: a reflecting glint off a powerboat's windshield, a gleaming stainless bow pulpit. Everyone was watching, he was sure. They stood inside darkened cabins, picking up cellular telephones, calling the police, calling Renkin.

True Blue rested securely in her slip and glistened with condensation. Lofton checked the gangway once more. No shrieking sirens, no flackvested guards pouring out of boats charging him with MI6s and Doberman pinschers, no Renkin with his gold-rimmed glasses.

He shook his head and turned on the dock to *True Blue*. She was dark, clean, no evidence remained of Howard Butler's trials and conquests at his helm earlier today. *True Blue* lay waiting for Butler's next adventure.

The Ericson's mooring lines squeaked in protest as he hopped easily over the lifeline. Her mast dipped, then realigned itself to the perpendicular. Canvas covered the top of the doghouse and the hatch cover. He unsnapped it, rolled it forward, and reached for the padlock. There was none. The hasp dangled on top of the hatch, useless.

Lofton sniffed. Some people just don't take precautions, he thought, as he lifted out the hatch boards and stepped down the ladder into the main cabin. He pulled the canvas over the cabin entry; he wanted to use his flashlight and didn't need to signal his presence.

The cabin was dark, yet warm; neat as he remembered it earlier in the day. The Seth Thomas clock on the bulkhead muttered along, the oiled teak wafted about him. He admired the shadowed symmetry of Howard Butler's small, selfcontained microcosm.

His attention snapped back to the GPS. The most likely place was the bilge. If the Butlers hadn't found it, it should still be down there among the keel bolts. He bent over, took out his flashlight, covered the lens with his fingers, then thumbed the switch. Enough light escaped between his fingers as he got on his knees and pried up the bilge cover. It creaked out and he laid it aside. Nothing directly below.

He bent further, nothing all the way aft, then forward, there! Near the mast step bracket! His olive-drab GPS receiver lay wedged under a heavy braided grounding wire.

He lay on his stomach. The GPS was just within reach. He stretched out his right arm.

A bolt of lightning suddenly ripped through his head. A shockwave of pain followed. His head would burst. He'd been hit, he knew. He struggled to his knees to get out, to--

This time the lightning bolt penetrated his right temple. He retched, then lost consciousness.

CHAPTER 5

Lofton's hand spasmed; he reached out.

"Oof."

"Thank God!"

Fire raged in his brain. Slowly it shifted to one side. He pulled a hand toward his head. A palm, not his, soft yet firm, guided his hand down. His stomach convulsed but he caught the retch with a choke; the nausea stopped midway and radiated for a moment. He forced it down. His mouth was dry, his tongue thick.

"It's OK, Matt, wake up." The voice drifted, the palm ran over his brow.

Lofton found his head; wet, seeping, swelling, sharp pain. A dagger penetrated both sides like--like the screwdriver through Thatcher's back! He opened his eyes; nothing, darkness. Blind?

He rose, a hand pushed him back. "It's OK. Don't move yet."

Shapes before his eyes, fingers. "How many?"

"Uh, seventeen."

"Try again. How many?"

He knew the voice. Shadows. A figure loomed over him in the cabin; medium-length straight hair, delicate features, fresh soap, cologne. A woman!

"Come on, how many?"

"Two. Uh, Bonnie?" he rasped.

"Very good. Look Matt, I'm sorry."

His head was in her lap. He distinguished the overhead, the teak grab rails, *True Blue*'s cabin. Bonnie dabbed a wet towel over his forehead and temple.

"Owww."

Bonnie in a blue-checked flannel bathrobe--a not unpleasant sight under other circumstances. He closed his eyes, then looked again as her eyes darted over his and to the top of his head, then back to his eyes. Her brow was knitted.

"What happened?" he asked.

"You happened. I was asleep in the vee berth." She nodded forward. "I was terrified. I forgot to lock the hatch from the inside. Actually, I hate to do that, it gives me clausto. When you came in and bent over the bilge I grabbed the first thing I could find." She brandished a gleaming, varnished three foot teak flagstaff. "I had to hit you twice. I think I sort of missed the first time."

"No."

"Oh, I'm sorry, Matt. I'm glad it wasn't, well, you know, the bogeyman or somebody like that, but someone I knew."

Lofton coughed, then lay silent for a moment. He focused, "I was in too much of a hurry. I should have known somebody was aboard when I saw the hatch wasn't locked. I'm the one who should apologize. God! my head!" He sat up, his head twirled. Bracing his palms to the deck he asked, "You all right?"

"Yes, how about you? Would you like something?"

"I should have knocked. You could have clunked me with a winch handle."

"I thought of that but they're stowed aft, you were in the way. Which leads me to ask, why are you here?"

She raised herself off the deck and sat on the pilot berth while she waited for him to answer. Lofton turned and looked up at her from the cabin sole, "Lost something here today. I had just found it when, uh, the lights went out."

"And what was that?" she asked, her voice cooler.

"In the bilge. It fell out of my bag today. Here, I'll...." He turned slowly and reached into the bilge. The flashlight was where he'd dropped it, shining directly on his RockwellCollins GPS. "Ugh." He stopped, his eyes blurred, then sat back. "I better wait for a moment."

"Are you sure? I straightened the cabin this evening before Daddy went home. Everything was put away." She knelt next to Lofton and looked forward into the bilge, "Oh, is this it?" She got on her stomach, wiggled, then withdrew the small cigarette-pack-sized box and handed it to him.

"What is it?" She drew close.

"A GPS."

"Say again?"

"Yeah, sort of an advanced copy, a half ounce receiver for the Global Positioning System--GPS. Latitude, longitude, anywhere in the world. It uses VHSIC and MMIC chips."

"Good God! Is it accurate?"

"Very. Plus or minus three yards." Bonnie's presence swept through him, her warm flannel robe, the soap; she seemed natural. And she wasn't wearing those glasses. "I owe you a double apology. For now, and again for this afternoon. That was an awful stunt."

She looked down, "It's all right. I'm afraid I was sort of a brat. Here I was on my own boat, and then this knowitall 'Joe expert' comes bursting aboard." She looked at him and smiled. "I guess I was resentful because 'Joe expert' really did know it all. Daddy talked to me about it after you left and I must admit his perspective on my shower was funny. I must have looked pathetic."

"No, very pretty."

Silence.

"What time is it?"

Bonnie turned to the Seth Thomas clock. "Twelve fortyfive." She got up and sat back on the pilot berth. "You were out for about five minutes."

Lofton shook his head gently. Better; nothing seemed to rattle, the pain was duller and the bleeding had stopped. He stood, pulling himself up by the teak grab rail. He willed the swirling to unwind. Finally, "Do you live here?" He looked around, the cabin seemed too neat for a live aboard.

"No, I'm just staying tonight. We live in Irvine and I have to make an eight o'clock presentation tomorrow morning in downtown Long Beach. So why fight the traffic?"

"Well, sorry I bothered you." Lofton pocketed his GPS, headed for the cabin steps and poked at the canvas.

"Sure you'll be OK?" she asked again.

"Yeah, I'm fine. Say hello to your dad and--" He stopped, then turned. "Presentation, you said something about the PW4000 jet engine today."

"That's right, we're bidding as a second source for the fuel pump."

"And you, your dad, Butler Engineering, makes fuel pumps for jet engines now?"

"Well, yes, at least major components. But we have a new system that we engineered ourselves. Daddy's very proud of it. It should--"

"Bonnie, let me ask you. Do you have an inhouse test facility?"

Lofton moved back into the cabin. This could be it. Come on, Bonnie.

She scrunched in the pilot berth's corner, drew up her legs and wrapped her arms around them. "Yes."

Lofton closed his eyes, then opened them. "What kind of fuel do you test with?"

"Jet 'A.' Matt, I don't understand--"

"JP-5?"

"Yes, that too, they're very close. We test with those two. We test with most varieties, including JP-8 and JP4. Why?"

God bless you! Lofton sat. "Look, can I talk to you for a moment?"

Bonnie Duffield pulled her legs tighter. "Well...I...it's late, Matt. I need sleep. Tomorrow is a big day."

He looked at her. "Five minutes?"

She studied him, "OK, you're here. Go ahead."

"I need about thirtyfive hundred gallons of either JP5 or Jet 'A.'"

"What?" Her mouth popped open. "Oh, I get it, you have a Lear Jet stuck on a deserted beach in Mexico with some white stuff aboard." Her words were staccato.

He put his head in his hands. How much would he have to tell her? "No, no, nothing like that. I need it here in Long Beach."

"Fine, call Long Beach Airport services. You can buy Jet 'A' at the pump there. Anybody can. About a buck ninety a gallon. Look, I'm tired.

I'm sorry I banged your head. But now if you don't mind, Mr. Thompson..."

Lofton nodded and stood up. He took a step toward the hatch, then-- damnit! He turned, "My name's not Thompson. It's Lofton, Brad Lofton."

She stared at him. "Figures. Nice to meet you--Mr. Lofton? Now please, let me get some sleep."

Lofton ground his teeth, then leaned against the galley. He needed the fuel, Jet 'A' or JP5, it didn't matter. Both of the simple cut kerosenes would do well in *Brutus*'s fuel cells. But Renkin would have staked out major airports throughout California by this time. Any unusual off-site purchases of Jet 'A' would be reported. He'd thought of renting a flatbed truck and buying the barrels he would need; sixtyseven of them at fiftythree gallons per barrel. But that was cumbersome. He couldn't move sixty seven barrels by himself; a full barrel of Jet 'A' weighed close to 360 pounds. Then how to pump each barrel into *Brutus*? Impossible! He needed thirtyfive hundred gallons in a tanker truck delivered to--he wasn't sure--but he had an idea.

He looked at her and smiled, his best grin, he hoped. "I still have two or three minutes."

"Damn, you're persistent."

Lofton sat down again. "Like I said, my name is Brad Lofton. I really am a naval architect and I work for the Marine Systems Division of Jenson Industries. Look, here's my ID and security clearances." He flipped open his wallet and handed it over.

"Here's what I can tell you..."

A sharp crack awakened Lofton. *True Blue* buffeted slightly, and the echo rumbled for a few more seconds. He sat up and looked at the Seth Thomas: 5:33. Almost daylight.

"What was that?" The door to the head flew open. Bonnie rushed to the doghouse window, leaned over him, and held the teak grab rail. Lofton shrugged out of his makeshift blanket, the spinnaker, and peered over her shoulder.

"What?" she said again softly. A black column billowed on the far side of the marina. Flames roiled, the early morning hue formed a backdrop for the smoke, the northwestern corner of the Long Beach Marina was bathed in campfire brightness.

Lofton's stomach churned. The Audi! It had to be; an explosion like that could only come from C4, not just gasoline or diesel fuel. He'd detonated enough C4 in his SEAL days to know what it sounded like. And the location was right. He sat heavily, then looked up to Bonnie as she peered out; faint flickers played over her face, her partially open mouth. Sirens began to wail.

"Matt--Brad, what's wrong?"

Lofton looked up to her, shook his head slowly, then leaned against the bulkhead. The C4. How could that have happened? The stuff is very stable except when an electric current--

"My Audi, that was my car, I think. It sounded like C4, like I told you last night. I don't understand what set it off." He looked at her; Bonnie's face was like alabaster as she stared out the window. "Bonnie?"

She turned to him, her eyes wide.

"Bonnie," he said softly, "sit down for a moment."

Bonnie Duffield looked back to the receding flames, then sat down slowly next to Lofton. The spinnaker cloth crackled under her blue flanneled bathrobe. "You were serious last night," she sniffed. "Oh, that sounds stupid." Her voice trailed, then, "Are you sure that was your car? How could that happen?" She grabbed his hand. Her eyes blinked.

Lofton sighed. "Carrington's people know their jobs; it wouldn't have gone off accidentally. I don't know, maybe somebody was trying to steal the car. You know, hotwire it and--"

He waved a hand. "Look, I better check just to make sure. If it was my car, they may think I'm dead and that'll give me some time." He stood.

"Come on, I'll take you over." She rose beside him.

"You don't have to, you should get ready for your meeting."

She grabbed a purse and was through the hatch before he could stop her. "There's plenty of time. Come on, Mr. LoftonThompson, you may be in the JP5 business, after all."

Lofton followed the blue flanneled bathrobe down the gangway, up the ramp, and to her red Chrysler LeBaron convertible. They got in silently. She asked as she started the engine, "How's your head?"

"Much better, only a dull ache. Thanks for letting me stay." He had called from a pay phone. Kirby's clinical tones commanded him to stay the night. He'd been right, Lofton was still woozy when he walked back to *True Blue.*

"That's OK, but to tell you the truth, I *was* thinking of calling the cops." She waited, two fire trucks whooshed by with twirling lights but no sirens. Pulling onto Marina Drive she said, "But I wouldn't have slept well last night, anyway. Too much going through my head. I woke up at five."

"Was it the PW4000 or the JP5?"

"Both. But for the time being it has to be the former."

He pointed. "Pull in this aisle. I don't want to get too close."

The LeBaron swung in and Lofton instantly saw that it was his Audi. Blueblack smoke still roiled but the flames were almost out. Bonnie switched off her headlights. They weren't needed in the overcast gray dawn. She pulled next to a dumpster three hundred feet away from the demolished Audi.

Lofton stared at what remained of his car. The glassless windows gaped, the two front doors were gone, and a rear one dangled from its hinge to the asphalt. The two front wheels were missing altogether and the rear tires burned. A black, glowing cinder, the trunk lid gaped open, there was no hood. They silently watched patrol cars roar in and disgorge policemen who milled among firemen spraying their foam.

Several policemen fanned out and begin picking up debris; a radiator hose, a door handle, but most of it was unrecognizable. Bonnie shook her head slowly, then started her engine. Lofton put out his hand. "Hold on for a minute. There, see the white car that just pulled up, the one with government plates? That must be the one Kirby saw. There, that guy--" Lofton slid down in his seat. "That's Underwood, the guy in the gray suit grinning at the cop, he's Carrington's lieutenant and head of security at our plant. Yeah, we better leave now."

Bonnie nodded. She turned in her seat to back up. "Damn, two fire trucks are back there blocking the aisle. Looks like they're just shooting the breeze. I'll have to go out this way. You just stay down until we get out of here."

Lofton squeezed all the way to the floor. He watched Bonnie who wore her thick glasses now. He could see her eyes; she looked vulnerable again, her full mouth, her chin jutted forward, defiant. He watched her eyes dart over the scene, heard the squawk of a fire truck radio as they rolled past.

Suddenly her head turned and her mouth parted. "My God!"

"What's wrong?"

Bonnie returned to her driving, her lips set, as she pulled onto Marina Drive and headed back to *True Blue*. Tears welled as she stepped on the accelerator.

"Bonnie?"

Finally, "They were...the cops...were picking up pieces, junk from the blast, I guess." She bit her lip. "The one closest to me was picking up a human foot--no shoe or sock--just a charred foot..."

Lofton uncurled and sat back in the seat. "Bonnie, I'm sorry. Maybe you better forget--"

Her head whipped toward him, tears running down her cheeks. "Well, Mr. JP5, or whoever you are. You're going to tell me everything or else I go back there and tell those cops everything."

Lofton sat wordless as she sobbed and drove back to *True Blue*'s gangway. She pulled up sharply. The car bucked as her foot jabbed the emergency brake. "Well?" she almost yelled. The engine ran.

"Bonnie, I--"

She tore off her glasses. "That was once a human being back there. Maybe it was just a common car thief, I don't know. All I know is he's dead and you're giving me cock and bull about some nameless, classified project, and a friend of yours who is supposed to be an orthopedic surgeon and-- and nasty little secret agents trying to kill you, blow you up. Well, what is it? Do you tell me or do we go back to those cops?" Her palm slapped the gear shift.

Lofton punched the dash padding with the heel of his hand, "Damnit, I can't, it's too dangerous. First Kirby, I had to tell him last night. He's my best friend; and now you." He looked at her, "I hardly know you but I don't want you hurt."

"What?" She looked at him. Then, "That's malarkey." She flipped the lever into Reverse. Lofton reached over and snapped off the ignition.

"Bonnie, It's not. If they catch me, they could make me talk about you with drugs. They could kill you."

She looked at him.

"Let's go back to the boat." He sighed.

"You'll tell me? Everything?"

He nodded.

Lofton spoke for fifteen minutes as the morning brightened through the overcast. Finally they got out and locked the car. He had to squeeze next to her so they could walk down the ramp together. His words rolled faster. At the bottom of the ramp they stayed close while she wiped at her eyes. His arm found her shoulder, it was natural and remained. Farther down the gangway they looked toward his Audi. Telltale smoke splotches rose over whoever died in it. By the time they reached *True Blue* her arm was around his waist.

"The way you talk you'd think I have a Teamsters card," Kirby muttered.

He stood easily at *Bandit*'s six-foot diameter stainless steel wheel as they powered to Newport Beach, twenty miles down the coast from Long Beach. The Cherokee would be returned to Kirby's house by one of *Bandit*'s crew.

Lofton sat in the cockpit well and propped his feet on the steering bracket. "It's all set up, Walt. We get to use the Butler Engineering truck and Bonnie ordered a load of Jet 'A' early this afternoon. It should have been delivered to the airport by now. All I have to do is go to the market, load your Cherokee with food, park near Berth 209 and--"

"You said a banana building?"

"Yes."

"I can't believe you're doing this."

"I wish I wasn't."

They mulled it over as the seventy foot *Bandit* rolled smoothly at eight knots through the swell. A ten-knot breeze blew over their starboard quarter. There was little relative wind and Lofton felt sticky under the marine layer; it had been stationary all day. He sighed. Usually the sun would nudge the clouds aside but not today, he thought woefully. And, if things went well tonight, he would be gone, en route to Soviet Siberia. He didn't know when he would see the sun again.

A small wave punched *Bandit*'s bow, spray shot up and spotted the foredeck. Lofton watched silently, wishing he was blasting downwind to Cabo San Lucas under the maxi's 2,450 square foot spinnaker.

They were abeam of Newport Pier as Kirby swilled a Corona. "What about this woman? Bonnie."

"What?"

"You sound soft on her."

"Come on, Walt, I've only known her for two days. Plus, she wears a gold wedding band."

"You spent the night with her last night."

Lofton's voice raised a notch. "Hell, she clunked me over the head with a flagstaff. It was you who told me to stay."

Kirby smiled. "Uh-huh. Come here, lemme check my handiwork."

Lofton glared at Kirby, then stepped behind the wheel.

"You drive, I'll check your head. I wish I could check what's in it, too." He turned the wheel over to Lofton, then pried up the bandages he'd put over his temple earlier. "Looks OK, except for the swelling. Should really have a couple of stitches."

"No."

"All right, you stupid jerk," Kirby secured the tape and sat down, "but make sure that bandage is still tight tonight when you go down to find your underwater hotrod."

Lofton caught Kirby's glare, his pressed lips. "Decision time, Walt. We can't put it off anymore."

"All right I'll do it. God knows, if that girl is dumb enough to--"

"Come on," Lofton broke into a grin.

"--dumb enough to fall for your line of crap then I might as well jump in, too." Kirby shook his head. " OK. Here's what I think we should do. Let's play both ends. First, we'll gas your hotrod and you take off tonight. Things are sticky for you around here anyway so it's just as well you're gone. That way, I keep you from stepping in your own dark-brown, smelly stuff. And I take care of things the right way. Do you still remember your Russian?"

"*Gdeh tooahlyeht?*"

Kirby snorted. "Down below, forward, second compartment on your left. And, please remember to flush it this time."

"What's the other end?"

"I know a guy."

"Who?"

Kirby rubbed his chin. "Nate Chandler. He's a patient of mine, an admiral. Met him skiing two years ago at Squaw Valley just after he tore up some knee ligaments. He had me do the reconstruction when we got back. We still stay in touch. In fact, he was at my party last Wednesday night. He's a helicopter guru on COMNAVAIRPAC's staff in San Diego."

"A zoomie?"

"Uh-huh. Nate's an interesting guy, flew A-6s off the *Hancock* and was shot down near Haiphong. Got interested in helicopters when they rescued him. From what he's told me he does a lot of drug interdiction and search and rescue, but it sounds like he's been mixed up in some spook deals, too.

"I'll head down to San Diego tomorrow after you shove off. Nate's a ring knocker and is well plugged into the Pentagon. At the very least, I'll get him to have an advisory message sent to the *Truman* so she can change her track. I'm hoping he'll know how to get to the Company and take care of that trawler. too.

"And Brad, he's gonna want to know why you couldn't talk to anybody. You must know quite a few people in the submarine business." Kirby looked at him with raised eyebrows.

"I tried. I called my old boss in Connecticut from the bus station pay phone. He was really cryptic, wanted to know where I was. He kept asking, `Where are you?' So then I talked to his boss. Same thing. I tried a Navy project officer, a full commander who I thought a pretty good friend, I used to sail with him out of Newport. He asked the same thing." Lofton shook his head. "You should have heard their voices, mechanical as hell, `Where are you?'"

Lofton wound some rudder to catch a ground swell. "Renkin has my personnel file. He knows who my contacts are and has found a way to either discredit me or at least shut them up. I don't know what he told them but they didn't sound scared or intimidated."

Kirby nodded grimly. "OK. Let's go over this again. What is it you want me to do?"

"Simple. We pick up some food and take it to berth 209 in the Cherokee. From there, we call a cab. I drop you at the Long Beach Airport fuel dump where you pick up the Butler Engineering truck. It's there now. I head back to your house, meet Bonnie, and we grab your Skipjack--is that all right?-- and zip over to Avalon. She'll bring your boat back while I shoot over to berth 209 with *Brutus*. Let's say we meet there at three-thirty with the truck. It should be quiet then. We load the Jet 'A' and the stores, and I'm gone."

They were still talking as Lofton eased *Bandit* into Kirby's dock. He backed the engine as Kirby wrapped the stern line on the cleat and stopped the boat. They secured the maxi and heard the phone ringing as they walked to the house.

"Let it go," Kirby muttered as he fumbled for his keys. "It's probably Mrs. Schmidlapp or whoever, sniveling about an itchy cast. Damn, I'm supposed to be off for the rest of the week."

The phone jangled while Kirby unlocked the door and punched his security system. Lofton followed him in, headed for the kitchen and popped a Pepsi. Kirby picked up the cordless phone with a scowl, listened intently and stepped next to Lofton. He motioned with a cautionary hand. "Slow down, Mary, tell me again. Who was it?" Kirby looked at Lofton, his eyes level. Then, "What kind of badges? Were you able to see where they came from?"

Lofton stood frozen as Kirby talked with his receptionist. Then he heard, "Tell Laura to calm down, it probably wasn't a shoulder holster...yes...yes...I know." He looked at Lofton again. "No, that's right. If they come back, tell them as far as you know I haven't seen Brad Lofton for several weeks. And tell them he missed the Catalina trip last weekend."

Suddenly, "They're what?" Then, "Didn't you explain I was out on the boat today?"

Finally, "That's their problem. I have a date with Nancy and am just leaving. They'll have to wait until tomorrow...fine... thanks, see you next Monday." He clicked off.

"We're outta here." Kirby growled. "Your friends are on their way."

Lofton needed no urging. He picked up his seabag. "How soon?"

"Maybe ten minutes. Come on, the jeep should be out front and--oh, one thing--quick, in here."

He led Lofton to the garage and opened the trunk of his Mercedes. "Here, my medical bag, you may need it."

"Walt, we have medical supplies on board."

"Take it, damnit. There's some stuff in here I know you don't have on board. I'd feel better if it went with you."

Lofton grabbed the bag. "Thanks."

They bolted to the jeep, started up, and headed down Bayshore Drive. Endless seconds passed while they waited at the guard gate signal. Finally, they sighed their relief as the light turned green, and Kirby whipped the jeep westbound on Pacific Coast Highway.

"Who did she say they were?" asked Lofton, looking back.

Kirby fumbled for the radio and clicked it on: country and western. He checked the rearview mirror, then relaxed. "She remembered one name, Underwood. That mean anything to you?"

"Um."

"Um, what?"

"One of Carrington's boys. He was at the Audi this morning after it exploded, laughing it up with the cops. It probably means they still think I'm alive, especially since they were just at your office."

"I don't think so. That was probably just a routine check to make sure you didn't spill the beans to anybody. No, the more I think about it, you're dead to them. It's going to take a while to identify whoever broke into your car and--"

Lofton held up a hand and cocked an ear to the five o'clock news.

"...even though most of the body was destroyed along with the Audi, federal investigators were able to match a lower jawbone fragment to the dental xrays of Lieutenant Commander Lester F. Thatcher of the United States Navy. Commander Thatcher was a submarine officer assigned to the submarine tender USS *William B. Holman*, currently based in San Diego, and had been reported missing for several days.

"The car's owner, Bradley P. Lofton, is also missing. The FBI and the Office of Naval Intelligence have been called in since a United States naval officer died in Lofton's car. The FBI announced late this afternoon that the statewide search for Lofton will be expanded to a nationwide basis..."

Kirby turned down the radio. "Jeeez!" he muttered and gripped the wheel. He turned to Lofton and stammered, "I saw that car, your car. Nobody was in it. They must have stuffed the body in last night or early this morning and set off the charge.

"Nationwide search; Renkin has a lot of clout."

"It was a signal, Walt," Lofton said grimly, "Renkin is finally letting me know. And he's moving fast."

"Jeeez." Kirby repeated softly. The setting sun poked momentarily through the haze. He pulled down his visor.

CHAPTER 6

Eastern Mediterranean, 1972

The new forty-seven-hundred ton Kashin class guided missile destroyer rolled drunkenly in the trough of a heavy northerly swell. The night was overcast, moonless, infinitely black as a thirty-six-knot wind tore at the *Odarennyy*'s superstructure. She slewed parallel to the waves. Her spider-like antenna swung through enormous arcs and her squat stern disappeared under dark, cascading comers only to shake loose again for the next onslaught. Things weren't better at the other end. Dark mountains assaulted her raked bow, which in calmer seas stood proudly and knifed easily at speed. Water had seeped through a faulty foredeck hatch gasket and shorted an electrical panel below decks. Power had been lost to the forward part of the *Odarennyy*. Her starboard anchor had been ripped effortlessly from the hawse pipe by a well-aimed rogue wave.

The pilothouse deck watch spread their feet; they clutched anything in reach and cursed as the *Odarennyy* bucked. Red instrument lights mixed with soft green CRT displays to cast a reptilian glow on their tense faces.

An apprentice seaman croaked loudly; a splattering sound echoed about the cramped, humid space. The deck watch bellowed an incredulous

roar of condemnation as the odor swept through. Orders followed to grab a
mop and remove the mess instantly.

As the young man gagged and swabbed at his vomit, the leading petty
officer muttered that the bow must look like a boar with one tusk. There
would have been soft chuckles under normal conditions. But they were
closed up to action stations and the missing anchor didn't concern them.
What concerned them was trying to find an American carrier group while
approaching the southern coast of Cyprus with one of their four gas
turbine engines down. Worse, the air search radar was acting up and the
surface search radar was inoperative.

Junior Lieutenant Anton Pavel Dobrynyn stood near the aft bulkhead of
the pilothouse and grabbed an overhead cable bracket just as the
Odarennyy lurched once again. The helmsman, one of their best, swore
softly and spun his wheel to keep them on course 290. The long, narrow
ship slithered along the front of a wave, paused, then pounded her way
across the back. Her nose finally buried in the trough. Dobrynyn heard but
couldn't see massive sheets of water engulf the weather decks and eight
souls who cowered under the starboard bridgewing bulwark. The captain,
the officer of the deck, the junior officer of the deck, three lookouts, and
two signalmen were out there sealed in leaking parkas and sea boots. With
dripping binoculars, they were trying to do what their radars couldn't for
the moment. Find Americans to the north, toward Cyprus.

A cigarette glowed next to Dobrynyn as its host took a drag. Captain
Third Rank Dimitri Lazo, the *Odarennyy*'s zampolit, political officer,
exhaled, then continued softly. "The Captain wants a firsthand report about
the number-three engine. Also, do you have any ideas about the surface
search radar antenna? Chernov is up the mast with that signalman,
Ullanov."

"In this? Chernov gets seasick."

Lazo eyed Dobrynyn. "I'm not sure about his seasickness. Don't worry."

"Anyone would get seasick up there now."

Seconds passed. Lazo measured his tones pedantically. "It is necessary for
the battle problem. That's why I sent Ullanov to help out. He's strong. They'll
be all right. But Chernov asked for you. The last word we got was something

about a broken waveguide. Do you know what that means? I can't get anything out of those idiots in main plot. They say they're too busy trying to work the battle problem off the air search radar. And the exec has the rest of the technicians up forward screwing with that damn electrical panel. Even a couple of radar people." He paused to watch the seaman work with his mop and bucket. "There is something else. You should know now since there isn't much time."

Lazo looked up to the six-two, thin, dark-haired Dobrynyn. "A fleet message came in an hour ago. You have orders. We're being refueled by the *Izhora* at noon tomorrow and you are to be sent over. You and Ullanov. They'll take care of you until she docks in Sevastopol in three weeks. You'll detach there and it's on to specialized training at the Combined Arms School. So have your gear ready."

Dobrynyn's jaw dropped open. He should have been surprised, he knew. He looked up, shadowy cables traced an indecipherable pattern in the overhead.It still followed him. He couldn't shake it. Political types had hounded him in school; he'd worked harder than most and graduated in the top five percent. Hadn't he proven himself? And he took his commission seriously, he was an officer in the Voyenno Morskoy Flot. The Soviet Navy. The new *Odarennyy* was the reward for his efforts. She was revolutionary. Her four gas turbine engines put her years, decades ahead of anything the Americans had. As assistant engineering officer, Dobrynyn was enjoying the prematurely recalcitrant propulsion plant. This was what he had worked for. He should be free.

He looked down to the barrel-chested zampolit and stammered, "But sir, I've only been on board for two months. Combined Arms School. That's Naval Infantry. I don't understand."

Lazo took another drag. His voice rose as he said, "Dobrynyn, remember what I told you when you first reported aboard. This ship's morale and political well-being are my responsibility. The last thing I need are countercultures in my midst. I'm having enough trouble as it is. You're not a natural citizen. The records say your father is an American." Lazo's eyes rolled up to Dobrynyn.

"Yes, but he disappeared and--"

"You were born in the West. All this linked with having an American brother creates a security problem and the fleet political directorate concurs with my--"

"I think I was born in what is now East Berlin--"

Lazo raised a hand and slowly rolled his thick head, "East. West. Berlin is Berlin to me. It doesn't matter and the record's not clear anyway. And I don't care if you just finished five years at the Dzerzhinskiy Higher Naval Engineering School. I don't care if you received high marks. And I wouldn't spare Stalin's last turd even if you are one of the *Rodina*'s greatest aspiring naval architects. No." Lazo shook his head." I just don't take chances. And since you'll be responsible for Ullanov at least until you get to the Combined Arms School, you should think about straightening out his Ukrainian line of shit.

"In any case, you are fortunate. You're to be given your second duty choice. Spetsnaz, isn't it? That's what you put on your duty preference form. You and Ullanov are headed for Spetsnaz training. You'll be heroes of the Soviet Union."

Dobrynyn drew himself up. "Captain Lazo. I like it here. This ship is a challenge and there is so much to do. Besides, I haven't seen my brother since we--"

The helmsman moaned.

Their eyes unlocked and turned to him. The wheel spun as the helmsman fought to keep the *Odarennyy* on course. He misjudged a wave, a monster, by two seconds. The destroyer took a heavy roll and the bow fell rapidly to port. Dobrynyn checked the inclinometer; the bubble traveled quickly to twenty degrees, slowed past thirty, and finally crawled to forty-one. The helmsman shouted. His wheel was useless. *Odarennyy*'s rudder rose out of the water. Her bow was buried.

Dobrynyn hung tight. He knew what would happen next.

Lazo didn't. The swell quickly slid under the *Odarennyy*. She snap-rolled through eighty degrees to starboard in two seconds.

"Eaaagh!" The zampolit screamed and crunched into Dobrynyn.

Books, charts, papers shot from shelves and scattered around the pilothouse. The bucket of vomit crashed to the starboard bulkhead, spilling its contents. Two decks below, shouts and curses drifted up to Dobrynyn as crockery burst from cabinets and shattered.

Lazo's mouth worked toward another curse as he groped in the dark for a purchase; his cigarette fell to the deck. Dobrynyn reached to steady him while Lazo fumbled after it. The ember tip spun, then trailed sparks toward the aft bulkhead. Lazo dropped to his knees, his hands flailed as it rolled toward a cabinet that had just disgorged its contents. The cigarette miraculously navigated between two thick fleet operations manuals and disappeared under the cabinet. Lazo scrambled in pursuit. Dobrynyn's hand shot up to the bracket for the next wave.

The starboard pilothouse door was undogged from the outside and burst open. Loose papers and charts stirred and whipped about as Captain Second Rank Vladimir Sulak jammed his fair, hairless babyface into the pilothouse, binoculars dangling from his neck. He shouted at the helmsman, "Damnit, Ledokil! If you can't keep us on course, I'll find someone who can. That last roll almost threw us in the drink."

"Sir! The fantail broke loose. I--"

"Lazo! What the hell are you doing on the deck?"

"Captain. We were trying to--"

"Is that a cigarette? Damnit! You know my standing orders. No smoking on watch. Anywhere. You Zampolits know how to give orders. Why the hell can't you follow them?"

Lazo's hand found the burning cigarette tip. He squeezed it shut in his palm, grimaced, then stuffed it in his pocket.

Sulak rolled his eyes.

Lazo caught his balance and managed to rise as the ship steadied in a trough.

"Dobrynyn," Sulak asked. "I hope you have good news about number three."

Dobrynyn shrugged, looked at Lazo, then said, " Sorry, Captain. We just finished opening it up. Catastrophic blade failure in the compressor section. It's a yard job. And we're having trouble with number four."

"What?"

"Yessir. Main bearings are overheating in the fuel control governor. Chief engineer recommends we shut it down so we can take a look."

"Damn that aft engine room. What's wrong with those people? Lazo, this is all your fault. How much speed will you be able to give me, Dobrynyn?"

"Twenty knots, Captain."

"Not enough. Keep number four on the line. We're closing with the Americans and we'll need more than twenty knots to maneuver. A lot more."

"Yessir."

The door closed then, reopened, "Lazo. What's the latest on the surface search radar? Have you heard from Chernov?"

Lazo said, "He thinks it's an antenna waveguide rotary joint. I sent him up the mast to have a look, Captain. He and a signalman."

"What?" Sulak stepped in and closed the pilothouse door. Hatless, his glistening fair hair was plastered to his head. Water ran down his splotched parka. "What about the air search?"

"It's still not giving us a reliable surface picture, Captain. The stable element is acting up now. With this rolling, we can only pick up the carrier every ten sweeps or so. And you said no fire control radar."

"That's right. Our orders are to close to visual distance with that damn carrier. Not start World War III."

Sulak wiped water off his brow. He tossed over his shoulder, "Quarter-master. What's the distance to the coast?"

A reply came through the darkness instantly. "The last radar fix was twenty minutes ago, Captain. Cyprus was forty-four kilometers away."

Lazo said, "If the Americans stay on this course, they'll run straight into Larnaca Bay."

Sulak checked the gyrocompass heading over the helmsman's shoulder: course 290. "No. We're not that lucky. I know they're close, just to the north of us. Recovering aircraft. In this crap, yet. I heard a jet go over a few minutes ago." He smiled. "Sneaky bastards. They're all darkened. No lights showing. No radar emissions. Radio silence. And they know we're here. Plus, they know that we know they're out there. The hunt is on."

He focused on the two and his smile disappeared. "No. They'll change course soon after they finish recovering aircraft. And that means they have to come left toward us on 260 or so to clear Cyprus. And that means we'll soon be right in with them. I have to penetrate that destroyer screen but I can't do it without radar, damnit!

"Lazo. Call the Exec up here immediately and get Chernov down off the mast. You know he gets seasick easily and he's no good to us puking his guts out thirty meters in the air. We need him well, damnit!"

"I sent him up there to make a point, Captain." Lazo grabbed a bracket, like Dobrynyn. "Chernov's a laggard. I think he feigns his seasickness. As I advised you before, you should put a letter of reprimand in his naval file. I've already put one in mine."

Dobrynyn winced. He and Alexander Chernov had been at the Dzerzhinskiy Higher Naval Engineering School together in Leningrad. Chernov was a year his senior. They'd met at Melekhov Hall as youngsters, and Chernov, a math wizard, had tutored Dobrynyn and helped him qualify for the prestigious Nakhimov Naval Preparatory School in Leningrad. Chernov *was* prone to seasickness and when commissioned, had applied for a shorebound assignment. He hoped to get an early start into shipboard electronics, just as Dobrynyn was striking for a career in naval architecture. Chernov didn't make it. The *Odarennyy* became his unsettled home a year before Dobrynyn received orders to her. Their hopes were to be assigned to the Zhadanov Shipyards in Leningrad after they finished their obligatory three year tours of at-sea engineering duty.

Sulak growled, "Captain Third Rank Lazo. You are not a line officer. Those decisions are up to--"

Shafts of bright white light pierced the pilothouse portholes, filling the area with an unreal gleaming brightness. They whipped their heads to starboard and shaded their eyes.

"What the--" Sulak grunted.

A metallic echo wafted to them. "...stand clear of me. I am in international waters. I am the privileged vessel..."

"No!" Sulak pushed the door open and bounded outside. Dobrynyn followed into what seemed to be broad daylight. He blinked his eyes, tears flowed as wind tore at him.

"...stand clear..." A mournful foghorn sounded six times.

"Hold course!" Sulak yelled in the pilothouse. "Quartermaster. Turn on your searchlight, you turd!"

Lazo elbowed his way out then shaded his eyes.

Sulak yelled, "Lazo, It has to be one of the American screening destroyers pinning us from the carrier. Get those men down off the mast. Quickly!"

Lazo's mouth worked, "But I--"

"Now! You idiot," The captain shrieked, "do you want them dead?"

"...I am the privileged vessel. You are standing into danger..." The foghorn sounded again, its six two-second blasts crisp, staccato. Closer.

The *Odarennyy*'s searchlight clacked on. A gray glistening hull shone, a hundred meters away, Dobrynyn thought. He judged her to be sailing ten degrees below the *Odarennyy*'s course. Her bow rose entirely out of the water and a hull number stood out: 792. It looked to be an older World War II type destroyer with single gun mounts and no missiles. As he watched, tons of green water shed under her bridge.

Then Dobrynyn knew. The American ship was smaller. Sulak would not change course.

He ran. Wind caught his back as he ran down the aft companionway. He ran. His hands caught glistening slick rails as he descended four levels.

"...STAND CLEAR OF ME..."

Twenty strides found him at the base of the midships deckhouse. He undogged a hatch, shoved aside a lifejacketed petty officer, and gasped up three decks. Another hatch. Dobrynyn flung it open and ran on deck.

A senior seaman stood wide-eyed looking at the closing American ship. Sound-powered phones were clamped over his fur cap.

Dobrynyn could see better. The *Odarennyy*'s bridge was the center of the American's attention, not this section.

He spun the man around, pointed up and yelled over the wind, "What are they doing?"

The ship took a roll to port, both had to grab the bulwark. "On their way down, sir. They just started."

Dobrynyn looked up. Two shadowy figures merged with the upper works in the blackness. They were about halfway down. One appeared immobile. Dobrynyn wiped his eyes and squinted. An officer! Chernov! The other figure grasped him with an arm and held tight as the ship swayed. They didn't seem to be moving.

Dobrynyn jumped at the small ladder and started up.

The American's foghorn blasted loudly six times.

Directly overhead, the *Odarennyy's* foghorn returned the fusillade with her own six blasts.

How close? He took a quick look over his shoulder. The American ship had grown to a massive, dark shape. It wasn't far, maybe a few meters.

"I AM THE PRIVILEGED VESSEL!"

He crawled, slipped. He racked a hand. Warm liquid ran inside his shirt sleeve. *Keep going!*

His head bumped a boot.

Dobrynyn looked up and yelled. "How is he?"

He barely heard, "Weak, sir. He's been puking the last half hour. Hasn't stopped."

"Are you Ullanov?"

"Yessir."

"Hold on. I'm coming up. We'll get him between us."

Dobrynyn heard a grunt, then started up again.

The *Odarennyy* rolled heavily to starboard. Then a shout from below mingled with water sluicing, washing, frothing. The American destroyer's exhaust blowers whined nearby.

Not us!

Instinctively, he wrapped both arms around the mast. The ships crunched loudly. Metal shrieked, sparks trailed along the starboard main deck amidships. He could hear the other ship. Feel it as it groaned alongside then bounced heavily away.

Dobrynyn slid down the ladder a meter. His foot caught a tread and he stopped and held tight. A boot kicked his head, scraped down his ear. Feet, legs spasmed down his back. He reached with a free hand and grabbed a wiggling collar. A second form bumped against his side. Someone shouted in his ear.

He turned to look as the *Odarennyy* started a roll to starboard. Alexander Chernov's hatless, pale face was within a few centimeters of his own. Chernov's eyes were wide, unfocused, vomit ran from the corner of his gaping mouth. Dobrynyn could only clutch the other man. The signalman groaned and shouted, his arm around Dobrynyn's back, holding Chernov's collar.

The ship wallowed through with her roll, another deep one.

The collar came loose, the coat tore. Chernov slid away, then plunged. Dobrynyn lost sight of him as he vanished into the dark, turbulent chasm between the two ships.

Both wrapped their arms around the mast and steadied themselves. Dobrynyn turned to look into the face of the man he'd just saved, the young face of Signalman Josef Ullanov.

CHAPTER 7

The skiff hit another wave and was airborne again. Lofton chopped the throttle and fought for control as the twenty-foot Skipjack ducked deep in the trough, then struggled through the next set of swells. He checked the compass and scowled; 223 was his course to Avalon but the compass card swung wildly on either side. The night was dark. All he could see were the bottoms of low churning clouds; they roiled an immediate warning of the sudden front as they scudded aft toward Newport Beach's light loom.

Lofton checked his watch. He'd been underway for almost thirtyfive minutes but he had only covered fifteen or so miles of the twentysix mile trip to Avalon.

Bonnie had tried dozing in the small veeberth up forward, but the ride had been too wild. Now, she sat next to Lofton in the cuttycabin jump seat. She had to yell over the wind. "Good God! How much longer?"

Lofton tried the throttle again and Kirby's runabout, *Them Bones*, gained speed; the knotmeter jiggled through 22, 25, 27...then--

"Hold on!"

Airborne, and, crunch! Water flared from the boat in all directions. He throttled back.

"Yeah, this should only be a fortyfive minute trip. But with this weather..." He wrenched the wheel to take a swell headon. "It's hard to tell. Maybe another forty minutes or so."

Bonnie reckoned they were nearing midchannel; the seas, even the whitecaps, were harder to pick out since they had cleared the coast. She was glad Lofton was steering, he seemed to be managing. "I'm not sure I can go back tonight, in this."

"I've been thinking about that." Lofton worked the throttle and wheel as they climbed the front of a large swell. It grew and grew, then they jumped over the peak and gaped into a confused, dark chasm twenty feet below.

He shouted as they slewed into the abyss, "Jesus! Did you see that? It almost broke on top of us."

The crests were high and the period between the waves short. Thirty-knot winds preceded the front, unusual for this time of year. He sniffed the air. Rain was on the way.

Another wave, a mountain, rose before them. He could hardly hear himself, let alone Bonnie, who scrunched tighter to him.

"We'll have to find a bunk ashore for you in Avalon somehow. Is your parka warm enough?"

"What?"

"Your parka! Is it warm enough?"

She put an arm around his shoulder and Lofton felt her lips on his ear. "The parka's fine. Where do I stay tonight?"

He turned and looked at her; her eyes, her full mouth. Her hair was wet again, like yesterday with the spinnaker, but this time the corners of her mouth were turned up slightly. They looked at each other. Then she chuckled in spite of the storm. "Watch the road, mister, or we're both in trouble."

In a quick glance, Lofton checked the wave pattern and his compass. The card bounced around 175. A wave towered above him; they were almost broadside to it, ready to broach. He yanked the wheel to the right and added power. The twin counterrotating screws linked to the single 230 horsepower Volvo engine bit the water just in time and pushed *Them Bones*'s bow around and up the wave. They got to the top. Wind shrieked in his ears, salt spray blew across his face and, yes, he tasted fresh water.

"Rain!" he shouted. Bonnie's hands pulled the parka hood deep over her face. She slid lower behind the small windshield and shoved her hands into her pockets.

"Good news and bad news," he yelled from the side of his mouth. He felt her move, his statement acknowledged. He laughed with, "I think we've punched through the front, which means the wind will die soon. It also means lotsa rain and I can't see a damn thing.

"Bonnie?" He tried again, "Bonnie?" He felt her shrug.

Another massive wave towered before him. He had to find his way up; too far to the right, he swung left slightly and found its top. Smaller humps eased their ride down the back. Rain and spray lashed his face, his parka, ran down his neck, his arms. Yet the Volvo purred on, the knotmeter held at around fifteen. Not bad.

The wind dropped ten minutes later. The waves were smoother, more predictable, and they weren't cresting as much. Lofton edged the throttles forward. The downpour was still hard; sheets of it drove against him as he tried to snake *Them Bones* around the larger moguls. Within another few minutes they reached the lee of Catalina and all he had to contend with was the late summer storm's rain.

The swells were almost nil; he firewalled the engine and the howling skiff gained her step and went flat out. Warm, large droplets tore around the small windshield and at his face. Lofton fumbled in the lazaret, found one of Kirby's old baseball caps, and jammed it over his head. He crinkled the bill into a vee with his thumb and forefingers, it helped divert the rain from his eyes.

Them Bones rode evenly, she barely bounced. Lofton checked the knotmeter: 34.5.

Bonnie sat up and leaned against him. "Where are we?"

He looked down to her and shrugged. Water smeared her glasses. How the hell could she see? Just as well, he couldn't either.

Lofton checked his watch. "Time to slow down." He pulled the throttle back to idle and *Them Bones* settled, her wake caught up, raising her stern and shoving her forward momentarily. "We're in the lee of Catalina. We should be close, I think." Except for the rain, his tone was almost conversational.

"Yes, but where? Why don't you try your little Captain Midnight box? That might be easier than waiting until we smash into the Casino."

Lofton already had his GPS out and was warming it up. Finally he punched the LAT/LONG button. The small backlighted display flashed:

33° 22'.07 N
118° 19'.11 W

"OK." He pointed at the screen. "We're here."

Bonnie said, "OK, Mr. Frogman, where's the chart? Show me the chart."

Lofton chuckled and tapped the tiny buttons. "Wait a minute, this gadget only takes quarters." He punched CS/DIST, then WPT 1. He wiped rivulets of rain off the screen as it flashed:

206/0.8

"Hm." He pointed to his left and edged the throttle forward. "This says *Brutus* is almost a mile that way. Here, take it and conn me along, OK? It says we have eighttenths of a mile to go."

Holding the GPS, she studied the little screen, then looked into the blackness. The wind blew the parka hood off her head. The rain fell harder as they gained speed but it felt good, warm, clean against her face.

"Talk to me, Bonnie."

She looked at the compass with a start. "You're way off course. That says you're on oneninety or so."

"You're reading the true course off the GPS, I'm steering magnetic."

"You didn't tell me that--"

"Don't worry." Lofton held up a hand. "How's the range?"

"Point two. It now says course twoohseven, then range point two."

"A degree to the right. Good, keep talking, you can bring us in. Four hundred yards to go."

The rain had eased to a downpour when they both noticed a light hue off their port bow. Bonnie looked to him.

"Avalon, probably the Casino."

"This thing's amazing." She turned the GPS in her hand and examined it. Finally she called in a low voice, "Less than a tenth, we're almost there."

"OK, we'll slide right through it as a check, then head for Descanso."

The GPS bleeped three times in Bonnie's hand, its red light flashed.

"Bingo! Hello, er, *Brutus*--is that what you call it?"

"Yeah." Lofton set his mouth. "Among other things." His stomach tightened. He'd be gone after tonight. *Brutus* was below, waiting; the minisub would rise at his command in the next few minutes. He would have to go, he would be alone. Riding with Bonnie, rotten weather and all, had somehow made him feel buoyant. They'd made a rough passage and someone else would have panicked, or would have been reduced to a sniveling wreck. But she'd done well sitting beside him. He hardly knew her, and yet...

Damn, she was married. He didn't want to...

Forget it. But why was she doing this? Why didn't she just tell him to fly a kite. He hadn't had time to probe her motives outside of his fast sales pitch early this morning.

The buoy line bobbed ahead. "Whoa," he said, half aloud, and dropped *Them Bones* in neutral.

"What's up?" Bonnie squinted through her glasses.

"We're here. Uh, yeah, here's W34." He swung right and paralleled the bobbing buoys, both rows empty. Finally, W37. They ghosted up to the white can and he snagged its ring with two fingers while the Volvo softly burbled in neutral. Then he stood, peeled off his parka, shirt, shoes, and topsiders.

"Be right back. Here, hold on to this ring, will you?"

"Wait, Brad, maybe you should--"

Lofton sat on the gunwale in dark swim trunks; then he winked and pitched over backward.

He was gone. Bonnie could barely see the beach. She looked around hoping no shore boats would blunder along.

A loud exhale. She looked aft. Two hands vised the transom and Lofton kicked over, gleaming, his hair matted, a white line clenched in his teeth. His back muscles shimmered in the gloom as he quickly stood, turned, and pulled the line after him. Finally Bonnie saw a large, sleek, black bundle work over the transom, then she heard the clunk of the weight belt and black tank.

He knelt to his bundle. Bonnie watched the grim set of his jaw. No easy banter now. He knew what he was doing and quickly worked at the straps.

He pulled on his weight belt and glanced at her.

"Shouldn't you use a wet suit?" she asked.

"Don't think so. I won't be in the water for more than five minutes and it's not that cold.

"Look, I'd like you to drop me off. But can you see the compass well enough to putt back to *Brutus?*"

"Of course." Bonnie took off her glasses and thumbed rainwater off the lenses.

"Yeah, OK. Steer the reciprocal, zeroonethree at slow speed while I finish with my gear."

Bonnie clunked the transmission in forward, swung right, and headed back into the rain and darkness. She bent to the compass, her face within inches of it, and caught the glow of the small red light. Peering through her dripping kaleidoscopic glasses, she coaxed a gurgling *Them Bones* to the lubber line. The blurred numbers looked right. She hoped it was, "zeroonethree," he'd said.

Finally, Lofton sat beside her. The seat groaned as his weight belt thumped against the backrest. He took the wheel and worked it with the throttle for a few minutes until they heard the GPS beep.

"OK, here we are again," he said quietly. He reversed for a moment, then cut the ignition switch.

The downpour pelted, almost roared as they drifted. It was cold, the rain not as warm as before. Bonnie pulled the hood over her head. Her jaw chattered as Lofton pulled something from his duffel bag: a black rectangular box, somewhat like a cordless telephone, except that no antenna protruded. He wiggled into his tanks and regulator, checked his mask and snorkel, sat on the gunwale, then put on his fins.

He spat on his face mask lens, rinsed it, then slipped it over his head and made adjustments. His voice sounded nasal with his nose covered. "Acid test time. We'll find out if this is going to work very soon." Lofton stuck in his mouthpiece, leaned back, and hit the water with a splash, his fins momentarily sticking straight up. Like a duck, Bonnie thought.

Them Bones listed while Bonnie leaned on the gunwale with her elbows and peered down. Nothing. Her glasses were useless in the rain. Water droplets popped around her as *Them Bones* silently bobbed. "Contacts," she muttered. Why hadn't she brought her contact lenses?

She heard a splash, a hand grabbed the rail within inches of her arm. Taking off her glasses she found Lofton's face in dim shadow with his mask on top of his head. "Well?" she whispered."That should be it. I pinged the daylights out of it. It may take *Brutus* a minute or two to put his program together. Otherwise, you and I go ashore and have a nice dinner."

The thought warmed her as they drifted. Bonnie watched the rain plop countless little craters on the nearflat water. Lofton's hand was next to her, rain ran down his arm as he studied the blackness beneath.

He said, "Could you check the other side? We may have drifted and-- hold on! Pay dirt."

A faint, soft, yellow light winked at them from beneath the surface like a haloed low-magnitude star. It grew larger as they watched, but not brighter. Enormous air bubbles rose and broke around them. Lofton looked up to her, the mask still on his forehead. "Here's my ride to Kamchatka. He should be close to thirty feet now."

He caught her eye. "Look, of course you can't take Kirby's skiff back tonight and I really can't see you going ashore in this crappy weather and trying to book a room, especially in those wet clothes."

He looked down. The yellowish light was stationary. "You better let me run you over to the mainland, then you or Kirby can pick up the skiff tomorrow or whenever the weather's better. We'll tie *Them Bones* to one of the buoys. OK?"

"You want me to ride in that thing?" she pointed down to the light.

"Yeah," he grinned, "hot showers, dry clothes, stereo, all the comforts of home. I can warm up a can of navy bean soup. We have scrumptious signature crackers by Nabisco and even a batch of Lofton's designer bug juice in the fridge. Doesn't beat the *Rex*, but..."

She caught his glance and mulled over her clausto. Her teeth chattered and she shivered again. *No. Not in that--what did he say--a sixtyfive-foot sewer pipe? Never.*

"OK." she bit her lip. "How 'bout fresh air?"

"What?" He paused, then, "Ah." Lofton studied the water, the yellowish light shimmered below, but they were drifting. He'd have to go soon. "Tell you what." He sliced a powerful forearm toward the beach, "Just steer that way, find one of the buoys and tie up. I'll follow you in, there's not much current, and pick you up. Then you climb aboard and I'll leave the hatch open. It might get a little wet inside near the hatch but *Brutus*'s bilge pumps can handle that. See if you can--ah, see if you like it. If not," he tilted his head with a smile, "Bonnie either goes ashore or she sleeps in *Them Bones*'s veeberth. How's that?"

She nodded slowly.

"OK." He pulled his mask over his face, then pushed from the skiff toward the light. "See you in a few minutes. Go ahead and tie up." He set his mouthpiece and rolled, the fins flashed in the air, then Brad Lofton was gone.

Bonnie started *Them Bones* and headed for Descanso Bay and the buoy line.

Bonnie shivered in the solid downpour as she searched for whatever Lofton was to bring alongside. *Them Bones* bobbed at W35 and her hands were raw, chafed, and still wet from cleating the bow and stern lines.

She had bent to finish snapping the canvas cover when she felt, but couldn't see, a presence. The water alongside had changed, it swirled instead of flowed, the pattern wasn't the same. Bubbles; she knew Lofton was close by.

There. A shaft perhaps twenty feet away rose into the night, fifteen, twenty feet high--a periscope. The water sighed, more bubbles, a long black sleek shape, a foot or so off the surface, nudged up to *Them Bones*. She squinted; *Brutus* was hard to see. Swells easily lapped over the submarine. It didn't seem to glisten or gleam as rain pounded and seawater lapped in small whirlpools.

She heard a clunk, then Lofton's voice through the rain, softly, "OK, hop on." His tone was quiet, yet immediate.

The skiff bounced in the wavelets and yielded her weight as she stepped off. The submarine's round topside by comparison was solid, rock-hard; it didn't bob. She edged aft around the periscope toward a low, dull shape. Lofton stood chesthigh in his hatch behind a small cutwater. He offered a hand and she grabbed it tightly as a swell raised, tore over *Brutus*, and pulled at her feet.

"Welcome aboard," he said quietly. "Come on, follow me, it's warm inside. Don't worry. I'll leave the hatch open."

Bonnie squeezed her eyes shut and inched down a small metal ladder. Her feet finally found the deck of Lofton's sewerpipe. Gripping the gleaming stainless steel ladder, she stood rooted.

"Well?" A chuckle.

She opened her eyes and scanned the long, tubular interior. Pipes, dials, gauges, a comfortable- looking pilot berth forward to her right. Across on the port side, a full conning station, except she didn't--

She stepped forward. It looked like a fighter plane's cockpit without the canopy. Four colored CRTs surrounded another large one and jumped with their displays; a joy-stick, a keyboard, a high- backed, comfortable leather armchair, even pedals like a fighter plane.

She pointed toward the pedals. "Is that for rudder control?"

Lofton, still dripping in his swim trunks, stepped aside and let her move forward. "No, those are throttles for bow thrusters, port and starboard. I had to use them to maneuver next to you. The joystick does all the rudder and stern plane control. The main throttle on the left side is for speed control and doubles as a shift for forward or reverse just like in *Them Bones*."

His voice rose a notch. "Look, I better back out of here before I snag a buoy line or run aground. OK?"

She nodded and looked back to the open hatch; rain and seawater cascaded down and swirled through a deck grate below the hatch.

Lofton took his seat, then pulled the throttle with his left hand. She felt a slight shudder but nothing else. More water poured through the hatch. A red light blinked frantically on one of the CRTs. She turned, sheets of water roared into *Brutus* as they gathered sternway. Then she caught Lofton's eye, his brow raised, the question unspoken.

"OK, close it, Mr. Lofton, and let's get out of here."

Lofton tilted his head slightly, got up and closed the hatch, then sat down again. It became quiet and her skin prickled; it was warm all right, but a little humid. He worked *Brutus*, she could tell, with the pedals--the bow thrusters--to swing around and head out to sea.

A digital readout on the large CRT--it was labeled "Master"-- checked with what she thought were compass bearings. Yes, a gyrocompass readout above the CRT console confirmed it. The compass swung, then steadied on 010. Lofton eased the throttle forward, then punched the keyboard before him. The master panel danced with numbers, geometric shapes, and instructions. A smaller CRT on the upper right side of the console, labeled "NAV" also flashed the same display. A gauge above the CRT console was labeled "Keel Depth" and read 8.90. She sighed and sat on the pilot berth as Lofton worked.

"I'm going to set up a program for," he checked his watch, "arrival at basin six in ninety minutes. That's when we're supposed to meet Kirby." He jabbed the keys, the console buzzed back.

She noticed the frantic red flashing light was out on the "Ship" CRT display. Of course, the hatch had been closed.

He nodded toward the bow, "The shower is in there, and I have a clean poopie suit ready for you."

Bonnie looked forward to an oval hatch labeled "Divers' Trunk." Dimly lit, it was small, cylindrical, about six feet high by three feet wide: more valves, pipes, metallic and threatening. The diving tank, regulator, and other gear lay on the deck. Lofton had entered *Brutus* through there; his wet tracks led aft on the green linoleum.

"I shower in that thing? Do I close the hatch? And what's a poopie suit?"

"You don't have to close the hatch," he said. "I'll try not to peek. Well, maybe...

"Come on!"

"And you'll find hot and cold water valves on the port side at chest level." He held her gaze, his eyes crinkled as his hands paused above the keyboard. "And a poopie suit is overalls. It's comfortable."

Bonnie sighed, "The hell with it, but the hatch stays open. And <u>no</u> peekee." She laid her dripping glasses on the small console table, then went forward, squeaked out of her soaked clothes and turned the valves. The nozzle gushed and steam billowed around her. It felt wonderful.

They sat at a small table built against the port bulkhead in the after part of the control room.

"Only one can of navy bean soup per passenger, we're out, actually. There's more bug juice, though." Lofton raised a plastic pitcher.

"What?"

"KoolAid."

She nodded and munched a cracker while he poured a refill. Sitting back, she drank, then drew her legs up in the little chair and propped her chin on her knees.

Lofton was in dry clothes; he'd showered too, and looked comfortable in a short sleeved faded blue sweatshirt, Levis and Topsiders. By comparison, she felt ugly in the overalls. She swam in them; they'd belonged to Thatcher, Lofton had finally told her. But she was warm, dry, and, she admitted to herself, cozy at the galley table, especially with the thought of the San Pedro Channel raging, how far?--she checked a bulkheadmounted remote depth gauge above her--four hundred feet over her head.

She ran a hand through her matted dark brown hair. "Where are my clothes?" she asked, taking another sip.

Lofton nodded aft to a round hatch just beyond the miniature cook top, "Back there in the motor room. I have our stuff laid out on a heat exchanger. It should be dry soon."

"That hatch looks awfully small. How big is it back there?"

"Oh, the motor room is big enough, all right, but it's crammed with all the power and air-scrubbing equipment. You'll find fuel cells, the DC motor, the reformer system; it's hard to move around."

Bonnie polished her glasses for the third time, held them to the light, then peered back at the hatch. "Why the tunnel?"

"The whole area is surrounded by fuel tanks."

"The JP-5?"

"Uh-huh. That and hydrogen peroxide."

"My God! That stuff is volatile."

Lofton explained the fuel systems's safeguards, then asked, "How did you know?"

"It's my business. Engineer, like you."

Lofton's eyebrows went up.

"Uhhuh, B.S. in mechanical engineering from UC Santa Barbara, class of 1977."

"What got you into that?" Lofton eyed a cluster of remote gauges above his head: depth 400 feet, course 023, speed 14 knots. They should be at the Long Beach entrance in another thirty minutes.

"My pop." She gave a thin smile. "He's a mechanical engineer and has been in the fuel business a long time. He worked for GE's jet engine division for eighteen years, then started Butler Engineering twelve years ago."

"Ah, and you're the secondincommand?"

She folded her hands on the table and leaned forward. "No, no. Nothing so grandiose as that. Butler Engineering is a solid eightyfive-million dollar company. I'm a Juliecomelately. But I've worked for my dad off and on over the years on a parttime basis. Marketing, mostly." She heaved her chest. "But now I've been on fulltime for the past four months. Daddy threw me into the PW4000 program and--"

"By the way, how'd your presentation go?"

"Good. Pratt & Whitney invited us back to their Hartford headquarters for a final proposal in two weeks. It's a real shootout. We're in the top three, now."

"Hey, that's great!"

Silence. She pressed her thumbs together.

"What did you do before you were fulltime at Butler Engineering?" he asked softly.

"Yeah." She sighed. "Married. Our son, Tim, he's ten now." She twirled her wedding band, looked up, and turned to Lofton. Then her gaze swept forward to the conning station, the pilot berth, the periscope, the....

"Bob is...was...a pharmacist. He did well, had two drugstores and a third was under construction." She paused. Her eyes were wide, empty, her voice was low. "He worked very hard. It was too late when we found out. That stuff is available, so tempting, all he had to do was grab it off the shelf. They audited him, the state. He'd been juggling the narcotics on his books and they discovered it. They threatened to revoke his license and put him on six months' probation. That's when I found out.

"He kept working but," she bit her lip, "he just went out and bought it on the street. We were already stretched tight and that's why I started parttime with Daddy. We couldn't pay our bills. Eventually, we lost the third store, which had become the most profitable. That really got to him. Plus he couldn't afford to stop working and he couldn't stop sniffing coke." Her voice trailed off.

"Then, that one night." She shook her head. "He bought a bad batch. Something was wrong, it was laced with--I don't know. They tried to explain it to me. He went crazy, it did something to him...it scrambled his brains..." Bonnie studied a scratch on the table, her fingers knotted together.

Lofton's chair creaked.

"He's been catatonic for the past four months. Not a blink, not a groan, nothing. His weight is down to about 110 and he's almost incontinent. We have him in a special home, a sanatorium. I had to sell our house and the drugstores. Tim and I live with Daddy."

"And, your mom?"

"She's gone, died three years ago."

"I'm sorry," he said, "I didn't mean to pry."

"You didn't. I...ah...I don't know, I just wanted to talk. Maybe it's this KoolAid or beetle juice."

"Bug juice," he said softly.

"What'd you put in it?" She looked at him, her eyes, black pools, glistened over a forced smile. "It's been a long time since I've talked to--to someone. I'm sorry, that sounds stupid."

"No."

Lofton looked up, then cocked an ear. Bonnie heard it, too: a low, deep, steady "whump, whump, whump."

She turned her face to the hatch and rolled her eyes down to him. "What's that?"

The whumps grew louder.

"Cargo ship, by the sound of it, single screw. Probably heading out."

"You sure?" She looked at him.

"Well, uh, I think so. I'm sure it's not a helicopter."

Bonnie grinned, then broke into a short giggle. Lofton watched her glow with a marvelous, gorgeous, genuine smile. It was lost to him when she covered her mouth but her eyes still crinkled. They listened as the cargo ship whumped on into the Pacific.

"You're going out there?" She nodded toward the fading propeller. "You have to?"

"It would be easy to say `no.' To stick around and let Kirby talk to his admiral friends. But that could take too much time. And they might lock Kirby up for all I know. Especially with Renkin out there and all his pull.

He tapped a finger on the small table. "Those sailors on the *Truman* are just twelve days from being blown up. And I need that defector. I can't leave it to chance."

"Brad." She reached over and took his hand, their eyes met.

"I have to, Bonnie," he said slowly. "It's the only--"

The control console gave a low, steady buzz.

"--way to be sure."

He rose slowly. "Duty calls. We're almost to the Long Beach entrance buoy. What say we go to periscope depth and take a look?"

Lofton took the console armchair while Bonnie sat across from him on the starboard pilot berth and watched. He tapped the keyboard, then touched the large master CRT.

He looked at her. "Like clockwork. Disengage autopilot." Then he grabbed the joystick and eased it back slightly. A stopwatch hanging by a lanyard from an overhead bracket swung toward her head.

She watched the depth gauge click off the distance to the surface. They'd been at four hundred feet. It changed steadily: 90, 60, 45, 35, 25, 20. It stopped at 15. *Brutus* rolled and pitched, but not uncomfortably. The stopwatch swung in lazy circles.

"Still crappy topside," Lofton muttered. "Here, let's have a look. There's nothing on sonar." He punched a button on the panel to his left, then pulled the periscope housing from the overhead.

Leaning forward slightly, he put his eye to the lens and slewed electrically with a trigger handle mounted under the housing. "Hm, how 'bout that?" he grinned.

"What?" She leaned toward him, away from the stopwatch. It had clunked her head a couple of times.

"Storm's blown over, no more rain, and the visibility is good." He hunched a shoulder and studied something. "Yeah, the channel is still rough. The Long Beach entrance buoy is about fifty yards off our port beam now. It's really bouncing around."

He paused. "The entrance looks clear. I can't see any traffic and the water inside looks fairly calm."

He checked his wristwatch, then looked at her. "We're in good shape timewise. I guess we better head in and see if Kirby's made it with your truckload of Jet 'A.'" Lofton went back to his eyepiece.

Bonnie sat on the edge of the pilot berth watching Lofton as he slowed to five knots.

CHAPTER 8

The thought hit her. Bonnie had known for the past fifteen minutes, but it finally sank in. Lofton intended to take *Brutus* submerged through Queensgate, the Long Beach Harbor entrance. How wide was it? Six, seven hundred yards, she couldn't remember. Big enough when you were on the surface. But down here? She hoped his aim was good as she recalled the thick jagged rocks that formed the breakwater on either side of Queensgate. She closed her eyes, then opened them again. The minisubmarine rolled and pitched gently but it was quiet, no swishing or gurgling sounds, no blooping and bleeping as in submarine movies.

She twisted her hands and looked at Lofton, concentrating, his eye jammed to the periscope housing. She rose with a start, leaned over his chair and watched the control panel. A televised display flashed on the master CRT, fuzzy in some spots, but she clearly saw the Long Beach breakwater rocks. Breakers tore at them, spray shot high in the air, and whole combers rolled over the top.

But Queensgate lay dead ahead. *Good.*

Lofton turned his magnification knob: derricks, cranes, towers, masts, a large pile of shipping containers took shape in the distance. A scale on the lower part of the screen blinked with: 357/05.

"Are you steering now?" she asked softly.

"Yes, the NAV system is in semiautomatic so I'm steering manually to the recommended course. But, like a DC-10, *Brutus* can do everything by computer, even land in a dense fog. I just feel better driving this thing." He waved a hand to the upper right NAV CRT. "That's the program. I 'match pointers' from either the screen or periscope displays." He grunted. "It seems to be working OK. Easier than when I left San Diego."

The computer bleeped, he checked the NAV CRT and went back to his periscope. "OK. We're through the breakwater." He moved the joystick.

Bonnie sighed as *Brutus* swung gently to the left. The rolling became less pronounced, then stopped altogether. She clutched her shoulders. It was quiet, very quiet. She heard her own breathing, a motor whirred softly back aft. Nothing else.

She checked the NAV CRT:

WAY POINT	CS	DIST	TIME			ETA-Z		
			d	hr	m	m	d	hr
1. Long Beach Buoy	—	—	—	—	—	09	14	1005
2. Long Beach Entrance	—	—	—	—	—	09	14	1021
3. Basin 6 Channel	310	1.4	—	—	17	09	14	1038
4. Mid-Channel	042	0.4	—	—	1	09	14	1039
5. Berth 209	316	0.6	—	—	7	09	14	1046
		2.4	0	0	25			
		SPD	=	5.0				
		DEPTH	=	15.0				

Lofton looked up again, then slewed the periscope. "Nobody is underway and we have another seventeen minutes to the basin six channel."

He rose, saying, "Tell you what. You sit here and keep watch through the periscope. I'm going aft to dig out your clothes. We must have you looking decent for Dr. Kirby."

"Me? Sit there?"

"Don't worry, it's dead topside, we have plenty of depth beneath us. Just yell if you see any ships coming or red lights start zapping on the console. Back in a minute."

Bonnie sat down. Her stomach churned as she scanned *Brutus*'s CRTs. Lights flashed, she tried to sort out which ones were imminent. She recognized a navigation subroutine, similar to the HUD displays she had seen in fighter cockpits.

It didn't take long for Lofton to negotiate the crawlway and return with her dry clothes. She changed in the divers' trunk and when she stepped out Lofton was at his periscope again, twiddling the high power adjustment.

He pulled away, ran an eye up and down, and went back to his eyepiece. "I liked you better in the poopie suit."

"Sorry, it didn't match my plastic jewelry."

Lofton twirled the magnification knob. "We have a tighter, more snug model in your size, with pink panels, purple piping and--whoa! Here we are. Take a look."

The computer bleeped and Lofton eased in right rudder. Docks, pilings, shipping containers flashed darkly on the screen.

A minute passed and the computer bleeped again. They turned to port and entered the triangular basin six. To starboard, a large bulk loader hovered over immense coal mounds. Towering cranes and conveyer belts stood silhouetted against the sky. Lofton flipped the scope to port quickly, the picture whizzed on the CRT, focusing finally on sprawling twostory warehouses.

Lofton checked the clock. "Three-forty. I told Kirby three thirty. Not bad."

He trained the periscope ahead. A wharf filled the screen. It had black, tightly packed pilings like creosoted rotten teeth. A building loomed above with a sign reading "Banana Terminal," and two rail cranes rose before it, their hooks dangling against the overcast.

Bonnie asked, "Is that berth 209?"

"Um, the Banana Terminal is 208; 209 is the empty space to the right just in front of that fenced parking lot." His hand waved. "Hey, look at that on the other side of 209."

Bonnie bent over Lofton's shoulder. "Tugboat. Moored outboard to a barge of some kind."

"A fuel barge, I think. See the hoses? Looks like nobody's home. All tucked away for the night."

"What kind of fuel, do you suppose?" She looked at him.

"Either diesel or, most likely, fuel oil for the big ships." He caught Bonnie's eye, her face inches away. "I don't think they have Jet 'A,' do you?"

"No." She drew back.

"I think we'll moor starboard side to, right aft of it. It'll be good cover."

He scanned the screen. "Ah, there's the jeep. No sign of Kirby, though."

"How close are we?"

"About a hundred yards, time to slow down." Lofton pulled the throttle through neutral and reversed momentarily. *Brutus* shuddered, then stillness. Lofton studied the wharf through the periscope. "No Kirby," he muttered, "nothing moving at all. He was supposed to park the truck next to the jeep. Damn!"

He took a full, careful sweep around basin six. Everything seemed frozen, no ships, no headlights, no movement of any kind.Drumming his fingers he said, "I'm going to surface and put us against the pilings. I have to see what's going on." He squeezed the joystick trigger. Air roared and gurgled. *Brutus* tilted, slightly noseup.

"You sure he knows how to get here?" she asked, watching the depth gauge until it stopped at 8.0.

"He knows. He was with me when we dropped off the jeep."

Brutus lurched as Lofton nudged him against the pilings. "Welcome to Long Beach," he said, then went aft to the hatch; it gave a small hiss when he spun the wheel. He eased the hatch open and slowly looked around. "Seems OK," he muttered and scrambled topside.

Bonnie followed him up the ladder, glad to exit the submarine. Topside, she was surprised the air didn't taste really different, just a bit sharper and colder from the rain. She realized the submarine's atmosphere hadn't been stale and close. She wrapped her arms around her waist. In fact, it had been a comfortable ride.

Enormous football-field lights glared from the bulk loading terminal, casting long, sharp shadows over the basin. A pair of long warehouses and a giant grain elevator stood on the basin's other two sides. The lapping oily water was thick with the basin's odors as Styrofoam cups, grapefruit rinds, apple cores, paper wrappers, and dunnage wallowed in the sheen. A barna-cleencrusted oil drum clunked against a nearby piling.

Fifty feet aft, the tug and barge sat mute, lifeless. Tiny wavelets slapped at the barge's twin rudder skags. A bloated, dead fish, its mouth wide, eyes popping, bobbed against *Brutus*'s hull. Rainwater dripped from the wharf while a storm drain vomited street runoff.

Lofton pulled a half-inch nylon line from a small deck lazaret and whipped it around a piling. Kicking open a twopiece recessed roller cleat at the bow, he tied the line's other end with quick half-hitches then swiftly padded aft and secured their mooring with a stern line. Finally, he looked up to the wharf fifteen feet above, his hands on his hips.

Nothing.

He brushed past Bonnie and disappeared down the hatch. In a minute, he returned with a coil of rope over his shoulder.

"I have to get up there. Something's wrong." He turned to her. "Would you mind helping with the stores? Kirby was supposed to hand down the food while we were refueling. I'm behind schedule and have nine trash bags full of canned goods, potatoes, cereal, condensed milk, even some perishables."

Not waiting for her nod, Lofton jumped to a piling, holding on for a moment as he tested the slick, creosoted surface. He shinnied up, slowly at first, then faster. His hands found the wharf, he threw a leg over and gained the top. Bonnie shuddered. It looked all too easy. She hadn't heard a grunt or groan from Lofton. Just up and over. Bonnie began to shiver; she tightened her parka and waited.

Lofton checked his Casio: 4:20. Where the hell was Kirby? What to do? Pull the plug and wait on the bottom for twentyfour hours? Sunup would be around six-thirty. He had to get moving.

Bonnie wrestled the last clanking bag of foodstuffs down *Brutus*'s hatch. She'd offered to pack it while Lofton waited for Kirby. That would take a good hour, at least, giving Lofton time to get the fuel truck situation in hand. But, where was the damn thing? Where was Kirby?

Pumping fuel would be no problem once he connected the hose. And the Butler Engineering truck was like ones found at smaller airports. Bonnie had said it was a black Ford that carried thirty-five hundred gallons and pumped 300 gallons a minute at forty pounds per square inch. *Brutus* could handle the velocity; Lofton had insisted on that capability in the design. All he needed was the damn truck, then twelve minutes to pump thirtyfive hundred gallons of Jet "A," and he'd be gone.

He looked down to *Brutus*. He had asked Bonnie to dim the interior lights so prying eyes couldn't see anything unusual, like a midget hitech submarine moored to berth 209. He heard clinking and the occasional rustle of a trash bag but that was it for basin six. Nothing else, except drain water gushing.

Maybe Kirby had forgotten. Lofton scratched his head. He began to walk through the parking lot to Panorama Drive. He stopped near the road, hovered in the shadow of the Banana Terminal, and studied his surroundings.

An immense, brightly lighted container terminal stood across the road that was part of the pier A east basin complex. Long rows of stacked container boxes stretched hundreds of yards in either direction and trucks zipped through the lot delivering them to a large ship. He squinted for a name on the ship's fantail: *Oriental Executive.* Standing proudly at pier A, dockside cranes roared and plopped boxes into her hold and abovedecks while trucks ripped through the yard hunting for more cargo. Some escaped to Panorama Drive without their trailers and snarled away like sports cars.

Lofton checked the road in both directions. Nothing except hotrod trucks tearing around with faceless drivers in their blacked cabins. He checked his watch, then saw a truck without a trailer pull from the gate and head toward him. He looked in the other direction. A guard draw a gate open, the truck barreled past and ground down through its gears. It turned right, exhaust blasted as it swirled through the entrance.

There! He'd missed it before. The truck's headlights had swept over the trunk of a fourdoor Lincoln. Its reflectors winked briefly and two figures inside were momentarily caught in the glare. He'd seen that Lincoln.

Where?

Carrington's! It was the government pool car he'd seen in front of

Brutus's San Diego pen. And now, two men sat inside. Lofton's mind raced; they must have figured it out. Computerized tracing of jet fuel purchases had probably led them to the Ford--Renkin had infinite resources. All he had to do was snap his fingers.

Bonnie--*Brutus*--he had to get out. He turned, then stopped. Wait. He bit a thumbnail while another truck caromed past. Lofton stooped to reduce his silhouette. Hold on. Those guys were hanging around for something. Maybe Kirby was close by. He could be hiding. Or maybe he was still on his way.

Damnit!

Lofton double-checked the road, looking for telltale reflections, dark silhouettes, a careless metallic glint. Nothing--Panorama Drive was clear except for the Lincoln; the two occupants sat motionless, like cameos.

He waited as another truck rumbled toward him. It drew abreast. He ran across the road through the van's swirling wake and gained shadows by a tall chain-link fence. He knelt, barely making out the Lincoln fifty yards on the other side of the gate.

The next truck trailer pulled out and roared past. Lofton stood and ran, hard. He reached the gate just as the trailer's taillights bounced over the potholed access road and into the cavernous yard. In the dark again, Lofton dashed across the road and ran at a crouch, then duckwalked the last twenty yards and dropped to his hands and knees. He crept to the right rear fender just as another truck swung through the gate. Its headlights flashed over the Lincoln and Lofton could see Dr. Felix L. Renkin's bald head gleaming in the passenger seat.

The road was clear again, there were no lights, it was quiet, except for growling trucks in the container yard. Renkin raised a twoway to his ear as Lofton crept to the front door. He heard Renkin's highpitched voice say, "Caper Two--Caper One. Any joy yet? Over."

The transceiver squawked. Lofton couldn't decipher the response.

Renkin spoke again. "Caper Two. It's almost five o'clock. I know it's a big area but that truck is in there somewhere. We saw it go through the gate. Have you tried the warehouse? Over."

Another muffled reply.

"What? Yes. A Ford. It's black. And tell that security guard you're on a government exercise; that you won't get in their way. Show 'em your Immigration ID. Do I have to think every minute for you? Over."

Renkin paused.

"That's Charlie, Caper Two. And tell Underwood to keep his-- er-- detector out of sight. I don't want anyone seeing it except whoever is driving that fuel truck. You have permission to use your detectors at that time. Do you understand? Over."

Squawk.

Detectors. Damnit! Lofton's nostrils flared as he checked the door lock button; it was up.

"Right, and hurry. We'll keep watch on the gates. Caper One--out."

Lofton rose quickly. He ripped open the passenger door. His left fist smashed Renkin's temple as he crawled across and reached for the open-mouthed man on the driver's side. With Renkin caught screaming and gurgling beneath Lofton's thrusting knees, he grabbed for the other man, whose hand went quickly under his coat. Lofton caught the man's tie with his right hand and pulled, smashing the head down on the steering wheel.

Renkin squirmed and shrieked under Lofton. "Osborne! ICyeaghhh!"

The other man dropped his hand from his shoulder holster, then grabbed Lofton's forearm with both hands; he was gaining strength. The blow hadn't been enough.

Lofton pulled the tie and smashed Osborne against the wheel again. Osborne shuddered, his hands still in a death grip on Lofton's forearm. From his contorted position, Lofton yanked again with all his strength. Osborne's head hit the steering column. Lofton heard a crack and the horn bleeped. He pushed sharply on Osborne's chest; the man's head lolled back, his eyes rotated to the ceiling, then closed. Blood ran from his mouth and from a gash on his forehead.

Squirming, Renkin was twisting free. His feet dangled outside the car, his heels drummed a tattoo on the dirt shoulder. He clawed at Lofton's crotch with a growl.

Lofton drew back from Osborne's inert form and grabbed the little bald man by the throat and sat on him. He easily pinned the wiggling Renkin in a schoolboy press. Renkin squirmed, his goldrimmed glasses crabbed askew on his face.

"Why?" Lofton roared. "Why are you doing this? Why did you kill Thatcher? And why, for God's sake, did you blow him up in my car?"

Renkin jerked and shoved under him.

Lofton's thumbs found Renkin's windpipe. "Tell me now," he shouted.

"Eaghh--we have to talk...I need you..."

"Talk! What the hell do you mean?" Lofton's thumbs dug deeper.

"Ugh...to help me. They want you to--ugghhh...." Renkin rattled, he began to turn blue.

"Help you? Who?"

"Caper One. Caper Two. We found the fuel truck. We're ready to move in. Was that you who tooted? Over."

Lofton's eyes snapped to the floor and the transceiver. Probably Carrington and Underwood. And they had found the fuel truck. Kirby!

He released his thumbs. Renkin's eyes were squeezed tightly shut with pain, they looked like x's. But color returned to his face. "Need me? Who?" he yelled at Renkin.

"Caper One. Caper Two. Over."

The transceiver lay there, demanding, as Renkin gurgled.

Lofton's fist smashed into Renkin's nose. He'd hardly noticed it was bandaged. Bone crunched, blood spurted, and Felix Renkin went limp.

He grabbed the transceiver and keyed it, then screwed his vocal cords up to what he thought would be Renkin's voice.

"Caper Two. What's your location? Over."

"Yeah, Caper One. Western end of the container yard. Actually about two hundred yards from you. Over."

Lofton bit his lip. *Delay*. "Caper Two. Wait one. Out."

"Caper two--"

Lofton reached under Osborne's chest and fumbled for the shoulder holster. There! A .38 automatic, neat, compact. He pulled it out and stuffed it into his belt while looking at Osborne, not knowing if he was dead or alive. He burned another fifteen seconds grabbing Osborne's handcuffs and linking his hand to Renkin's through the steering wheel. Then he quickly pulled the hood release under the dash and threw away the ignition and handcuff keys. He jumped out of the car. Renkin moaned but Lofton didn't have time to shut him up. He lifted Renkin's legs and jammed him back in the passenger seat.

Lofton picked up the transceiver, then locked and slammed the door. One last thing. He ran to the hood, raised it, and ripped out all the wiring he could see. He found a battery cable and pulled furiously. It didn't give. He braced both feet on the bumper, reached down and gave another yank. The cable popped off the terminal. The Lincoln was dead, maybe Osborne too, Lofton thought, as he brought the hood down. Should he kill Renkin? He hadn't killed anyone, even while he was in the SEALS, although he'd come close to it.

No time.

He peered in the passenger compartment for a moment. Both bodies were still. Lofton was tempted to reach in and throw away Renkin's glasses but the transceiver would be asking more questions soon. Questions he didn't know, and he'd recognized Carrington's voice. *Hurry.*

Lofton trotted toward the gate. He followed a truck through, then turned and broke to a dead run toward the container yard's west end.

Row upon row of boxes rushed past him as he slogged over water gorged potholes. He slowed to a trot knowing he'd run more than the two hundred yards, and he was out of breath. Looking ahead, he saw a warehouse and, through its gaping doors, the wharf and bay. He'd gone too far. He turned and ducked down an aisle between stacked containers just as a container truck, its drive wheels spewing mud, rumbled past. "...get your ass outta here...stupid sonofabitch..." he heard from the cab, and the truck was gone.

The containers were heaped four high and glistened with runoff. Lofton slipped down the aisle to the next road, then peered around the corner. Nothing. He moved on, faster.

Some areas were bare; muddy outlines testified to where containers once stood. One section looked like Stonehenge, with the rectangular boxes spaced evenly around an imaginary point. Lofton dashed across another road and down an aisle, his head twisting, trying to see between the formidable ranks.

Another aisle. Nothing. He dashed across a road and doglegged to the next. There was no pattern to his search, he became frantic.

Something caught his eye--he stopped and turned back. There! Four rows down, between container boxes; a glint of a windshield, that had to be it. He had to check, but how? Carrington had reported they'd found the fuel truck. Renkin's batman and Underwood were close by.

Lofton peered around the containers and checked the reflection again. It had to be the fuel truck. Maybe Kirby had stashed it in one of those empty areas.

Up, he decided. The cargo containers were stacked only two-high in this section. He propped a foot on a container's tailgate latch, reached a foot across to the next container row, and braced himself up, steadying his climb with his hands.

He reached the top and peered over. Nothing seemed out of place, no one, only small puddles of water gleamed. Farther away, he saw the *Oriental Executive* with her dockside cranes howling and clanking. He stood and tiptoed over the containers' frames, not wanting to stick a foot through the middle or have the metal bow inward and signal an alarm.

Lofton reached the far edge and peered down.

Yes, there was his fuel truck! Stubby looking, a large stainless oval fuel tank was mounted over the Ford's rear axle. The door label read "Butler Engineering, Inc.," with a small, red sticker underneath saying `Jet A.' He hoped it was full to its rated capacity.

He could see through the side window. Nobody was inside. Where the hell was Kirby?

Something creaked behind him. He turned, too late, a figure-- someone--shoved his back and he tumbled into space.

Lofton twisted and made a decent landing in soft mud. He rose quickly and looked up to his former perch.

A man stood on top the container holding a pistol loosely at his side: Underwood, grinning. Lofton turned for the shadows.

"Don't move, Brad." Close by, off to his right, he recognized Carrington's voice; he would have a gun, too. Carrington favored the compact M10 Ingram machine pistol. One squeeze of the trigger and all thirtyfour nine millimeter rounds could leave the silenced weapon in just over two seconds.

Carrington's voice was businesslike. "Turn around and back up. That's it. Now, turn again, put your hands against the trailer and spread your feet. And don't screw with me."

Lofton's heart sank as he slapped his palms against the container, slowly shifting his feet apart. Carrington would find Osborne's pistol soon. Then Renkin, then...

"OK. Come on down, Kevin." Carrington gave Lofton a quick search. "He's tame for now. Well, well, a .38 automatic and--damnit! What's this? A transceiver!"

A searing blow slammed Lofton's kidney, then another. Pain exploded in Lofton's back and raged through his belly. He dropped to his knees.

"Kevin, where the hell are you? Get down here. This bastard has Renkin's transceiver and--"

A neatly placed kick in the nape of his neck sent Lofton's head bouncing against a steel container, then his face plopped in wet earth. He doubled up and tucked in his knees, waiting for the next blow.

Carrington's hand grabbed his sweatshirt and twirled him in the mud, their eyes inches apart. Lofton felt a gun barrel in his chest. "Where's *Brutus*? And what did you do to Dr. Renkin? And Osborne?" Carrington shifted his gaze up for a moment. "Kevin? Will you--"

Lofton felt a rush of air, a whoosh; a foot connected near the muzzle of Carrington's Ingram, which cleared Lofton's chest. The machine pistol coughed as it left Carrington's hand. A line of bullet holes stitched a container as the Ingram twirled in the air.

Lofton struggled to his feet while two figures whirled in the ooze. A hand raised, a short steel pipe silhouetted momentarily against the sky. It came down with a crunch. Carrington fell on his back, groaned, and was still.

Kirby stooped over Carrington and searched quickly while Lofton caught his breath. The orthopedic surgeon handcuffed Carrington to a container latch rod and picked up the .38, the Ingram, and the transceiver. Stuffing the pistols in his belt, he turned to Lofton. "You're getting careless."

Pain flashed through Lofton's lower back as he tried to stand erect.

Kirby reached and thumbed one of Lofton's eyelids. "You look like hell. How do you feel?"

"You keep saying that. How'd they find you?"

"Followed me. Didn't realize it until I was almost here. So I turned right instead of left, lost them in this yard."

"Did they--ugh." Lofton finally straightened up, his breathing more regular. "Did they see you? Can they identify you?" He took a step and stumbled.

Kirby gently pushed him against the container. "Hold on a minute, Brad. Clear the cobwebs."

"Gotta go."

"In a minute."

Kirby prodded the unconscious Carrington with a toe as Lofton slouched, then tucked the .38 into Lofton's belt. "No, they didn't see me. I was out of the cab long before they found the truck. I waited near the rim of the boxes just like ol' Kevin up there. Somehow they got the idea something was up. Carrington kept yelling into his walkie-talkie, then he sent the other guy--"

"Underwood. Kevin Underwood."

"Underwood, yeah. So anyway, Mr. Underwear is up there watching and waiting between the boxes just like me, not on top like you. And, sure enough, here comes old John Wayne along the top with his spurs clanking. You could almost hear them, 'ching, ching, ching.'"

Kirby shook his head. "You're getting careless in your old age. I'm surprised you didn't slice a hole in the roof and fall through. It would have been great to see you wallowing in all that baby powder, or whatever's in there. But Underwear got to you before I could stop him."

"Thanks. Where's Underwood now?"

Kirby scratched his head. "I popped him with this," he held up the pipe, "and he fell off the container. When I jumped after him, he ran toward the gate." He pointed.

"He's loose then?"

"Yeah, but long gone."

"We better get out of here."

"You OK now?"

"Yeah." Lofton wiped mud off his face and arms.

They got into the Ford and Kirby started up and pulled into an access road behind another truck. Kirby went left when the other went right and muttered, "These guys are kamikazes. All we need is a nice headon."

"I know." Then, "Did you get a full load?"

"Near as I can tell. The guy at Long Beach Airport gave me a copy of Butler Engineering's bill. Three thousand five hundred and twentyfour gallons. The bill was for well over seven grand with taxes and everything."

They bounced through the gate and quickly howled down Panorama Drive. Their headlights whipped across the Lincoln. Two inert mounds were just visible below the dashboard. That's three out of four, Lofton thought. What would Underwood do? He'd find the Lincoln all right, but that would be a lost cause. So he'd probably run for a phone and call in reinforcements. Time enough, he hoped. Fifteen--twenty minutes at most to hook up, pump fuel, disconnect, and shove off.

He said as much to a nodding Kirby, who downshifted and pulled into the Banana Terminal.

Lofton checked his watch. "We need to hurry. It'll be light soon." He pointed at the wharf's edge and Kirby drew up. Lofton jumped out and quickly inspected the pumping system. It looked easy, nearly like the one in San Diego. He showed Kirby how the mechanism worked.

"By the way, Bonnie's aboard *Brutus*." Lofton jerked a thumb.

Kirby's eyebrows went up. "Yeah, I'm not surprised. How'd you two make out under the Catalina Channel? A little stereo, spin down the lights. No place to run thousands of feet below--"

"Damnit," Lofton held up a hand. "Nothing happened. Come on." He filled Kirby in on their stormy crossing. "*Them Bones* is tied up to W35 in Descanso. Sorry to leave it there but you should dig it out in the next couple of days before the Avalon harbor master impounds it."

Kirby studied the truck's pumping valves. "I'll take care of it. You better move."

Lofton turned for the wharf and stopped as Kirby asked, "How long will you be gone?"

"Two--three weeks. I haven't calculated the whole trip yet. It's over four thousand miles to Kamchatka."

"OK. I think I'll leave the boat at W-35. So when you get back to

Catalina, you don't have go ashore and wait around for the cattle car to the mainland.

"The harbor master charges thirteen bucks a day, last time I checked."

"He'll get an offer he can't refuse."

"Thanks. Oh, yeah, could you haul Bonnie up while we're pumping?"

Kirby fiddled with valves, his back half-turned. "See? I was right. I'll wait 'til you two finish pumping before I haul her up."

Lofton fought an impulse to kick Kirby in the pants, then shinnied down the piling to *Brutus*'s casing.

Bonnie's head popped out the hatch. "My God, I was worried! Where have you been? What happened to your face?"

"In a minute." He turned and whistled up to the wharf. Kirby gave a thumbsup and lowered the thick fuel hose with the rope. Lofton wrestled it down the hatch to the trunk near the aft tunnel. He opened the trunk, flipped the retractor lever, then plugged in the hose. Setting the valve, he moved forward to the master panel and tapped in the fueling routine. Venting, air scavenging and spark control were important, and he cut all unnecessary electrical machinery. He checked the lower right display, labeled "Power": The digits were all highlighted in green.

He swung to the ladder, climbed halfway up the hatch and gave two sharp whistles. The fuel hose surged and become stiff. Jet "A" fuel flowed into *Brutus*'s tanks.

He stepped down and leaned against the stainless steel ladder. Bonnie sat against the galley table with her arms crossed. He'd forgotten about her.

"Bonnie, I'm sorry, I'm in a real rush. It'll be daylight soon. Kirby will haul you up to the wharf. He'll explain what happened. You two have to move quickly. You take the jeep and Kirby will return your truck."

He paused. "I don't know how to say this, I don't know how I can return the favor. I'll repay Butler Engineering for the fuel and I think--" He stopped.

She stared into him again, just like--"Will this take long?"

"Another ten minutes, and...thanks for stowing the chow." He looked around, everything was neat and organized. "I'd like to get a sling around you now. Once I disconnect, I have to cast off."

"When do you return?" She stepped closer, her glasses in her hand.

The hell with it! He moved the two paces, grabbed her shoulders, then bent to kiss her. She turned her head, his lips brushed a cheek. They stood awkwardly. The fuel hose shuddered nearby.

Lofton started to break but she raised a hand and wiped grime from his eyes, his cheek. He stopped. Both her hands slid down his back and roamed under his mudsoaked sweatshirt. He looked at her. Bonnie. Their lips met in a prolonged, swaying, tightly embraced kiss. They parted, then kissed again, harder this time; searching, longing. Unspoken words flowed between them.

"Brad." She felt the small of his back. "A gun. Brad, damnit."

"Yes, damnit, we hardly know each other, Bonnie. Why? Why have you helped me? I don't understand--"

She put two fingers on his mouth. They kissed again, and then once more.

He had to let go, to release her. His mouth found her ear. "I'll be back. Two to three weeks, no more. We'll have time together, then."

She looked up to him, her eyes glistened. "Yes. Make sure you come back."

They heard a whistle from topside. Lofton quickly kissed Bonnie on the tip of her nose, then both cheeks, and led her topside.

The rope dangled near the casing. Lofton fashioned a sling under Bonnie's arms. "Keep your feet against the piling, it'll go easier. Here." He stuffed her glasses in her parka.

Her head jerked in a nod.

Lofton whistled and slack went out of the rope. He patted Bonnie on her rump as Kirby heaved. She caught a piling neatly with her feet and Kirby had her up and over in ten seconds.

He heard another whistle and grabbed the hose. It no longer vibrated. Full tanks, he hoped, as he bolted down the ladder. Underway in two minutes. He stepped to the pilot station and checked the "Power" CRT:

Jp5: 3566 - 95%

Good enough. He stepped aft, disconnected the fuel hose, and whistled through the hatch. The hose snaked out of *Brutus*. Lofton followed it topside and ran for the bow line.

He stooped at the cleat and was unwinding the line when something caught his eye. The hose had dropped to water level, the nozzle swung back and forth, grazing little wakes across the viscous surface. Lofton stood and looked at the wharf. He gave a short whistle. Nothing.

He whistled again. A gull shrieked and a diesel fired up in the bulk-loading terminal. A subtle gray hued the eastern sky. The port of Long Beach was waking up.

The Ford started above him, its engine raced, and it clanked into gear. The fuel hose snapped up and sprang over the wharf.

Lofton looked to his mooring lines. Something was wrong. He jumped for the piling, shinnied up quickly, found the top, and stood. Bonnie and Kirby were stepping from the jeep Cherokee with raised, awkward hands. The black truck had nosed into the jeep's rear bumper, a hand protruded through the window, it held a pistol.

Lofton squinted. Underwood! He crouched, yanked out the .38 and chambered a round. With a twohanded grip, he aimed and fired. The bullet slammed through the top of the truck's door.

Underwood's pistol clattered to the asphalt. His head whipped around. He grit his teeth and the Ford's transmission clanked.

Kirby ran around the jeep and pulled Bonnie to the pavement as the truck backed away.

Lofton yelled, "Walt!"

The truck jerked to a stop facing Lofton, then bounced ahead, the clutch going in and out as the engine raced. Underwood was searching for the proper gear.

"Back in the jeep! Now! Go!" Lofton backhanded his arm toward Panorama Drive. Kirby and Bonnie ran for the jeep as the truck roared and picked up speed. The Ford tore at him; seventy, sixty, fifty feet away. Underwood was crouched behind his wheel. Lofton saw his hunched shoulders, his eyes.

Underwood wanted Lofton. He didn't care if the truck pitched over the wharf. Renkin's agent could jump and save himself, not realizing the Ford would crash onto *Brutus*.

Lofton turned right and ran. Bollards, enormous cleats flashed by. The fuel truck snarled closer as Lofton sobbed with frustration. A ten foot chain link fence stood to his left. The wharf was only ten feet across at this point and the moored fuel barge lay to his right.

Underwood had him.

One thing left. He stopped, turned, pulled out his .38 and took aim. A grinning Underwood slid down, knowing the engine would protect him.

Lofton snapped off four rounds. The windshield starred near the top of Underwood's head. He dropped his aim slightly and sent two more rounds through the top of the hood toward the dashboard. Fifteen feet; the truck's engine sputtered but still rushed him.

He lowered the .38, found the right front tire, fired his last round, and sprang for the chain-link fence. The tire popped and hissed. The truck swerved violently to the right, barely missing Lofton in midair.

The engine coughed and died as the truck slowed. The right front wheel, its tire now flat, caught a huge cleat. The wheel ripped away as the truck lurched to its right. The Ford drunkenly pirouetted off the wharf and crunched loudly onto the fuel barge, its nose buried in a fuel bunker. The Jet "A" tank dislodged, smashed through the truck's cabin, and came to rest, its seam split.

Lofton ran to the edge and peered over. Fumes! Jet "A"!

He dashed for *Brutus*.

Sirens. Someone from the bulk loading terminal had probably seen the wreck and given the alarm. Making sure the jeep was gone, he edged over the piling and onto *Brutus*. Racing, he tore off the bow and stern lines, recessed the cleats, jammed the lines in their lazaret.

Shouts wafted from Panorama Drive as he dropped through the hatch. A truck, more trucks, screeched to a stop above him. Jet "A" fumes, heavier than air, found his nostrils just before he clunked the hatch shut. Spinning the wheel, he lurched forward. How much fuel was left in that tank? He wondered, as he jammed himself in the pilot's chair and kicked the right bow thruster pedal. Twenty--thirty--gallons of Jet "A" sloshing around now, maybe mixing with the barge's fuel oil? More than enough.

Nothing happened. He kicked the right bow thruster pedal again. *My God*. Reconnect power. His fingers flew over the electrical panel. The CRTs blinked on, status boxes winked from red to green. He kicked the pedal again. *Brutus*'s bow nudged away from berth 209.

His thumb found the flood button on top of the joystick. *Brutus* settled as the ballast tanks roared and accepted seawater. The bow dipped and Lofton jammed on full throttle, kicking in left full rudder. He'd taken on stores and a full load of fuel but there hadn't been time for a trim dive. Paying the price, he fought the controls as *Brutus* bucked between ten and thirty feet.

"Just don't broach," he urged.

He managed to catch the minisub at fifteen feet and slowed to five knots. Deciding to take a chance, Lofton raised his periscope and peered aft.

Brutus was in the middle of basin six when the fuel barge exploded, vaporizing Special Agent Kevin T. Underwood, along with much of the Ford. Flames roiled three, then five hundred feet in the air. Chunks of the truck and whole sections of the barge flew in every direction. The tug rolled on its beam, then miraculously righted itself, strangely devoid of her super-structure. Flames raced through her exposed length.

The shock wave quivered past *Brutus*'s periscope as igniting fuel oil spread from the barge. Creosoted pilings caught fire, an isolated blaze leaped from the roof of the banana terminal. Its windows were blown out. One of its rail cranes had been flung off the tracks and leaned crazily against the building.

The carnage disappeared behind a promontory as he cleared the basin six entrance and eased in right rudder for the Long Beach outer harbor. Something there! He flicked the stick right and dropped the periscope. Two fire boats flashed toward him, were soon overhead and gone. Their twin screws buzzed furiously.

He raised the periscope again. All clear. Almost daylight and almost time to swing left and head for Queen's Gate. He checked in the distance. A thick column of black smoke rose over the receding warehouses. He adjusted his focus and watched for a moment.

Something caught his eye on the basin six promontory, now about four hundred yards aft. He flipped the lens to hipower and found a jeep Cherokee silhouetted by the early dawn and towering black smoke. Two figures leaned against the front fender, their heads swivelled from the smoke to the basin six channel. The taller figure's hands were jammed in its pockets. Its gaze swept over *Brutus*'s camouflaged, almost wakeless periscope, then back to the smoke again.

Lofton chewed a thumbnail. They didn't know if *Brutus* had escaped. He quickly twirled the periscope through 360 degrees. Nothing close by, although a bow wave charged directly toward him about a mile east. Probably another fire boat from the Queen Mary area, he supposed. He pulled hard on the joystick, hoping it would be enough. Large red letters blinked on the "master: CRT:

Broach - Broach - Broach

Brutus lurched to the surface; he could stay there for only ten seconds or so with his nearnegative buoyancy, it was all the exposure he could afford. The two figures' heads kept turning as they receded in his lens.

Here I am. Hurry up, not much time left.

Brutus wallowed and lost speed. Lofton shoved the stick forward and added power.

There! The taller figure nudged an elbow, pointed toward him, and jabbed an extended thumb in the air. The shorter figure waved both arms over its head furiously as *Brutus* swam back to periscope depth.

Lofton watched as long as he dared, then swung the periscope to Queen's Gate and put *Brutus* on course. Seventeen minutes to the entrance at five knots, he remembered. Time enough to set up a track to Kamchatka.

He punched the keyboard and watched the NAV CRT scroll through the "Alpha Select Sailing Directions" program.

He let the cursor illuminate Poluostrov Kamchatka and found a subtable for Mys Mayachnyy, a cape that guarded the entrance to Petropavlovsk harbor. The fifty-third parallel, he noted, bisected the city's downtown section. Biting his thumbnail, Lofton sat back for a moment. What kind of track should he take and how long would it be?

He leaned over his keyboard again and slewed a linear cursor across a Pacific Ocean gnomic projection. It wouldn't be a true great circle route. *Hmmm.* He checked the closest points of approach to land masses from the computer's projected track. Clear the west end of Catalina by six and one half miles. OK, it's deep there. Then clear the west end of San Miguel Island, Point Bennett, by twentysix miles.

Good. Clear Rat and Near islands in the Aleutians by ninety miles to the south. OK. Finally, clear Komandorskiye Ostrova by one hundred thirtyfive miles to the south, then zap toward Petropavlovsk on final course 274.5. And the hell with fuel efficiency; he had plenty on board now. He needed speed and punched in thirty knots.

Lofton switched the program to the master CRT:

WAY POINT	CS	DIST	TIME				ETA-Z	
			d	hr	m	m	d	hr
1. Long Beach Buoy	—	—	—	—	—	09	14	1222
2. San Pedro Ch. Dogleg	226	10	—	—	19	09	14	1241
3. 33 40'.0 N — 121 00'.0 W	272	137	—	04	34	09	14	1715
4. 50 00'.0 N — 180 00'.0 W	309	3145	4	08	50	09	19	0205
5. Mys Mayachnyy	287	935	1	07	10	09	20	0915
		4227	5	20	53			
		SPD	=	30.0				
		DEPTH	=	1000				

He sighed, then checked his periscope. *Brutus* was almost to the Long Beach entrance. He looked at the projected track again. Almost six days. Time enough to locate PARALLAX and PITCHFORK, then run south and disarm the CAPTORs before the *Truman* nosed through Chetvertyy Kuril'skiy Proliv. He jabbed "Set" on his computer and locked in the NAV program.

Queensgate passed abeam. He took a last look at the thick, black smoke column rising over Long Beach.

Exhaustion swept through him. With the back of his hand, he shoved the periscope to its overhead bracket and punched "Auto." *Brutus* accelerated smoothly to thirty knots.

Lofton's head fell to his chest.

PART II

Lo! Death has reared himself a throne
In a strange city, lying alone
Far down among the dim west,
Where the good and the bad and the worst
and the best
Have gone to their eternal rest.

Edgar Allan Poe,
The City in the Sea

9

Karlskrona, Sweden, 1981

Karlskrona, one of Sweden's four major naval bases, guards the southern approaches to the Baltic Sea. Malmö lies 170 statute kilometers to the southwest and dominates the Danish Straits, which provide access to the Kattegat and Skagerrak. Stockholm, which lies on Sweden's eastern coast, is approximately 390 kilometers north of Karlskrona.

The Union of Soviet Socialist Republics' landmass, directly across the Baltic, begins only 220 kilometers east of Stockholm. And Leningrad, home port to the Twice-Honored Red Banner Baltic Fleet, is situated another 510 kilometers into the Gulf of Finland. The USSR's view of Sweden, her neutrality notwithstanding, borders on paranoia. In time of "national emergency," Soviet fighting and essential support units could be bottled up in the Baltic, denied access to Western Waters, and worse, destroyed by Swedish air and naval forces. Thus, strategic planners of the Twice-Honored Red Banner Baltic Fleet lose more sleep than they care to admit when it comes to hard choices on how to deal with Sweden's offensive and defensive capabilities, particularly their substantial submarine capability. And Karlskrona is a major submarine base.

Hard information, indeed, on-site reconnaissance is in constant demand for Soviet strategists. In other words, how can the Swedes' strike capability be quickly neutralized? How can Soviet access be guaranteed to the North Sea, then to the Atlantic? How can the Central Committee be assured that the Baltic Fleet, which represents 16 percent of the Soviet Union's naval forces, will not end up on the bottom?

Karlskrona is favored by an archipelago just offshore that parallels the coast and provides a secure, natural defense for hardened submarine pens. Many of the islands are bases for secret naval activities, and the whole area is highly restricted. Ashore, "No Aliens" signs are posted in the partly wooded, low rocky hills and on navigable channels outside the archipelago. The rocky beaches, cliffs, and headlands are heavily patrolled by aircraft, elite troops, dogs, and electronic surveillance equipment. The seaward approaches are covered by observation posts on the strategic larger islands, which coordinate patrol boat and helicopter activity. An interesting network of bottom mines is controlled from various shore stations.

Reconnaissance, therefore, is the food, the main ingredient that allows Soviet planners to make their hard choices.

The Voyenno Morskoy Flot *Podvodnaya Lodka (PL) 673* was one of 236 variations of the Pskovskiy class attack submarine built in the 1950s. Known by the NATO code word Whiskey, most of the class had been scrapped except for forty units that had been handed over to "client" navies. Rendered obsolete by advanced nuclear designs, remaining submarines of the Pskovskiy class were workhorses; they were still useful for coastal defense work, training, and reconnaissance.

The 673 typified the class appearance with her World War II German U-boat's general dimensions and silhouette. She didn't carry a deck gun and the lack of other topside clutter gave her a submerged speed of thirteen knots. Her surface speed hadn't improved over her predecessors, though: seventeen knots. At periscope depth, a snorkel fed air to her two 4000 horsepower diesel-electric engines, which were coupled to twin screws. And she sported four 533 millimeter torpedo tubes forward and two aft. She usually hauled a full warload of ten standard and two nuclear-tipped torpedoes.

Until six months ago, white figures had proudly announced hull numbers on her conning tower. However, the 673's assignment required full stealth advantage. The large numerals contrasted too brightly. The numbers were obliterated, covered in black to match the rest of her conning tower and topside surfaces.

Captain Second Rank Vladimir Zuleyev stood on his cold, cramped bridge as the 673 crept on the surface under an overcast nighttime sky toward the Karlskrona Archipelago. He peered into blackness and wondered about stealth. With the gyrocompass acting up who cared if the damned numbers were on the conning tower or not? The moon would rise in another two hours but that didn't matter now. He shook his head and again checked the red illuminated gyro repeater. The compass card drifted fifteen degrees either side of their intended course.

They were under strict emission control, radar was prohibited, and without a gyro they couldn't navigate accurately.

"That's it." Zuleyev cursed softly and threw up his hands. " We're lucky. Five kilometers to go, it could have been worse. I'm not going in there without a gyro. Not in this." He ordered left full rudder and, steering course 165 by magnetic compass, dashed for the Swedish territorial twelve-mile limit at flank speed. When they crossed into international waters, Zuleyev submerged to thirty meters and made turns for five knots. He kept his boat on course 165, stood down from action stations, and set the regular watch.

Anton Pavel Dobrynyn sat in the officers' mess, empty now except for two junior officers who, exhausted from the previous night's midwatch, snored in bunks jammed to the port bulkhead. Dobrynyn's black coveralls bore the military insignia of captain, equivalent to the naval rank of captain lieutenant. He and Ullanov had just removed their equipment and scuba gear lay stacked about.

It sounded as if the pressure was off. He'd heard the quartermaster report to the captain that an immediate gyro repair was unlikely. Zuleyev told him to try anyway.

The Zampolit, finally happy for something to do, rubbed his hands together and went to work. He commandeered Zuleyev's stateroom just aft of the officer's mess, summoned Ullanov, and drew the green curtain. Dobrynyn insisted on being there but Captain Third Rank Pyotr Kapultichev, a superior officer, ordered him to stay put. He was to be interrogated next. Dobrynyn had been through this sort of thing before with Ullanov, who usually handled himself well with political officers.

As he waited, Dobrynyn realized he was alone for the time being, a rarity on a submarine. His thoughts drifted again to the letter, the one that had come just before they shoved off. He'd already picked through it five times in the last two days. Like a volatile substance, it fascinated him. It seemed a missive of morbidity; a chronicle of perpetual damnation. A summation.

He ran a hand through his dark full beard and chewed a thumbnail. With a sigh, he reached into his ditty bag and pulled out the smudged envelope. Cheap paper crackled in his hands. He thumbed the torn flap open, then hesitated as Kapultichev's voice bellowed through the corridor.

"Sergeant! Brace yourself to attention. Don't look at me. Look at that bulkhead."

"Sir!"

Dobrynyn heard Junior Sergeant Josef Ullanov clamp his heels together. His feet would be at the precise forty-five degree angle. Ullanov's thumbs would be jammed along the seams of his black overalls. His face, Dobrynyn knew, would settle to the unfocused, totally subordinate expression of a military recruit. But when he stood before Zampolits, Ullanov's eyebrows would be slightly knit upward. And his eyes would glisten. Ullanov would weave slightly; his whole powerful stature would be an exquisite portrayal of "up yours, sir."

Kapultichev launched into his harangue. Dobrynyn grunted, pulled out Irenna's letter and unfolded it. His eyes found the scrawl.

Dear Anton,

This is very hard. I'm leaving. I know you're not surprised. I tried to call before you left but they wouldn't put me through or tell me anything.

Do you know how much time we've had over the past 2 years? I figured it out. 5 weeks and 4 days. That's all. And that includes our 6 day honeymoon in Riga. I still don't understand why you didn't want to go to Havana. Viktor could have fixed it for us. He has connections. What do you have against Havana? The only time we seem to enjoy each other anymore is when we are in bed. Always in bed. Or jogging or dancing to the jazz records. You're so alone. Why don't you just talk to me?

You're away too much and my own career is at stake. I don't know what a <u>Spetsnaz</u> does except jump out of airplanes or submarines on dark nights and sneak up to desolate beaches with all that scuba gear on. I wish you could tell me more. I wish you would wear your decorations more. Then maybe Viktor and the others would shut up.

"Sergeant! I asked you a question. Where did you get the stuff?"

Dobrynyn looked at the overhead. Not bad. Kapultichev was boring in. He visualized Kapultichev's handsome features, his square jaw, short-cropped red hair and well-defined build. He was a political officer, who had spent his entire career in Moscow, and the Leningrad-based 673 was his first, long overdue tour of sea duty. As in Moscow, Kapultichev quickly ascended to the top of photographers' lists when they needed a model of a typical Soviet naval hero. Propaganda photos found him standing dockside before ships or under massive statues, looking wistfully up at clouds. But Kapultichev was never sent out to speak. Instead of a solid Soviet rumble, his voice was high, almost castrato, soft. When his anger rose it became shrill.

Dobrynyn thought about it. How far could Kapultichev go? Zuleyev would back them up, of course. Zuleyev was the captain, he outranked Kapultichev. And he couldn't afford not to support Dobrynyn and Ullanov.

For Zuleyev had given them the idea. He, Dobrynyn, and Ullanov had been drinking in the Sphinx the night before they shoved off. Known for its good booze and entertainment, the Sphinx was the latest in-place, a converted powerhouse on the Neva River. The deep, cavernous dynamo bed had been converted to an orchestra pit, then a disco chamber. As music pounded, Zuleyev reminisced about how he'd seen it done once when he was a gunnery officer in the Caspian Sea Flotilla. The results were glorious.

Morale shot straight up. Josef sat there, nursed his beer, and nodded dumbly. Then Dobrynyn caught the slight tilt of Ullanov's head. Their eyes met briefly, the decision instant. Ullanov would know where to get the stuff. Dobrynyn knew where to put it. And later that night, it was done.

He went back to his letter.

And when we are together, you never talk to me and Ullanov is always around. I don't mind telling you. That man is dragging your career. Why is a sergeant, a junior sergeant at that, your best friend? And his girls. Like the one he brought to the party aboard the *Grozny* that night. She looked like someone from one of those Amsterdam bordellos you hear about.

Dobrynyn's ears perked up when Ullanov finally admitted it.

"...off the tender, sir. A friend of mine is a second-class petty officer. A pharmacist's mate."

Now they were getting down to it. The best part of the drama. Men, both officers and ratings, stood watch in the control room directly aft of Kapultichev's temporary chambers. Their heads were pitched forward, their ears cocked. Zuleyev hovered among them, suppressing the hacking coughs, sneezes, and rippling giggles as Kapultichev's rantings ascended through upper octaves.

"...methyl blue?" Kapultichev's squeal seeped through the curtain. "Some petty officer just handed a liter of methyl blue over to you?"

"Well, sort of sir. Uh...it was...er...when he wasn't looking."

Actually, Dobrynyn had distracted the man while Ullanov slipped behind the counter and pinched it.

"How did you introduce it into the fresh water system? I didn't realize *Spetsnaz* had such intimate knowledge of a submarine's plumbing. Such intimate knowledge of..." Kapultichev paused, the electric propulsion motors softly whirred aft, "...of naval architecture." Kapultichev recited this evenly for Dobrynyn's benefit. A preamble to his own interrogation.

"Been around submarines for a long time, sir. Actually I--"

"You're still at attention. Damnit!"

"Sorry, sir. I had a fourteen week tour on the 992 in the Caribbean once and I..."

I have made a decision. I took the Aeroflot job. I'm through with coaching.

I told Viktor yesterday. All my life has been on the ice dancing with Viktor and now, teaching new little Viktors and Irennas to skate their little hearts out. And that's what is going to happen to all but a few of them. No hearts. Since I was ten years old, I can't remember anything else except skating. And for what? An alternate in the Lake Placid Olympics? Maybe it's just as well I didn't go. The Afghanistan business made things messy for the team. And Viktor says you and your sergeant friend must have been there. Were you?

But guess what Viktor told me a couple of months ago. The real reason I didn't go to Lake Placid was because they were worried about us even though we were only engaged. It was about your people there. That I might try to contact your brother or father for you. They thought I might even try to defect. How do you think I feel about that? Now it turns out I could have actually skated in the Olympics. But instead, they reclassified me down to second alternate, which means nothing. You should do something about your family problems once and for all.

"Sergeant. This is going to go badly with you. You've damaged state property. Everything's blue. My teeshirt is blue. All our underwear is blue. The macaroni is blue. Our skin's turning blue. Blue -- blue -- blue. The chief engineer says we won't be able to purge the fresh water system for another two to three days, you bastard!

"And," Kapultichev's fist slammed on the desk, he gargled at a high tone, "everyone's piss is blue.

"You two thought we wouldn't figure it out until you were ashore, didn't you? What if the gyro hadn't broken down? What if you were ashore now? What makes you think we would have come back for you? The Swedes would have hung you both by the balls first, then shot you! No questions asked."

I'm going to Moscow. Viktor found a place for me there. Aeroflot has me scheduled for the Warsaw shuttle after flight attendants' schooling. And they promised to put me on the waiting list for the Havana run. But that takes two to three years.

I've taken my things. The place is yours. I never did like Leningrad anyway, I'm sure you're not surprised at that.

I'll get the paperwork started. I know you don't have any time.

Sincerely,

Irenna

P.S. I took the Count Basie, Quincy Jones and Johnny Keating records. You can have the rest.

Kapultichev's fist slammed again. "You're going back to Afghanistan, damnit. I'm making sure that--"

Something changed, the boat took a slight up angle. Dobrynyn heard a light tap outside the Captain's stateroom.

"WHAAAT?" screeched Kapultichev. Then, "Sorry, Captain."

In muffled tones, Kapultichev said, "What? It is? Yes sir, right away. Ullanov. Did you get that?"

The wardroom curtain ruffled, and Zuleyev stuck his head in and said quietly, "Gyro's fixed, Anton. There's still time tonight. We're going to try again. Back into your Sunday-suit."

Dobrynyn looked up and nodded aft.

Zuleyev grinned, "Don't worry about Josef. I'll fix it with Kapultichev later. And I'll get him off your back, too. I didn't think he'd pull something like this."

"Could be he's still nervous about submarines and being this close to the Swedes. Having a bladder full of blue piss at the same time probably scared the hell out of him."

"Don't worry. I'll have a talk with him."

"I think he could blow, Vladimir. You'd better watch him. Maybe even tonight. His first time in."

"Yes. I've thought about that. He needs something to do. But the control room people were bitching to me about him earlier. He stumbled into an electrical panel just before we surfaced a couple of hours ago. Nearly shorted power to the dive planes." Zuleyev studied the deck for a moment. "How about sticking him in the conning tower with the plotting party? Plenty of air in there. He'd be close to the bridge and you and the Chief can show him the charts so he can see what's going on."

"For as long as I'm there. Josef and I exit. Remember?"

"That's OK. I think he'll be all right after you two start out. He'll have seen two Soviet heroes go over the side in the name of the motherland."

Dobrynyn chuckled.

The skipper shook his head slowly, "Only a gag. That's all I wanted. Something to make these poor bastards laugh. Why do you think I let it slip the other night? Do you think I was that drunk? I knew you two were game."

"More like had."

"Yes. Perhaps." Zuleyev spotted the letter. "Forget her, Anton. Can't you remember what I said yesterday? It never was right."

"I know."

Zuleyev turned and went back to the control room. Ullanov walked in and glanced at Dobrynyn. He snorted and sat to pull on his gear as the *673* rose to periscope depth.

Dobrynyn and Ullanov suited up, and each double checked the other's equipment. By the time they waddled up to the crowded conning tower the *673* had turned north, surfaced, and quickly approached the Karlskrona Archipelago.

.   .   .

Rumbling diesels powered the 673 over a flat, viscous surface at fifteen knots. Action stations-surface were set and Zuleyev stood on his bridge with the exec, a third class quartermaster, and two lookouts.

The moon had risen and softly backlighted a descending overcast. Landmass shapes were barely smudged before them and surface visibility settled to about fifteen kilometers. Zuleyev wiped a hand over his jaw. Good for navigation now, not so good for stealth.

Zuleyev peered through his binoculars but his mind was on his objective. Which objective? Their primary target was the torpedo base at the western end of the island group. What if an alarm had been raised during their earlier attempt to penetrate that area? And their op-order warned of heavy patrol activity near Karlskrona in the central section. Stay at least twelve kilometers east of the main base, he decided. The Gåsefjärden area, the eastern section of the archipelago would be the one. Zuleyev set course zero-two-one and mulled over their chances of safely conning the 673 through the eastern section.

He was fidgety as he swept with his binoculars. He and his lookouts hadn't seen any patrol boats. He didn't think any were running darkened and he'd always seen one or two on previous trips.

Strange.

He turned to make sure his lookouts searched their sectors properly. "Anything?" he asked quietly.

"Clear starboard."

"Clear port."

Zuleyev's thoughts drifted back to targets. Which island? he mused.

The 673 rumbled on.

The exec and his quartermaster looked for navigational points toward shore; one's finger would jab at the night, the other would nod. White lights winked at them from irregular, ebony islands. Distant main channel navigational buoys illuminated by red and green lights danced in their binoculars. An occasional headland or charted rock revealed itself, barely silhouetted against the blackness. Sometimes the two disagreed on which was which but quickly moved to another point rather than lose time arguing.

Left to right, the exec sighted his bearings and spoke in clipped tones,

"Beacon, three-four-seven; Hasslö, left tangent, three-three-two; Utlängen, right tangent, zero-four-six." The quartermaster noted the time, scrawled numbers on a small pad then called them to the plotting party below in the conning tower.

The conning tower reeked of garlic, sweat and diesel oil as men crowded against one another and bent to their tasks. The open hatch to the bridge did little to dispel the stench in the afterpart of the space. Even as the 673 now prowled along at five knots the air flow seemed less than usual. Dobrynyn figured they moved with a following breeze. Ullanov made a face, eased under the hatch, and took deep breaths. Dobrynyn saw him shift into darkness, away from the small, crowded navigation table and as far as possible from Kapultichev who lurked at the aft end of their cramped quarters.

Dobrynyn peered over the shoulder of a deeply wrinkled, scarecrow-shaped chief quartermaster. The man nodded and wrote on a small pad as his talker, a young seaman, murmured data from the bridge, "Sturkö, left tangent, three-two-four; Danaflöt, zero-two-four point five; Inglängen, zero-eight-seven." The Chief licked his lips and quickly, accurately penciled three lines across the chart. Close now, Dobrynyn saw. The lines intersected about a kilometer south of Danaflöt, a small island that partially guarded the entrance to the Gåsefjärden.

The 673's gentle rocking ceased as they entered the channel's smooth waters. The bridge talker held his hands to his earphones, nodded, then turned to Dobrynyn, "Captain says Danaflöt is abeam to port. He plans to take you right up to Ornö Island, sir."

Dobrynyn nodded.

Ullanov spat. "Ornö. Nothing but the best. I thought the 531 scouted that last month?"

"They did, but apparently they didn't get everything," said Dobrynyn.

Kapultichev's soprano tones wafted across the space. "Secondary target, Sergeant. Underwater mine control center."

Ullanov ignored him. "Why the hell haven't they heard us? The way this floating turd coughs and farts, they'll blow us all to hell before we get to Ornö."

Kapultichev cut in. "Sergeant! The captain has good reason to..."

Orders were relayed to the control room. Zuleyev had the diesels shut down and shifted to electric power. Then he called for ballast. The tanks hissed momentarily and the 673 rode with her decks awash. Only her conning tower remained visible.

Kapultichev tried again. "You should--"

The chief quartermaster said loudly, "Flaggskär Island abeam to starboard, plot recommends--"

"Don't interrupt me," said Kapultichev.

The talker blinked and said, "Bridge wants a course to steer."

"Zero-two-four," said the quartermaster. "It's shallow in here, too." He checked the fathometer: seven point four meters. "Bottom's rising. Tell the captain I think we should go in dry."

Kapultichev edged in between the talker and the quartermaster. "You mean pump our ballast back out again? The captain gives orders on this submarine. Why do you think he did that? So they can't see us."

The talker started to relay the quartermaster's recommendation but Kapultichev covered the mouthpiece. "Hold on. Chief, I asked you a question."

The talker rolled his eyes. The chief quartermaster turned red. Silence swept the conning tower as incredulous, open-mouthed faces turned to Captain Third Rank Pyotr Kapultichev.

The zampolit looked at the quartermaster, then squinted at the chart. A fan whirred above them.

The talker held a hand to an earpiece. He said to the bulkhead, "Bridge wants to know what is going on, sir."

Kapultichev stooped over the chart, then eyed the fathometer. "Yes, all right. One moment. Chief, what does this mean?"

A voice echoed down the hatch, "Josef, give me a fathometer reading. I can't get anything out of plot."

Ullanov eyed the instrument, "A little over seven meters, Captain."

The low-pressure blowers whined. Ballast was evacuated from the tanks.

Kapultichev looked at Ullanov. "Sergeant! Who said you were qualified to--"

"Don't talk, Kapultichev. We're in the channel." Dobrynyn said sharply.

The zampolit mouthed, "You cant'--"

"It's tight in here. We can't turn around if something happens. You're interrupting the plot. Stop talking. Now." Dobrynyn's eyes were cold, gray.

"I'll see that you're--"

Ullanov pushed next to the table. "He means shut up you little zamp. Your crap isn't helping."

The chief quartermaster eyed the bulkhead chronometer. "Thirty seconds late. Tell the bridge to come left to zero-zero-six. Now."

"That's insubordination, Ullanov. You're going to prison." The talker relayed the message. Dobrynyn watched the rudder angle indicator swing left.

"Did you hear me, Sergeant? Your ass is going to--"

The boat heeled slightly to port. They heard a loud clanging down the starboard side.

"No!" shouted the Chief.

The 673 lurched again, heavily. Sailors pitched forward, then shouted, then tumbled. One thousand and fifty tons of a Voyenno Morskoy Flot Podvodnaya Lodka, NATO Whiskey class submarine kept going. Her five knot-inertia carried her over rocks, boulders; she plowed through sand, then screeched over more rocks.

"All back emergency!" Zuleyev roared down the hatch.

The 673 jinked on drunkenly. Her momentum slowed, but she bumped and thudded more heavily, sharply. Their vision blurred. Light bulbs shattered. Dust jammed the compartment; papers, books, charts spilled.

She creaked once more and gave a final gasp.

Silence. It was over.

Sailors moaned and cursed. They reeled and picked themselves up.

Dobrynyn rose with them and checked the depth gauge: three point five meters, one and a half meters above their five meter draft. High and dry.

The 673 shuddered as Zuleyev started the diesels. They thundered with full astern power. The boat worried like a shark; her screws churned frothy water onto the rocky beaches of Torumsk Island.

Something dug into Dobrynyn's back. He whirled. A dark, crimson face, Kapultichev's, was close to his. He looked down. The zampolit's Makarov, an eight shot semiautomatic, was pressed in his belly. The safety was on.

"You," Kapultichev growled. "You were behind this. It's because of you that--"

Dobrynyn backhanded the pistol. It crashed to the bulkhead and clattered to the deck. He took a half-step back and grabbed Kapultichev's collar with his left hand. His right fist, swift and powerful, buried itself against the zampolit's nose. Bone crunched, teeth shattered, blood spurted as the man's legs gave way.

Dobrynyn released the shirt. Kapultichev sagged to the deck.

Zuleyev stood in the aft end of the bridge, looking out the channel, into the Baltic, willing his command, his 673 to take hold and find freedom. All she could do was shudder as her skipper shouted, screamed over his bellowing engines. He pounded both fists. He urged.

His 673 could only pathetically wiggle.

The talker shouted in his ear again, then shook his captain's shoulders. The chief engineer had advised, then screamed to the bridge talker that their thrust bearings were overheating. They would burn up soon.

Zuleyev waited another sixty seconds, hoping, willing. His shoulder slumped, he nodded. He ordered all stop and secured his engines.

First light was at five-thirty-five. At five-fifty, *Kristine*, a ten-meter fishing boat, weighed anchor and chugged out of a small cove in Hästholmen Island. She powered on a southerly course out of the fog shrouded Gåse-fjärden toward the Baltic and her fishing grounds.

A misty Torumsk Island slid down the port side as the *Kristine*'s skipper gulped hot coffee and blinked sleep from his eyes. He looked to his port instrument console to check the DECCA. The LED wiggled as it usually did when it warmed up. He punched the LAT/LONG button to verify its alignment. It read:

56° 04'.3 N

15° 44'.1 E

He studied the digits but something else swirled into his view just over the top of the console. His eyes flickered, then focused. Through the windshield. The long, black matte shape was enormous. Rust streaked down from limber holes. A periscope extended above the conning tower, its mirrored lens glinted toward him. He gulped. Fifty meters away. On Torumsk! *Jesus!*

"Rolf! Wake up. Rolf! Jesus!" He jumped from the wheel, ran aft and shook his partner in his bunk. "Rolf!"

10

Admiral of the Red Banner Pacific Fleet and Hero of the Soviet Union Yeofofey D. Belousov studied the message, then leaned back in his chair and considered the odds. He could let it go, do nothing. Possibly it wouldn't be exposed before he moved on to Moscow and his next job. It seemed minor, and yet...

His chair squeaked as he turned and gazed out at the hills and harbor. On this misty September day, bustling Vladivostok was jammed full of merchant ships from all over the world. Likened to San Francisco in many ways, Vladivostok was known as the "Ruler of the East" and was easily the Soviet Union's largest Pacific seaport.

Vladivostok was also homeport to Belousov's powerful Red Banner Pacific Fleet, whose newest additions included two forty-three-thousand ton *Kiev* class carriers, the *Minsk*, and the *Novorossiysk*. Onethird of the Soviet Union's strategic missile submarines fell under Belousov's administrative control, although they were operated by the KGB out of Petropavlovsk to the north. Belousov's command had well over thirty percent of his country's major surface warships and also deployed the largest fleet air arm. As a surface warfare specialist, he'd fought hard in the Defense Ministry's cloakrooms and finally received the brand new twenty-four thousand ton nuclear battle cruiser *Frunze* two years ago.

But now, things were different. The Rodina wasn't the same as in the old days. Elected civilians in Moscow were wresting control of allocations long coveted by the military and were threatening to build TV sets, food machinery, and plumbing fixtures rather than completing modernization programs for the Voyenno Morskoy Flot, the Soviet Navy. And enlistments were down, meaning the Navy had to depend more and more on conscripts, ones not hyped on drugs or alcohol, for key technical tasks. His Red Banner Pacific Fleet, in particular, had almost intolerable ethnic, language, and cultural problems. Belousov sighed, realizing that these days he wasted more and more of his time grappling with hideous administrative realities he had never envisioned when he entered the navy thirty-one years ago.

And now this problem. The message was a Faxed information copy routed to his own Pacific Fleet Intelligence Directorate from a Second Division line agent in Washington, D.C. His blunt fingers carefully placed it beside an open folder labeled Jet Stream and he bent to read it again:

TO: SPILLOVER
FROM: MAXIMUM EBB

IMPERATIVE WE MEET SOONEST LOS ANGELES. UNABLE TO TRAVEL. POSSIBLE USSR DEFECTION EX P/P. JET STREAM IN JEOPARDY. MAXIMUM EBB IN JEOPARDY. AVAILABLE COM STA 213.

Belousov snorted at the phrase, "Jet Stream in jeopardy." Eighteen months ago MAXIMUM EBB--Felix Renkin--their American asset in Washington, D.C., had told SPILLOVER, Belousov's line agent, Yuri Borodine, that U.S. submarines had been sneaking into the Sea of Okhotsk for the past five years, listening to cable traffic between Petropavlovsk and the mainland. In a way, he admired that, right under the noses of his Red Banner Pacific Fleet. What audacity, what ingenuity, and all in international waters, too.

The American intrusion required a counterintelligence operation and Belousov set up Jet Stream, which poured disinformation over the cables when U.S. submarines were known to be in the area. It was a game, the

Americans had to know that now. His intelligence staff was running out of ideas and was putting out such absurd crap over those wires. The really secret material went by satellite, guard mail, or courier to circumvent the U.S. Navy's operation--what did they call it? He ran a thick forefinger through the folder--Ivy Bells.

He frowned at the phrase "Possible USSR defector ex P/P." Who? In his command? In Petropavlovsk? Never!

Something else tugged at the back of his mind, a far deeper problem. He still wasn't sure why he'd inherited MAXIMUM EBB/Felix Renkin from the KGB two years ago. Upon reflection, the KGB had been uncharacteristically happy to hand him over. Their rationale was that a naval line agent, such as Borodine, the one Belousov had in Washington D.C., would do a far better job extracting technical information. The only requirement was for the usual reports. The asset had not balked at the transfer of control and continued to provide priceless information. But it had been too easy. Now, as Belousov drummed his fingers, he thought he knew why.

"Maximum ebb in jeopardy," the message said. The KGB had dumped the man on Belousov because they had been afraid of a blown cover. Belousov knit his brow. With great visibility, the Americans were unearthing Soviet agents right and left. True, some had been arrested due to plain bad luck, but others had gotten careless. American/Soviet relations were threatened at the highest levels and new policy directed that only the most efficient and noncontaminating agents be used. Emphasis was directed, for the time being, to passive methods, like the American listening operation, Ivy Bells.

Belousov understood what they meant by 'non-contaminating'. Someone would hang if another agent were arrested.

He drummed his fingers. Felix Renkin "in jeopardy." What kind? How imminent? Renkin, now highly placed in the U.S. government, had been on the Soviet payroll for several decades. If caught, he *would* be a major embarrassment.

Belousov considered his options. Perhaps MAXIMUM EBB should retire before things came to a head, and well before Belousov got stuck with an international clamor that would cause his own premature retirement. He could offer Renkin a comfortable villa. It had to be somewhere in the

West since defection to the Soviet Union was out of the question these days. Yes, he would instruct his line agent to ask the man about retirement after the Petropavlovsk defection problem was sorted out.

Belousov rubbed his jaw and undid his collar. He examined the message again, finding the routing fortunate. Keep it in the family, in his own intelligence command and away from the GRU, or worse, those ghouls in the KGB. It would get tricky if they learned of a potential defector in his command. They would quickly shove it up to Medvedev, the Navy's chief political director in Moscow, directly under his commanding officer, Viktor P. Kolomeytsyev. Then, crap would fly.

He flipped the message over and checked the date-time group. It had been endorsed and forwarded from the Soviet embassy in Washington, D.C., over five hours ago.

Belousov decided to permit Yuri Borodine's travel and expenses for the meeting in Los Angeles. He needed answers. He rang for Perelygin, his deputy chief of staff, to send the authorization.

Captain Second Rank Yuri Borodine was happy to be on the ground. The flight to Los Angeles had been hectic. The football team, their victorious élan, their exuberance, had filtered through the entire coach section. Riding on an overcrowded DC-10, he'd been squeezed next to a monstrous, thicknecked, grinning boy with pimples and short blond hair. The youngster had continually bellowed to his pals in the row forward, something about their season opener and how they'd slaughtered the other team.

Borodine, on the other hand, had done his best to be quiet, to minimize conversation, and he had studied the same five pages of *Popular Science* all the way from the Dallas/Fort Worth Airport, where he'd transferred from his Washington D.C., flight. He was glad to be on the ground and in the modern, cool Delta Airlines terminal, away from gouging elbows and hacking, impetuous laughter.

Those cretins. Those super soccer players or football players, or whatever they were, seemed no different from the ragtag, drug- sniffing ruffians his Soviet society produced nowadays. Jealous of their athletic acumen and contemptuous of their empty heads, thirtysix-year-old Yuri Borodine was glad he'd never indulged in sports. How could he with a five-foot-six-inch frame that carried 132 pounds, and an atrophied right foot?

Borodine had suffered a severed Achilles tendon in a motorcycle accident shortly after graduating from basic officers' training. About to be cashiered, Borodine demanded a hearing, citing his high marks. Reluctantly, they agreed to keep him on but only as a staffer, with no sea duty. This was to his liking, a way to make up for his physical deficiencies. In subsequent schools he always had the highest marks. Then his superiors handpicked him for the A. S. Popov Higher Naval School of RadioElectronics and later, the Kiev Higher Naval School. He graduated from both at the top of his class. He went on to language school, where he gained fluency in English and its American dialect. After several more schools, Borodine found himself in a niche of his own where his knowledge and wits would serve him better than any idiot's physical strength.

He'd fallen into this assignment by accident. Borodine was billeted with the Red Banner Pacific Fleet Intelligence Directorate, Fifth Division--the electronics intelligence section where he excelled, as usual. They'd decided to send him to temporary duty in Washington, D.C., under the cover of a cultural attaché, to help support an ongoing ELINT operation against the U.S. Navy in Norfolk, Virginia. It was temporary duty, three months at most. That was five years ago.

Yuri Borodine had grown up in Russia's ancient and magnificent Novgorod. Small, with slick jet-black hair, a pockmarked face, deeply sunken cheeks, and full lips, he looked less than pathetic. Borodine was ignored, people felt sorry for him, he never attended the "right" social functions and, indeed, was not invited to join the circuit in Washington; his looks forbade it. He was allowed to blend into the background.

But his work was always impeccable. After three months in Washington they'd transferred him from the Fifth Division, Electronics Intelligence, to the Second Division of the Pacific Fleet Intelligence Directorate as a line agent. Yuri Borodine became a spy, and a very good one. He didn't have to worry about political infighting since the other United States based agents were mostly KGB, interspersed with a few GRU types and one or two Moscow-based naval intelligence agents. Borodine was the only one from any of the four Fleet Intelligence Directorates. And Borodine, like the others, was now engaged in passive surveillance, marking time to see which way the political winds blew in the Rodina.

Borodine dodged a foursome of uniformed cabin attendants. Reviewing the message, he recalled Belousov's priorities had been to first, take care of the defector problem then, if conditions made it feasible, explore the question of MAXIMUM EBB's retirement. But the retirement question was difficult, since it affected Borodine's operation. He had a good relationship with the asset now and the man had promised something in a year or two that could be a major intelligence coup. This would be good, possibly very good for Borodine's career.

Borodine sighed as he dragged his foot along to the phone booth. He would see to the defector problem, all right. Retiring the asset was something that perhaps could be mentioned, then put in abeyance. If the man did produce, Borodine would finally get the position the Naval Personnel Directorate in Moscow was discussing, a prized one: head of the Fifth Division, Intelligence Directorate, for the TwiceHonored Red Banner Baltic Fleet in Leningrad.

Leningrad, the Hermitage, the Venice of Russia, the Neva River, the parties, his old friends and, best of all, only 160 kilometers northwest of Novgorod, with his favorite retreats, the Volkhov River and Lake Ilmen. Yuri Borodine would give thought to joining the cocktail circuit and working his way up socially. Until then...

He picked up the phone and closed his eyes, recalling the digits, and punched up the 213 COM STA code for the week. The phone relays clicked and growled at his ear. With a sigh, he identified two satellites keying in. He wanted to sit, but his good leg would fall asleep, so he leaned against the partition and waited ninety seconds while the connection worked its way around.

Borodine eyed the LAX crowd automatically. The last of the football players from his flight folded into the horde. He saw his seatmate, the blond crew-cut grinning kid, bowl his way down the long hall dragging a duffle bag, his shirttail hanging out. The kid had his arm around a flight attendant's shoulder.

"Two five two one."

Borodine immediately spoke in his deep, compelling bass. "Good afternoon. Worthington Hatch here. I'd like to talk with someone about the Chagall we purchased last week. It appears to be damaged and they sent me to discuss it with you."

"Yes. Where are you, Mr. Hatch?"

"I just arrived and have my own transportation, thank you." Borodine would rent a car, he didn't want to be at Carrington's mercy. They would meet on neutral ground, without Carrington hulking around the table he hoped. "We could meet later at the Bonaventure in downtown L.A. if you like, say, about four o'clock?"

"Sorry, Mr. Hatch, the Bonnie's out. Like we said, we have a mobility problem."

"Serious?"

"Very uncomfortable, but otherwise OK." A pause, then, "I'd like to pick you up."

"No, that won't be necessary." Borodine's mind raced ahead. He didn't want to be at their mercy, without transportation. "I'll come out there. Let me have your address, please."

"Mr. Hatch, I have instructions to pick you up."

Time to get serious and quit jousting. "Ah, yes, we can always send the Chagall back. It's still in its crate. We're sure the frame and canvas are just as you packed them."

Borodine smiled as he heard the mouthpiece covered on the other end. Muffled tones followed, then silence.

The hand squeaked off the mouthpiece. "Yes, all right, four o'clock here. We're in Newport Beach."

"Thank you. Where?"

"Number twelve, Oakmont Lane. That's in a gated community called Big Canyon. We'll leave word with the guard." He gave directions.

Borodine relaxed. The safe house near the coast sounded all right. Neighbors, probably children playing, a golf course nearby. It sounded authentic.

"Four o'clock, then." Borodine hung up, then headed toward the main concourse. It would be an hour and a half drive and there was time for a quick bite. He was hungry now. Borodine checked his watch and found he could just make it.

Borodine walked to a restaurant, sat down and ordered a cobb salad. While waiting, he went over MAXIMUM EBB's--Felix Renkin's background in his mind. The doctor spoke French, German, and Italian fluently. His undergraduate degree was in political science and, in 1950, had joined the U.S. Navy, where they made him a courier. Based in London, his routes took him through Rome, Frankfurt, Munich, Brussels, and Berlin. An agent of the Soviet NKVD, predecessor to the MVD and active in Germany before the KGB took over, had blackmailed Renkin, photographing him *in flagrante delicto* with a Berlin prostitute who was a known NKVD informer. Renkin turned over his courier pouch for photocopying in return for a set of negatives, which, he realized without being told, was a duplicate batch. When Renkin learned the prostitute was pregnant with his child he bolted, getting himself transferred to Seventh Fleet headquarters at the Yokosuka Naval Station in Japan.

The Soviets used discretion in selecting Renkin's Far East control. They recognized his intellect was counterbalanced by immaturity, and that he was a loner in need of friendship. His Far East control propped up the ensign's ego and started him with easy assignments, such as reporting ship movements and photographing less sensitive documents marked "confidential" and "secret."

At his release from active duty in 1958 the Soviets turned Renkin inactive. He was to devote his energy to developing a civilian career. By this time he had risen to full lieutenant and had become very confident, almost arrogant. Occasionally, his control had to remind Renkin that he was an agent and that they could blow his cover. The control also told Renkin that the prostitute had died in a bomb blast and that he'd sired not one child, but identical twin boys. The KGB man--by this time the KGB had replaced the MVD--told him one had been adopted by an NKVD sergeant and was being raised in Leningrad while the other was living in California.

Lieutenant Renkin was incredulous that his issue was now an American. The control told him the boy had been adopted by an Army demolitions corporal, Willard Harrison Lofton, who had married a young German girl. They came to Minneapolis in 1953 and were divorced almost immediately. She disappeared and Corporal Lofton kept the baby and moved to

California, where he was killed in an auto wreck in 1954. The toddler was consigned to San Diego orphanages.

The shock was enough. Renkin agreed to be responsive to any future summons, knowing the boy's existence might be used against him, especially if he rose to prominence in adulthood.

Renkin returned to the U.S. and proceeded to earn two Ph.D's, almost back to back. One was in political science, the other in international finance. After serving three years at RayTran Corporation, a think tank based in Washington D.C., he taught for another two years at the U.S. Naval Postgraduate School in Monterey, California, in matters of national security.

The young instructor lived in the BOQ and rarely strayed, not wanting to mingle with (Borodine remembered the direct quotation in Renkin's dossier) "Californians and suffer their free-thinking, undirected, cow college mentality." His impatience with outsiders and passion for study served him well. A major step in his career came when he met Dr. Fulton Dowd, a fifty-five-year-old electronics and first-generation computer sciences expert who taught Navy communications programs. Like Renkin, the reclusive Dowd stayed close to his books and slide rules. Renkin learned that Dowd had ideas for the U.S. Navy's proposed Extremely Low Frequency (ELF) communications program, a strategic program to communicate with submerged Polaris ICBM submarines anywhere in the world.

The submarines, Dowd explained, needed a "bell-ringer." Something that would tell the submarines's captain to rise near the surface at his discretion, where he could safely receive a more high-speed, conventional message via high frequency or satellite link. At seventy-six hertz Dowd's ELF could "bell-ring" any submarine in the world at any depth. All he needed were favorable rock formations in the US that could accommodate an antenna *twenty-eight miles long*. Under those conditions, Dowd could produce a wavelength not measured in millimeters or centimeters or even meters. His wavelength would be *two thousand, five hundred miles long!* Renkin, sensing an opportunity, pitched in and discovered the perfect site near Grovers Mills, Wisconsin.

Their collaboration flourished. They completed their teaching contracts and formed FLR Industries (Dowd, a modest individual, had no

desire to have his initials as part of the logo), a consulting company special-
izing in secure defense communications. Renkin shrewdly took options on
contiguous real estate near Grovers Mills and knocked on doors in the
Navy Department while Dowd hovered with slide rules in a rented one-
room office in Silver Spring, Maryland, refining specifications.

FLR won a large second-tier consulting subcontract, meaning the prime
contractor had to put up the money and suffer the risk while conforming to
FLR specifications. The major problem, ironically, was not in the technology or funding or development. It came when Renkin exercised the real
estate options he had signed over to the Navy. The populace of Grovers
Mills became angry when they learned the U.S. government intended to
tear up their pastures and forests to lay miles and miles of cable, all
protected with miles and miles of chain-linked fence and security patrols.
Renkin worked eighteen hours a day with residents and local government
officials to insure the Navy had its way. His weapons included logic, patriotic appeal, and hard negotiations. A few gave in to payoffs. Two were
evicted on trumped-up court orders.

Renkin's efforts won him the recognition of Congress's House Armed
Services Committee in addition to the Navy Department's gratitude.
Dowd's plans for a more efficient system, one with a fifty-six-mile-long
antenna, were virtually complete when he died at his desk of heart failure
in late 1968, six months too soon to witness the first successful test of his
ELF system in Grovers Mills. It functioned as expected and U.S. ballistic
missile submarines trailing long, neutrally buoyant antennas no longer had
to approach the surface to search for instructions.

But Renkin needed to expand. Larger ELF orders were coming in and
he needed capital to hire staff and build testing laboratories. His problem
became acute when the bankers capped his credit line, saying they had
problems extending so much money to a company working on "black
programs" of which they had only a vague understanding.

In desperation, he approached his KGB control in Washington D.C.,
about the same time the KGB were thinking of awakening him. Borodine
remembered the year a matured, far more stable, and far more valuable
Renkin worked out his agreement. It was 1969, eighteen years after he'd
been recruited. A bargain was struck and the KGB provided a "loan"

through a legitimate U.S. venture capital group. The loan payments, less interest, reverted to Renkin when the venture capital company made deposits to a series of offshore bank accounts the Soviets had set up for Renkin's access. In turn, Renkin turned over plans for the fifty-six-mile antenna system the Navy was building in Michigan. The irony was that the Soviet Union, with ideal geological conditions in several locations, didn't have its ELF system functional until 1986 because of technical and cost problems.

The ELF contracts lead to related submarine programs, including follow-on strategic evaluations of major SOSUS (underwater listening arrays that detected submarines' movements and transmitted the data to shore bases) updates. Other consulting assignments followed: RDSS, an air-dropped deep-water listening barrier and FDS, a fixed distributed system as a successor to SOSUS with vastly improved fiber-optic upward looking sensors.

Renkin recruited the best scientific minds to carry on Dowd's tradition. He was hard pressed to find committed recluses like Dowd and ruthlessly fired those who didn't work twelve-to fourteen-hour days, including Saturdays. He overpaid those who did. The Soviets never overpaid Renkin for information on deployment and technical characteristics of SOSUS or RDSS or FDS. They just paid well. And Dr. Renkin didn't marry, absorbed by building FLR Industries to a seventy-five-million-dollar, staff-intensive organization, which he took public in 1972.

FLR's reputation become impeccable as Renkin met all projects on time and on budget. His reputation also grew on Capitol Hill, where he testified in behalf of the Navy and his prime contractors with a staccato highly informed precision. His direct, no-nonsense approach, quick mind, and limitless energy won the attention of elected officials and political appointees, especially Justin Cromwell, the director of defense policy for the National Security Council.

Renkin's file had been specific about their approach. It was straightforward, Borodine remembered. They met at the Burning Tree Country Club where Cromwell stated the National Security Council needed an individual of Dr. Renkin's education and government know-how. Simply put, the National Security Council could use a man of his skills to keep the

Congress off their backs and let them do their jobs. Would Dr. Renkin mind, he asked, taking a two- year sabbatical from FLR and acting as director of a new office entitled special projects? He would be privy to full disclosure of the council's affairs so that he could properly anticipate and deal with congressional problems.

Renkin accepted in 1977. Two years later, he received his permanent appointment, director of congressional liaison, and sold his FLR stock. The proceeds from that, of course, remained in U.S. banks but didn't come close to approximating the large balances he had well-hidden overseas.

In 1984, Renkin came to the public's attention when he was tasked with placating a budget-conscious Congress about cost overruns on the MX missile. The press discovered Renkin was the one solidly contributing to the idea of shifting arms control goals from limiting the number of vehicles to limiting the number of warheads. Selling this plan to Congress helped obtain approval for MX funding. It was more difficult pacifying an irate Capitol Hill during the Iran-Contra affair, of which, ironically, he knew nothing. In that case, he could only act as an information conduit, hoping the matter would burn itself out. It didn't, but the nation's attention quickly shifted to the principals, and that left Felix Renkin with a job and an unscathed reputation.

Borodine had inherited Renkin from the KGB two years before and, proud of his unique challenge, initially spent more time overcoming Belousov's reluctance than effectively working the asset. After a review of both the twins' careers, an opportunity became clear to Borodine, and he lost patience with those who failed to immediately grasp his vision. In a flurry of messages, Borodine presented the concept to Belousov; a concept that would have been a masterstroke for the KGB had they been smart enough to identify and exploit it; a concept that would elevate Borodine quickly in the Soviet naval hierarchy.

Lofton.

Belousov endorsed the Lofton concept, as it became known, after an exasperating six months and Fleet Intelligence in Moscow took another two months to approve it.

Borodine was finally able to put it to Renkin. "We would like you to look into the possibility of recruiting your son, Bradley Lofton. You both have

strong knowledge of naval matters and some day perhaps you could pass
the torch when you retire."

Renkin balked. But Borodine pressed, saying Lofton's background was
perfect. He had graduated cum laude from the University of Michigan's
School of Naval Architecture in 1971 and served with distinction in Vietnam
as a SEAL. And since 1977 he had been with the Marine Systems Division of
Jenson Industries.

Borodine purred that Lofton didn't have to know who his father was
right away. Renkin could decide when the time was right.

Renkin gave in, having really no choice. He looked for an obscure
program where it would be possible to observe Lofton closely. He decided
on the X-3 project in San Diego and had him assigned as soon as the NSC
took over. Borodine was pleased and didn't press for immediate information on the X-3. Perhaps Lofton, a naval architect with program management experience on the 688 attack and Ohio ICBM class submarines, could
provide data once he agreed to work for his father.

Borodine finished his salad and sat back. In the final analysis it was a
man's motivation that concerned him. Renkin's profile was perfect, very
American. In essence, it consisted of money, manipulation, and flexible
ethics. In Doctor Renkin's case, money easily became greed, and the means
to gain power. Manipulation came from his intelligence and the fact that he
was a tireless worker who took advantage and demanded the best from
those around him. His ethics were heartless rationalizations designed to
accomplish his distorted goals.

Borodine sighed. Felix Renkin was heir to ancient and immutable traits.
Through the ages, somebody was always available. He hoped Lofton would
be as easy.

The gate guard smiled. "Yes, Mr. Hatch, you're expected. Please go right in."
Directions to Oakmont Lane were given, the button was pushed, and the
barrier silently raised. It was 3:56.

Borodine discovered Oakmont Lane was not a narrow, tree-shrouded
dirt road as the name implied. The safe house lay nestled among trees, all
right, but was accessible via a meticulously maintained culdesac complete

with speed bumps and large, beautiful homes, which looked out on fairways. Security signs were posted throughout.

His shriveled foot, the right one, was tired and he'd had to drive with the left for the past fifteen minutes. He braked at the bottom of the hill, with both feet. Pins and needles shot up his right leg.

Number twelve was a low, sprawling onestory house with dark wooden siding and large decorative tropical shrubs. He got out and stood for a moment while circulation returned to his leg. Then he walked to the double entry doors and pushed the button.

Silence. He looked for the TV camera that was sure to be hidden: ah, there, nestled among the eaves. He held his head down, wishing he'd worn a hat.

Finally, the door eased open and Carrington, with a bandage over the side of his head, stood in the entry. "Hello, Mr. Hatch. This way, please."

Borodine followed through a tastefully appointed living room and down a long, silent hallway to another double-entry door. Borodine waited as the man knocked. There was a muffled reply, then both entered a high-ceilinged master suite done in pastels, which contrasted well with a pleasing oriental bedspread and matching furniture fabrics.

Perched in the middle of the kingsized bed was his asset, Felix Renkin. To Renkin's right was a PC with a laptop keyboard. Books, papers, huge directories, and volumes surrounded him. He wore a light blue terrycloth robe and sat erect. His nose was heavily bandaged and both eyes were very black. Shiners, as they said in American Westerns, as if he'd been in a barroom fight.

Borodine took the initiative. "Good afternoon, Dr. Renkin." He looked about. "You were right. This is a nice place to talk."

The man accepted the handshake lightly. Borodine fixed on Renkin's eyes. They were cloaked behind thick goldrimmed glasses, which did nothing to obscure the shiners.

"Thank you for coming. Please sit down." Felix Renkin pushed aside a yellow pad and pencil. "How was your flight? Do you need anything, a drink perhaps?"

Borodine selected a deep comfortable club chair and shook his head.

Renkin looked up and nodded. "That's all for now, Carrington." The man turned and walked out. The door clicked behind him.

Borodine moved ahead. "What happened to your face, your nose, Dr. Renkin?"

"I was struck twice within a week's time by your Mr. Lofton."

Borodine picked up on "your Mr. Lofton." He realized it would serve no purpose to say anything about kinship at this point. "Yes?"

"He and his accomplice also beat up Carrington." Renkin waved a hand toward the oak-paneled double entry, "and killed one of my best assistants. Lofton is one of the reasons we're meeting today."

Borodine feigned sympathy with clicked teeth. "Why did Lofton do that to you?"

Renkin explained.

Borodine sat forward. "*You* killed Lieutenant Commander Thatcher? Why? I heard about that in Washington."

"Thatcher assumed too much, Mr. Hatch, and he was correct in his assumptions. He figured it out from the disks aboard the *X-3*. I had no idea the man was that intelligent. He was a mustang, up from the enlisted ranks. During his trip back from the Kurils he had time to pull the disks and back into a solution that told him the CAPTORs were live, and that I had ordered them to be laid automatically."

Borodine crossed his leg over his knee and propped his chin on a fist. "Interesting, this *X-3*. A fuel cell submarine. Revolutionary, if you come right down to it. Can you give us details?"

"Of course."

"Thank you." Borodine leaned forward. "Shall we return to the business at hand?"

"Yes. The CIA has an asset in Petropavlovsk--"

"Yes, the message--"

"--who wants to defect."

Borodine recrossed his leg. The right one was falling asleep. Soon he would have to stand and walk around. "That, of course, interests us. Who is this man?"

Renkin shook his head slowly and pursed his lips. "I don't know. The CIA reports to us are terribly sanitized, just like ours to them. We don't trust each other. What I do know is that the man is military, he's stationed in Petropavlovsk, and is aware of both of the Ivy Bells/Jet stream operations. He wants out and the CIA has promised to extract him via one of their people on a Japanese trawler that fishes near Kamchatka regularly."

Yuri Borodine sat back, at a loss for words. The matter was worse than he had anticipated.

Renkin caught it, and his shoulders straightened. "Apparently the CIA has an asset, a native Japanese, on the trawler. The asset has been in contact with your defector. They plan for the trawler to offload fish at the Petropavlovsk commercial dock. The defector is supposed to jump aboard and hide, and the trawler, the *Kunashiri Maru*, will put to sea." Renkin looked down, then said slowly, "The *Kunashiri Maru* is to rendezvous with the USS *Truman* and transfer your man, er, the defector, near the Kurils."

Borodine stood and tried to pace. It was hard at first, those needles in his leg distracted him. He had to concentrate as Renkin explained the rest of the CIA transfer plan.

Renkin ran a finger over his bandaged nose. "But then Thatcher figured out that the CAPTOR was a live drop. He also figured out the targets and rendezvous, and now that idiot Lofton has the X-3 and has the potential to screw everything up. He's a SEAL, he knows how to disarm those CAPTORs. That's why I need your help."

Borodine sat down again. "Dr. Renkin. Have you thought about what could happen if Lofton is successful?"

"With your assistance, he won't be."

Borodine nodded. "But, we're concerned. What if he is? What if something else happens? What would you do?"

"You mean if it came to..."

"Yes."

Renkin looked about the room and waved his arms. "Come to you, I suppose."

Borodine sensed from the tone of Belousov's message that that wouldn't be acceptable. "Have you thought of retirement?"

"Absolutely not. I--ah. You're worried about my cover being blown. About what would happen on an, ah...executive level."

"Mmm. That and public opinion. Yes."

"We have some other business to finish, Mr. Hatch. Perhaps we should conclude those proceedings, then speak of retirement?"

Borodine stroked his chin, knowing Renkin dangled a carrot. He thought it over and decided to take the chance. Fortunately, Lofton's impetuous run to Petropavlovsk could be easily nullified. But Belousov would have to know right away so they could authorize the counteropera-tion he had in mind. He mused over pressed palms. "All right. We'll wait for the time being. What else do you know of this defector?"

"The information is very sketchy. All I know is what I told you; that the candidate defector is military, that he knows of both Ivy Bells and Jet stream."

"Well that narrows it down somewhat." Borodine rubbed his leg, the needles went away, it felt better. "Petropavlovsk. A military man there with knowledge of both operations would be one of a select few."

"Fleet Intelligence, perhaps?" Renkin grinned slightly.

"Perhaps. Also, it could be someone in the KGB. They're responsible for land line signals." He paused. "But then, this will be our job to find out."

They stared at each other. Borodine finally caught on. "But this must mean Jet stream is compromised, if your CIA is aware of it."

"I don't think so. From what I can tell, they're aware of the code word. But I don't think they know what it means."

"But Ivy Bells?"

"No, they only know the defector is aware of an American listening operation near Kamchatka. That's my interpretation. The name Ivy Bells wasn't used. But Jet stream, your code word, was."

Borodine said, "Then it's possible both operations can continue for a while."

"Yes, I think so. As long as the business on both our ends is taken care of."

"Good. Now, Dr. Renkin. Can we return to the subject of Lofton?"

"I think we should."

"Your reports highlight a very capable engineer who has strong poten-tial for us. But we're vague on his personal characteristics. What is he like? What are his habits? How does he enjoy himself? Have you approached him about working for us, yet?" Borodine's questions were staccato.

Renkin shook his head. "As a transition, I talked to him about working directly for me, but he refused.

"As far as Lofton's personal characteristics, I've found him to be very reliable, intelligent, and a good manager. He works long and hard. He's a bachelor. There was a marriage in 1979. It only lasted two years; they separated. And now, he dates a girl for six or seven months, drops her, and goes on to another. His one hobby is sailing, yacht racing, he does a lot of that. He's half owner of a seventy-foot racing sloop that's moored here in Newport Beach."

Renkin sighed. "But his habits, who is he? I don't know. He has friends, but he lives alone in an apartment near Point Loma. He reads a lot and plays chess."

"Drugs? Alcohol?"

Renkin shook his head. "No, nothing as easy as that. He's just a loner."

Borodine looked into the distance. Renkin's presentation was convincing and it was evident the Lofton succession scheme was finished. Plans had to be made to salvage what was left and keep Lofton from ruining things. Borodine would also have to think of another successor to Renkin when the time came. "He's dangerous."

"You can tell that by looking at my face. Can you take care of him?"

"It's difficult. We've been ordered to cut way down on wet jobs. This is a period of *perestroika*."

"You needn't remind me. But I still need your assistance." It was the closest Renkin would come to groveling.

Borodine stood again and walked to the large bay window. There was a nook he hadn't noticed where a small fireplace lay nestled among bookshelves. He looked out the window and admired the flowering shade plants. Azaleas, he thought. "You're sure Lofton is coming to our side of the Pacific?"

"Positive. He took my briefcase. He can learn a great deal. And the file says he is proficient in Russian; he would be comfortable putting in to Petropavlovsk before he heads for the CAPTOR site."

"Really?"

"Yes, there were papers in the briefcase that may compel him to contact the defector."

"All right. I think something can be arranged. When do you think he will arrive?"

"We laid a track. The *X-3*'s best cruising speed is thirty knots. That would put Lofton in Petropavlovsk on the twenty-first or early on the twenty-second, that is, if he was able to get a full load of fuel. There was so much confusion. We're not sure if he topped the *X-3*'s tank, because the fuel truck blew up. If he didn't top off he'll need more before he attempts the crossing and we're watching for that, believe me. Carrington has a special interest in him also."

"I believe you." Borodine turned to Renkin and examined him. The bathrobe, the rumpled sheets and bedspread, he couldn't see any sign of legs or feet. Renkin's torso seemed to grow out of the enormous bed.

Borodine put his hands behind his back and limped toward Renkin. "I think it will be rather easy. At least, here is what I shall recommend to Pacific Fleet Intelligence."

11

Lofton's heart pounded as adrenaline surged through his veins. *No!* He dropped to his knees and blinked his eyes, not believing...and yet... He peeked past the number-three decomposer and aimed the flashlight.

Damnit! Right there on the master control solenoid valve. Rust!

Frantically, he reached for the tool kit, yanked it open, spilling sockets on the motor room's deck grate, and hooked up a long extension to a ratchet handle. He arched his back, reaching for the fuel block.

Who built this piece of junk?

He was less than twelve hours from Petropavlovsk. One thousand feet down in the cold North Pacific, and he'd almost been blown to smithereens. His routine inspection schedule had been primarily to keep busy, he had not expected trouble. Aft in *Brutus*'s motor room, this was to have been his last swing through before he closed the Kamchatka Peninsula. He'd almost missed the problem. *Lucky.*

He put the wrench aside and stripped to his skivvies, perspiring. It was going to be tricky.

Go easy.

He eyed the aluminum fuel block, finding galllike corrosion granules that grew into the master control solenoid valve. There, it had converted to plain rust. It took a half hour to remove the solenoid and juryrig a polyfluorinated hose to the hydrogen peroxide fuel block with two stainless steel clamps. In disgust, he threw the solenoid aside. He would eject it after he installed the new unit.

The repair took another two hours and with two more bolts to tighten, he lay on the deck grate and stretched his arm past the decomposer. He aimed the socket, a nine-sixteenths; it seated and slid home. Relaxing for a moment he wiped his brow. The temperature was well over a hundred, both tunnel hatches were clipped open, yet the airconditioning system barely kept up.

Tired, almost done.

Soon, the hydrogen peroxide fuel transfer system would be back in shape. After a quick check with the inspection mirror, he could get out of here; dog the hatches, take a shower, and jump in his bunk while the air system lowered the temperature to a comfortable seventytwo.

The wrench fit perfectly. He twisted the ratchet--

"Damnit!" The wrench slipped off the nut, ripping two knuckles. Try the other side. He rolled to his back, scooted aft, and worked his left hand to the fuel manifold.

Don't touch the decomposer.

It cooked at four hundred degrees inside and was still plenty hot outside. He'd already burned his wrist.

He found the nut, held his breath, and slowly turned the ratchet. It was going to work, it had to. Sweat dribbled into his eyes; he blinked.

Rust! How, he didn't know. Perhaps electrolysis of some sort. If rust, an organic substance, worked inside the solenoid to the valve, it would contaminate the hydrogen peroxide fuel. Then, an irreversible reaction. Auto heat. The fuel, all of it, would become hot and explode--violently. Just a little bit would be enough. He'd seen no warning on the master panel, the damned thermo displays still registered in the green. He'd have to work out an autoaccelerate detection routine if he ever returned to...to normality.

Lofton shuddered while he torqued the manifold nut. *Damn!* Why hadn't he thought about corrosion problems in the design phase or even during prototype buildup? It was a materials problem, a fairly simple fix; he should have caught it. His mind wandered back. The Germans had lost a few type XXI Uboats, which used Walther cycle engines, to autoheat. And early postwar hydrogen peroxide torpedoes had been a disaster. One had exploded in a British submarine during dockside trials, killing everyone in the torpedo room. The original American X-1 had blown up dockside, killing three technicians. The problem wasn't the fuel-burning cycle itself, where the energy was converted. It was the fuel storage and pumping systems that caused the problem. Improper handling anywhere along the line could cause a violent and usually lethal explosion.

What else could go wrong? He'd discovered more bugs, more than he would have expected, during this trip. Everything was so damned new. *Brutus* really hadn't had a proper shakedown before Renkin placed him into service.

Lofton tested the pressure and read the gauge. Tight enough. He eased the torque wrench off.

One more nut to go. He wiped his brow, then carefully seated the socket. Another sixty seconds and he'd be finished.

"Ow!" Skin on his elbow seared and crackled as he was thrown against the decomposer unit. *Brutus* leaned hard, his rudder jammed to port. *Damn!* He hadn't heard the beeper on the control panel. The bow took a sharp down-angle and the minisub went into a corkscrew death plunge

Adrenaline pumping, Lofton yanked his arm free, spun on his knees and grappled at the tunnel hatch. How long? Sixty--ninety--seconds to scramble through the twenty-foot tunnel, lurch to his feet, and dive for the joystick at the control panel. If it was ninety seconds he'd be well below crush depth. *Blotto!*

Lofton found his knees and lunged through the circular hatch. A foot connected with the rusted solenoid, it bounced and clanked down to the bilge. *Later.* On hands and knees, he flashed down the tunnel as *Brutus* wove through his deadly tailspin.

Faster!

Lofton flew out the forward hatch checking the depth gauge over the galley table as he ran: The digits zipped past 2677. Five paces, an eternity. A vent riser flange joint gave a loud clang toward the bow.

Lofton's belly caught the back of the armchair. He leaned over, punched "Override" on the master panel, yanked back on the joystick and chopped the throttle. Lights blinked on the displays; some amber, the rest red. *Brutus* shuddered. A loud pop, then a resounding thump, aft this time; another flange seating itself. He hoped neither had cracked, otherwise that would be it.

He lurched into the seat as *Brutus* straightened from his nosedive. Finally, zero angle, then slowly up again.

Depth: 3086. His mind raced the calculation; *roughly 1364 pounds per square inch!* The bow rose further, speed fell to ten knots. The ballast tanks rumbled, somehow anticipating a casualty. Long ago, the computer should have hit the chicken switches and executed a "blow everything and get to the surface" emergency program. Lofton would have to fix that, too.

He nursed *Brutus* back to one thousand feet and resumed course. His face and chest were drenched and he paused, letting his breathing return to normal. He punched temperature on the Ship display:

SEAWATER: 44° F

INT. ATMOSPHERE: 106° F

After ten minutes, he reset `Auto' and allowed the NAV system to resume control.

This was the third time. During the first, he'd been asleep in the pilot berth just before he'd crossed the International Date Line south of the Aleutians. *Brutus* had gone into a sharp right corkscrew, throwing Lofton from his bunk. On the second occasion, *Brutus* had jammed into a helical *left* turn. All three times coincided with a course change on his great circle route, minus one hour. A software bug, a bad chip; he had no idea how to correct it outside of setting a beeper on the control panel one hour before course changes. Lofton shook his head. The beeper tone was too soft to have been heard while he was changing the $H_2 O_2$ solenoid valve in the motor room.

He checked the displays, all green, then spent five minutes interrogating *Brutus*'s subsystems: ballast tanks, fuel tanks, through hull fittings, electrical, hatches, valves, piping--on it went.

All OK.

Lofton slumped for another ten minutes trying to empty his head. Was the sweat rolling down his chest and onto what was supposed to be a comfortable leather armchair caused by heat from the motor room or was it that his submarine had nearly penetrated crush depth and imploded like a watermelon being squashed by a bulldozer?

They say you don't drown. Instead, you burn to death. Very quickly. Seawater, under tremendous pressure, enters the hull as fast as a piston thrusts in a diesel engine. The horribly compressed air mixture at the top of the cylinder becomes very hot and incinerates nonmetallic matter-- human beings.

Lofton rubbed his chin and studied the plot. Eleven or so hours to Petropavlovsk.

Get going.

Tighten the last manifold nut, shut the hatches, and cool down the main compartment. Then, food. He was hungry. He would eat, take a shower, and get some sleep. He would have to be alert in a few hours so he could quietly transit the Soviet seabed, especially when he closed to within a hundred miles of Petropavlovsk

With a sigh, Lofton heaved from his chair and started aft. He winced at the singed patch of skin on his elbow and looked into Kirby's medical bag. He found a tube of burn salve and rubbed on the ointment. After a quick bandage, he trudged toward the motor room hatch. *Brutus* arrowed on course 267 at one thousand feet for a headland called Mys Mayachnyy.

Lofton wore a dark blue turtleneck sweater, a clean set of Levis, socks, and dark blue sneakers. He didn't know what the day would bring but, he chided himself, this wasn't Southern California, it would be cold topside. If *Brutus*'s navigation system had been accurate, he should be about ten miles due east of Mys Mayachnyy. A large bay, Avachinskaya Guba, lay beyond Mayachnyy, roughly circular and eight miles in diameter. Petropavlovsk lay nestled on its eastern shore.

Lofton twirled a knob and the local chart popped onto the screen. Avachinskaya Guba was accessible through a four mile long passage bracketed with rocks, shoals, drying reefs and small islands. It was about two thousand yards wide at the entrance and indicated depth was fine: thirty-nine feet. But the passage funneled at the other end to a five-hundred-yard width.

Tricky. He needed good visibility to navigate the channel and he didn't want to key his periscope radar around a major Soviet naval base. He decided to approach manually by periscope and use the pilotage program on his NAV display as backup.

Brutus crept at periscope depth. Speed: ten knots. Very quiet; Lofton listened to his breathing, checking his watch: 0508 local time. Petropavlovsk time, Soviet time! Soon he would be in the midst of one of the most powerful fleets in the world.

He bit his thumbnail and checked again: 0508.

Another ten minutes before he would lift the periscope. He checked the master display and called up his passive sonar. Nothing. No fishing boats, no destroyers, no ASW helos or sonobuoys or torpedoes, just...nothing. He shook his head. He could be in a black hole as far as he knew. Still quiet on this--what day was it? His Casio said Monday, the twentieth, which meant local time was Tuesday the twenty-first. He'd crossed the International Date Line. *Brutus*'s original ETA at Mys Mayachnyy had been set for five- fifteen the previous afternoon, but repairs and helical spins had slowed him down. Just as well, he would have had to loiter and wait for daylight.

0517. Good enough. Lofton swung the periscope housing into place, then raised the scope to full height. Depth: twenty feet. He wiggled the joystick slightly and worked up to eighteen feet. He wanted just the periscope's tip above water; six inches, that was all, no wake. He pulled the throttle back and watched the speedo. There, three knots, time to peek. No--one more thing. Check the passive sonar; all green? OK, all clear.

He tapped the joystick back slightly: seventeen feet. Good. Lofton put his face to the eyepiece, his first look at the outside world in six days.

Brutus's periscope was still underwater. The water was gray, lighter toward the surface. Sediment zipped past his lens, a few bubbles, the surface was mirrored just above. It looked calm, no thundering rollers or breakers, just a softly undulating upside-down silver smoothness.

He eased a slight up-angle. The periscope broke the surface, skipped through a wavelet, churned bubbles, then held above the Pacific.

Overcast. The cloud's bottoms looked to be about five thousand feet. The North Pacific was calm; he trained the periscope left of his heading.

A sharp, angular moonscape jumped through the lens. Three mountains, two conical, the third, the nearest one, a large amorphous mound; gray, yet alive, glistening, waiting. A coastline, still dark, rose on the horizon. Jagged features came into focus as he flipped to high power. No ships or watercraft. He flipped back to low power and rotated the periscope through a careful 360 degree arc, then checked the sky. Nothing. Quiet. No ships, no fishing trawlers. Maybe the Russians had taken the day off.

He trained ahead again, wanting to identify those peaks. First, the big one to the southwest. He punched Nav-Pilot-Ident on the CRT, then checked the screen:

VULCAN VILYUCHICK - EXTINCT VOLCANO 254/54 nm

Desolate, threatening. Lofton's throat became dry as he went back to the periscope. The next was a cone-shaped peak. White slabs of snow ran down its sides. Closer, its base was almost visible. He punched Ident again:

SOPKA KORYAKSKAYA EXTINCT VOLCANO 262/36 nm

He checked the third peak, the high mound:

SOPKA AVACHINSKAYA ACTIVE VOLCANO 268/22 nm

Another full sweep with the periscope showed all clear. Then he checked the promontories. They were large, enormous; some were sheer cliffs, hundreds of feet high. A high-power view of the shoreline showed rocks and reefs, white water tossed at their bases. He saw a few sandy beaches, yet no greenery to speak of. Maybe it was too early to see trees and shrubs.

He checked the NAV screen, watching landmarks scroll on the Ident program as he slowly trained the scope: Bukhta Sarannaya, Ostrov Starichkov, Mys Bezymyannya, Kamniri Brata. There! Stop! Mys Mayachnyy, his last way point. From this angle it looked like a continuous shoreline.

Lofton took a deep breath and dropped the scope. Those monstrous cliffs: He'd have to draw closer before he found the channel. It ran on a northsouth axis and wouldn't be visible until he was almost on it. Lofton retracted the periscope housing, then pushed the joystick and dove to five hundred feet. He nudged the throttle up and *Brutus*'s speed climbed evenly, quietly to fifteen knots. He reset Auto, then checked the clock: 0519. He would take another look in twenty minutes.

Lofton sat back and peered at the squiggly lines on the passive sonar CRT: OK. He checked the NAV display and watched the range to Mys Mayachnyy click down. His mind rose to the surface and what he'd seen through the periscope. The vision flashed; those tall, graywhitish, hulking volcanoes, straight out of Disney's *A Night on Bald Mountain*. Interesting, the composer was Russian, Mussorgsky, he must have had Sopka Avachinskaya in mind for Vulcan's redoubt.

A dry tightness clawed in his stomach.

Do it! Skip Petropavlovsk!

There was still time to change course to Chetvertyy Kuril'ski Proliv, disarm Renkin's mines, then get the hell out. It would be easy, just flip in some left rudder and head southeast. He punched the coordinates on the NAV screen:

CAPTOR SITE:
49° 39'.2 N
156° 02'.7 E

A simple doglegged track flashed on the screen: only 264 miles from Mys Mayachnyy. An amber light flashed the interrogative. All he had to do was punch "Auto" and *Brutus* would swing left to safety. He could run down there in ten and a half hours. And then: home.

Do it, Brad.

Lofton tapped a thumbnail on his teeth. Petropavlovsk, was it worth it? He thought of Felix Renkin, of Les Thatcher, of the screwdriver...

He slapped the armrest. Petropavlovsk was infinitely more dangerous, but yes, worth it. And it would have to be tonight. There wasn't much time to save the *Kunashiri Maru*. He would scout Petropavlovsk Harbor, find her, then lie in a remote spot and rest until this evening.

0539. OK. He checked NAV:

MYS MAYACHNYY 269/3 nm

Three miles off the beach, no time for an Alka-Seltzer. Lofton sighed and reached for the joy stick. He flipped off "Auto", then pulled back gently. *Brutus* swam to periscope depth, seventeen feet, at nearneutral buoyancy. He punched another button and checked his displays. Still green, all clear. He slowed again and waited until the speedo settled on three knots. Finally, a deep breath and up periscope.

There it was, directly ahead; stark, desolate, damn near a sheer cliff. He checked NAV. Yes, Mys Mayachnyy. The headland stood almost five hundred feet above the Pacific Ocean, guarding the eastern entrance to Avachinskaya Guba. It was dark, glistening, with steep, precipitous sides, the point descended to rolling breakers and a treacherous reef on the channel entrance side. He quickly slewed the scope left. There. Mys Bezymyannya, well over six hundred feet high, rose with whetted, reddish sides. He flipped to high power momentarily; a sharppeaked rock pillar was perched atop Bezymyannya, almost like a cartoon. It seemed to jeer at the gray dawn.

The channel began to unmask from the other side of Mayachnyy; he would be turning right soon. *Brutus* lurched a bit as a wave lapped over the scope. The swell seemed more pronounced as he neared the coast. Current. He'd have to be careful.

No contacts forward. He flipped to low power and trained aft. Nothing, a clear ocean. He did a sky sweep: OK. Sonar: clear.

Still time to turn around.

No, he was committed. He'd go, he had to try.

Train forward again. Those cliffs. Look at the guano on those dead reefs over there. But where were the birds? What was that? He flipped to high power; three basalt pillar rocks, each one over a hundred feet high, stood on the right side of the channel. He scrolled NAV for an ID:

KAMNI TIR BRATA

The scrolling disappeared and NAV advised him *Brutus* would be at midchannel in thirty seconds.

He took a final sweep. Where the hell were all the Russians? He felt like yelling. His stomach knotted.

Bleep! NAV flashed course 346. He moved the joystick and came right to the recommended course.

Lofton could see well into the bay now; a few dull, nondescript structures, some bright lights at the far end. Fog obscured low peaks surrounding Avachinskaya Guba.

Another full sweep, all clear. He was almost abeam of Kamni Tir Brata. He concentrated forward again. At the end of the funnel, Poluostrov Izmennyy, a low peninsula with a sheer base, jutted out four miles away on the eastern side. That was where the shallows were, that was where he'd have to be very careful. After that, he'd be clear. Plenty of room to hide.

A formation came into view on the left side of the channel. NAV told him it was Babushkin Kamen, a rocklike islet over two hundred feet high that looked like a tall, black cap. And just to the left of Babushkin Kamen, boats! Fishing boats. People! Lofton smiled and waved into the periscope. Four anchored dories bobbed in the swell between the islet and two whitish guano-covered rocks closer to shore. He flipped to high power. A man smoked a pipe. He was bundled in a parka and sat aft on a thwart with--

Ping! His scope suddenly blinked with digital displays, red warnings flipped through the lens. He checked NAV. it was OK. More red lights blinked on the Master display. That couldn't be a mechanical or electronic sound from *Brutus*. It must be from outside the boat.

Ch-ping! Another one, definitely outside *Brutus*. He punched Master to overlay sensors in his periscope, then peered ahead.

The power of that thing. Was it shore-based? Did they have him? If so, the helos or frigates could be on him in minutes. He checked aft, all clear.

An ELINT classification program scrolled in the scope as he scanned from side to side. The fishing dories were still anchored off Babushkin

Kamen. The lone man was there, smoking his pipe, he didn't seem concerned. Lofton trained forward.

Ah, whitish foam dead ahead. He flipped to high power: a bow wave. Yet not a veeshaped bow wave, but a plowing sort of one, like a barge--no--a submarine! Outbound.

Ping!

Identification:

TAMIR 22L SONAR, 3 KILOHERTZ

The powerful Soviet sonar hit *Brutus*'s hull like a hammer. Yet, the period wasn't regular, Lofton remembered. It wasn't keying at a particular rate, not as if it were on automatic. Maybe the Russian sonarman was testing as part of his underway procedure. Surely the water was so shallow that all he'd get for such a tremendous burst of energy would be a cluttered return, like shining klieg lights into a dense fog.

The computer stopped scrolling and blinked its solution:

TYPHOON CLASS SUBMARINE

"My God!" Lofton whispered as the stats popped in his periscope lens. One of the world's largest and most deadly submarines was headed directly toward him, probably en route to a Pacific patrol station. At this range rate they'd meet near the Izmenny narrows.

A Typhoon. She was the size of a heavy cruiser, twentyfive thousand tons submerged, 557 feet long, the length of the Washington Monument. Beam: eightytwo feet. Draft: fortytwo feet. Two pressurized nuclear water reactors delivered one hundred thousand shaft horsepower each to twin, sevenbladed propellers.

Lofton risked a pulse with his fathometer: fiftyfive feet. The Soviets must have dredged the channel for this giant from the thirtynine feet shown on the charts.

More of the Soviet boomer hove into view. Bulbous, oval lines grew above the foamy bow wave. The Typhoon had bow planes, her curved sail was arranged on a streamlined yet awkward-looking, fairing. It made her look squat, like a giant pinheaded football player. Missiles, twenty vertical launched SSN20s, rested in watertight silos forward of the sail instead of aft as on U.S. missile submarines. Each missile was fortynine feet long with a range of four thousand five hundred nautical miles; each carried six MIRV thermonuclear warheads.

Ping! He hoped the Soviet sonar couldn't see through *Brutus*'s anechoic coating, but Lofton nevertheless decided to sit this one out. There should be enough room at this point, the channel was about a thousand yards wide. He eased the joystick to the right and vented his tanks for negative buoyancy, hoping he could find a sandy bottom while twentyfive thousand tons gushed past.

Ping! The Typhoon's machinery noise penetrated *Brutus*'s hull. Master flashed the range: 250 yards. He flipped on the audio, set the volume, and cocked an ear. No propeller irregularities. He heard a high-pitched growling interspersed with an occasional bubbling sound.

Brutus settled with a petit crunch, then listed to one side. Lofton took more ballast quietly. He didn't want that monster's wake tearing the minisub off the bottom and spinning him around.

One hundred yards, almost abeam. The Typhoon was quiet for such a large power plant; still no whumps or propeller noises. He visualized the machinery above: giant reactors, distilling plants, condensers, feed pumps, lube oil pumps, turbines--enormous ones, turbogenerators, primary steam loops, secondary steam loops, two hundred thousand horsepower.

The Typhoon was abeam, he could hear better and tweaked the volume. There was something like the low growl of a diesel locomotive without the pumping reciprocation sound. Then a high whine, loud. Lofton smiled; this Typhoon, one of the USSR's finest, was noisy abeam. He wished he had the equipment to record her acoustic signature.

The Typhoon's wave nudged *Brutus* but he stayed put. Even without the sound, Lofton felt the presence of the ship's churning and her 150 souls.

It drew behind him, quieter from astern, he could tell. Then the Typhoon was gone. Silence. Lofton exhaled, flipped off the audio, and waited for twenty minutes.

He checked the sensors: clear. NAV: ready. Ship: two thousand pounds negative buoyancy. He squeezed the joystick trigger and blew to slightly positive buoyancy, then kicked *Brutus* off the bottom with ahead one-third. With speed on, he flooded back to neutral buoyancy and swam the minisub to periscope depth. Clear ahead. He checked aft. No sign of the Typhoon. Off to his left the four dories still bobbed off Babushkin Kamen. Another man had joined the pipe smoker. This one carved wood as they talked.

Back to three knots, *Brutus* drew close, then abeam of the large peninsula on his right, Poluostrov Izmenny. Ahead, Petropavlovsk hove into view, three miles away and slightly off his starboard bow. Tall gangly cranes, water towers, brownish steaming smokestacks, and warehouses blended into a grayishblue hue on Avachinskaya Guba.

A downtown section with blockshaped buildings rose behind the waterfront, then merged with square and rectangular apartment buildings in the hills. He studied an oniondomed church close to downtown. Nearby, a slag heap rose three stories high and a two-story hospitallike structure crouched next to it.

Lofton punched temperature on his control panel:

SEAWATER: 46° F
EXT ATMOSPHERE: 54° F
INT ATMOSPHERE: 71° *F*

Fog still camouflaged the peaks surrounding the large bay. He checked the far side of Avachinskaya Guba: A navigation beacon winked at him from Mys Kazak.

Merchant ships rode at anchor ahead of him. He flipped to high power, finding a dark blue Polish freighter that sulked behind her anchor chain, brown stack gas rising above her funnel, straight up. No wind. An Italian freighter sat two hundred yards away. Two Soviet merchantmen bobbed closer to shore. One looked like an icebreaker and the other, military, a high, slabsided repair ship of some kind. Lofton checked her fantail; the Soviet Red Banner naval ensign drooped from its staff. A small work boat trudged around the point to his right and picked its way through the nearby Rakovaya Shallows.

Down scope. Lofton checked the clock: 0655. He'd give himself until 0800 to find the *Kunashiri Maru*. By then Petropavlovsk would be fully awake and he'd have to pull away and sit on the bottom until twilight. He increased speed to eight knots. The anchored merchant fleet gave enough machinery noise so he could navigate among them on passive sonar.

Lofton rubbed his chin and checked to the north. A forest of masts and radar antennas, the Soviet fleet, sprouted like weed tufts. Massive cranes towered over the Frenza ship repair yard. Adjacent was the V. I. Lenin submarine base and repair facility. The most likely place for the *Kunashiri Maru* would be at the commercial docks in Petropavlovsk's inner harbor. He'd try there first, then across the bay on the western side.

He raised the scope. A lumber barge lay anchored close to a quay wall. Two tugs maneuvered around it, their screws churning. He was close to Mys Sigal'nyy and Petropavlovsk's inner harbor; it looked small. Fortunately he could--

Oh oh! Down scope.

Two patrol boats blasted from under the stern of the Italian freighter and overtook him. Soon, their screws ground past at two hundred yards slant range. As they raced by, Lofton punched Ident:

STENKA CLASS PSKR PATROL BOAT
LENGTH: 129 FEET
SPEED: 34 KNOTS

Petropavlovsk. Kamchatka Peninsula. Soviet Siberia. USSR. Forty-two hundred miles from home and he'd almost been caught by the two Stenkas because he'd forgotten to check aft; a miracle they hadn't spotted him. He wiped his brow and waited.

A minute passed; he raised the scope and made a careful, full sweep: All clear. He slewed and tracked the two Stenkas. They were about five hundred yards away, had slowed and approached the docks, toward a medium-size freighter. She was moored in front of an enormous wooden structure, which nearly obscured the ship. He flipped to high power and checked her flag: Cuba. The wooden building looked like a cannery.

He slewed forward and studied the two Stenkas. With low freeboard, they looked swift as they idled past the docks. Twin thirty-millimeter machine gun turrets, one forward, the other aft, comprised their main armament. Without the humpbacked deckhouse amidship, the Stenkas appeared as large versions of the old American PT boats. But harsh super-structure lines robbed them of grace and lent them a sinister cast.

Lofton turned cold as he checked their colors. These patrol boats flew the green ensign of the KGB Border Maritime Troops.

The Stenkas hove to and swung lazily; he could see their white hull numbers just below their bridges: *831, 726.* Their turrets were trained inshore. Where was their target? Lofton squinted; a shape was silhouetted against the shed. Twin masts, but it was still too dark to pick out details.

Lofton dropped the scope and ran at ten knots for two minutes, then slowed for a closer look.

He could see better now; the Stenkas rode easily one hundred yards offshore and the building indeed was a cannery. Conveyors, crates, and pallets ranged below blackened windows.

Something stirred on the docks. Lofton recognized four BTR60 armored personnel carriers swooping down the quay wall. They bounced over a shallow trench, then disappeared behind a dark shape, a ship. One BTR60 was still visible and disgorged a dozen naval infantry. They quickly, professionally fanned out from the stern of the lowslung fishing trawler.

Dawn was breaking, the light improved, he could make out the ship. Two masts, forward well-deck, black hull. She had a white deckhouse aft with a rusty, stubby-looking stack. She flew the Japanese merchant ensign. As more Soviet troops arrived and stalked about, he picked out the name on her fantail: *Kunashiri Maru.*

12

Libya, 1986

The Libyan patrol boat *Waheed* burbled her way toward the minefield at five knots. Nine hundred meters inshore, water beamed like a black mirror. Range lights winked at them from stumpy silhouetted hills above the Sidi Bilal training compound. The sky was dust-laden, a quarter moon filtering through to cast a soft sheen on the graceful, low gray hull. Waheed's forty-nine meters alternately squatted and rose with the gentle quartering groundswell.

A high pilothouse stood across the *Waheed*'s seven point one meter beam, giving her bridge crew a broad view forward over the domed seventy-six millimeter Melara single automatic gun mount. A look amidships revealed four fixed Otomat surface-to-surface missile canisters. Another enclosed mount near the *Waheed*'s fantail contained dual forty-millimeter Breda/Bofors automatic guns on a raised barbette. With four MTU 20V538 diesels, her four propellers could drive the French La Combattante-II class patrol boat to a roaring thirty-nine knots.

Anton Dobrynyn leaned on the bridge bulwark. The range lights had been turned on for their entrance. He examined them, then shifted his glance to Gholam Aziz, the *Waheed*'s skipper. Aziz seemed to be doing well. Their course looked good for the minefield channel. But Zuleyev. Damn! Holding Aziz's hand was Zuleyev's job. Not his.

Dobrynyn double-checked his landmarks. The Bilal tomb stood darkly on a low rise just to the right of the range. It was a sprawling, Moorish structure with a commanding dome. He promised himself he would walk up there soon and look it over. Closer, he picked out the single wharf with its corrugated Marine Guards shack. The fairway buoy was a joke. The *Waheed* should have been passing it now, as it was intended to help mariners navigate the channel. Instead, it had been moved inside the minefield where it swayed pitifully thirty meters off the pier.

The downtown lights of Tripoli winked at him off the port side. Clearly visible, even at this hour, were the sawtooth battlements of the Tripoli castle with its large dome. The belfry of the Santa Maria delgi Angeli church punctuated the skyline and glowed softly above a street light. Strange, a church here. He wondered if they were allowed to hold services. Then the city slid behind a dark headland.

Dobrynyn checked his digital watch: 0147. He ran a hand over his forehead and wiped away perspiration. The water had felt invigorating during their demolition exercise, and the ride back was cool before they slowed for the minefield. But now, with no wind, stagnant air hung oppressively on the bridge. Aziz had predicted the Ghibli, which brought dust out of the desert, would soon be offset by northwesterlies. The skies would be clean again. But not tonight. Dobrynyn's shirt clung to him; he unbuttoned it further but it didn't help.

Ullanov clumped up to the bridge and stepped next to Dobrynyn. "Sir?"

"Both starboard engines are out, Josef. They need you down there again."

Ullanov cursed softly and said, "What is it this time?"

"Sludge, I think. Both engines. Simple. Go down and give it one of your five-minute jobs. We need to get through the minefield."

Ullanov swore again.

They watched Aziz hover behind his helmsman and check compass headings. The helmsman muttered as he worked his wheel against the offsetting thrust of the port engines while another sailor alternately goosed and retarded his throttles. For the third time in as many minutes Aziz looked to Dobrynyn with a plaintive smile before he went back to his conning.

Dobrynyn nodded to Aziz then said quietly to Ullanov. "He's too stubborn to ask. He needs at least one starboard engine on the line, Josef."

Ullanov grunted. He was tired, his head throbbed. He didn't look forward to climbing down into the *Waheed*'s sweltering engine room and fighting with that imbecile chief engineer again. Besides, the place reeked of vomit. The engineering gang was always seasick. Conscripted men of the desert didn't seem to adapt well to the sea, even these waters close to the Libyan coast.

Ullanov's ears still rang. Tonight had been difficult, a night exercise with live limpet mines. The dive on the wrecked freighter had gone as planned until O'Toole, that damned IRA fire-eater, had set his limpet for ten instead of thirty minutes. The thing went off, predetonating seven other mines in ripple fire. An erupting Mediterranean heaved Dobrynyn, Ullanov, and their entire eight man team off the rubber boat. Water and shrapnel rained among them. The only casualty was the dark, silent one. Rameriez, a Honduran, had an ugly red gash across his forehead. Still, he helped right the boat, scrambled in, and wordlessly tied a splotchy wet rag over the wound.

And now Ullanov had to undo a simple wingnut under the fuel filter and run his finger around a perforated basket. Both engines. Damnit! Would those idiots down there never learn such a basic job? Why did they use such cheap fuel to begin with? And what if it wasn't fuel filters? What if it were something more serious, like clogged injectors? Then they'd be in the middle of the minefield without the damned starboard engines and all their skins would be on the line.

Ullanov asked, "How about the tug?"

"Can't raise them. Radio's acting up. Static everywhere. We're on our own."

Ullanov watched the *Waheed*'s bow wave gurgle down the port side.

"I'd go myself Josef. But Vladimir's flat on his back again and there's no one else to watch Aziz. Somebody has to do it. Go down there, show them how to clean strainers once more, and you'll be a hero before the colonel's eyes. He'll pin a medal on you just after Captain Aziz docks the *Waheed* without ripping out half the wharf."

Ullanov spat over the side. "OK." His voice dropped a notch. "What's with Zuleyev."

Dobrynyn dipped his head in the gloom. He didn't know how well the rest of the bridge crew understood Russian. "I don't know where he finds the stuff. He got completely plastered while we were out setting limpets. And right under the noses of these people, too. Lucky his breath doesn't smell too much. I found him while you were pulling the boat out of the water. I stuck him in Aziz's bunk and posted O'Toole outside."

"Must be some way to dry him out."

"I don't know. He just doesn't seem to care any more. He would have been a captain first rank by now. Submarines were his whole life. This shit detail is, *was*, his last chance. But it's probably too late. I think they'll kick him out, soon."

"It's probably our last detail, too. I wouldn't be surprised if they throw us out with him." Ullanov shook his head. "That filthy zamp deserved it. If you hadn't decked the sonofabitch, I would--"

"As I said, too late to worry about it now."

Ullanov paused. "OK. Let's take Zuleyev back to Tripoli tomorrow and lock him up."

"Where? Got any ideas?"

"How about the Uaddan Hotel? One of us can take a couple of days off. Tie him to a bed and let him sweat it out."

"Two hundred rubles a night, Josef."

Ullanov grunted. "That's true. A month's pay. Too rich for my blood, Major. You should be able to handle that."

Dobrynyn grinned. "Me?" He pointed to a ring that had materialized on Ullanov's finger three days ago. A gold filigreed "U" was set over a large black onyx. "Tanya. Right?"

Ullanov smirked. He had been dating a nineteen year old communications rating aboard the *Kotel'nikov*.

"How much did your weekend at the Uaddan cost, Sergeant? Did she--
"

A shout reached them. Voices babbled. Aziz called over in stilted Russian, "Major Dobrynyn. The radar is off. We can't get a picture on any of our repeaters."

"What?" Dobrynyn stepped over and looked at the radar console. The PPI wasn't blank, as Aziz implied. The cursor swept around a snowy, pale green scope. No blips, no land, no targets. Nothing.

Of course! The radios were out, too! Static! Why hadn't he thought about that?

He looked up. "Captain. Is the ECM gear on?"

Aziz's darting eyes betrayed him. No, the ECM gear wasn't energized as required. He flipped switches on the bridge intercom and fired rapid Arabic interrogatives to his operations officer below. He digested the response, then said, "All radars are still off, Major. And the ECM operator reports jamming on a northerly bearing." Aziz paused, his eyes found the deck. "I would feel more comfortable if Captain Zuleyev were here."

"All right. I'll get him in a minute. He's not feeling well." Hell, yes. This is Vladimir's territory, not mine. I'm just a glorified frogman and that clown Zuleyev is dead drunk in your cabin.

Dobrynyn turned. "Sergeant!"

"Sir!"

"Clean those fuel strainers, now. And tell the team to assemble their gear and prepare to debark, fast. I think Captain Aziz will want to get back to sea as quickly as possible."

"Sir!" Ullanov ran for the ladder.

"Americans." Aziz spat. His eyes narrowed. The memory was fresh. He had lost a cousin when the U.S. Navy sank three Libyan patrol boats last month; one was a La Combattante-II class sister ship. A coastal radar site near Sidra had also been bombed out.

Dobrynyn said, "I suggest you sound action stations and douse your navigation lights, Captain."

Aziz fumbled at the button. He finally found it and pushed. A klaxon wailed, feet shuffled, dark shapes materialized around Dobrynyn and donned helmets. The forward mount unlimbered with a whine, trained back and forth and elevated her cannon.

Aziz ordered half speed. The *Waheed*'s helmsman cursed as the boat, with more power on the port side, crabbed against the rudder.

They had just entered the minefield when the throttleman nodded at his headphones. Aziz sighed as the outboard starboard engine roared into life. The throttleman worked his lever. The engine bellowed while the helmsman coaxed the *Waheed* to a more precise course.

The blaring diesel masked the first explosion. Their heads snapped to the left. A brilliant flash illuminated the horizon toward Tripoli. Then another and another.

A loud "crumff" enveloped them. They felt it in their ears. Another explosion followed, much louder this time, the pressure wave was thicker.

Dobrynyn looked east toward the promontory. "Forty-four-hundred-kilo bomb. The first ones must have been eleven hundred."

The *Waheed* cleared the minefield, slowed and approached the wharf. More "crumffs" mixed with the sound of screaming jet engines. Bright flashes, on the horizon, surface-to-air missiles, leaped from launchers and disappeared in the haze.

Aziz ordered `all stop' and let his boat drift. His concentration on the pier broke as his eyes darted toward the east where more bombs flashed and thudded.

Dobrynyn followed his gaze. The flashes came from the direction of Colonel Qaddafi's bunker complex. "Looks like they're hitting the Azziziyah Barracks."

"No!" Aziz shouted. "They--"

"I hope they've turned off their street lights." He looked toward the wharf, fifty meters ahead. Men stood in scattered groups, their mouths agape, watching the bombing.

He said to Aziz, "Can we get word to somebody over there?" They should douse the pier lights."

"They wouldn't dare to--"

A string of bombs, five or six, Dobrynyn couldn't tell, salvoed forty meters aft, walked right abeam of them and across the pier in two seconds. The night was filled with an impossible brilliance, thunder, his lungs felt as if they had caved in. Shrieking metal, cordite, human screams. The *Waheed* reeled like a wounded bull to her beam ends. Aft, men wailed incredulously as they pitched into the water. Shrapnel, indescribable hot chunks, pieces of the corrugated Marine Guards building rained over the boat as she righted herself.

Dobrynyn picked himself up. He'd been thrown against the port bulwark. Shouting men were jammed against him. The decks were wet. Some was plain Mediterranean seawater. But a thick fluid oozed around a prostrate sailor.

Aziz knelt next to him, shouting in his ear.

Dobrynyn shook his head. "What?"

The man's lips moved, flames leaped above the pier and reflected off Aziz's teeth. Dobrynyn blinked, roaring still echoed in his head.

"Where is Zuleyev?" he heard.

Dobrynyn rose as another bomb string charged up the beach and fell in the motor pool. The fuel dump erupted and flung him to the deck again. Flaming tires spun high overhead. A T-54 tank turret, its one-hundred-millimeter gun obscenely bent, arced lazily skyward as the blast carried over them, bounced among hills, and washed over them again.

He lay on the deck, on his back. Coughing. His ribs. Pain, his shoulder. It grated. His lungs were filled with noxious smoke. He gasped and tried again. No oxygen.

Aziz crawled next to him again.

Dobrynyn tried to sit as a string of secondary explosions from the fuel dump enveloped them. "Let's get out of here," he shouted.

Aziz reached for Dobrynyn's collar. "Incompetent, this is--"

"What the hell are you talking about? We have to move. Do you want to get blown up too?"

The hand clawed at his shirt. Dobrynyn slid back, seeing blood running from the captain's mouth, ears, and nose.

"--all your fault. You let this happen," Aziz's voice rasped. You're afraid of the Americans."

"What the hell do you mean?" He crawled next to the captain. Aziz's hand fell. Dancing flames from the fuel dump glowed on their faces as Dobrynyn grabbed Aziz's shoulders and screamed, "We're in this as much as you are! Why do you think I..."

Aziz's eyes rolled into his head, he fell unconscious and slumped into Dobrynyn.

More fuel exploded. No! It was the ammo dump. Hot, projectilelike shrapnel surged skyward as he lowered Aziz to the deck.

"Uhhh!" He wobbled to his knees, then rose. "Josef!"

Dobrynyn stumbled aft toward the gangway. His lungs screamed for air as explosions reverberated around him. Shock waves slammed him against the pilothouse bulkhead. He pitched toward the ladder, his hands in space.

The next thing he knew, he was sprawled on the main deck amidships among a tangle of writhing, screaming men. Their eyes were wide, imploring, they looked to the skies. Dobrynyn leaned up, then pulled his legs underneath. The engine room hatch gaped seven meters aft.

Dobrynyn cast aside arms, wiggling legs. A voice roared a strange language --Farsi?-- in his ear.

The hatch.

He pressed a hand on his knee, struggled to his feet and lurched aft.

The hatch.

Even as he wobbled toward it, a pair of hands, then a shrieking head rose through the hatch. Half of the face was blown away, the man's gelatinous jaw was dislocated to one side. He screamed again and again as his hands spasmed for a grip on deck.

Dobrynyn reached for the creature. He heard a whoosh and looked up. A bomb salvo sprinted directly toward him. An incredible flash, spinning, screaming. End over end. He couldn't breathe.

Dobrynyn sweltered under an open tent. He leaned against an oil drum and looked at his watch: twelve-thirty. Dark smoke roiled above him. The news wasn't good from Tripoli either, as smoke rose from that direction, too. The sun occasionally winked through and added more heat to the still blazing fuel dump. His ribs hurt and his left arm was stiff. In order to look around the Sidi Bilal compound, he had to swivel his body.

Thirty or so corpses lay under a common tarp for later identification. The mixed nationalities had been quickly arranged side by side: North Korean, North Yemeni, South Yemeni, Pakistani, Indian, Filipino, Japanese, Italian, Guatemalan, Cuban, Irish, West and East German, Honduran, Panamanian, Iraqi, PLO, even an American.

And Russian. Captain Second Rank Vladimir Zuleyev's body had bobbed its way to the beach during the flat, calm morning. He was one of five known Soviet advisors killed in the raid. Two others were missing. The Soviets lay under the tarp, too.

And Libyan. Captain Gholam Aziz, whose ship, *Waheed* lay fully capsized in ten meters of water, was stretched out with twenty-one countrymen beneath a separate tarp.

Charred wreckage was cast about as if thrown by an enormous, cosmic hand: burned out trucks, two wrecked helicopters, twisted light attack vehicles, parts of metal buildings, concrete chunks, and paper. Hundreds of sheets of scattered paper.

Where the hell did all the paper come from? Dobrynyn wondered. If wars were organized with paper, this one was over, he thought dully. He prodded a sheet with his boot: It was stamped "TOP SECRET." The bold title suggested a tome on neutralizing radars at civilian airports.

He sipped a can of fruit punch, the first nutrition he'd taken since yesterday evening except for hurried gulps of water. He couldn't shake the exhaustion, and yet he knew he had to consolidate the base command and above all, make sure the perimeter was secure against another attack. His pauchy eyes swept the hills again, checking his distribution of the mobile radar units and the remaining ZSU-23-4 self-propelled air defense guns. Four of the tracked vehicles, with quad twenty-three-millimeter radar-guided cannons, had miraculously survived. Five other demolished heaps were still neatly parked side by side in a gully.

His eye caught one ZSU as it trailed dust atop a low ridge line, then slowed in a palm grove. It was quieter now, the whine and snorting of the ZSU's engine reaching him faintly as it jerked among trees. It stopped, exactly where Dobrynyn had ordered, and swung its turret out to sea. The driver switched off the engine.

Silence reigned for a moment, a gull squawked. Then an auxiliary generator coughed into life. Dust stirred once more as trucks rumbled in from Tripoli with food and medical supplies.

Finally, reluctantly, he rotated his body toward the bay. The water was incredibly flat. A smooth, viscus surface, nothing moved except for light ripples around the gunboat. Ullanov's tomb: steel, air-conditioned, modern, it used to travel at thirty-nine knots. Very different from Bilal's timeless brick and mortar tomb perched on the ridge.

The *Waheed*'s stern protruded a meter or so above the surface. Her propellers and rudders clawed at the sky and diesel oil glistened around the hulk. An assortment of cans, life jackets, Styrofoam cups, strips of wood, a whole tree, a blackened car seat stretched over the minefield. Rainbow crystals danced off the oilslick and pierced his eyes.

Dobrynyn squinted. Still no horizon and Fata Morgana had given them two silhouettes so far. The first looked like an American frigate and all guns blazed for sixty seconds at the mirage. Dobrynyn let them shoot, it helped relieve their frustration as their rounds fell uselessly into the Mediterranean. The second time, he called a cease-fire at once.

He looked again knowing the hulk would be gone soon. Their command ship *Kotel'nikov* had warned the Marrobbio was on its way. It was an unexplained surge in the coastal water level near Tripoli, and would cover the *Waheed* for a few hours, maybe until tomorrow. Just as well, he wouldn't have a chance to pull Ullanov's body out until things quieted down in another two or three days.

Ullanov. Damnit! He'd sent Ullanov down there with all those seasick engine mechanics. They hadn't a chance. They--

Ripples.

He stood up and peered at the *Waheed*. Ripples, tiny ones expanded from the hulk in concentric rings. Some bounced through occasional air bubbles.

Damn! Ripples!

He yelled, grabbed two nearby men, one a naval infantry private, the other a Spetsnaz corporal, and ran for the demolished pier. They commandeered a rubber boat, jumped aboard, and paddled furiously.

It took five minutes to gain the hulk. They slipped and slid up the *Waheed*'s crusted bottom and tied the painter to an outboard propeller shaft.

The other two knelt with Dobrynyn as he put an ear to the hull and said, "Quiet."

Something metallic thumped inside. Yes a rhythmic clanging! "Someone's alive," Dobrynyn shouted. He pressed his ear to the slimy hull again and listened.

A strange, weak rhythm. A tattoo. Somewhere, he thought he recognized a cadence. He listened again. It sounded like a hammer, possibly a heavy sledge.

"Clang-clang", then, "CLANG."

The letter "U"! "Yes!"

Dobrynyn stood and thumped a "D" several times with his boot. Then he knelt again and listened. Silence. Good. Save your air, Josef.

Other boats bumped against the hulk. Men scrambled up the flat bottom and joined them. Soon, fifteen were packed around the *Waheed*'s propellers. Most were Soviet naval infantry, but a few Libyans thumped, slipped, and cursed among them as they grabbed propeller shafts and rudders to keep their balance.

And the Marrobbio inched its way over the hulk. The group became more tightly packed as the Mediterranean made its temporary demand. Their feet sloshed as they argued over how to extract survivors trapped inside the *Waheed*'s engineering spaces.

Dobrynyn, still on his knees, looked about frantically. All their diving gear was on the bottom with the *Waheed*. What else?

Yes!

He grabbed a naval lieutenant's sleeve. The man had a portable radio. The message was sent.

An excruciating twenty minutes passed before the torch arrived. The acetylene and oxygen bottles bobbed in the boat. Hoses snaked under slipping feet to the cutter's torch. The yellow-toothed demolition expert sparked the flame and knelt to the plates. His hood was up as he asked Dobrynyn, "Where?"

Double bottoms? Engine mounts? Ammo stowage? Pyrotechnic lockers? Fuel tanks? Dobrynyn had no idea what was beneath, what they would burn into. Something could explode. But their choices were limited. Only half a meter of the *Waheed*'s transom protruded above sea level now.

He checked an area between the port propellers. A deep alley should run longitudinally between the shafts. With the heel of his boot, Dobrynyn drew an outline perhaps half a meter square. He would have liked to have a larger opening but the water was close. It lapped within a meter of the welder's Reeboks.

"There!"

The welder flipped down his hood. He turned a knob and the flame became an intense roaring blue.

Water crept up higher.

The torch snapped and sputtered as it attacked bottom plating. Slime and sea growth sizzled and smoked. Wisps trailed above the blue flame as the cutter followed Dobrynyn's rough outline.

It was done. A sledge was produced, a burly, bare chested sergeant with thick matted hair swung. The hammer clanged and bounced.

Nothing.

Dobrynyn grabbed the sledge, but the welder reached up and held his arm. "Wait!"

Even as water lapped at the crack, the welder bent for thirty seconds and worked on two corners. He rose, lost his balance, and slid back. Men caught his elbows as the torch fell sputtering in the water. He shouted, "Now!"

Dobrynyn stood over the plate, took a two-handed grip and raised the sledge high over his head. He swung, the head arced down and hit with a bang. The section gave way and quickly disappeared with a soft splash.

They all yelled at once and crowded the opening. Dobrynyn dropped the sledge and shoved in among them. Dark, oily water glistened forty centimeters below as the Marrobbio freely poured in.

"Flashlight," Dobrynyn shouted.

Inside, a hand appeared, waved, then was gone.

Dobrynyn's heart surged. The hand wore a ring with a gold "U."

Four out of a ten-man engine room crew came out alive: three Libyan naval engineering ratings and Senior Sergeant Josef Ullanov, who was hoisted out last. All were unconscious as they were whisked to shore, their faces white, their mouths hanging open as rich oxygen tempted their body chemistry.

Just as he was laid on the stretcher, Ullanov coughed loudly. His chest surged and he pulled great lungfuls of air. His lips moved.

Dobrynyn knelt to listen. He cocked an ear then, shook his head. With a hand on the sergeant's shoulder he said, "Later, Josef. Rest now."

Ullanov rasped, his eyes flickered.

Dobrynyn bent again.

"...Major...You can tell Colonel Qaddafi...I fixed *both* his damned fuel strainers..."

13

The lumber barge was anchored five hundred yards off the *Kunashiri Maru*'s port quarter. *Brutus* crept at half a knot, minimum steerageway, toward it. At a range of twenty yards, Lofton reversed, stopped, and hovered so all six inches of his periscope blended into the barges's rusty freeboard. It felt comfortable here, he was in deep early morning shadow within two hundred yards of the quay wall and slightly forward of the Cuban freighter. Lofton could follow movement on both sides of the *Kunashiri Maru* and still remain safe from the two Stenkas which, with their twin 30-millimeter mounts trained on the trawler, growled back and forth offshore.

Three more eightwheeled BTR60s, pulling great clouds of dust, roared down the quay wall, crunched over the ditch, and drew to a stop before the trawler. Men dismounted wearing black tunics with blue and white striped teeshirts, black trousers, boots, and black berets set at a rakish angle. They carried the newer, more lethal AK74 automatic assault rifles instead of the AK47s, which the Soviets were quietly surplusing to "client" nations. The men looked confident, casual, and sure of their equipment. Lofton checked their lapel patches. Full and junior sergeants dominated the group; these weren't pimply faced recruits. A few laughed, but most were serious. Their beret insignia identified them as Soviet Naval Infantry, similar to the U.S. Marines.

Another vehicle swooped in: a T55 medium tank. Its commander stood waisthigh in the hatch, his hands braced on top of the jiggling turret. It lurched to a stop amidships of the trawler. Then, to Lofton's disbelief, the tank trained its hundred millimeter cannon on the ship's bridge.

The activity was not lost on the *Kunashiri Maru*'s crew. They siphoned out of hatches and doorways in ones and twos, pulling on shoes, coats, and sweaters. Some rubbed their eyes while others sipped at steaming mugs. Twenty or so men and a few women lined the rail and stared at the Soviet Naval Infantry staring at them.

Was one PARALLAX? What had happened? Surely a nighttime barroom brawl would not have brought out ten BTR60s, one hundred elite Naval Infantry and a T55 tank.

The Soviets meandered about their positions while the Japanese fishermen leaned on the ship's rail. Conversation rippled among the Japanese crew; a few shook their heads and shuffled inside but most lingered on deck.

A stout, gray crew-cut man walked on the *Kunashiri Maru*'s starboard bridge wing and stood on a platform with his fists on his hips. He wore a short-sleeved plaid shirt and dark trousers. Slowly, deliberately, he rotated his torso, surveying the Soviets and their fighting equipment. He raised a megaphone. A few Soviet heads looked up, then ignored him. The Japanese skipper tried again, the megaphone arcing back and forth over the Soviets. Nothing. They didn't pay any attention. The man in the plaid shirt stood at his bridge wing, the megaphone dangling at his side. He accepted a mug from a pea-coated sailor and sipped, watching the Soviet Naval Infantry pace about their positions.

Bleep! A printout splayed across *Brutus*'s lens. Lofton heard it at the same time, a deep, pumping sound on the other side of the lumber barge:

ROSLAVL CLASS PELAGIC TUG
LENGTH: 147 FEET
SPEED: 11 KNOTS
ENG: DIESEL ELECTRIC
RANGE: 6000 nm

The gray tug had approached from the other side of the barge. He watched her boil past, then slow and pick her way between the Stenkas and ease alongside the *Kunashiri Maru*. White froth kicked up under her stern and she stopped, then drifted in her own swirl. Her skipper stepped out of the pilothouse and examined the trawler. They were about the same length.

The tug's arrival galvanized the Soviets. About thirty infantrymen ran up the trawler's gangway and split into two groups. One group dashed quickly forward out of Lofton's view. The other ran aft to the deckhouse and disappeared inside. Soon, two or three popped onto the bridge. The captain yelled at them; Lofton saw his arms wave. They ignored him and moved inside. The trawler's crew followed the first Soviet group toward the bow and out of Lofton's sight. The skipper on the bridge picked up the megaphone and faced forward; his elbows pumped as he mouthed the device. Ten more troops loped aboard.

The tug crept ahead to the trawler's bow. A messenger line snaked through the air and landed on the tug's low aft deck. Soon, a large manila hawser was pulled aboard the trawler. The Soviets disembarked and milled on the dock, nervous. A few had their AK74s in their hands. Their heads swung toward the trawler's bow.

They're going to tow that ship. Even as Lofton watched, two sergeants worked the stern line off the bollard and threw it in the water, not caring if it wasn't hauled aboard; they simply walked away. The gangplank must have been taken in or thrown aside because the *Kunashiri Maru's* bow drifted from the wharf.

The Roslavl's stern frothed, she took a strain on the hawser and maneuvered perpendicular to the dock, her nose pointed directly into Avachinskaya Guba. *Kunashiri Maru* was underway. She rotated from her dock and obediently followed the tug as scope was paid out to her.

PARALLAX! The defector! Where were they going? To a customs dock? Arrest? To Prison? Lofton hovered next to the lumber barge as the tug and tow gained headway. The KGB Stenkas looked mean, deadly, as they took station fifty feet off either beam of the *Kunashiri Maru*. Their gun mounts were now trained fore and aft but their crews were alert; they wore helmets and life preservers and crouched in the bridge area and at their weapons stations. Except for the man in the plaid shirt, Lofton couldn't see any of the *Kunashiri Maru*'s crew.

The trawler rode behind the tug with perhaps three hundred feet of scope on the towline. They cleared the anchored merchant fleet and picked up speed--Lofton ran a solution--ten knots or so. He'd wait another few minutes, then follow them to their new mooring. He needed the distance so when he poked up his periscope now and then, the wake wouldn't be obvious. Fortunately that was less of a danger now. A northwesterly breeze had kicked a light chop on Avachinskaya Bay. The feather wake off his periscope would be less conspicuous, he could go a bit faster. Still, it was full daylight: 7:27. *Be careful.*

He swung the periscope. The day had grown brighter as the overcast burned off, rugged mountains surrounding Petropavlovsk poked through the mist. He checked his watch. Almost time to shove off. He decided to take another look.

Except for the Naval Infantry, the only other people he saw were two sailors on the Cuban freighter's main deck. They leaned on the rail in conversation; one spat over the side.

The BTR60s and the tank prepared to move out. Troops scrambled aboard, exhausts belched and filled the air with blue smoke. The T55 jerked, spun a half circle on its right tread, and headed down the quay wall toward an access road that corkscrewed up a hill.

Lofton looked up the road as the tank spun left and jiggled onto the thoroughfare. A BTR60, several troops, and two jeeptype vehicles stood across an intersection two blocks up the road. People milled about the far side of the crossroad. A few bicycles and an occasional car passed. But no civilians came near the dock. The Naval Infantry had blockaded the waterfront.

That was it, there were no civilians about. Roadblocks had been set up to keep out casual observers. Lofton whistled under his breath. He'd arrived in the middle of what was proving to be an elaborate operation; Naval Infantry, BTR60s, a T55 medium tank, two KGB Stenkas and the Roslavl tug.

He swung the scope. The *Kunashiri Maru* convoy was aimed for the Avachinskaya channel entrance. That was odd. He reversed *Brutus* for thirty seconds, cleared the barge, and kicked the minisub's nose around with his bow thrusters. He lowered the scope, checked sonar, then set a course through the merchant fleet at ten knots. He'd look again in two minutes. He'd thought the *Kunashiri Maru* was being towed to another dock, perhaps across the bay. Why into the Pacific Ocean?

They were getting rid of the trawler for some reason. A dispute of some kind? A bad load of fish, a persona non grata situation, or worse, they'd caught PITCHFORK, then ejected the ship. But if they released the *Kunashiri Maru*, he could follow. Perhaps raise them by radio when they were well clear of Kamchatka. His heart lifted. If the *Kunashiri Maru* was at sea in international waters, he wouldn't have to worry about Russians. And he still had a chance to contact PARALLAX. Maybe he could set up a meeting after he disarmed the CAPTORs. Then run for home and do something about Renkin.

He checked NAV; *Brutus* was clear of the merchant anchorage. Lofton slowed, raised the scope, and took a quick but careful visual sweep. Yes, dead ahead, there was his convoy. They had swung left and already stood abeam of the Poluostrov Izmennyy narrows. The convoy had a five-knot speed differential but he'd catch up soon. And the Stenka ID program showed limited antisubmarine detection gear, so he could go to flank speed once they cleared Mys Mayachnyy. The trawler would most likely turn south once the tow was dropped; the *Kunashiri Maru* couldn't do more than twelve knots or so, *Brutus* could overtake her easily. Lofton would dog her until twilight, then make radio contact.

The console bleeped, a red warning light flashed in his periscope lens. *Brutus*'s computer burped, a ship's ID program scrolled:

KRIVAK III CLASS FRIGATE 348/I.I nm

Lofton whipped the scope around and trained on the bearing dead aft:

SPEED: 12 348/l.o nm

A small bow wave--there--beyond that container ship. A thin shape appeared with a tall mast. A radar antenna twirled on top. He switched to high power and searched for the shape. Yes, there it was, a graceful new Soviet frigate with a clipper bow. Her bridge windows glinted in the morning light. He punched the Krivak III subroutine and let it flip through his periscope display:

DISP. 3900 TONS
LENGTH: 377 FEET
BEAM: 46 FEET
DRAFT: 15 FEET
SPEED: 32 KNOTS
PWR.: 2 GAS TURBINES, 2 BOOST TURBINES
2 SHAFTS 48,000 HP EA

She's coming right at me. Time to park.

SPEED: 12 - 348/1550 YDS

Lofton lowered the scope and headed for the bottom. She was a Krivak, a third-generation ASW platform, deadly, she was no ship to tangle with. He arched an eyebrow as the Krivak's characteristics continued to zip down his Master CRT:

SONAR:
HERKULESMED FREQHULL MOUNTED 6 KILOHERTZ
TAMIRMED FREQVARIABLE DEPTH 12 KILOHERTZ

WEAPONS:
ROCKET LAUNCHERS: 2 RBU6000
TORPEDOES: 821 IN(2 QUAD MT)

GUNS:
1/100 MM/70 CAL DP
230 MM CLOSEIN
(2 MULTIBARREL)

Depth: 45 feet. Lofton slowed, then reversed a bit to stop *Brutus*. He thumbed negative buoyancy and settled toward the bottom.

HELOS: I KA27 HELIX
RADARS: I BRASS TILT (FIRE CONTROL)

The Krivak III was new, built in 1985; she bristled with electronics, but that main gun with its hundred millimeter bore--Lofton did some quick calculations as *Brutus* crunched on the bottom--a four-inch gun. DP meant dual purpose, surface and air capability.

SPEED: 12 - 349/950 YDS

He listened to the Krivak grind and clank, her screws beating the water with a freight train sound. Why wasn't she pinging? Lofton looked up toward the rumble and added more ballast.

SPEED: 12 - 349/400 YDS

The TYPHOON notwithstanding, maybe they were not supposed to key their sonars in the bay. The U.S. Navy had similar rules. The big sonars were so powerful they actually cavitated and boiled the water around the ship. Fish died and bellied up.

SPEED: 12 - 349/250 YDS

Almost overhead. A roaring whining swelled around him; the screws swished loudly, one sounding uneven, perhaps from a nick in the blade. The Krivak plowed above Lofton's raised head at no more than thirty yards slant range. Finally, a frothing, gurgling sound and the Krivak was past; her wake tugged at *Brutus* for a moment. Then it became quiet.

He waited thirty minutes, then blew ballast. *Brutus* rose off the bottom and swam back to periscope depth. Sonar showed all clear. He raised the scope and checked. Visibility was good, he was almost to the Izmenny narrows. The bay looked clear, docile, with minimal maritime traffic. The

Krivak's wake churned about three miles away. She was almost abeam of Mys Mayachnyy and was no longer a threat. The frigate would be concentrating on her entrance into the Pacific.

Lofton wound *Brutus* up to fifteen knots. He checked NAV, then punched up a subroutine:

EBBTIDE 09210942 2.5/SSE

Good. He'd have a two-and-a-half-knot current to shove him out, his actual speed would be close to eighteen knots, and he'd clear the channel in fifteen minutes or so. He set Auto, then sat back, poured a cup of coffee, and waited.

Ten minutes later he slowed to three knots: up scope. *Brutus* was making good time, the two-hundred-foot-tall black cap island, Babushkin Kamen, lay slightly aft on his starboard side. Seven fishing dories now heaved on their anchors as the tide pulled at them. Bundled men stood in their boats and cast fishing lines. Lofton couldn't find the pipe smoker but he waved anyway. *So long, nice knowing you.*

He trained slightly off his port bow, NAV scrolled:

KAMNI TIR BRATA

Perfect. *Brutus* was in mid channel. The recalcitrant NAV system seemed to be working all right in this mode.

He looked straight ahead to see the Krivak's fantail disappear behind Mys Mayachnyy. She was beam on to him, froth boiled at her stern as she increased turns. *Good.* She had swung left and headed north to clear the area. Down scope, dive to thirty feet, and back to fifteen knots.

It was going to work. Lofton felt better than he had in days. He relaxed for another five minutes before bringing *Brutus* up to seventeen feet and raising the scope.

Mys Mayachnyy was almost abeam, but much of the five-hundred-foot cliff was obscured as a fog settled at the entrance to Avachinskaya Guba. He checked to starboard, making sure he stood clear of the Stanitskogo Shallows, an area dominated by two drying rocks. Breakers tore at them. *Goodbye, Petropavlovsk*. Lofton dove to fifty feet and went back to fifteen knots.

He checked his sonar, looking for Stenkas and the *Kunashiri Maru*. They should have been south at a range of three or four miles. But the bearing was clear in that direction. He scratched his head.

Lofton sat up and peered at his CRT. Nothing. No Stenkas, no tug, no Japanese fishing trawler. He expanded the sonar to a full passive sweep. Nothing except the Krivak grinding to the northwest--and it was close, only two miles off his port quarter. She must have reduced speed.

Two miles? Lofton punched Sensors, then shifted the readout to the Master CRT:

KRIVAK CLASS FRIGATE 054/2.0 nm
STENKA CLASS PSKR PATROL BOAT 055/2.1 nm
STENKA CLASS PSKR PATROL BOAT 055/1.9 nm
ROSLAVL CLASS PELAGIC TUG 055/2.1 nm
UNK VESSEL 055/2.1 nm

What? Lofton banged the throttle back, his speed dwindled. Come on, come on. What the hell are they all doing over there--he checked NAV--two miles off Toporkov Island? His speed dropped to three knots and he climbed to periscope depth. Up scope. There, Toporkov Island, another islet monster; steep, slabsided, 150 feet high. It was shrouded in fog, and he could just see its irregular toothy summit. He slewed to the right, finding shapes in the mist. The Krivak was wakeless, she lay wallowing, dead in the water, light brown haze rose from her stack. Big groundswells marched past but they weren't breaking, and there was no wind, just the grayish, dull ocean and a hoary, rolling mist.

Fog swirled around the ships, he lost sight of them. He eased in left rudder, lowered the scope and checked Sensors:

KRIVAK 052/2.4 nm

Brutus steadied on 052 and he checked the other targets. Same bearing.

Go easy. Brutus crawled at four knots while Lofton thought for a few moments. He punched NAV and risked a single fathometer ping:

DEPTH: 377 FEET

Something was missing. Pinging! The Krivak still wasn't pinging. Either her sonar was down or they were out for a holiday. Maybe the sonarmen were drunk on vodka. *Fat chance.* He knew he could outrun the Krivak's design speed of thirtytwo knots with *Brutus's* actual thirtyfive knot dash speed. He was sure the frigate couldn't track him on sonar at thirtytwo knots. But her twentyone-inch ASW torpedoes had a fortyfive-knot capability and packed a nine-hundred-pound high-explosive warhead. No, the Krivak wasn't pinging. Fine.

Five minutes passed. He rose to scan the ships in the mist. A shape became the *Kunashiri Maru*, rising and falling with the swells. Then he picked out the Roslavl backing toward the *Kunashiri Maru*. She stopped, her stern a few yards from the trawler's bow. A pair of heads popped over the *Kunashiri Maru's* bulwark near her hawsepipe. The eye of the towline snaked through the hawsepipe and plopped into the water. It was reeled in by the Roslavl while her twin screws churned up the sea. She swept away in a wide turn and disappeared into the fog. Her bearing drew rapidly left. Back to Petropavlovsk, Lofton supposed.

Lofton felt strange, displaced, for some reason. This wasn't right. Why the Krivak and the two Stenkas?

He checked his range, seven hundred yards, then slowed to half a knot, bare steerageway. The faint, howling whine of the Krivak's gas turbines was audible as she lay to.

His eye roamed the frigate's aft superstructure. Her corrugated hangar gaped open. The Helix ASW helicopter, her folded blades looking like cockroach antennas, lay tucked in the white, brightly lit space. He checked the hull number under her bridge, 059. A look at the foremast told him this ship also flew the KGB Maritime Border Troops green flag. Something tugged in his stomach. The Krivak, the two Stenkas? A KGB operation? Not the Soviet navy. He lowered the scope. Maybe it was a port clearance problem. Wait it out, that was all he could do.

A new sound came from the group of ships. He cocked his head toward an irregular yet continuous plopping. Another sound, a low rhythmic pumping. Then, a loud metallic screech!

Up periscope!

Smoke, shrapnel greeted his eyes. Chunks of the *Kunashiri Maru* flew in all directions. Even as he watched, her forward mast buckled, shook against her shrouds, then fell into the water with a large splash.

"No!"

Lofton slewed the periscope to the Krivak, astonished. The Stenkas were lined up fore and aft of her in a column, all guns trained abeam. The Krivak's hundred-millimeter main gun pumped fifty-pound armorpiercing projectiles at eighty rounds per minute into the *Kunashiri Maru*. Her starboard side 30-millimeter six-barrel gatling gun spurted at a hideous thousand rounds per minute per barrel. The Stenkas joined in with their four dual mounted 30-millimeter gatling guns.

A KGB maritime firing squad, they were killing the *Kunashiri Maru*.

"Nooo!"

The Krivak and Stenkas kept at it. Large pieces, then part of a lifeboat shredded from the trawler. Heads bobbed up and down the deck. The *Kunashiri Maru* lurched drunkenly. Large holes angled up her stack, then the stack was gone as a one-hundred-millimeter projectile obliterated it, along with much of the deckhouse just forward. A small fire spouted aft and just as quickly went out as another large round slammed in. He saw a man run forward; the skipper in the plaid short-sleeved shirt. He grabbed the rail of his bridge. His mouth formed an "O," and a round tore into him, severing his torso.

Lofton didn't realize he'd retched. He grabbed an oily rag and wiped spittle off his chin and went back to the periscope.

Shrouded in a pall of cordite, the Krivak and the Stenkas maintained their deadly fire. Flames bursts from their guns. Water kicked around and beyond the *Kunashiri Maru* in large frothing columns as more chunks were torn from her; innumerable tree-stump size holes punctured her port side.

Suddenly the trawler lurched, almost involuntarily. Time to get it over with, she seemed to moan, time to die.

Slowly at first, then faster, the *Kunashiri Maru* rotated to port and capsized. Ten or so figures, Lofton picked out two women, were miraculously alive and scrambled up her sides. They found handholds on the barnacles, the prop shaft, the gleaming bilge keel. Their last hope was to make it over the keel and cower in the limited safety of the other side, away from the lethal, raking fire of the KGB Maritime Border Troops.

The firing squad kept at it. The terrified fishermen, some waving their arms, were blown off the ship's glistening bottom as if hit by huge, hydraulic fists. Others were merely vaporized as large rounds slammed into them.

Lofton squeezed his eyes shut, unable to watch. They'd set it up; the Naval Infantry, the sealed waterfront, the KGB ships. The fog, nobody could see from the beach. Yet here was a killing ground two miles offshore, well within Soviet territorial waters.

It was a premeditated operation. But they would tell the press that a military transit zone, or something, had been ignored. Apologies would be made to the Japanese government six months later. He ground his teeth.

Renkin! This was Renkin at work; how, Lofton didn't know. But only a man with such power, such influence, money, international stature, could casually order the death of thirty or so innocent Japanese fishermen and, along with them, PARALLAX and PITCHFORK. Renkin!

The loud pumping sounds stopped but he heard smaller rounds still at their work, along with great screeching, ripping noises as the *Kunashiri Maru* broke up. There was a prolonged groan, then a gigantic crash; it had to be her diesel engine coming unbedded and falling through the overhead to the ocean floor.

The *Kunashiri Maru*'s bow was down, almost submerged, fifteen feet or so of her stern hung in the air. She would slide to the bottom in a minute or two. And no sign of life; bodies splayed in the water with crates, vegetables, a deflated zodiac, large pools of oil.

Another noise, a steady growling sound. He checked the scope. The *831* and *726* were both underway and headed directly toward him! They'd spotted his periscope either visually or on radar. Damnit!

PING!

The Krivak had lighted off her sonar. Then he heard large propeller noises. *Get out of here, the Stenkas were almost on top. Move!*

PING!

The Krivak was underway, maybe generating a solution for those forty-five knot torpedoes. He couldn't rely on his anechoic coating or his speed, the KGB frigate was too close. He had to obscure the Krivak's firing solution.

A chance, he had to take it. He lowered the scope, jammed *Brutus's* throttle to flank speed and eased to one hundred feet.

Sonar painted a target directly ahead: the *Kunashiri Maru* still wallowed in death throes on the surface. He could put her between *Brutus* and the Krivak. All he needed was a couple of minutes at dash speed, thirtyfive knots, to clear the area.

It would be close. He chanced a ping on his active sonar:

UNK VESSEL 064/450 YDS

His speed climbed nicely, passing through fifteen knots.
PING!

KRIVAK CLASS DESTROYER 275/1500 YDS

Hull number *059* was on his tail, Lofton heard her screws beat through the water. The Stenkas buzzed well behind now, they'd lost the scent.

DEPTH: 100
SPD: 18

He passed under the *Kunashiri Maru*, hearing crackling and tearing overhead. A red light flashed on Sensor. Datum! He was clear! Lofton eased back on the stick a bit.

Suddenly, *Brutus* lurched, then skewed to one side. Something clanged against the hull. Incredibly, the minisub shuddered to a complete stop. The five-bladed propeller thrashed wildly, *Brutus* corkscrewed and shook.

Speed zero. *What the hell is happening?* A huge roar and hiss behind him, more metal shrieks, bubbles. He thought he heard a prolonged human scream. The *Kunashiri Maru* was going down.

Lights blinked, all the CRTs shouted at him. Speed zero, yet he had full RPM. *Brutus*'s prop shaft began to wobble.

Lofton cut the power and bit his lip. He knew what it was, he would just have to ride it out. Quickly he checked depth: 355. He might be able to do it, bottom *Brutus*, then exit in his diver's rig. He would need just five minutes to cut the dangling line that had reached out from the dying *Kunashiri Maru* and fouled his propeller.

The dive planes! They were jammed to full dive. With a loud prolonged hiss from the air flasks, *Brutus*'s overtaxed computer gave up and called it a day. All chicken switches were activated and three thousand pounds of air quickly blew water from the ballast tanks. *Brutus* ascended even as Lofton frantically jabbed his CRT panels and keyboard to override the emergency program.

Forty-six feet. He frantically jabbed at keys. *Brutus* rose faster, the air flasks defiantly roaring as ballast disgorged.

Twentytwo feet, he'd pop out like a cork. He tried the throttle again. A low pathetic thumping answered him from the motor room. One or two RPMs, then the shaft ground to a full stop. He pulled the throttle to neutral as *Brutus* lurched through the surface like a dead, bloated whale.

A buzzing sound echoed toward him. He checked the periscope. Both Stenkas swooped in, drawing close to either quarter. Four thirtymillimeter gatling guns were trained directly at *Brutus*. In the distance he saw the Krivak's bow wave as she sliced nearer with her howling gas turbine engines.

He tried to swallow. There was a lump in his throat. It was too much to believe. All he wanted was to expose Renkin and disarm those CAPTORs in the Kuril Straits. Never had he planned to face the damn strutting Soviet Navy, certainly not the KGB. He hadn't foreseen thirty dead fishermen, nor Underwood, nor Thatcher.

The computer blinked at him and indicated reset. It had figured out its mistake. Having panicked without interrogating sensors, artificial intelligence had given way to a convoluted survival instinct. *Brutus* was ready now, all green except for propulsion and dive planes. The damned computer was now willing to take a chance, sit on the bottom and wait for the Stenkas and Krivak to go away.

Lofton shook his head, he'd be dead meat if he moved. The Stenka's gatlings would chew *Brutus* to pieces before he could get under. He sighed, then reached forward and flipped switches to "off." The CRTs went blank, lights blinked out, the air stopped circulating. *Brutus* wallowed, his systems died one by one. The minisub became inert, like Lofton.

He fumbled in the dark, found his duffle and yanked out his sailing jacket. He grabbed the ladder and stood dumbly for two minutes, his head down as *Brutus* rose and fell with the waves. Finally, he reached up and popped the main hatch open. Siberian air and a tinge of cordite greeted his nostrils.

Lofton climbed the ladder onto *Brutus*'s dripping casing. He put his hands in the air.

A thunderstorm boiled over the Kalorama Circle area of Washington, D.C. Ted Carrington knocked on Dr. Felix Renkin's door. He entered and quietly clicked on the bedside light.

"Yes? What is it? What's the time?"

"Three-thirty, Dr. Renkin. A Watkins man came to the door and left this for you."

Renkin turned to his bedside stand, fumbled, then put on his round gold-rimmed glasses. Rain pelted outside, then he saw Carrington's outstretched hand.

"Thanks, Carrington, I didn't realize you were staying the night."

"Had to work late. Been talking to Vito. He's still cleaning up from the hit on that guy Kirby--"

"Is Calabra all right? Can they trace anything back to us?"

"No sir. He just went down hard and Vito is making sure it looked like an accident. And we're double-checking that Kirby didn't talk to any of his Navy friends."

Renkin stared into space.

Carrington said, "Think I'll use the guest room. Don't want to go home in this." He waved a tired hand to the window.

Renkin regained his focus. "Very good. Let me decode this. Go back to bed."

Carrington shuffled out, the door closed softly. Renkin opened the envelope and looked at the five letter groups on the common sheet of stationery. He sighed, then rose from his bed, donned a bathrobe, and went to his desk. He snapped on the light, spun the two combination dials, and opened his small armored wall safe, making sure he bypassed "destruct."

He sorted out the small, onetime pad and decrypted his message. It was a long one the rain drummed as he worked and he poked at his nose bandage. It itched from blood clots drying inside. *Damn Lofton.*

Finally he sat back. The message was dated two hours earlier. Not bad.

TO: MAXIMUM EBB
FM: SPILLOVER

OPERATION A COMPLETE SUCCESS. TRAWLER SUNK 092121113Z. BOTH ASSETS TERMINATED. WISH TO CONTINUE JET STREAM AND PROPOSE RECOVER OR KILL CAPTORS PRIOR TRUMAN'S EXIT KURIL STRAITS. PLEASE SEND LAT/LONG ASAP. ALSO X3 CAPTURED WITH SKIPPER. NOW IN DEEP SOLITARY. UNODIR WILL TERMINATE.

Felix Renkin pursed his lips and studied the phrase, "UNODIR WILL TERMINATE"--unless otherwise directed will terminate. Yes, yes, you clods. Shoot the sonofabitch, and now!

He scowled. They'd probably send Lofton to one of their "psychiatric institutes" first. Squeeze all the submarine hitech data out of him--then kill him with no trace. Fine, just be quick about it.

Except...Lofton's capture presented intriguing possibilities. Renkin sat back and rubbed his chin. He could rid himself of both albatrosses, there was still time. Maybe talk to Hatch, the art dealer. Yes.

He looked at the message again. Nothing referred to the return of the X3. But then, why bother? If the damn thing did show up there would be too much to explain. Fair enough. Keep the minisub, shoot Lofton, and get it over with.

Meticulously he checked a folder, then drew out a blank sheet and wrote:

TO: SPILLOVER
FM: MAXIMUM EBB

CAPTOR SITE: 49° 39'.2 N 156° 02'.7 E.

IMPERATIVE WE MEET

There. He felt better and coded it into five-letter groups. He rang for Carrington and, while waiting, burned the original message and the plain-language draft of his reply. The toilet gurgled with the ashes as Carrington knocked. Renkin sealed his message in an envelope and handed it to his nodding, bleary-eyed assistant director with instructions.

Finally, Carrington gone, he turned off his lights and crawled deep under his covers as rain cascaded outside. He slept until nine-thirty.

14

En Route Baikonur Cosmodrome, Kazakhstan Steppe, USSR

The Mil'-8 helicopter bucked and groaned as it flew northwest twenty meters above the humid Caspian Depression. Lieutenant Colonel Anton Dobrynyn clutched the back of the pilot's seat to keep his balance and his eyes flicked over the instrument panel. Many gauges he didn't understand, but he could tell the Mil' had burned over half its fuel. The bouncing, weaving helicopter, with ten combat-loaded Spetsnaz, still had 270 kilometers to go before it reached the Baikonur Cosmodrome.

He shouted, "What now, Boris?"

Naval Captain Lieutenant Boris Orbruchev yelled over his whining twin Isotov turboshaft engines. "Headwind, Colonel. Almost twenty knots. We'll get the tailwind on the way back, though. Should even things out."

Dobrynyn simply nodded. Orbruchev and his copilot, Lieutenant Eduard Ritzna, needed their concentration at this altitude.

A clear three-quarter moon helped visibility and though the land was flat, dust clouds kicked up below, disorienting them. Through the haze, he caught occasional glimpses of the meandering Volga River to starboard. Aside from maintaining altitude the real worry was electrical transmission towers. Earlier, they had crossed their fingers when they plotted the towers on their charts.

The headwind taxed their 370 kilometer combat radius. If it held as Orbruchev believed, they would get a boost on their return trip to their refueling stop, Ostrov Nizni Oseredok, an island off the northwest shore of the Caspian Sea. And from there, they could finish the 590 kilometer return trip to Baku safely.

But now Dobrynyn doubted that outcome. This felt like a snap cold front, one of Mother Natures's late September hurry-up jobs. The wind could veer, they could end up with it on their nose for the return flight.

They had planned the raid down to the last drop of fuel. Orbruchev and his flight crew had even stripped the tired Naval Infantry issue Mil' for a 10 percent contingency factor: armor plate, guns, rocket launchers, even NAV equipment, which included Orbruchev's terrain-following radar. It should have worked with the long range fuel tanks, except for this unseasonal headwind.

The Mil' jounced as Dobrynyn peered out the windshield. He saw an occasional flash of rotor blade and roiling dust cloud and nothing else.

His tongue seemed thicker. He licked his lips, then rubbed his palms together: dry, ionized air. No humidity. They must be out of the Caspian Depression. Occasional lights whipped past but there was nothing else to see at--he checked his watch--1:34 in the morning. In another five minutes or so, they would discover if Orbruchev remembered his dead reckoning. Kharabali, a solid checkpoint, was due to pop up ten kilometers on the starboard side. Otherwise, land at a rural gas station, ask directions first, then smash some pump locks and steal fuel. Orbruchev had boasted about doing it before. But that could be messy, regular gasoline played hell on the engines, diesel fuel would be better. Dobrynyn hoped it wouldn't come to that, he wanted a clean raid with no loose ends.

Particularly this raid. Flotilla headquarters in Baku had organized it. *Unusual.*

He bit his thumbnail. Dobrynyn's Spetsnaz operation orders normally originated with the GRU's Main Intelligence Directorate in Moscow, then were endorsed and coordinated through Naval Headquarters in Leningrad. His brigade, stationed in Baku as part of the Caspian Sea Flotilla, had been assigned to a top secret program to assure tight security at strategic bases. Surprise raids were staged on major installations hundreds of kilometers from home base. Guards were overwhelmed and tied up, officers pushed around, a few windows smashed, desks overturned, files upended, and simulated demolition charges set. The last thing was to call the base commander as he settled to his evening television, even better if they tracked him to a mistress. Then they would slip away, untraceable, before the sputtering officer showed up.

But most of Dobrynyn's work had been with swimmer and minisubmarine raids, which, along with undersea habitats, were his specialties. Aside from training exercises, this was his first helicopter assault.

Unusual.

And this time, Baku Naval Headquarters had requested the operation, but the raid was endorsed by the GRU. Reading between the lines, Dobrynyn supposed a flag ranker at Baku wanted to embarrass the KGB garrison in Baikonur. Rumors of these things, sometimes ugly, with loss of life, reached the Spetsnaz. Politics. The KGB had probably beat up on somebody in Baku Headquarters recently.

Out the right window, a pair of red radio tower lights winked at eye level, a light loom glowered in the dust. Kharabali ten kilometers to starboard. Orbruchev turned and Dobrynyn saw a thin smile. The pilot nodded at Ritzna, then went back to his work. Another two hundred kilometers to Baikonur, a little over an hour to go.

Baikonur Cosmodrome. A sprawling eleven-hundred-square-kilometer complex, Baikonur was one of the Soviet Union's major rocket research and manned space centers. Nine hundred forty kilometers southeast of Moscow, the Cosmodrome easily absorbed millions of rubles daily to staff its research centers, control complexes, launch pads, manufacturing and final assembly plants, fuel dumps, rocket test firing stands, telemetry, computer, materials, instrumentation, tracking, building, and maintenance facilities. Leninsk, thirty-seven kilometers to the south, was exclusive home to Baikonur's seventy-five thousand workers. Situated over flatlands on the Kazakhstan Steppe, Baikonur was crisscrossed by hundreds of kilometers of railroad track. Construction towers, radar antennas-- hundreds of them-- organized into large farms, competed with thousands of telephone poles for skyline space. Packs of wild horses meandered at will over the arid cosmodrome and somehow survived temperatures from minus forty to over 110 degrees Fahrenheit.

Sputnik I had launched from Baikonur, then Gagarin, then Titov, then Shatalov. The Soyuz manned space flight missions originated there. Heroes were made in Baikonur.

They died there too. *Pravda* had recently printed a story about fifty-four scientists and technicians who were killed in the early sixties when an erroneous signal touched off the first-stage rocket they worked on. An enormous monument had been built in Leninsk, its stone engraved letters read, "Eternal glory to the military who heroically died while fulfilling their duty." Dobrynyn was surprised to see it in *Pravda*. He had read about the mishap, and others, in classified literature, but it seemed strange to see it in the press.

But success still followed success at the Baikonur Cosmodrome. *Mir*, the orbiting space station, became a reality, as did the Energia and Proton heavy lift boosters. And Buran. The Buran manned space shuttle, when strapped to an Energia booster, could orbit the earth and carry a payload comparable to its American counterpart.

Tonight's target was the Buran number-one launch pad. The complex was toward the north extremity of the Cosmodrome. The main technical center, Baikonur's core, lay forty kilometers to the southeast. Dobrynyn looked at the fuel gauges and shook his head. Another sixty kilometers to the Buran pad, 120 round trip. Fuel for the return trip was a major problem.

But intelligence had predicted things would be quiet at the Buran pad for the next week or so. They had stood down for maintenance to the liquid oxygen and liquid hydrogen fueling systems. The Energia was already stacked for the next mission but the Buran shuttle was not scheduled to be strapped to its booster until next week. Not many people around now. Getting in and out should be easy.

He saw a dim reflection inside the windshield, someone moved forward -- Ullanov. His adjutant was in full battle gear, an AK-74 slung over his shoulder. Like Dobrynyn's, his face was blackened. Ullanov's eyes and teeth shone like spotlights in the murky interior.

Ullanov checked his watch, then nodded toward Ritzna. "Isn't it about time?"

"Late, I think. Leninsk should have interrogated ten minutes ago."

"All this nonsense about transporting critical machine parts. I wouldn't buy it if--"

Ritzna raised a hand, then reached up and flipped switches overhead. He pressed a palm against his helmet and keyed his mike. His lips moved. The copilot nodded, then shook his head, then nodded again. He looked up to them and shrugged.

Two minutes passed. Ritzna put his hand back to his helmet. He turned with a grin. "Leninsk Airport has cleared our flight plan, Colonel. I gave them an ETA of an hour and a half, said we were having generator problems along with the headwind."

"Do they have us on radar?" Dobrynyn asked.

"No, sir. And they bought the IFF malfunction. I reported our position over Orlovski. Even with this headwind, we should be in and out by the time Leninsk expects us."

Dobrynyn glanced at Ullanov. The master sergeant's expression was darker than his face camouflage.

"I think you're right, Josef. That was too easy." Dobrynyn said.

He bent to the pilot. "Orbruchev. This whole thing stinks. We'll hit the secondary target."

Orbruchev nodded, the Mil' came left slightly.

Dobrynyn rubbed his chin and said to Ullanov, "South side of Baikonur. Liquid oxygen distillation plant, Josef. Eh? They make liquid hydrogen too, right?"

Ullanov looked aft. "Yessir. I'd better brief the men."

Dobrynyn put a hand on Ullanov's forearm and said loudly, "Rocket fuel, Josef. Liquid oxygen, liquid hydrogen, hypergolics, all kinds of fuel. Don't you think they would have a few drops of kerosene?"

Ullanov and Orbruchev looked at each other, their eyes crinkled. Then Ullanov turned and went aft to tell the men about the change in targets.

Orbruchev grinned up to Dobrynyn. "No fun stealing gas in Baikonur, Colonel. No windows to break, no screaming babushkas to piss off."

· · ·

The Mil' swooped over a hoary, spiked landscape sixty-five minutes later. The wind had unaccountably stopped and it was clear now. Dobrynyn looked out the port window as they shot over a low white wall, Baikonur's southern boundary. He checked his map and squinted at a group of lights. Yes, Tyuratam, Baikonur's original village, lay nestled six kilometers to the west. The liquid oxygen plant should be about nine kilometers north. He turned aft, caught Ullanov's eye and raised a fist. Two other Spetsnaz rose beside the master sergeant, they checked one another's gear.

Ritzna looked up to Dobrynyn. "Leninsk Approach Control wants to know our intentions, Colonel."

"They used that word? Intentions?"

"Yessir."

"And they still don't have us on radar?"

"That's what they said, sir."

"Don't believe a word. They know exactly where we are. Tell them we're fifteen minutes out." He looked ahead and nudged Orbruchev's shoulder. "There!"

The pilot nodded as an antenna farm whipped underneath. Then he eased the Mil' among a group of prefabricated aluminum buildings. Fuel trucks were parked in long rows behind a wire fence. A double railroad siding gleamed in the moonlight.

Seven meters, four, one. The Mil' came closer, downwash billowed dust clouds around them.

The side door opened, three figures jumped, then Orbruchev raised his helicopter again and headed north.

Dobrynyn stepped aft among his squad as the Mil' slowed for another descent. He checked them quickly, slapped backpacks, then went to the open door as the Mil' dropped her tail and squatted six meters over an asphalt courtyard. As they descended into dust, Dobrynyn picked out two large distillation towers in the distance; closer, he saw a low concrete barracks building, and their secondary target, the three-story combination fuel distribution and administration building. The valve control and distribution center was on the second floor.

...the second floor...something nagged at the back of Dobrynyn's mind as Orbruchev eased the Mil' down.

A meter off the deck. Dobrynyn jumped with Corporal Smirnitskiy and the pair ran for the control center's side door.

Three quickly jumped after them, sprinted fifteen meters, and knelt. They fired gas grenades into the barracks, donned gas masks, then dashed into the smoke. As the Mil' settled to earth, the last two Spetsnaz jumped, both laboring with heavy backpacks. One stumbled. His partner raised him by the armpit and the pair raced toward the liquid oxygen distillation towers.

As expected, the control room side door was metal-shielded and double-locked. Dobrynyn stood back. Smirnitskiy shouldered his AK-74 and fired a five-shot silenced burst. Then another quick one. Bullets screeched and ricocheted inside. Smoking holes took the places of the knob and lock mechanisms. They yanked, the door crashed open, and they sped inside.

There. Dobrynyn spotted the main stairway five meters ahead. He dashed for it, caught the bannister on the run, and whipped onto the stairs, his legs pumping.

Six submachine gun muzzles stared at the two from the top of the landing. They stopped in disbelief halfway up the stairs. Feet shuffled behind them, as four more men armed with submachine guns took positions on the first floor.

Then it hit Dobrynyn. There had been no resistance, no guards, no workers walking around. Not even a damned stray cat! It had been too easy.

Outside, the Mil's engines spooled down with a mournful whistle. It was quiet for a moment. Dobrynyn heard shouts in the courtyard, then screams of pain. He recognized his men's dismayed voices. He looked back to the group on the landing.

An officer, an oval-faced captain with pinched, close-together eyes and green KGB shoulderboards, smiled thinly. He waved a hand. "You are late, comrade."

Gun barrels and shouts prodded the pair into the first-floor cafeteria. They searched Dobrynyn, then handcuffed, gagged, and threw him into a plastic chair. Leg irons were snapped around his ankles. Smirnitskiy was quickly disarmed and made to brace against a far wall with his feet spread.

Presently, the rest of his squad, including a wide-eyed Orbruchev and

Ritzna, were booted through the door. Two Spetsnaz, the demolition squad, struggled among the soldiers. They were beaten and kicked. One of the men's arms dangled obscenely as they roughed him to his feet and shoved him along.

Dobrynyn looked around, incredulous. His men. It had only taken sixty seconds. All bled from gashes around their heads, faces, and necks; even the erudite Orbruchev had a long slash down his cheek; Ritzna's eye was almost swollen shut, and blood ran freely from his nose. Their gear was tossed into a corner and the team joined Smirnitskiy against the wall.

The KGB captain pointed at three men. Their legs were kicked out from under and they pitched to the floor. One soldier planted a foot, pinning their necks, while other soldiers kicked the downed men in their backs and stomachs. Soldiers laughed as they stood over the man with the broken arm. A boot pinned his wrist while another soldier brought a rifle butt down on his hand. Bones crunched and the Spetsnaz screamed shrilly.

Over the next ten minutes Dobrynyn raged through his gag. Yet nothing inhibited these animals as they moved from man to man kicking, yanking, gouging. The KGB captain strutted among them, his hands behind his back. He looked at Dobrynyn once, shook his head, then watched the squirming Spetsnaz, nodding at their screams.

Dobrynyn counted thirty or so assailants. Their rifles were slung over their shoulders as they grunted and stomped and booted. All wore green KGB shoulderboards--these weren't the Army or Strategic Rocket Forces men that garrisoned Baikonur.

"Stop!"

An officer stood in the doorway. He wore an overcoat and his shoulderboards indicated a KGB full colonel. Dobrynyn looked at the insignia: Medical Corps. Full face, wide-spaced pointed teeth, sandy hair, the colonel walked in and stood before the captain in silence. "This was unnecessary." He shook his head slowly.

"We've waited for this for a long time, Colonel. These people have been-
-"

"Captain, that's enough. We've accomplished our mission. Load these men and take them to the dispensary. Keep them under guard but don't touch them anymore. I'll take care of this one." He nodded toward Dobrynyn, then walked up to him, his hands on his hips. "You should have tried the launch pad. Things would have gone easier. We had Army personnel waiting for you."

Dobrynyn looked into cold, brown eyes, a freckled face. Except for crow's feet around his eyes, the colonel could pass for twenty.

"My name is Sadka. I've been trying to find you for the past twelve hours. And, believe me, it was hard to convince the GRU to let us in on what you were doing. When I finally learned of your whereabouts, you were over the Caspian and headed this way.

"There is no time. No time at all. I flew directly from Moscow to intercept you here." He reached and pulled down Dobrynyn's gag.

Dobrynyn shouted, "You bastard! What the hell do you want with us? Why go to all the trouble of setting this up, then tipping it off?"

"In a moment." Sadka nodded to two men. "In there," he ordered.

The soldiers dragged Dobrynyn's chair into a small room. It had a long drainboard, a porcelain sink, blackened range, and refrigeration equipment. The men left. Sadka and Dobrynyn were alone.

"What is it, Colonel?" Dobrynyn demanded. "What is so important that made you mangle my men? You or whoever set this up could have recalled us when we refueled at Nizni Oseredok. Why did you let this go so far?"

Sadka raised a hand. "I needed you to come to me. We saved at least--"

"Saved what?"

"--three hours, possibly four. I didn't anticipate what these people would do. It took me a while to get here from the Buran launch pad--"

"I don't expect apologies out of you. And believe me, we'll take care of your people later. And what is a doctor-colonel, or whatever the hell you are, doing here in a command function? Are you a zamp in disguise? And what is so damned important that an entire mission is compromised? It's a useless waste!" Dobrynyn roared.

Sadka waited as Dobrynyn glared. He leaned against the sink and folded his arms. Finally, "Your brother."

"What?"

"I said, `your brother.'"

Dobrynyn was silent.

"Yes. I thought that would get your attention." He paused, then, "Haven't you wondered about him and your father? Hasn't the legacy given you enough trouble?"

"Major! I demand you release us. I want our weapons returned and--"

Sadka stepped to Dobrynyn and backhanded him across the cheek. Dobrynyn's head whipped.

Sadka yelled, "Listen to me, you idiot. There is no time. This is really about your brother and you have a chance to do something about it!"

They locked eyes. Men murmured and groaned outside, an occasional shout cleaved through the door.

Sadka went back and leaned against the sink. "Well?"

Dobrynyn sighed, "All right, zamp."

"All right, what?"

Dobrynyn shook his head. "I don't understand any of this. My father and brother. Yes, they follow me everywhere. You must be aware of that already. If you aren't, read the damn file. But it means nothing. I never knew my father. My brother and I were separated when we were very small, a year old, I think. And what's it to do with all this?"

"Everything and nothing. If you must know, your raid was to be compromised, anyway. GRU wanted to test your reactions as well as those of base security here. But I needed you quickly. That's why we were forced to do it this way.

"There is no time. You will be leaving within the hour." Sadka tapped his coat pocket. "I have your orders. Your adjutant too, if you wish. You rate one. As far as your colleagues in Baku will know, you have been placed in temporary command of the garrison. That's your cover. It's been all arranged. It will be done quietly."

Dobrynyn struggled against his cuffs. The chair bounced. "I don't understand a word of this. What garrison? And whose orders?"

Sadka waited until Dobrynyn settled, then reached over and patted him on the shoulder. "An exciting opportunity for each of us, comrade. And I am not a zampolit. My field is psychopharmacology. Yours is, in a manner of sorts, espionage and assassination. Together, we can run the perfect operation--"

"Speak clearly, damnit! What operation?"

Sadka almost pouted. "Your brother. You are going to become your brother."

"What? How?"

"That's what I've been trying to tell you. We have him. In Petropavlovsk. You are going to study him. His every facet. His every nuance. It will be a crash course. Your English will become perfect. You will learn your brother's American dialect, and then..."

"What?"

Sadka snapped his fingers, "...take his place. In America. He is a naval architect like you. Although he doesn't know, he is slated to be a leading program manager on the SSN-21 program. Have you heard of that?"

Dobrynyn nodded. "Their next generation attack submarine for the twenty-first century."

"Yes. That's where I come in. I will help you learn what your brother knows. When you go to America in his place you will find out more about the SSN-21 program and anything else you can discover. But we must do it quickly. Your brother can't be missing too--"

Sadka's head twirled to the door.

They heard "plop-plop" sounds in the cafeteria. Dobrynyn recognized the hissing of tear gas canisters. Then gunfire, a quick burst, raked outside. They heard screams, rasping coughs, and gurgling. Glass shattered, feet shuffled, and voices shouted hoarsely. Sadka pulled a Makarov from under his coat, his eyes grew wide. More gunfire, smoke seeped under the door.

Dobrynyn and Sadka coughed, then they retched.

The door crashed open. White smoke poured in. Dobrynyn's eyes ran freely and he coughed in rasps, his lungs white-hot.

Sadka stood at the sink dousing a handkerchief when a shape merged behind him. A rifle butt swung and smacked his head. Sadka slumped to the floor. His pistol clattered beside him.

Keys jangled, then worked at Dobrynyn's cuffs. His hands were free and a gas mask landed in his lap. The wraith bent to work at his leg cuffs. Dobrynyn fumbled the mask on, blinked several times and took deep breaths. He recognized Ullanov's black curly hair as his master sergeant worked furiously at his ankles.

Another shape blended before him, a man in a flight suit. Orbruchev also wore a gas mask.

Dobrynyn was free. They grabbed his armpits, dragged him to his feet and toward the door.

"Josef," Dobrynyn coughed behind his mask.

They kept moving, in the middle of the room now, toward the main hallway. Other shapes stumbled with him, his own men, all with masks on. They shuffled among writhing, coughing, whimpering, reeling soldiers. Without masks, the KGB couldn't ward off kicks and blows as they groped down the hallway.

Finally, outside. They breathed in sobs as Ullanov and three other Spetsnaz conked emerging, coughing KGB soldiers and threw them into a shed.

Dobrynyn tore off his mask and breathed deeply. The air was clean, cold, sweet, but his lungs still rasped. "Josef," he gurgled.

Ullanov ran up and lifted his mask. "I've set up a perimeter and Orbruchev says he can fly. He's starting the chopper now. I have Ritzna and Barguzin pumping kerosene off the truck. All we need is two more minutes. Then we have to move, fast. Some of those dumb turds dove out the windows and got away."

Dobrynyn ran wheezing back to the building.

"Where are you going?" Ullanov yelled.

"That KGB colonel. I'm taking him with us."

Ullanov summoned two Spetsnaz and they caught Dobrynyn at the door.

Ullanov said, "Fine with me. Might as well grab that captain and throw his ass in the Caspian, too. I wonder how high the sonofabitch will bounce after he falls five hundred meters?"

The four donned their masks and ran into the smoke.

15

They hauled Lofton over Stenka 726's fantail and searched him, taking everything except, surprisingly, his watch. Two sailors shoved him against a bulkhead and pinned his arms while other crew members turned their attention to *Brutus* bobbing alongside. One officer held a pistol, loosely, speaking to the bridge via a hand-held radio. Another shouted at his men, exhorting them to make a sling and fenders around *Brutus* to keep the minisub from bumping the patrol boat's starboard side.

The Stenka wallowed. Her crew gathered in knots, speaking conversationally as if they were on a Sunday jaunt. The two sailors relaxed their grip and Lofton stood between them almost casually. But, he smelled the cordite, and his eyes caught the *Kunashiri Maru*'s oil slick, flotsam bobbed in ground swells. *More than fifty men and women.* The man next to him, a heavy-set gunner's mate, pulled a half-peeled orange from his pocket. He began munching, his thin red lips sucked at the rind, juice ran down his chin and dripped on his parka.

Lofton wound up and hit the gunner's mate solidly in the left temple. He hardly saw the man go down. Huge fists pummeled his face, his kidneys, back, stomach. He toppled to the deck and groveled among empty thirty-millimeter shell casings covering his head. Finally, mercifully, they tied his hands and threw him into a paint locker where they almost crushed his wrist in the hatch. Fortunately, the ropes and stainless watchband absorbed most of the hatch's impact.

His jaw ached, pain shot through his head when his tongue jabbed the tooth they'd loosened. His ribs hurt, blood caked his face and sweater. He lay among buckets and pails for well over an hour and listened to Stenka 726's three great diesels idle as she rolled in the ground swells. The Krivak's gas turbines whined nearby. Shouts filtered down to him. The KGB crews were standing by for instructions.

The hatch ripped open, and Lofton blinked at the brightness. A lanky, yellowtoothed figure moved in, jabbing a knee in his chest, and laid a cold pistol muzzle on his nose. Lofton couldn't distinguish his captor's face, just teeth and the round, white outline of an officer's combination cap; the man's parka smelled of diesel fuel and fish.

"Americanyets, we know. Selfdestruct? Explosives?" His head nodded outside.

Damn! Why hadn't he thought of that? It would have taken thirty seconds to arm those limpets. *Brutus* should have been blown to bits by now. Instead, his minisub was about to fall into Soviet hands. He jerked against his ropes.

"Explosives?" the enraged voice repeated, the knee pushed harder.

Lofton shook his head.

"Good."

The officer got up pressing his weight against Lofton's chest. Then the hatch slammed and was dogged shut.

Soon, there were more shouts. The Stenka's three M503A diesels rumbled, backed, stopped; transmissions clunked as the boat pirouetted. The KGB was setting up a tow for *Brutus*.

The trip to Petropavlovsk seemed to take hours. Diesel exhaust and paint fumes swirled around a coughing, gasping Lofton. Keeping his head close to the deck didn't help. He retched over and over until he fell into a lethargic, toxic sleep.

He awoke when the diesels dropped to an idle. He felt a small, almost tentative bump. Shouts, thumping of boots, and the slap of heavy manila lines told him they were docked.

The hatch banged open; quickly, they yanked him to his feet, a blindfold was wrapped around his face and they prodded him off the Stenka and threw him inside a large, vehicle with a strong, wide floor. When it moved he could tell it was one of the eightwheeled amphibious BTR60 troop carriers. A boot pressed firmly against the small of his back during the five-minute ride.

They dragged him out and stood him against the BTR-60. Nobody spoke. With his blindfold, he felt alone in a blackened world. A gull cried and a ship's forced draft blowers wailed nearby. *This is it. That yellow-toothed officer is lining up ten guys at twenty paces. They'll cock their AK-74s any second now and pull their triggers.*

Someone grunted, a hand pushed him up a short flight of stairs, he stumbled through a door. Feet shuffled, a chair scraped on a wooden floor. Voices whispered as he passed through a room: pencil shavings, it smelled like a schoolhouse. A heavy door rumbled and Lofton was eased down a deep flight of wooden stairs by his armpits. His ribs screamed with pain, one or two felt broken. At least three men surrounded him, one on either side and another behind. Wordlessly, they shoved him along a hallway and into a small, sturdy room. A door clanged shut behind him.

Alone.

Sinking to his knees, Lofton lost his balance and fell heavily on his side. "Owww!" He bounced six inches off the dark, cold cement as if he'd been jolted by defibrillating paddles. Everything: ribs, tooth, face, jaw, belly, sent unbelievable messages of wretched anguish to his overloaded brain....

Lofton woke several times. His throat was dry, he couldn't see or move his hands. Once, he tried to roll and swung his feet. A cold thick wetness seeped out of his trousers as his own stench greeted his nostrils. Shivering in his excrement, he dozed and waited. Sleep came fitfully as his ribs shrieked.

For company, he set his digital watch alarm and counted Forty six double "bleeps" interspersed with forty-five single "bleeps": almost two days.

Footsteps. The door banged open, men entered the room and muttered in soft voices.

The blindfold was untied. He blinked. Gray light filtered through a high, barred window. Yes, three shadows merged into figures. One of them blended to the likeness of an officer. Lofton squinted at his shoulderboards.

They were green, the man was a KGB full colonel. He swung his head to find a wooden bench and a crude concrete cell, perhaps eight feet square. The other men were Naval Infantry with black berets. Their boots were planted wide apart on the rough floor, a pool of stagnant water glimmered in one corner.

"Up!" from the KGB colonel.

"Huh?"

"Sit up, Comrade Thatcher. We want shirt, pants. You have smell."

Hands grabbed his armpits, he was lifted to the bench. The soldiers untied him. He bit back the pain as they tugged off his jacket, then the rest of his clothes and threw them aside. Naked. Cold. He sat and hugged his shoulders.

The two Naval Infantrymen were silent, confident. One was a tall, oafish blond corporal, the other a master sergeant with dark curly hair and intelligent eyes. AK74s were slung over their shoulders. He didn't recognize the badge on their berets. Their boots squeaked, shiny, strong. The master sergeant caught Lofton's eye, then looked away.

The KGB man stood over him. "My name is Sadka, Commander, Colonel Sadka. OK, please be relaxed and lie down. I examine." The shoulder patch indicated the KGB colonel was a doctor.

Lofton's tongue was thick as he tried, "My name's not Thatcher. You've got it wrong. I'm Lofton."

Hands shoved him back. The master sergeant easily pinned Lofton's shoulders to the bench and stared at him.

"Yes, that's OK." Sadka bent over and thumbed the cuts on Lofton's face. He said softly, "Where are you all right?"

Lofton blinked, then answered, "The ribs and the wrist." He pointed to them.

"OK."

Lofton watched the doctor probe; he had sandy hair, a full face, wide-spaced pointed teeth, and freckles. He looked too young to be a colonel. He pushed at Lofton's wrist, rotated and flexed it. Then Sadka poked his ribs, watching Lofton grimace.

"OK." Sadka produced a stethoscope and gave him a quick onceover.

"OK." The wrist and ribs were quickly taped. Sadka stood and reached into his bag. Out came a Nikon and he snapped six pictures of Lofton's blood-encrusted face. Then he repacked the camera, closed his medical bag, and turned to leave.

"I'm a civilian. Can I speak with someone from the U.S. embassy?" Lofton blurted.

"OK, shirt, pants clean. Not smell--they come to you."

"No--. I mean yes. Thanks. Can I see someone from the U.S. Embassy, please?"

The master sergeant stopped as he bent to pick up Lofton's clothes.

"OK. Three days to patch up. We need you rested, then we are to Kubinka--"

"--I can't believe this." Lofton's voice rose. "Yes, I made a terrible mistake coming here. I'm sorry. But it's not like I'm a POW. I mean our countries are...are..."

All three stared at him, their faces like stone.

Colonel Sadka's lips worked to a thin smile. "Good-bye." He walked out.

With a thumb and forefinger, the sergeant slowly handed the turtleneck, trousers, and skivvies to the corporal. The sergeant kept his focus on Lofton as he tossed the jacket in his lap. Their eyes locked until Lofton turned his head and put on his jacket.

Squirming into sneakers and socks, Lofton felt absurd before the sergeant and corporal. They sported slick creaking boots, wellcut black trousers, spotless blue and white teeshirts under black tunics, and close haircuts.

The sergeant nodded to the corporal; they quickly snapped handcuffs and leg manacles on Lofton while he watched dumbfounded. The corporal walked out; the sergeant paused and slowly backed away, his eyebrows arched. Then the door thumped shut.

He slept until the early evening when the corporal returned with clean clothes. The infantryman waited patiently while Lofton put them on, then replaced the handcuffs and manacles. Surprisingly, the corporal produced a tray with weak potato soup, a slice of bread, and tea. He stood outside the door until Lofton finished, then took the tray. Lofton was still hungry. The soup made him ravenous and thirsty.

Lofton's watch bleeped twice, waking him: 3:00 A.M. *Where am I?* His belly rumbled. *Forget it*. He couldn't and was tempted to lap at the pool of water in the corner. A green viscous surface beckoned. *It's stagnant--forget it.* He cocked an ear while he waited for sleep. Doors opened and shut over-head, the building felt small, it must be a working facility, with his present quarters a holding cell. A guard shuffled in the hall occasionally. Even at this hour, voices, boisterous shouts drifted from outside, a tank rumbled past, other deep-throated vehicles drew up and left. His tooth still hurt, but his head didn't explode when his tongue nudged it.

Lofton shut his eyes to go back to sleep; but his mind wandered. Suddenly, he was wide awake and sitting upright with his eyes wide open. He bit his lip. In just two days, the USS *Truman* would be blown apart by Renkin's torpedoes and splattered over uncharted acres at the bottom of the Kuril Straits. One hundred twentysix American officers and men would be dead. And *Brutus*. Dr. Sadka had called Lofton "Commander Thatcher." That meant they must have been inside *Brutus* and found Thatcher's personal effects.

He gritted his teeth. Those bastards had been crawling in his minisub. He imagined grinning, white overalled technicians with thick paws ripping out wire harnesses. At this very minute, they could be peering into cabi-nets, pushing switches, running their fat hands over his fuel cells, studying the anechoic coating. Why the hell hadn't he set the limpet charges? How could he have forgotten?

And Sadka had said Kubinka. Lofton knew of it from his SEAL days. Kubinka was a major Soviet Air Force base north of Moscow. But why not one of Moscow's civilian airports, like Sheremetyevo? Or Domodedovo? Or Vnukovo?

Lofton's stomach churned. His tongue was dry and he swallowed rapidly. Kubinka! A maximum security air base. No civilians. Minimal bystanders. He could be secretly whisked to--to one of the KGB's "psychi-atric Institutes" nearby. With unlimited clinical resources, Sadka could work him over. Then Lofton would simply disappear. Three days, the doctor said, then Lofton would be well enough to travel to Kubinka--

--a door banged open. Soft voices filtered down the hall and stopped at his door. Lofton checked his watch: 3:27 A.M. Men talked with the guard, then the key rattled and the door swung open. There were two, both wore berets and were silhouetted in the dull hallway light.

A flashlight snapped on. Lofton covered his eyes, then lurched to sit up. "*Nyet.*"

The flashlight was close to his face now. The man's other hand held a pistol close to Lofton's head. He recognized the glint of a nine millimeter automatic Makarov PM.

He propped himself on his elbows, frozen. The flashlight and Makarov came closer, then stopped twelve inches from his face. The beam's reflection cast a faint glow, allowing him to identify one of his jailers, the master sergeant. His ribs hurt. He started to rise again.

"Don't move!" the sergeant barked in Russian.

Lofton froze.

The other black beret slowly walked into his cell and stopped in cameo five feet away. Lofton caught the reflection of an officer's cap device; a shoulder insignia told him this was a lieutenant colonel. He couldn't see any features except for the outline of a beard.

Trembling, he did his best to control his breathing and counted to twenty: *Will it be quick?*

Forty: *Do you hear the sound? Do you feel the blast just before a nine millimeter slug tears through your brain?*

The flashlight wandered down his chest, his hands.

Fifty-seven: The light flicked back to his face. He squeezed his eyes closed. *Is it painful? Will my head feel like it's bursting? Exploding? Will my life flash before me--*

"Pull the trigger and get it over with, Ivan!"

The sergeant's chuckle startled him. He opened his eyes to see the officer tap the master sergeant on the shoulder.

The pistol and flashlight were withdrawn. Both berets backed out of the cell. The door locked, their boots receded down the concrete hallway.

The doctor showed up the next morning, probing and pushing. He sniffed and pulled a face. "How are you feel, Commander?"

"Fine, Colonel Sadka--"

"Dr. Sadka."

"Yes, Dr. Sadka. Look, it's important that I speak with the American consul. This is all a big mistake. I'm a civilian and I never intended to--"

"OK, Commander, very good. Ribs seem better, maybe not split. Two days now." Sadka stood up. "You clean up. We don't like crap. You wash. I return tonight. Look tomorrow too. OK." Sadka picked up his medical bag and held it before him with both hands. He tilted his head slightly, smiled, then walked out the door.

The door remained open. Lofton caught a soft exchange in Russian down the hallway between Sadka and one of his guards.

"This man's injuries have put me way off schedule and you're not helping things. I left orders yesterday for him to be cleaned up, and not just his underwear. He stinks. How can I work with a patient who stinks, you idiot? You may do things differently in Petropavlovsk but where I'm from, people follow orders. I want him clean. Do you understand?"

"Yes, Dr. Sadka."

"What's your name?"

"Ullanov, sir."

"Who is your superior?"

"Lieutenant Colonel Dobrynyn, sir."

"You report to Dobrynyn?"

I'm his adjutant, sir."

"Spetsnaz. You look familiar. Have we met?"

"Uhh. Briefly, sir. Baikonur."

"You! You tried to throw me out of the helicopter!"

"Thought you were a spy, sir. You compromised our mission."

"Nonsense!"

Silence. Lofton heard a nervous shuffle, he felt darkness. Spetsnaz? What the hell did Baikonur have to do with all this?

Sadka spoke in a level tone. "We'll talk about Baikonur later, Ullanov. After I'm finished, you could well be patrolling the Bering Straits by dogsled. In the meantime, get this man cleaned up!"

"Sir!"

Footsteps receded up the stairs, the door creaked open and slammed.

An enormous redheaded Naval Infantry brute filled the doorway, his eyes like slits. He unslung his AK-74 and beckoned. Lofton shuffled out carefully, turned left, and almost bumped into the master sergeant. The black-clad soldier unlocked the cuffs and leg manacles, then nodded to a gray-painted alcove at the end of the hallway. Lofton saw a drain; a fire hose with a long, thin nozzle was coiled on a rack. The sergeant handed over a bar of soap. It felt like the heavily pumiced kind mechanics used to clean up. The rifle prodded his back. "Go!"

Lofton took off his clothes and stood over the drain while the redhead blasted him with a heartstopping cold spray for a full minute. He soaped as best he could. The shivering helped him swipe the rough bar over his body. It chafed his skin and he wasn't able to raise any suds. He washed his face, scraped at his hair, then endured another sixty-second blast of cold water.

The sergeant peered at him, then nodded to the open cell door. Lofton picked up his clothes, tossed the soap on the floor and walked back. They waited while he drew the clothes over his wet bandages and body, then remanacled him and slammed the door. He sat on the bench, drew up his knees, and shivered.

His Casio bleeped: 1:30 A.M. He'd won a Rolex in a regatta but never wore it. The Casio was with him at work and did well when he raced on *Bandit*. It was with him now as he sat on the cold concrete of his darkened cell, his elbows rested on drawn up knees. Maybe that was why the KGB hadn't taken it; after all, it was just an inexpensive fortyseven dollar-and-fiftycent watch with a stainless expansion band.

Lofton held his head. *What are they going to do to me?* He couldn't ignore that he'd blatantly trespassed into sovereign Soviet territory with a foreign naval vessel, one meant for covert activities. And now they were flying him to Kubinka. That jivetalking Sadka was no doubt rubbing his hands together waiting for the moment when he and his team could start probing with their needles.

A cockroach skittered over Lofton's right foot, then stopped at his left, unsure. He raised his hands, his wrist throbbing as he watched. This was cockroach number fourteen. Lofton had made up names for them but ran out of ideas after number ten had cruised by. Eventually, they all became Colonel Sadka.

A vehicle stopped next to his window, the engine rumbling above him. Lofton recognized the sound of a BTR60 and caught a whiff of diesel exhaust. The driver revved it once, then switched off.

Will they kill me? Torture first? Or do they simply beat the hell out me and let me rot? No, not now. Everything's changed in the Soviet Union, hasn't it?

Bonnie! Her soft, full lips. They were both surprised, it was so spontaneous, so wonderful. She'd kissed and hugged him aboard *Brutus*. Bonnie with her glasses, wideapart green eyes, and thick sandy hair. The way she looked at him. She understood when he talked shop, she liked to sail. The look on her face that Sunday afternoon. Her chin had been set just so when she stood at the mainsheet with *True Blue* death rolling and on the verge of a gybe-broach. She wasn't afraid and spilled the vang, then the main, just in time.

Bonnie: drenched under the wet spinnaker, damnit. Bonnie: waving from the basin six promontory as she stood alongside that insane Kirby. Bonnie: in her bathrobe, snug in *True Blue*'s main salon, talking to him. She smelled so good. Lilacs? Bonnie: reading...

And here he was, crammed in a cell in downtown Petropavlovsk with cockroaches for company. He looked down to see Colonel Sadka waddle across the cell.

And Kirby, renewing their friendship. Lofton had even bought into that crazy Santa Cruz 70, *Bandit*, with Kirby. What was it Kirby had once said as they sat at his dock with their feet dangling in the water? They'd finished puttering with *Bandit*'s steering cables. One beer became many as the horizon flattened a setting sun on a hazy, warm Saturday evening. The subject had turned to women and Kirby's troubles with Nancy, a woman who was becoming an elusive fiancee. Suddenly he popped out with it. "You know, Brad, we're pretty lucky here. If you really work hard you can have damn near anything you want. Wealth, power, women, all the goodies." Then he smirked. "Trouble is, you can't have it all at one time. No way." Then, "Sheeyat."

Kirby.

Two bleeps on his Casio: 2:00 A.M.

Kubinka: Renkin wanted him dead. He probably gave the order, or at least let it happen. Lofton bit his thumbnail. *But why not just kill me?*

Then he knew. The realization washed over him in cold, penetrating waves. *Sadka wants to look in my head first.* And when he does that, he'll find a wealth of highly classified data.

He hugged his knees tightly, put his head down and moaned. As he saw it, there were no choices. *In his laboratory, Sadka buttons up his lab coat and gives me a starter IV solution of sodium amytal. When I'm properly sedated, he runs some amphetamines through me and I'll blab like a drunk on New Year's Eve. After that they put a bullet in the back of the head and throw me down the sewer. Here, they just shoot me and throw me down the sewer.*

Sadka would be happy to practice on him, Lofton knew. Without political dissidents, the population of the USSR's "psychiatric institutes" population was probably greatly reduced. Sadka would welcome a new, healthy subject like Lofton.

He recalled a class from his SEAL days. They had all tried to duck it, the subject repulsed them, it went against their grain, but attendance was mandatory. The name on the syllabus stood out morbidly: *"Autoeuthanasia Methods"--ways to commit suicide when under extreme torture with no hope of survival.* Two techniques came to him; they were desperate, crude. One was to bite the tongue and drown in your own blood. It worked best when your hands were tied behind your back so you couldn't involuntarily clear your airway with your fingers.

The other was a breathing exercise. How did it work? Something about overdosing on your own carbon dioxide. Lofton smirked. They'd called it an exercise. When does an exercise cease to be an exercise if you are trying to kill yourself? He tried to recall it.

A door opened upstairs, and he heard footsteps on the landing.

What was the carbon dioxide method?

Two sets of boots tapped down the wooden stairs.

Damnit! He purposely hadn't listened to the lecture, the subject was just too hideous. But he realized why they taught it. They were dead serious, yet he'd joined the SEALS because he was a good swimmer in top athletic condition. A lark, showing off for the dollies--until now.

The boots reached the concrete and walked toward his cell.

Bite your tongue. Where? Toward the back, there's a big vein or artery there.
They came closer.

He lumped his tongue and probed with his molars. Then he remembered, you had to bite almost all the way through. It took a while to drown in your own blood. Where was that vein? Maybe in front, that would be easier.

The key grated in the lock and the door opened. Too late. He'd try it later, maybe on the plane when the interior lights were low. It would be a long flight...

The flashlight clicked on, blinding him. Two men stood in the doorway, the same ones as last night, but the lieutenant colonel carried the flashlight. The man, about his own size, wore a beard.

A hand reached out, it touched his right cheek lightly. Lofton jumped, then steadied. The master sergeant stood in the doorway, he unshouldered his AK74, and aimed it loosely in Lofton's direction.

The hand touched his right cheek again. "Even with your black eye, I wouldn't have believed it."

What? That was his voice. But the lieutenant colonel spoke Russian much better than he ever could.

"You are Ernst Lubeck." The man swung the flashlight into his own face.

Lofton's mouth dropped open. Exactly the same. The lieutenant colonel was his double; the salt-and-pepper hair, the eyebrows, gray-blue eyes with the light crow's feet. He wore the same beard he'd shaved off almost two weeks ago. Even the lower incisor was crooked.

Lofton blinked several times, his mind whirled, and yes, that was his voice, yet he hadn't spoken. He worked his tongue, his lips. "What the hell is this?"

"Many times, I wished you were dead. Hadn't existed. Until last night, I'd hoped they would kill you. Since I've been here, I've thought of killing you. Yet, now..."

Lofton tried to stand, but the colonel's hand restrained him with, "Are you aware of me? Are you aware of your...our heritage?"

"What heritage?"

"You mean you don't know?"

"All I know is that you and your quacks are going to stick me with needles and then kill me, Ivan. Maybe you've stuck me already. Is that why I see my double? Maybe it's just a good cosmetic job." Lofton jabbed a thumb and his manacles rattled. "Hollywood is four thousand miles that way, Ivan. And what--"

"Your Russian is much better than Sadka realizes."

"What do you mean by heritage?"

The master sergeant moved in with a scowl, his AK74 ready. "Colonel? Is this all right?"

"Go have a cigarette, Josef. He'll be fine."

"Like hell I will," Lofton sputtered. Somehow, he didn't know why, he felt an easing deep inside, an incongruous warmth that shouldn't have been there.

The master sergeant slung his rifle over his shoulder. "Yes, sir. But we don't have much time until Donuzlay returns."

"I know, Josef. Please wait in the hall."

The master sergeant grunted, then stepped outside, leaving the cell door open.

The colonel turned back to Lofton. "Do you know where you were born?"

Lofton sniffed, then settled against the wall. "Minnesota, I think. But nobody knows for sure."

"Well, I do, you idiot!" Dobrynyn yelled, grabbing Lofton's sweater. "Berlin. Our mother was a whore!"

Lofton gaped. He tried to move his lips, but nothing came out.

"Yes. They made sure I knew that. They keep reminding me. I am--was Manfried Lubeck. You were Ernst. She was killed and I went East. You went the other way--

"A whore? Ernst? No--"

"--Yes! A sleazy kraut whore! And, guess what, Ernst. Our--your father," Dobrynyn jabbed a finger in his chest, "was an American! He ran when he learned our mother was pregnant." Dobrynyn's face was near, Lofton saw the dark rage.

"It's followed me all my damned life. Screwed up my career. You and my father, damned Americans. Have you enjoyed your fast cars and disposable razors?" Dobrynyn flung him against the wall, his brother's head bounced.

Lofton groaned and rubbed his head while Dobrynyn stood back. His eyes scoured the ceiling.

The Casio bleeped: 2:00.

"And digital watches," growled Dobrynyn.

Ullanov shot in, his rifle ready.

"Sergeant. Get the hell out of here!" Dobrynyn roared.

"Sir!" Ullanov disappeared.

Lofton tried to clear his mind. Images swam, but it wasn't the blow to his head. Something was there, it faded in and out. He rubbed his temples. "Berlin? A whore? You--"

"Yes! Haven't you ever thought about it?"

It welled deep within Lofton. He couldn't have stopped it if he wanted, out of control, a primordial eruption. "Anna," he shouted.

Dobrynyn's fists doubled, he turned, surprised, his mouth worked dumbly. "Yes! ...Yes. That's right. Her name *was* ...Anna." His shoulders slumped. "That's right. I didn't know...hadn't remembered until now."

"My God, Anna! Ernst!"

"That's right, Comrade Thatcher-Lofton." Dobrynyn stood with his hands on his hips. His eyes glistened. He bit his thumbnail and shook his head slowly. "You are me and I am you."

Turning, he walked out of the cell.

A minute passed. The door swung shut softly.

Lofton tried to lie back. He couldn't and blinked in the grayness. Anna. Ernst.

Manfried.

The door was kicked open. Lofton jerked awake; he was stiff, his ribs hurt, he couldn't rise.

"Up!" A shout.

"Uhhh."

"Up, you turd!"

He turned his head. The nocturnal master sergeant stood over him with a crude wooden tray while the blond corporal leaned against the doorway, grinning.

Lofton tried to rise. The master sergeant onehanded the tray and grabbed Lofton's armpit, helping him to sit.

The thick, barrel-chested Spetsnaz clattered the tray on the bench, bellowing, "I hope you enjoy this, Sir. Sorry it's four days old but the cook just pissed in it to make it nice and warm for you." Lofton stared blankly as the sergeant stalked out. The door slammed and was locked.

He sat with his head in his hands. He felt stiff. He stretched his legs out and rotated his ankles. The Casio read 7:05 A.M. Dull, gray light found its way through the barred window.

He'd slept hard, his face was crinkled--

--that Russian Spetsnaz! A lieutenant colonel. Had he imagined last night? A horrible dream? Born in Germany with an American father? A whore for a mother? A twin, identical? What had the man said? "You are me and I am you". Lofton bit his thumbnail.

He sniffed and looked down at the tray. It smelled good. Had the cook really pissed in it?. A generous portion of dark, thick soup steamed beside him. Borscht. Potatoes and beets bobbed on the surface. Next to the bowl, half a loaf of dark, rich bread, butter and a pot of coffee beckoned. He tried it; borscht with sour cream--marvelous! He burned his tongue but it took just four minutes to eat everything.

Lofton dozed with his hands behind his head, listening to early afternoon traffic and light rain splattering outside. His cell shook slightly when two tanks blasted by, their treads creaking.

The Casio had just bleeped 1:30 when the upstairs door grated open. Footsteps clattered down the landing. Lofton cocked an ear. Three men, he thought. Their muffled voices became more audible as they drew near. The key scraped and the door banged open.

Sadka strutted in, a smile on his face. "OK, you look good. How you are today?"

"What's it matter?" He sat up with a groan and looked into the hall. The blond and redheaded corporals stood outside the door, their AK74s slung over their backs, casual, yet alert. Their eyes missed nothing. No master sergeant this time, he noticed. The doctor waved his hand and the corporal came in and unlocked Lofton's handcuffs.

"Off," the gattoothed doctor gestured, and Lofton took off his sweater.

Colonel Sadka probed and tapped while he clicked his teeth and pummeled Lofton with his odorous breath. He looked in Lofton's ears, eyes and mouth, and even checked his knee reflexes with a rubber hammer. Then he retaped Lofton's ribs and wrist, reloaded his medical bag, and zipped it shut. "I think ribs, hand, been OK, soon," he muttered.

"Ah." Sadka ran his hand over his face, then reopened his medical bag and took out his Nikon. "O.K., smile. Last time you look crappy. Blood smeary. Now we need good pictures." He clicked off six frames as Lofton glowered. Then the camera was repacked while Lofton drew on his sweater.

"OK, you got well. Real hot. Rest now. Dinner on plane soon."

Lofton had just pulled his head through the turtleneck, his elbows were up, his ribs shrieked with pain. "What? When?"

Sadka grinned; his pointed teeth glistened. "Tonight. You and I. Fly to Kubinka. Home for me, you too. Nice plane, Tupolev16. Two big engines. We make it fast."

"When?" He managed to pull his sweater over his waist just as the corporal ratcheted the handcuffs back in place.

Sadka walked toward the door. "Good patient. I may give something before takeoff." He patted his bag.

The door slammed, their bootsteps receded up the stairs. He heard a creak as a guard arranged himself in a chair outside his door.

Lofton sat. His knuckles turned white as he gripped the bench between his knees. The cabbagebreathed doctor was talking about tonight, a day early. Somehow, that day seemed important, precious.

Kubinka. Sadka and his needles. Damn.

He wished he hadn't had the borscht, wished he didn't feel better, wished he hadn't met that damned Spetsnaz...his...his brother. In six or so hours, if the doctor was right, he would be high over the Soviet Union flying west in total darkness at close to six hundred knots. And he'd probably be pumped full of Sadka's chemicals. He imagined himself strapped in one of the medium bomber's jump seats, his head lolling through the turbulence, eyes feeling like sandpaper, the crew laughing and talking about liberty in Gorki, or wherever they hung out.

No! He stood and looked toward the barred window. The rain had become a downpour. He checked his watch: 1:54. No!

Something else came to him. It was 1:54, six hours after the USS *Truman* was to have transited Chetvertyy Kuril'skiy Proliv.

One hundred twentysix officers and men were dead now, crushed, vaporized by the ocean's enormous hydraulic pressure. By the time they'd heard the whine of the Mark 46 torpedo rising from the ocean floor it would have been too late. No time to open the throttles wide and evade. No time. Surprise would have turned to horror. The explosion would have been aft, probably near the reactor or the engine rooms, the boat sinking, imploding compartment by compartment. Or maybe all at once. No time. One hundred twentysix men dead! He sat heavily and clasped his hands.

"Carrington. Take a look at this."

"Yes, sir?" Carrington walked around Renkin's desk and peered over his shoulder. A threebyfive glossy color photograph lay on the blotter. "Was that in the envelope that just came?"

"Yes."

Carrington bent further. The head and shoulders of a single figure lay sharply defined on a crude wooden bench. Gray concrete formed a back-drop and emphasized the man's debilitated appearance.

Carrington studied it. "Jesus, it's Lofton!"

"Yes."

"Wow. They really beat the crap out of him, didn't they?"

Renkin's bald head swivelled to Carrington, his glasses shot bolts of light.

"Uh, sorry. But that black eye, it's almost closed shut. And, look at his mouth, all that blood." Carrington grinned. "His beard is gone, just like I thought when I saw him in Long Beach. He must have shaved it off. You wouldn't know it's good old Brad Lofton."

"Now look at this." Renkin picked up an earlier Jenson Industries ID photo of a bearded Lofton, stuffed the two in an envelope and sighed. "The message said Mr. Lofton will be flying to Kubinka soon."

Carrington mimicked a female falsetto. "Thank you for flying Aeroflot, Mr. Lofton. Hope you enjoy your tour of Kubinka. Photographing MiG-31s is strictly prohibited."

"Yes. This picture was a courtesy. They seemed to recognize our rather carnivorous interest in this matter. However, I've asked them for a more recent photo. I'd like to see what he looks like without all that blood splattered about. Mr. Hatch's message did confirm that the CAPTORs were neutralized. Apparently they had some trouble, the water is close to six hundred feet deep there. One was recovered and the other was destroyed; they had to get in and out quickly before the *Truman*'s arrival. He also said that the *Truman* safely transited the Kuril Straits just after his team cleared the area."

"Close."

"Yes, but we're back in business." Renkin leaned in his deep leather armchair, then spun to his safe. He hadn't mentioned the retirement question to Carrington. It might not be necessary. His control hadn't brought it up since the California meeting.

"Bye-bye, Brad." Carrington grinned.

"Not yet, Carrington. Mr. Lofton has some tutoring to do, which includes saying a few words to his captors about the SSN-21 program. After that, we can say 'bye-bye'."

"I don't understand."

"Here." Renkin flipped a picture on the desk, another three-by-five color glossy.

Carrington snorted, "Lofton. An old picture. He's--what? Dressed as a Spetsnaz. This is his brother?"

Renkin nodded.

Carrington handed back the picture. "Jesus, a lieutenant colonel. Beard and all. Exactly the same. When was that taken?"

"Two years ago when he was promoted. Now, I want you to do some research. I need their data confirmed and I need it quickly."

"Whose data? I don't understand what is happening."

"We're doing a switch, Carrington." He arranged the photo-envelopes in the safe.

"What?"

Renkin explained as he closed his wall safe and twirled the dual combinations. His nose itched, and he nudged the bandage with his finger. Not good enough, he couldn't make the itch go away.

16

Lofton checked the Casio: 4:57. Rain drummed outside, he was hungry, he hadn't seen anyone since breakfast. Breakfast...the borscht...why had they decided to give him a decent meal? Maybe his last? Maybe something to raise his energy to make him talk, to make pain, any sensation more acute....

I can't do it here, not in this damned cell. Wait 'til later. Besides, my hands are cuffed in front, I can free my airway with my fingers.

When? Maybe on the airplane. No, I might be drugged by then.

Do it now.

Bite my tongue? Drown in my own blood? Kill myself for what? So they won't be able to empty my head.

They're going to kill me anyway.

Put it off. Wait 'til the airplane.

No! Do it now before they come.

He tried to roll his tongue between his teeth. There. His tongue lay jammed between the upper and lower teeth on the left side of his mouth. Everything from the molars to the incisors were ready to go.

Now, bite! Hard!

Do it now, Brad, before Sadka comes.

A tear ran down Lofton's cheek. He relaxed his jaw.

Physical torture? Tear out my fingernails, gouge my eyes? Do they cut me up or use electrodes or pliers or fists? OK. So I jump out a window, fall under a tank. But then...if they tranquilize me right away, I turn to a talking vegetable. I won't know what I'm saying, I won't be able to move.

How long to live? A few weeks to get everything out of me, probably.

Then some dark, cold, rainy night one of Sadka's boys, a whitecoated 250-pound drooling Ivan with a single-digit IQ and rimless, round glasses comes into my room on squeaky, two-inch rubber soles. He's testing the plunger on a gigantic syringe; it has a six-inch needle and he grins while enormous drops glob onto the shiny linoleum floor.

That might be too sophisticated, maybe the goon just snaps my neck between thick, hairy paws. If the guy really lacks subtlety, he slips a knife between my ribs or puts a bullet behind my ear.

The upstairs landing door squeaked. Lofton heard footsteps. Still, he was relieved, he didn't have to do it now, he'd get to his tongue later. The key scraped in the lock, his cell door opened and the gattoothed Dr. Sadka walked in, rain dripping off his greatcoat and cap.

"OK, Commander, you're good. Time we to move." He waved over his shoulder and the burly redheaded guard came in with a long, thin section of towel and quickly blindfolded Lofton. They jerked him to his feet, then removed his leg manacles. His jacket was stuffed under his armpit.

"OK, Commander, you need feet, not eyes. Not to run, please. We go to an airplane."

A hand pushed his back, others grabbed his elbows and guided him down the hall and up the stairs. The door rumbled open, he heard typewriters, smelled pencil shavings, a telephone chimed over muttered conversation.

"Silence, please," Sadka's voice ordered from ahead. A hand at each elbow guided Lofton through a room, then another, down some steps and into the rain.

They waited quietly in the downpour. Seconds stretched to minutes. Five...seven...ten? Lofton lost count.

Ridiculous. "Could I put my jacket on?"

A fist drove into Lofton's back. His rib cage screamed in pain, and he fought for breath as his knees gave way. Falling to his side he reached in mud to steady himself and rose shakily. His jacket plopped to the ground.

"Quiet, shithead," from behind in Russian.

The message was plain enough in any language. Lofton forgot his jacket and concentrated on staying on his feet and holding down the nausea.

A wet, soggy lump was stuffed under his arm. Sadka said, "OK, Commander, you stay warm sooner. Put on sometime. The car will--Ah!"

Lofton heard a car's tires on the pavement. They squished to a stop beside him. A door opened and he was shoved in. Strong hands grabbed his elbow and roughly pulled him down. To his right, Sadka said, "OK, Commander, problem fine. We are late but please hang out. Real hot."

A man on his left growled across him. "No, idiot, the trunk lock is broken. The doctor's luggage goes in front beside the driver."

That Spetsnaz Colonel! The voice next to him belonged to his brother. Lofton jerked. The man groped for his elbow and squeezed hard as the luggage thumped into the front seat. The door slammed shut.

"Right, let's go, Sergeant," Sadka commanded.

The car jerked and moved away with scraping windshield wipers.

"Damn summer storm," muttered Sadka. "Where were you?"

The Spetsnaz next to Lofton said, "Sorry, Doctor Sadka. The car pool assigned me to a vehicle with a dead battery. I had to requisition another. Didn't Captain Noya call?"

"Nobody said anything. Did you contact the airport?"

"Sir?"

Sadka's breath reeked of garlic as he leaned across Lofton. "Rakovaya Airport, you dunderhead. They are on a strict schedule and I want to be on time. This car was to be equipped with a phone. Where is it?"

"No, sir, this car is a replacement. It's as I said, I had to--"

Sadka yelled, "Damnit driver, slow down. I want to arrive in one piece."

"Sir!" from up front. The master sergeant--Ullanov, the man was driving fast. The car lurched and its engine growled, the rear end lost traction when the doctor yelled.

"I'm sorry, sir," the Spetsnaz continued, "It took a while to draw another vehicle. Those clerks over in the Twentyfifth aren't used to working after three o'clock."

Another curve. They swayed to the right.

Lofton felt Sadka lean before him. He caught his whisper.

"...inject this man as soon as we arrive at the air..."

Lofton's heart plunged to his stomach, cold waves of nausea swept over him.

The Spetsnaz replied softly, "...good idea...sir, I wonder if we can--"

"Driver!" Sadka yelled. "Sergeant! Slow down, I said, at once. What's your name?"

"Pardon, sir?" from Ullanov.

The Spetsnaz Colonel suddenly jammed his shoulder and elbow into Lofton's chest. Lofton's right foot was kicked forward and raised against the front seat, then the left. The car swayed wildly.

"Your name, idiot," roared Sadka.

"Ullanov, sir."

"How long have you been driving?"

The car lurched to the left.

"Six months, sir."

"Colonel, what's going on? This man is incompetent!"

"There was no one else, sir. The pool's duty driver is installing a new battery in the other car." The Spetsnaz braced his feet alongside Lofton's.

The car whipped sharply to the right.

"Look out," Sadka screamed. "Stop!"

The Spetsnaz pushed hard against Lofton. The car seemed to recover, but gravel crunched beneath and it left the pavement.

"Eyachhhh. Don't--!"

Sadka's wail was cut off in the whitehot grinding of rock, undergrowth, glass, and steel. They hit something. Metal shrieked. The car bounced, teetered on one side, almost rolled, landed upright, and stopped with a loud crash.

Silence. Rain drummed on the car's roof.

"Colonel?" from up front.

"Fine, Josef." The colonel relaxed his feet and arms. "How about you, Mr. Lofton?"

"Not sure...I'll live."

The colonel grunted and reached across. "I'd better check the doctor."

Lofton heard Sadka groan, then a hard pop. The groaning stopped.

"OK, let's move, we're late," Dobrynyn said.

Lofton's blindfold was untied. He blinked at gray-black surroundings. Enough light remained to distinguish a large, wet boulder on the car's right side and an enormous tree trunk that stood before the radiator. Sadka's limp form lay beside him, his mouth gaping open.

The colonel was bending to unsnap Lofton's handcuffs while Ullanov got out and ran to the rear of the car. The colonel jumped out. "Mr. Lofton-- Ernst. Pull the doctor from the car while Josef and I take care of this. Drag him over to that gully." He joined Ullanov and they fumbled at the trunk.

Lofton sat dumbly. "What...what the hell's going on?"

"Get out. I can't hear you."

Lofton leaned out the door. Water dripped down his neck, shocking him. "Why are you doing this?"

The two men raised the trunk and bent in. Dobrynyn shouted, "Move."

Lofton shook his head and got out of the car. Weaving for a moment, he reached to the doorjamb and steadied himself. Rain cascaded over him, roaring, stimulating. He looked around, seeing no more than twenty or thirty feet. Muddy car tracks trailed back in the mist, trees and boulders surrounded him.

"Mr. Lofton!"

He reached into the back seat, heaved on Sadka's belt and pulled. The KGB colonel's head flopped against his shoulder. Blood ran from his nose and mouth, and a deep, three-inch gash oozed on his forehead. Lofton felt his neck and found a pulse. He arranged Sadka's hands over his head and yanked him out of the car.

He'd almost made the gully when he stopped, out of breath. As he rested he saw the master sergeant carrying a naked, inert human form, a hawknosed man about his own age with a shiny white face. The man's thin arms dangled. His head hung back and his mouth was stretched wide open to the rain.

He dropped Sadka's arms and jogged back. "Is that man dead?"

"This is the new Commander Lofton. Take off your clothes." Dobrynyn threw Lofton a bundle. "Your watch, too, I'm afraid. I just hope they don't find a way to check dental records."

Lofton ripped open the bundle, finding ordinary workman's clothes, boots, and a jacket.

"You're going home."

"What?" Lofton stood dumbly.

"Later. Put that stuff on."

Lofton stripped in the rain and tossed his clothes and watch to Ullanov. "Who was he?"

"A transient welder, a drunk. He fell this morning at the Frenza Ship Repair Yard and broke his neck. A body switch was the only thing I could think of when I heard of Sadka's schedule change to ship you out tonight instead of tomorrow. We had the devil's own time diverting this body from the crematory. Josef kept talking to the undertaker and distracting him while I rolled the man out a window. I even had to stuff pillows under the sheet. Then we helped the undertaker burn two other bodies; there were supposed to be three. The records are correct. We used KGB uniforms and posed as auditors. Those people remove the gold and silver fillings from their--uh--clients, and make a small profit after a while. We wanted to make sure the state was getting its share. That's why we were so late."

Lofton pulled on the clothes while Ullanov splayed the body across the back seat. He peered through the rain, seeing the road embankment fifty feet away. "Where are we?"

"Coast road on the way to Rakovaya Airport. The main gate is about a mile and a half north of here."

"Is this the main road?" Lofton asked. "I don't hear any traffic up there."

"They closed the road this morning because of a train derailment in the Nalacheva Tunnel. Sadka didn't know that.

"Josef, are you ready?" Dobrynyn called.

"Another minute, Colonel." Ullanov had the man dressed in Lofton's clothes. They heard the handcuffs ratchet, then Ullanov went to the trunk and hefted two large gas cans. He went back to the car and splashed the contents on the body, then over the back seat.

"How do my clothes fit?" Dobrynyn asked.

"Yours?" Lofton held out his arms. "Amazing. You'd think I'd bought them."

"Thought so. But I'll have the boots back before the evening's over."

Ullanov worked quickly in the car. A white-pink liquid spewed from the gas can.

"How is this going to work?" Lofton asked.

"You were a SEAL weren't you?"

"Yes."

"We're putting you on a Be12, a seaplane. You're going to swim ashore to Rebun Island. It leaves in forty minutes. That's why we're in such a damn hurry."

"Rebun...where? How can I just get on an airplane?"

Dobrynyn's turned. "Josef?"

"Almost finished, Colonel."

Watching, he said to Lofton, "The pilots owe me a favor; in fact, plenty of them. Josef and I worked with them in the Caspian Sea Flotilla. They dropped us near shore for incursions into Iran. They're good, brave men but the fools were caught smuggling marijuana. I found out and destroyed the evidence. Still, they were relegated to Petropavlovsk. Now, they fly the evening guard mail run to and from Vladivostok.

"And you should know their route; from here they fly south over the Kamchatka Peninsula, then the Sea of Okhotsk, then over the southern part of Sakhalin Island near the Soya Strait. At that point they will develop engine trouble, dip down below radar coverage, and land within one to two miles of Rebun Island, the westernmost of two Japanese islands just off Hokkaido. You jump out and they take off immediately, as if they had never landed, and only a minute or two behind schedule."

Dobrynyn adjusted his beret and smoothed his tunic. "I checked the La Perousse weather two hours ago; it's clear down there, with a moderate chop. Water temperature is fiftyfour. We have an immersion suit for you." His shoulders slumped. "It's the best I can do. By this time tomorrow you should be with your own people."

Lofton's mind whirled. Fifteen minutes ago, he'd been in jail. In hours, he was to have been in Sadka's Moscow redoubt where the doctor would shoot him full of drugs, brainwash him, kill him. Now, Lofton was going home. "I don't know what to say."

Dobrynyn stared at him. "I can only...."

"The body is set, Colonel," suggested Ullanov.

Dobrynyn's head snapped to Ullanov. "Where's the pistol?"

"Right here." Ullanov pulled a single-shot large bore-flare pistol from his belt.

"The gasoline, Josef?" Dobrynyn asked.

"Well laced with naphtha, Colonel. It will be a hot fire. We should do it now before too much rain gets in there and--"

"Stop, all of you! What is this?"

Their heads spun. The KGB doctor swayed in dimness ten feet away. He was hatless, and rain ran down his face and mixed with blood. His automatic pistol was raised.

Ullanov tensed and growled. His thumb caught the sling of his AK74.

Dobrynyn grabbed the sergeant's elbow and said in a low voice, "Not now, Josef."

Lofton took a step to the side.

"Stay right there, don't move. What are those fuel cans for?" Sadka weaved up to Ullanov. He shook his head and his eyes focused. "Who is that man in the car? Why are you just standing around?" He turned and saw Lofton, then jammed the pistol in his stomach. "My prisoner! Where are his handcuffs?"

He jumped behind Lofton, shoved the pistol in his back and clamped an arm around his throat. "Drop your weapons. You, there, Sergeant! It's obvious that flare gun isn't going to be used to summon help. What is this all--"

Lofton jabbed backward with his elbow. The pistol muzzle arced away from his spine and fired into the rain, but Sadka's arm gripped his neck tighter. Lofton twisted. He grabbed Sadka's wrist, forcing the pistol straight in the air as it fired again. They were eye to eye. Lofton's ribs shrieked as his right hand found Sadka's chin and nose. Then he crawled his palm over the doctor's gaping mouth and worked his fingers toward the bulging eyes.

Two other hands grabbed Sadka's wrist--Dobrynyn's--and brought the pistol slowly down. Dr. Sadka bent his knees slightly, then raised up with a growl. Dobrynyn pulled the pistol down further. Ullanov stepped in and fumbled at the automatic just as Lofton, five inches from Sadka's nose, threw a knee hard in his groin.

Sadka gasped in pain. His wrist came down suddenly to his head. The pistol barked.

The KGB doctor's face ballooned slightly and a rush of white and deep red spewed from his left temple. Sadka's eyes glazed, one rolled back. He went limp and the pistol fell with a splash.

"Jesus!" Lofton muttered, then dropped Dr. Sadka in the mud. They stood over the body, their mouths open.

Ullanov spat, "Clinic ghoul! He runs a floor, he has--had thirty patients, if that's what you call them." His eyes bored through Lofton. "I don't care if you are American, Russian, or Bolivian; this man got what he deserved."

"Maybe so," Dobrynyn said, "but it wasn't supposed to happen this way. We were supposed to save him from the flaming car with just a few burns, then haul him unconscious to the main gate and send him to the dispensary."

"What now?" Lofton asked his brother.

They looked at each other and nodded silently.

They bent to pick up the corpse, but Ullanov nudged them aside. "I'll take care of it. It'll be my pleasure." He looked at Lofton again. "Really, Commander--uh--Mr. Lofton, this man was the KGB's own devil. Don't let his slang fool you. On his orders, his squad ruined one of my men's legs at Baikonur. They had to amputate. It was needless. And a friend of mine, an old platoon sergeant, went through his program and was one of the few this man released. The sergeant's close to being an idiot now. And I think you realize now that you were to be Dr. Sadka's star pupil."

Ullanov shook his head, carried Dr. Sadka to the car, and bent to place him inside. "Colonel, do you mind if I fix his skull to obscure the bullet wound?"

"Hurry. We've only thirtyfive minutes."

Crunching sounds reached their ears through the rain.

Lofton winced. "Where was I held?"

"You were a guest in the old Petropavlovsk waterfront town hall, built in 1910. It's now Spetsnaz Brigade HQ. Had you chosen to arrive five months later, you could have stayed in the new KGB building, now under construction. The ELINT Department will be on the top two floors, executive and administrative offices are on the next five. You would have resided in detention cells, interrogation chambers and experimental laboratories in the subbasements."

Lofton stiffened. "You're Spetsnaz. Were those your men who barricaded the docks around the *Kunashiri Maru*, boarded her, and cast off her towlines?"

"No. I just got here. Sadka told me about it, though." He toed a rain puddle with his boot, "Naval Infantry boarded the ship, wrecked her radios, then cast off the dock lines. The rest was a KGB operation." Dobrynyn looked at Lofton. "Did you see what happened?"

Lofton nodded.

"Ready, Colonel," Ullanov said.

The brothers stared at each other.

Lofton paused. "It was horrible. All those guns blasting away. Those poor people didn't have a chance, there were women aboard, too." He looked down.

"I really don't understand it," Dobrynyn ventured. "Sinking the trawler was very unusual. I heard even those KGB clods were skittish about it."

Lofton grit his teeth. "Renkin."

"Who?"

"A man back in the US. He--"

"Colonel?" Ullanov walked up.

"Go ahead, Josef. We'd better move back."

The three stepped away about thirty paces. Ullanov drew the flare pistol from his belt. He flipped open the barrel, chambered a cartridge, snapped it shut, took a careful stance, aimed, and fired.

Ullanov's flare sputtered through a graceful arc, ricocheted off the door post, and landed just outside the car.

"Another?" asked Lofton.

"Don't think so," said Dobrynyn.

The car went up with a bright whoosh. They jumped back from the magnesium bright explosion. Then the fuel tank blew up with a concussive "whack" singeing Lofton's hair. They ran for the embankment. He still felt the whitehot intensity at his back as he gained the roadway, out of breath.

They turned and looked back. A sodden tree, its branches hanging over the wreck, had caught fire and threw off steam; it hissed and crackled in the rain. The car glowed orange and red, the tires were aflame, and all four doors were blown open. Nothing inside looked recognizable.

Lofton thought of his Audi in the Long Beach Marina. It seemed like decades ago. "Thatcher," he said softly.

Ullanov spat, then picked up his two empty five-gallon gas cans. He would dispose of them later.

"Let's go," Dobrynyn said, "we're running out of time." They turned north and started up the road into the rain.

Lofton trotted behind the other two. His ribs ground in pain; he tried the balls of his feet, weight forward. It was a little better, but his chest hurt if he took a step wrong.

The rain eased, he could see a darkness, the bay, off to his left. How much time? He looked for his Casio. Gone, melted down, along with the poor derelict who last wore it.

The road curved right. "Nalacheva Tunnel's that way." Dobrynyn threw a thumb, then swung left. They abandoned the road and headed straight for the beach. A large mountain rose through the mist, cliffs plummeted to the waterline where wavelets lapped at the beach. Their feet sank in saturated sand, slowing their progress, as they began to weave among tank sized boulders.

Dobrynyn slowed to let Lofton catch up. "About five hundred yards, Commander."

"Brad," Lofton puffed.

Dobrynyn eyed his brother. "After that, we've got a clear beach. There's a hole in the fence and another two hundred yards to the seaplane ramp. We should just make it."

Lofton's lungs raged as he frantically scrambled up a large rock behind the other two.

"How was your obstacle training, Brad?" Dobrynyn tossed over his shoulder. He perched on top of the rock, then jumped a wide gap to another huge boulder.

"It was--eyuhh." He was dizzy but managed to follow Dobrynyn, over a twenty-foot chasm.

The rain had stopped, light glowed around the bend. The air base. Maybe another fifty yards of these monstrous rocks.

Dizzy, rasping, he vaulted for another boulder and stumbled. His hand found the boulder's ridge but granite tore at his fingernails as he slipped, then fell into the blackness.

He knew he'd bounced; he sat up blinking, his head whirled. Where were the airfield lights? He couldn't see. Where--yes, between the boulders.

Hands on his shoulders; a face, his own. He squinted. Me? A beard?

He heard, "Let's wait two minutes, Josef, then we'll carry him."

He was too winded to speak. Nothing wrong except those damn ribs. They felt broken. Sadka was a quack. He'd pronounced them healed. The man really had been in a hurry.

"You've been a civilian too long, Brad," Dobrynyn said

"My...damn ribs..." Lofton sputtered.

"That's right. I'd forgotten. They're broken. Sadka didn't give a damn. He wanted us to get going right away."

He looked up. "Us?"

"Yes. I was to go with you, study you, become you--"

"Become me?"

"Yes. They wanted to send me back in your place. Sadka was..." Dobrynyn checked his watch. "Damnit. Come on, Josef, let's go."

They hoisted Lofton to his feet and guided him through the remaining boulders. Soon, they crunched on gravel. He raised his head and saw the airfield's lights stretching off to his right. Buildings and enormous hangars rose on the other side of the field. A row of sleek, sweptwing MiG29 Fulcrum fighters glistened with rain, their light gray tails probed the sky.

"Five minutes before Alex starts engines. There, see? You can see his plane through the fence."

Lofton was too woozy to keep his head up as he stumbled along. They pushed him down; his shoulder scraped on fencing wire.

Ullanov asked, "How is he going to do a two-mile swim, Colonel?"

Lofton managed, "No problem, I'll be rested by the time I get there. Immersion suit will give me buoyancy. Float, kick, rest, float, kick.... Just hope for an onshore current." He trudged between them, thankful he was past those enormous boulders.

"I'll have Alex give him a one-man survival raft. He'll be all right. Look, we're almost there. Alex said he would meet us behind this shed--hold on," Dobrynyn growled.

They heard the high pitched whine. Lofton peered around the two Spetsnaz. A high gull-wing amphibian squatted on a concrete ramp. Facing them, its port turboprop wound up to full power for a moment, then dropped to idle.

"No," Dobrynyn shouted. "Where's Alex? He said he would wait for us here, and we're on time." He checked his watch. Both engines were turning. The twin-tailed plane, it looked like an old P5M with a thin torpedolike radome, sat on its landing gear, its propellers flashing arcs in the soft ramp lights.

"Look." Ullanov squeezed them into the shed's gloom. Headlights probed the concrete pad, then a jeeptype vehicle, spewing mist, ground down the access road, swung a half circle and stopped next to the fuselage.

A man jumped out. Lofton squinted to see the shoulderboards of a captain second rank, who pounded on the fuselage near a waisthigh hatch. Propeller blast tore at his overcoat. He held his combination cap on with one hand, the other gripped a shiny briefcase. Something glinted; the briefcase was chained to his wrist.

Dobrynyn bit his thumbnail and sagged. "A courier, damnit! They must have manifested him at the last minute."

The fuselage door pushed open against the propwash. Two hands reached out and pulled the scrambling captain through the hatch. The Be-12's turboprops wound up for a moment, it moved forward, then braked on its right main and rotated toward the ramp.

The three stooped in mud as they watched the Be-12's running and landing lights wink on. She waddled down the ramp and splashed into the bay, where her turboprops wound to full power. The Be-12 nosed into the light chop of Avachinskaya Guba and was lost in propwash during her takeoff run. In thirty seconds she was airborne; her navigation lights gracefully skimmed the water for a moment, then gained altitude and blinked toward the channel entrance.

Lofton watched the Be-12's lights recede over Mys Bezymyannya and the Pacific Ocean. He looked at Dobrynyn.

"Tomorrow night," Dobrynyn muttered. "We'll try it then."

17

At 1:45 P.M., Ted Carrington's green Jaguar XJ-S pulled from the brick house in Kalorama Circle and turned on Massachusetts Avenue. It eased through light traffic and headed downtown.

It took fifteen minutes to reach the Executive Office Building, a gray, Civil War era structure on the White House grounds at the corner of Pennsylvania Avenue and Seventeenth Street. Carrington parked his Jaguar a block away and pushed through the early afternoon crowd.

Inside the EOB, he pinned his ID to his breast pocket, chatted with the lobby guard as he signed in, and caught a packed elevator to the third floor.

He walked to the office. The door's brass lettering announced:

Dr. Felix L. Renkin
National Security Council
Department of Congressional Liaison
Suite 386

With a nod to the receptionist, Carrington walked through a paneled double door to a large, wellappointed anteroom. Renkin's secretary eyed him, then went back to her word processor.

"How long, Martha?" Carrington stood before a Queen Anne sofa and thumbed a copy of *Fortune*.

"Soon. He's finishing with Senator Phillips. I just buzzed him."

"I need twenty minutes."

"Five."

"Martha, it's important."

"Five, Ted. He's due at the Pentagon in half an hour to meet with General Marquette."

"I'll drive him. He doesn't know it yet, but we have to stop by the house."

"OK, ten minutes. But first I need him for three minutes myself."

The door opened and young Senator John Phillips's well televised six-foot-five-inch frame and shock of prematurely white hair filled the entrance. Behind him walked a sportcoated aide. Felix Renkin, ever the friendly host, managed to nudge his guests through the foyer with small talk.

Renkin looked at Carrington. They nodded curtly. Carrington casually dropped a large manila envelope on the coffee table, turned his back, and flipped through his magazine.

Senator Phillips's face angled down toward Renkin. "This has been most helpful. I really appreciate your time, Dr. Renkin, and--what?"

Phillips's aide whispered in his ear.

"Oh, yes. A minor thing, I almost forgot. The V-22 Ospreys. Are you aware of the situation?"

Renkin nodded.

"Well, the issue still isn't settled. There just has to be a better way. I may be new at this, but Armed Services wants a complete accounting of your opplan, and I understand GAO has asked the same thing. Plus, we have to know, must know, what the president's intentions are. We've gone along with you so far, but there are too many contingencies."

Renkin took a half step back and folded his arms. "For example?"

The senator's eyes darted to Carrington, then to Martha. She avoided his glance, tapping at her word processor. His voice lowered as he put his hands on his hips. "Well, why do you want the V22s in the first place? That's supposed to be a Marine program and we still haven't funded a production run. DoD may kill the program without us and yet you have a coproduction order with...with..."

Phillips's aide whispered in his ear.

"--Federal Technologies for three of them. Do you plan to napalm a Central American jungle?"

"You told us to buy them, Senator."

"What?" Phillips's face colored. He dropped his hands.

"Yes, that's right," Felix Renkin said mildly. "Your committee recommended last year that we buy five, not three, as a loss leader, even though it was evident we didn't need them. We have plenty of hovering equipment."

Phillips looked at his aide.

The man nodded slowly.

"I wasn't aware." Phillips took a deep breath and looked to the ceiling. "Is it too late to rescind the purchase?"

"No, of course not, but it will take full council action to reverse the process. The V22s have been committed to clients."

"Which clients."

Renkin smiled slightly and shook his head.

"All right." Phillips ran a hand through his hair. "Will a recission require the president's vote?"

"Not in this matter. And as far as the National Security Council goes, only a deputy or an authorized representative from each department would have a voice in this situation. That includes," Renkin ticked off his fingers, "the Departments of Defense Policy, Intelligence, National Security, Geographic Areas, and Legal Counsel. Also, the president's assistant for national security affairs has to review the action, along with an undersecretary from the Departments of State and Defense. But those are just confirmations, endorsements so to speak."

Renkin looked up to the senator. "You understand, John, that those slots more or less form our administrative quorum. Of course, I'll be glad to carry the ball here for you at the Congressional Liaison Department." He palmed the senator's elbow, and the aide snapped the door open. "If it were of an operational or threat analysis nature, John, then each of the directors would have to vote on the action, along with the chairman of the Joint

Chiefs and the director of the CIA and, oh, yes, the president." A smile drew across Renkin's lips, light caromed off his baldness.

Carrington grinned to himself and switched to a copy of *Time*.

Senator Phillips walked through the door. "Thank you, Dr. Renkin. I'm glad we don't have to bother the Oval Office with it."

Renkin gripped the knob. "I appreciate your coming over, Senator. Say, how are you and Gladys enjoying Washington? Are you settled yet? We should have dinner at the Jockey Club some evening."

"Well, yes. We would enjoy that."

"Fine John. Let's do it soon."

The door closed. Renkin stared at it, his hands behind his back. "Yes, Carrington."

"We have to talk, Doctor. I have the research."

"Can it wait?"

"I don't think so, sir."

"Martha?"

She spun in her chair, "You're due at General Marquette's in twentyfive minutes. And I need--"

"Call over there and postpone for an hour." Renkin waved Carrington into his office, followed him in, and shut the door. "Go ahead. What is it that won't keep until this evening?."

"This, Dr. Renkin. I finished a little while ago and it has me concerned." Carrington drew a thick report and handed it over. "This operation has a lot of loose ends. I've been worried from the start and now--"

"I don't have time to go through all that."

"Just the three marked sections, sir."

"Very well. Please sit."

It was an extensive clinical document. Renkin flipped pages quickly while Carrington took the sofa. "Yes, the studies of identical twins separated as infants." He eyed Carrington, turned to the summary section, and sat in a leather armchair. He reached over his desk, poured water from a silver carafe, and sipped.

Carrington had highlighted a section that stated: "identical twins raised together develop traits to establish individual identities between them-selves. Those raised apart have nothing to inhibit their genetic behavioral preferences and turn out with strikingly similar personalities and predilections."

Renkin looked at Carrington and flipped to the next marked page. The highlighted section asked: "Is our behavior influenced primarily by our culture? Our environment? Our creeds and nationalities? Or is our behavior influenced by our genetic structure as these studies suggest?"

Renkin looked at his watch and lay the report on his desk. "I'm due at Marquette's office. What's on your mind?"

"Two wingnuts. Not one. Lofton's double, his brother, will be exactly like him: unreliable. He may pull something like Lofton did in San Diego or even Long Beach."

Renkin snapped, "Yes, but they grew up in totally dissimilar countries. Don't you think they would have overriding cultural differences?"

"Possibly, sir. But we don't know how vast the differences are, or for that matter, how similar. We do know the other twin is a Spetsnaz. And Lofton's a SEAL. To me that goes in line with what the report is saying about 'genetic preferences.' They're dangerous and unpredictable."

Renkin rubbed his chin.

"And that's not the worst part."

"Yes?"

"I almost missed it. Chapter Three, as marked. It says that twins' finger-prints are not identical--"

"What? Hatch assured me his people said there were no problems in that area."

"I realize that. This happened so fast, my guess is they were careless and missed it. But when I saw that," Carrington waved a hand at the report, "I put a call in to an FBI friend. He just called back and confirmed that iden-tical twins *do* have distinguishing fingerprints. The differences are small, but subtle, so there *is* a way to tell them apart. That would trigger any decent security check, especially the Jenson Industries security force. They're top-notch."

Carrington exhaled loudly. "My recommendation is that we get out and cut our losses. Tell Mr. Hatch to get rid of Lofton. Now. The twin should be killed, too, if he's spent any time with Lofton. Something could get back to us." Carrington sighed, his shoulders sagged. "Besides, this genetic stuff has me worried. It's a weird feeling. Lofton could become close to his brother. If one dies, retribution, maybe? We don't need that."

Renkin muttered, "Two Loftons. The Soviet could be as intractable as his brother."

"Yes, sir." Carrington crossed a leg. He imagined closed eyes behind Renkin's glasses; the mind would be superactive.

Renkin sat forward, bent his head, and massaged his temples. "You were right to come. The switch must be called off. I'll go home and draft a message to the art dealer."

Carrington relaxed. He had received a pat on the back.

Renkin rose and walked around his desk. "I'll have Lofton taken out immediately. And his twin, too, if he has been exposed to Lofton and the *X3* operation."

He picked up his phone. "Martha? Please call General Marquette's office and reschedule our meeting to tomorrow. Something has come up."

"Sir. A second message is coming in for you. Do you--"

"Yes. I'll wait."

At 5:05 P.M. in the Washington, D.C., Soviet embassy, Captain Second Rank Yuri Borodine closed the door and walked behind the crypto clerk to watch the coding machine decipher another message. A yellow light blinked and the machine stopped. The page scrolled up, was torn off and handed to him.

TO: SPILLOVER
FM: MAXIMUM EBB

OPERATION SWITCH CANCELED. TOO MANY CONTINGENCIES TIED TO TWIN ASPECT ON THIS SIDE. FULL REPORT/ DEAD DROP 43. IMPERATIVE YOU ELIMINATE LOFTON ASAP. RECOMMEND ELIMINATE TWIN IF DETAILS OP SWITCH KNOWN TO HIM PARTIC-ULARLY THE LOFTON/X3 ASPECTS. PLS ACKNOWLEDGE.

Borodine took a secretarial chair, sat heavily, and wiped his brow. Relief swarmed over him. Yes, cancel operation switch. He'd gone too far with Renkin's adventuresome plan in the first place. Especially in light of the "Most Secret" message he'd received from Belousov five minutes ago. Belousov! Until now, the admiral had never contacted him directly. Usually Perelygin, Belousov's deputy chief of staff, signed correspondence and issued his orders.

Borodine whipped the admiral's message from the folder:

TO: SPILLOVER
FM: COMRBPACFLT

INTERROGATIVE:
1. OPERATION SWITCH.
2. MAXIMUM EBB RETIREMENT, STATUS
ADVISE ASAP.

The first question, when juxtaposed with the second, meant Belousov was itchy about switching the brothers and was telling Borodine to tactfully drop the whole thing. Fine. Euphoria over the X-3's capture had motivated Borodine to go along with the proposed exchange. And it kept Renkin happy. But later, Borodine had grown nervous about it. Belousov must have felt the same way even though Sadka's reports had been extremely positive. The Psychopharmacologist was enthused, he wanted to get to work right away and had accelerated the schedule.

Borodine absently rubbed his leg. It tingled and fell asleep as he looked back to Renkin's message:

CONTINGENCIES TIED TO TWIN ASPECT

He would have to read Renkin's report to find out what had actually gone wrong, but that didn't matter now. He would cancel the ill-conceived venture at once and learn the details later.

His eye jumped down to another line on Renkin's message:

IMPERATIVE YOU ELIMINATE LOFTON ASAP....ELIMINATE TWIN....

Renkin's tone was immediate, almost urgent, and Borodine reminded himself to look into that, too. He checked his watch. Sadka and his subjects were airborne and were due to arrive at Kubinka Airdrome in another two hours. All Borodine had to do was send the order and Sadka would have to kill the twins within minutes after landing. Belousov, reluctant about dealing with Sadka and his KGB holdouts in the first place, would gladly endorse the command. The admiral's clout would override any hesitancy from the men with green shoulderboards.

Rubbing his knee, Borodine considered the ramifications of Belousov's second question. He hadn't pushed Renkin's retirement as Belousov originally intended. Borodine would have to figure a way to further delay it until after his intelligence coup--his ticket to Novgorod.

For Dr. Felix Renkin was going to deliver a brand-new Bell-Boeing V22 Osprey, an advanced-technology rotarywing aircraft, which cost millions to develop. It featured state-of-the-art composite materials, the newest electronics, and revolutionary tiltable twin Allison T406-AD-400 turboprop engines with 6150 shaft horsepower each.

The National Security Council had five of the tiltrotor aircraft on order, two of which were scheduled for black missions in South America. They could do strikes like the one the U.S. had done in Panama, but more efficiently, with far greater range and larger payload than helicopters. Renkin agreed that a V-22 would conveniently be shot down in a remote spot, with Borodine's people waiting close at hand.

Renkin had negotiated hard; $8.5 million with an advance deposit of $250,000. Belousov must have forgotten about the advance, which was a lot of money for a delivery two years hence. The coproduction order was a stroke of genius. If the V-22 program were canceled, Borodine would still have an Osprey from the NSC's inventory now secretly under construction at Federal Technologies.

In his mind, Borodine sketched his reply to Admiral Belousov. So far, results were positive. Thanks to Dr. Renkin, they'd rid themselves of the defector and a CIA asset, one who had effectively penetrated Petropavlovsk and could have become even more dangerous; they had saved the Ivy Bells and Jet Stream operations and as a bonus had captured the *X-3* with all its marvelous secrets free of charge. That alone was worth $250,000 and he would point that out to Belousov.

On the other hand, Borodine assumed Belousov was worried the KGB had dumped Renkin on the Red Banner Pacific Fleet Intelligence Directorate to avoid terrible recriminations if Renkin was exposed. Belousov's thick mind would conjure up an embellished macro picture of negative world opinion; losing most-favored-nation trading status with the U.S., losing lines of credit, losing face, and tarnishing the *glasnost* image.

But Belousov didn't know the man as Borodine did. Dr. Renkin was a highly experienced asset incapable of taking an impetuous step that would blow his cover. The man was just too careful for that. He handled himself well and was intelligent enough to ask for help; he'd done so in California. Surely he could last another eighteen months or so. Enough time to consolidate the V-22 situation.

Pins and needles coursed through Borodine's leg. He stood and almost lost his balance. By all means, cancel Operation Switch, eliminate the twins, and take care of Doctor Renkin, his ticket to Novgorod. The retirement question would be broached in another two to three months. That should satisfy Belousov for the time being.

He stumbled, catching the crypto operator's raised eyebrow. "Yes, I'd like to dictate two messages. The first goes to Pacific Fleet Intelligence in Vladivostok."

Dobrynyn handed Lofton a steaming mug of tea and walked to the window. "Don't worry. Alex does his guardmail run six days a week. You'll get out tonight."

Lofton, wanting the practice, answered Dobrynyn's Russian. "All right. You said you were married? What was her name?"

Dobrynyn lifted the curtain and peered out. Petropavlovsk would wake up soon. "Irenna." He sighed. "She was an ice skater...Olympic caliber. They wouldn't send her to the Lake Placid Olympics...."

"Why?"

Dobrynyn studied the street, almost dawn, no unusual activity. He eased the curtain back, finding his fists were doubled. "You. They were afraid she would contact you. That somehow, both of us would defect."

"That's ridiculous. I had no idea."

Dobrynyn tried to relax. "Doesn't matter now. It wasn't a good marriage anyway."

"What happened?"

"She left me and joined Aeroflot. Married a pilot, divorced him, and married her skating partner. They run an ice-skating gymnasium now."

"The Lake Placid Olympics. 1980. Is that when she left you?"

"No. 1981."

"A bimbo. Me too, 1981. But, her name was Ann. I got a `Dear John' letter after she cleaned out our checking and savings accounts." Lofton filled his lungs, his ribs felt much better. Ullanov had done a good job of taping them.

"Dear John?"

"You know, when a woman dumps on her serviceman husband. She sends the letter and he's reading it just as a bad guy crawls to the edge of his foxhole with a live grenade in each hand. In my case, I'd been working almost three weeks solid. I came home late one night and found the letter on the bed."

"Yes. I know about `Dear John' letters." Dobrynyn told him about Irenna's, then asked, "Your wife's name was Ann?"

Lofton said, "The marriage lasted almost two years. It was strictly physical, although I didn't realize it at the time. We must have been in bed eighteen of those twenty-four months."

"What happened to her?"

"Married a dentist, cleaned him out, and moved to Florida. Last I heard, she'd married a seventy-two-year-old real estate magnate with a private island in the Caribbean."

They fell silent. Dobrynyn sat in a creaky wooden chair and looked around the apartment. A lucky find. What was the girl's name? The one stationed at the submarine base? Tanya, Ullanov's girlfriend. The hot, blond communications clerk the sergeant had met in Libya. One of Ullanov's intercontinental string of women, she'd given him the signet ring he still wore. It had taken Ullanov only hours to reestablish their relationship after they'd flown in with Sadka.

Tanya's place was sparse: a kitchenette, a small living room, and a pull-down bed. But she had somehow wangled a bathroom with a shower; a luxury.

Dobrynyn checked his watch: 5:37. Ullanov was due back soon. Dobrynyn had sent him to contact Alex's crew chief and check the situation at the Spetsnaz brigade HQ after their wild, threeman motorcycle ride from Rakovaya. His brother had showered and now rested comfortably on Tanya's perfumed sheets.

Dobrynyn asked, "Why did you leave the SEALS? You would be a major or a lieutenant colonel now."

"That's military rank. The SEALS are Navy. I would be a lieutenant commander or commander, maybe even a captain." He looked at Dobrynyn. "But, if the truth be known, I hit an officer."

"What?" Dobrynyn's jaw dropped.

"Yeah." Lofton looked around. "On the way back from Vietnam. We stopped in Honolulu for our first real liberty and decided to start at the O Club for cheap drinks before we hit town. A drunken reserve colonel was pawing the cocktail waitress. The guy ran his hands up her dress, she was just a kid. I don't know," Lofton exhaled. "I saw red."

"I hit 'im. Broke his nose. The guy had served a term in Congress. He knew enough people to make sure I was passed over for lieutenant commander. Charges were never pressed, but he got it done and I resigned from the Navy. So, I--Anton, what's wrong?"

Dobrynyn rocked forward on his chair. "Do you know why I'm in this hole of civilization?" He waved an arm. "Volcanoes, rain, granite, snow, forty-knot winds, ice, cold ocean, three movie theaters for two hundred thousand people. Plenty of bars, though, and thousands of liters of vodka, even narcotics."

"I thought you were stationed in Baku. That Sadka brought you here for a switch."

"No. Petropavlovsk is typical of the assignments I've had. I've always been marked because I...we were German born. And I was marked because I had an American brother. They never let up."

He looked at Lofton and caught his gaze. "I also decked an officer, as you say. I broke the bastard's nose and would have killed him if it hadn't been for Josef. That sealed *my* career."

It was Lofton's turn to look amazed.

"Yes, yes," Dobrynyn drove his left fist into his right palm. "His damned nose."

"What was it about?"

"Did you hear about one of our submarines running aground near the Karlskrona Naval Base in Sweden? It was in 1981."

"Sure. The 'Whiskeyontherocks' incident. Made all the front pages. It took a few days to get the thing towed off, as I remember."

"Guess who was aboard as a young Spetsnaz?"

Tanya's apartment grew lighter as Dobrynyn told the story. "When we returned, the executive and operations officers were relegated to menial duties. The *zampolit* was cashiered also, but he got to me first. He had friends like your colonel, who set up something special for the captain, Josef, and me: They sent us to a terrorist training camp in Libya. You, I mean Americans...bombed us. Zuleyev, our captain was killed. Josef was almost killed, too.

Lofton traced a finger over Tanya's pillow lace.

"That's when we were transferred to the Caspian Sea Flotilla. Baku." Dobrynyn opened his hands. "They like to send us on raids into Iran when we're not keeping the Armenians at bay."

"You're like outlaws?"

"Umm."

"You grew up in Leningrad?"

"Yes. I even had a foster father, once."

"So, you took his name."

Dobrynyn's eyes grew unfocused. "No. It wasn't that simple. Theo Kunitsa adopted me in Berlin..."

"Kunitsa? My foster father was Lofton. How did you become Dobrynyn?"

"I was known as Manfried Lubeck when I lived with him. Kunitsa was an NKVD sergeant who was killed on some sort of bungled spy mission in the West. I was sent to an orphanage, which wouldn't accept someone so openly of

German heritage, and they wouldn't let me take Kunitsa's name. So their first step was to assign what they said was a decent, proper Soviet name. Dobrynyn."

Lofton shook his head. "Orphanages were not fun."

"I was at several, actually. The first one--" Dobrynyn cocked an ear and stood, hearing a soft tapping. He went to the door and opened it. Ullanov quickly walked in, his face flushed. He was out of breath.

Dobrynyn closed the door softly. "Josef?"

Ullanov sat at the small kitchen table, snatched off his beret, then unshouldered his AK74 and propped it in a corner. He cocked an eye at Lofton. "How do you feel, Commander?"

Lofton sat up. "Civilian--the name's Lofton, and I feel fine."

"Josef, what's wrong?" Dobrynyn stood between them.

Master Sergeant Josef Ullanov looked up at Dobrynyn. "They... there's a general alert out for you, an arrest order. The KGB, Fleet Intelligence, the GRU--everybody. I don't understand it. Even Department Sixteen is in on the act. They sent a team from Moscow to interrogate you. They're due to arrive in two hours or so."

"Sadka," Dobrynyn muttered and sat on the bed. "A botched job. We didn't have time to plan correctly." He looked up. "What about Alex?"

"I couldn't get on the air base. It's--"

"Shhh," Lofton said. Footsteps, two pairs of boots thumped down the hall. Lofton jumped from the bed and put on his shirt. Ullanov grabbed his AK74 and eyed the door. The boots squeaked by, muttering voices receded. A door opened and slammed at the other end. The three looked at one another and relaxed. Lofton finished buttoning his shirt.

"...sealed tight with patrols and dogs. We can't do now what we tried last night." Ullanov shook his head, "This is something much more. It's big. I sense it. The local KGB teams would have investigated the wreck and sifted evidence to assure Sadka's and," he threw a thumb, "Lofton's demise. But that takes time. Yet there is already an arrest order for you specifically from the main Naval Intelligence Directorate in Moscow. That couldn't have happened so soon just because of a car wreck."

"I had to buy time, so I tossed the message. Then I saw a copy of the same message addressed to the KGB with Admiral Belousov's endorsement.

Can you believe that? The admiral of the Red Banner Pacific Fleet endorsing a KGB order to arrest you? And Belousov hates those people, we all know that!

"I couldn't toss that message, it was delivered by messenger directly to Major Pechenga. He showed it to me and asked where you were. I said I didn't know and slipped out the back door a few minutes ago.

"Apparently the local KGB has already sent a team to your quarters, and the brigade HQ is in pandemonium. Pechenga doesn't know what to do. There's a GRU colonel there right now sitting in his office watching every move."

"Good God!" Lofton said.

Dobrynyn nodded to his brother, then eyed Ullanov.

"I don't know, Colonel," the sergeant said, "it might have to do with your brother but..."

"Go on, Josef."

Ullanov sighed. "I have a feeling they don't care if Mr. Civilian here or Dr. Sadka are dead or alive right now. They want you. Period."

"And what about you, Josef?"

"I'll be all right, sir."

"Josef?"

Ullanov looked at the ceiling.

"I see. Are you absent without leave, Josef?"

Ullanov shrugged.

Dobrynyn stood and took a step toward his sergeant.

Lofton said quietly, "Anton."

"What?" Dobrynyn's head whipped to Lofton.

Lofton nodded toward Ullanov, "It looks like he's made a decision. Three, not one or two naval careers are wrecked now."

Dobrynyn tried again. "Josef, damnit, I don't matter. What about your mother? What about," he sputtered, "Tanya? You have people. How can you just walk out on the Navy? You have almost twenty years."

Ullanov turned. "I haven't seen my mother for twelve years. We write, yes, and exchange gifts. But she has terminal cancer; she'll be gone in four to six months." He waved a hand. "Tanya, no, we never were serious, although it seemed so at one time. She's due to be posted to Sevastopol next month and that will be that. No, there will be other girls.

"And, speaking of Tanya, she gets off duty within the hour. In a situation like this, her loyalties will definitely be with the men from Moscow. We should be out of here by then."

Dobrynyn shook his head and stepped close to Lofton. "I still don't know why...all I wanted...was to save you from Sadka, to keep you from that man's drugs and his filthy interrogation chambers."

He turned to Ullanov and spread his palms. "I couldn't help it, Josef. This man--he's my brother. We're the same." He slammed a fist on the table. "And now my life is really botched. They want to arrest me--why?"

"Renkin," Lofton said.

Dobrynyn ran a hand over his face. "Who? You mentioned that name before."

Lofton did the telling quickly. He added details about his own theft of *Brutus*, the refueling and shootout at berth 209, and why he chose to come to Petropavlovsk first to intercept PARALLAX and PITCHFORK aboard the *Kunashiri Maru* before he ran south to disarm the CAPTORs. "Renkin is a powerful man in America. He's the reason I'm here and because of him one 125 American sailors are now dead along with those on the *Kunashiri Maru*."

Ullanov said, "Commander--"

"Please. It's Brad."

"All right, Mr. Brad." Ullanov arched an eyebrow. "I may have some interesting news for you."

The twins looked at him.

"A strange message on Pechenga's desk caught my eye this morning. It was mixed in with Colonel Dobrynyn's arrest order. A pink information copy, it was a message addressed to the Pacific Fleet Intelligence Directorate from Submarine Rescue Squadron Eight. It said Rescue Eight retrieved one of two U.S. Navy CAPTOR mines from the ocean floor near the Kurils yesterday morning. They used the *Alatau*." He looked at Dobrynyn, who nodded. "They had trouble grappling the second CAPTOR so they blew it up, because, and this really seemed strange to me, they were on a strict time schedule. They had been ordered to clear the sector by zero five hundred and apparently just made it."

Lofton smiled, then beamed. "That's wonderful news!" He sat on the bed, then lay back and threw his fists over his head. "Ouch, damned ribs." With a grimace, he rose and massaged his side. "Those guys are still alive, aboard the *Truman*. That means Kirby got to his Navy buddy. It's amazing they let you guys retrieve it. They must have gone through diplomatic channels. And that tells me Renkin could be in deep trouble by now."

They looked at the floor for a moment. "We're in the muck here, too." said Dobrynyn. "We need to think about how to--"

"Do you guys want to get out?" Lofton interrupted.

They stared at him.

"Take me back to *Brutus*. If they haven't screwed him up too much I can get us out of here, anywhere you want to go."

Dobrynyn cast an eye to Ullanov before replying. "That is out of the question."

"Why?"

Dobrynyn looked down. "I know this Spetsnaz brigade well. In fact, I trained many of them. They're a minisubmersible group and were assigned the task of preparing your submarine for transport. I inspected their work. Your submarine is secure now and ready for towing to Vladivostok. From there it goes aboard a special rail car across country to the Leningrad Naval Yard."

"Soviet naval headquarters?"

"Yes, the plans are to disassemble it there."

"Have they been inside yet?"

"Two men took a quick round of photographs. A shipyard engineer went through to make sure everything was shut off. Besides that, they had orders not to touch it."

"Where is it now?"

"Aboard a barge under tight security in the KGB naval basin. They made a wooden cradle, covered it with canvas and chained the submarine to the deck. A fake superstructure was built around that to disguise it as cargo barge because of your," he twirled a finger in the air, "spy satellites. It's in the KGB naval basin under tight security. It's due to be towed out tomorrow."

Lofton stood and paced for a moment. "All right. Sounds like we have nothing to lose."

Dobrynyn exchanged glances with Ullanov. "What?"

"Let's swim in. It's not as if we don't know how. We can blow the barge out from under *Brutus* with limpets."

Dobrynyn rubbed his chin. "Not a bad idea, except for the swimming. The people in the KGB naval basin are on a full-time war footing."

"Why?"

"Belousov ordered a battalion sized assault three months ago. We do this all the time." He explained about the Baikonur raid and how they had met Dr. Sadka, adding, "And here there were fistfights, stabbings, and unfortunately, a fatality--a shooting." The new dawn softly illuminated Dobrynyn's smile. "One of theirs, an officer.

"The KGB commander was fired and the new one is an animal. He's just finished building guard towers around the perimeter, the fence was electrified. Machine gun nests are set up with overlapping fire and are manned on a twentyfour-hour basis.

"That's why your submarine is in there. And the reason we can't swim in is that they installed underwater sound detectors and lights. Small boats patrol around the clock and they throw hand grenades into the water at the slightest provocation." Dobrynyn spread his palms. "Even without that, swimming is extremely difficult. The currents are treacherous through the entrance. Sometimes three to four knots."

Lofton muttered, "Damnit! If only there was a way to get in there, we could do it." He bit his thumbnail and looked up. "How about a disguise? Maybe...maybe steal a truck. Go in with the meat delivery. Or dress as shipfitters and--"

"--There may be a way." Ullanov raised his eyebrows.

They looked at him.

"Tanya and I took a walk on the waterfront yesterday morning. I saw one or two scows, garbage barges. T-4s. They're serviced at the public docks, in front of an abandoned paint factory. The scows make their runs at night."

"You're sure the paint factory is abandoned?" Lofton asked.

Ullanov nodded.

"All right. We hide there today and grab the scow tonight."

"A garbage scow." Dobrynyn rubbed his chin.

"It'll take us right up to the barge where *Brutus* is, won't it?" Lofton said.

Dobrynyn and Ullanov looked at each other. They nodded. Dobrynyn said, "Let's go."

18

Seaman Second Class Vasiliy Bubnov was angry. It was past time to shove off. Instead, he stood waiting in the canvas-topped pilothouse of his sixty-two-foot landing craft. At seventy tons, the Soviet T-4 closely resembled an overgrown U.S. Navy LCM6. The well deck had been designed to carry a mediumsized tank or eighty soldiers, both launched off a retractable bow ramp, which, on this boat, had been welded open parallel to the waterline. Bubnov's T-4 looked as if it had never been maintained. Her well deck was half full of garbage they had collected from merchant ships this afternoon. A small bulldozer lurked in the aft section to push the refuse off the ramp when at sea.

Where the hell was his crew? First, Yablochkov was missing, and now Kubchek. Idiots! Bubnov checked his instruments. The battery levels looked tolerable for once and they had just topped their fuel tanks. If the starboard engine wasn't too bad, they might do the trip in the allotted four hours instead of the six or seven it had been taking.

Come on! Looking at hulking, run-down waterfront structures, Bubnov ran the back of his hand over his nose and wiped it on his parka. The cannery had been abandoned three years ago, replaced by a new one across the bay. And now, the paint factory was shut down. Labor costs. They simply closed them, and with each closing he lost some of his best customers, people who liked the coke and hash he provided, courtesy of the Cubans. He had to depend on Navy customers now, but that made him nervous, and he vowed to cultivate a new group of civilians, soon.

Where the hell were those two? Yablochkov had simply wandered off. Kubchek said he was going to take a piss. Maybe they'd found a card game. Maybe they were smoking some of his stuff. If they were, he'd kill them. They knew that, too.

Bubnov wiped his nose again, jumped off the T-4 and walked up the dock. Wet, overcast, deserted; nobody was around. Deep shadows cast from downtown lights fell over the wharf. He checked his watch, an imitation Cartier. Damnit! They were due at the KGB naval basin entrance now.

"Kubchek!" he yelled.

Nothing.

Swearing, he walked across two railroad spurs to the paint factory. The offices were on the facade. Kubchek had a mattress stowed in one of them , for the occasions when he became serious about his recreational drug habits.

Peering in a smashed window, Bubnov saw a few cardboard cartons, an overturned chair, and water pooling on the cement floor. Kubchek's mattress lay in the corner, empty.

"Yablochkov, damnit! Kubchek!"

Something creaked. A side door, a barrel-chested man came out. A deep voice rumbled, "You all right, Comrade?" He moved closer.

Bubnov's skin prickled. The man wore a Naval Infantry uniform. No! Spetsnaz! *They're on to me.* He took a step back. "Uh, no. I...was just looking for my detail. We're late."

The man moved closer, within four paces. He grinned with broad white teeth. "Two guys?"

Bubnov swallowed. He tried to speak but could only nod.

"Yeah, I saw them walk by. Said something about going down to the cannery to strip brass."

Impossible! Bubnov, Yablochkov and Kubchek had checked the cannery months ago. There was no brass. Frightened, he turned and--two dark shadows, men, stood before him. An arm swung a short pipe...

. . .

"He's the senior petty officer. Looks like I'm stuck with him," Dobrynyn said. They picked Bubnov up and hurried inside.

Lofton sniffed. "And the smelliest. Glad he's yours."

"Get going. Start the boat." Dobrynyn striped off his shirt.

"Do you need help?"

"No. Hurry, before those guards come back."

"OK."

Lofton and Ullanov ran out. Dobrynyn quickly changed, tied and gagged the sailor, and dragged him down a long dark hall. He didn't know where Ullanov and Lofton had dispersed the others. No matter. He found a door. A closet. He shoved the sailor in and, slamming the door, left him naked except for his underwear.

He quickly ran outside toward the docks and--no! Dobrynyn ducked under a wooden stairway. Two guards with rifles over their shoulders were talking to Ullanov, who stood in the pilothouse. Lofton's dark form hunched over the instrument panel, behind the sergeant. Although the T-4 was moored starboard side to, Dobrynyn heard her port engine ticking over. It looked as if Lofton was trying to start the starboard engine while Ullanov talked with broad gestures.

Dobrynyn cocked an ear. The starboard engine cranked and cranked. Black smoke drifted from her exhaust but the engine didn't catch. One of the guards propped a foot on the gunnel as Ullanov blabbed and waved his hands. The guards laughed. Dobrynyn recognized the pattern of Ullanov's hand movements. It was one of his crudest jokes.

The starboard engine sputtered and caught with a bellow. An enormous cloud spurted from her exhaust and nearly consumed the guards.

Belching a thinner bluish smoke, the engine roared as Lofton jazzed the throttle. The guards spun away from the cloud, coughing and yelling. Ullanov raised his eyebrows and held out his palms. One guard flipped him the finger, his mouth worked. Even in the poor light, Dobrynyn could make out his reddened face before both walked off brushing their uniforms.

Dobrynyn waited until they rounded a corner. He sprinted across the tracks and down the dock and tossed off the bow line while Ullanov undid the stern. The engines roared. Lofton spun the T-4 and idled into Avachin- skaya Guba as Dobrynyn climbed the ladder to the pilothouse. He edged next to Lofton while Ullanov climbed up and propped his AK-74 in the corner.

"It's yours," Lofton said, stepping aside.

Dobrynyn cranked both throttle levers to full power. The twin screws of the flatbottomed, sixtytwo- foot garbage scow bit the water, taking the vessel to its full speed of ten knots. Wavelets thumped under the bow ramp, fine salt spray settling on condensation-covered decks. Twirling the helm, Dobrynyn asked, "How does your new uniform fit, Seaman Lofton?"

"Tight." Lofton tucked in his shirt and zipped the parka. "The guy was taller and much thinner. And, pheeew, it smells." In spite of this, a release swarmed through him, almost overwhelming. His feet were planted on a deck again, it didn't matter what kind, even this odorous wreck.

The black waters of Avachinskaya Guba kicked the bow ramp as Lofton zipped tighter. His breath condensed to mist and he blew on his hands, looking at the nighttime shapes and lights. Water gurgled past and swirled into a long, white wake where Petropavlovsk's downtown lights danced astern. He saw nothing, blackness, to port. To starboard, a low promontory gradually swept away to the narrow plain that accommodated Rakovaya Airport. Overhead, a grayish cast bloomed. No moon, no silhouettes. Thank God for little favors.

"This was a good idea, Josef." Dobrynyn had to shout over the twin diesel's roar. "But we pay a price. I never knew anything could reek like this."

Ullanov lit a cigarette and shouted back, "My father always said, 'why walk when you can ride?'"

"Is there a chart aboard?" Lofton asked.

"Should be." Ullanov rummaged in a shelf under the instrument panel. He pulled out a stained document with a thumb and a forefinger. Unfolding it, he sniffed. "Here." He jabbed a finger toward a thumb-shaped bay in the northern reaches of Avachinskaya Guba. "That's the KGB naval basin."

Dobrynyn scanned the chart in the dim light, switched his eye back to the compass, and adjusted their course slightly left.

Lofton, looking into blackness, asked, "Where is it?"

Ullanov pointed.

Lofton picked out a few low hills off the port bow. Abeam to starboard he recognized Mount Nalacheva near the area where Dr. Sadka and the derelict welder had been cremated in the sedan. Forward of that he saw the runway lights and buildings of Rakovaya Airport and, yes, the seaplane ramp where the Be12 had launched and taken off. Directly ahead, from the darkest, most remote part of Avachinskaya Guba, a flashing red light winked out of the void. A dim light loom glowed behind it. "Looks like a channel marker. Is that it?"

"Yes, it's a breakwater light."

He studied the light. Hills emerged out of the gloom while the T-4 plowed closer. The light became clearer; it stood on the right side of the breakwater, blinking at three-second intervals. "How wide is the entrance?"

Ullanov bent over the chart. "Looks like a hundred feet or so."

"Should be all right."

Dobrynyn nodded and throttled to half speed. "We're getting close." He pointed off the port bow. "That's the main control tower up on Mount Tamleva. They should see our running lights soon. They'll either call us by radio or send out a guard boat. Maybe both."

He turned to Ullanov. "OK, Josef, go on up to the bow, slouch on the ramp, scratch your balls, and look dumb."

The sergeant grabbed his rifle and made for the ladder. "An easy task, Colonel."

"And, Josef--"

"Sir?"

"If we're stopped by a guard boat and they get on to us, don't hesitate. Fire a burst into the pilothouse, then jump. I mean it, jump! Don't wait for us. Head for the beach to starboard, outside the breakwater. We'll meet at the toolshed near the amphib ramp."

"Sir." Ullanov's broad head disappeared down the ladder.

"OK, Brad, your job is to do the same thing. If a guard boat stops us, and I'm pretty sure they will, stay up here with me. When we get inside the breakwater, go below and handle the stern line." He smiled. "You're going to learn how to handle good, solid Soviet garbage soon."

"Can't wait." Lofton bounced on his toes and did some arm stretches; he tingled. Action. Old feelings swarmed through him; Coronado, Cuba,

Lebanon, Sidra, Tripoli, the Red Sea, the Mekong Delta. He rotated his back, testing his ribs. Ullanov had retaped them but he still felt small, fresh bursts of pain. He hoped that was it.

A searchlight blinded them, followed by a shout. The pilothouse glared in hoary light as Lofton covered his eyes. Dobrynyn quickly shoved the gearshift handles down through neutral to reverse, twisted the throttle grips and backed full. He timed it perfectly. The T4 slewed to starboard before it stopped, and with a slight breeze over their port quarter, great clouds of diesel smoke from the sputtering starboard engine wafted toward the searchlight, engulfed it, and turned it to a dull brown. Dobrynyn shifted to neutral and idled the engines. The T4 kept swinging slowly counterclockwise.

"Bastards didn't have their running lights on," Dobrynyn muttered. "I didn't see 'em."

Lofton joined his brother as they leaned out the pilothouse to starboard.

A small patrol boat's prow emerged from the smoke. A man shouted, "Bubnov, you idiot! What the hell are you doing? Haven't you fixed that piece of junk yet? You're late!"

The patrol boat, about fifty feet long, gurgled to their starboard side. KGB soldiers with carbines slung over their shoulders stood on deck about a small amidships pilothouse. Two men slouched by a single twentyfive-millimeter cannon on the foredeck.

Dobrynyn leaned over the rail and shouted down to them. "Bubnov's sick tonight. He's got the trots. They said he was eating garbage. We were assigned this duty at the last minute."

"Who are you?" A different voice from the pilothouse.

"Yushchenko, Sir, Petty Officer Second Class. They detailed us off the *Sposobnyy* only two hours ago."

"Wait." Two officers in the pilothouse put their heads together.

Dobrynyn muttered from the side of his mouth, "In case they say anything, Brad, the *Sposobnyy* is a guided missile destroyer, Kashin class."

"I know."

Dobrynyn arched an eyebrow and continued. "She's from the Baltic Fleet on a goodwill cruise and just got in three days ago from Hanoi. She's anchored midstream down by the naval base. And try not to say too much. Your Russian is good, but your accent is somewhere between a Riga slaughterhouse and a Turkish bordello."

"That'll be one thousand rubles, sir," Lofton squeaked a female falsetto.

"Brad, damnit--"

"Hold on, we're coming aboard." An officer shouted from the patrol boat's pilothouse. The transmission clunked and whined as the fifty-foot craft twisted on her twin screws, water frothing at her stern. Four soldiers, carbines over their shoulders, jumped onto the bow ramp. One stopped and talked to Ullanov for a moment, then followed the other three aft. They approached the heap in the well deck. One grabbed a gaff hook and poked and shoved the trash.

A garrison cap rose up the ladder, green shoulderboards identified a KGB master sergeant. He stopped at chest height, silhouetted by his patrol boat's searchlight. "You people stink. This whole damn boat stinks, and don't screw around with us again with that starboard engine!"

"Sir," Dobrynyn replied.

"Where are you from?"

"Leningrad, sir."

He eyed Lofton. "And you?"

"Kalinin, sir."

"You been ashore yet?"

"No, sir," blurted Dobrynyn. "We're supposed to take on fuel and provisions in the morning. We sail for Nikolayevsk day after tomorrow, sir. They didn't schedule us for liberty here, sir."

The master sergeant shouted forward, "Well, Corporal?"

The reply drifted over rumbling engines, "Nothing, sergeant, just the usual crap."

"Very well, go on back." He waved them to the bow ramp; the three KGB soldiers quickly scrambled and squished their way forward where Ullanov helped them jump to their waiting patrol boat's fantail.

The master sergeant looked up to them. "Just as well you can't make it ashore. Petropavlovsk is a hell hole anyway." He grinned. "This detail is the best liberty you'll draw here." He looked at Lofton. "Kalinin, huh? I used to know a girl from Kalinin. Let's see, her name was Ludmilla. She--"

"Sergeant!" from the patrol boat.

"Coming, sir," he shouted across.

The garrison cap ducked, then reappeared. "And, Yushchenko, fix the starboard side light on this turd. It's out and I'm going to write it up. Somebody will hang by their balls if this boat comes back tomorrow night without a starboard side light. And that means you!" He jabbed a thumb, eyed them both, and descended.

"Sir!" shouted Dobrynyn.

The master sergeant made a long, graceful jump to the patrol boat's midships section. It burbled off into the dark, open bay.

Lofton looked at his brother. Both exhaled with the same thought. Lofton offered, " IDs. He didn't check."

Dobrynyn shrugged. "A flaw in our plan. We were lucky."

"Maybe it *was* the smell."

Dobrynyn jammed the T4's shift levers forward and twisted the throttles to half speed. With right rudder, he set the scow on the basin entrance.

The breakwater's red beacon flashed across their faces every three seconds as they rumbled through the entrance. Guard towers stood on either side, and as he looked up Mount Tamleva's blunt face, Lofton saw the glassed-in control station on its peak. He imagined the uniformed guards inside, studying their sensors, watching every move through night vision binoculars.

Inside, Lofton judged the basin about five hundred yards wide. He could see all the way to the end as it curved gently to the left. Docks, ships, buildings, and warehouses stood on the starboard side. Nothing to port except a perimeter fence and there, Ullanov's target. Two large and two small camouflaged fuel tanks, surrounded by their own perimeter fences, rose darkly into the night. He squinted. Three guards strolled inside the chain-link fence. A refueling pier and small boat docks stood at the water's edge.

Lofton nodded toward the tanks. Dobrynyn said, "Right, the two large ones carry jet fuel for the gas turbine ships, the smaller ones are for diesel." He throttled back. "Here, we better service this icebreaker first."

He swung toward the fantail of a stubby, high superstructure ship with a helo platform on her aft deck. Cyrillic letters were painted on her stern--

Neva. The T4 backed, twisted nicely under the helo deck, and bounced against her rubber tire fenders. Ullanov threw a bow line, Lofton scrambled down and tossed up a stern line.

They looked up as the T-4's engines idled. A loud voice announced, "Dinnertime, Bubnov." Flashes of garbage and trash rained into the T4's well deck with clatters, clanks, and soft plops.

Men drifted away, except one. His voice drifted across softly, hoarsely. "Hey, Bubnov, got any hash tonight?"

Dobrynyn looked out from under the tarpaulin top and gave a thumbs down. Rotten turnips splattered about his feet as he ducked back under.

They cast off and roared to their next customer--two new supply ships nested together. Dobrynyn nudged the T4 between their sterns. The garbage rained, but this time no one hailed Bubnov.

"Hey, Brad, did you see it?" Dobrynyn called down.

Lofton coiled the stern line. "No, where?"

"Wait 'til we back out of here."

Their pickup completed, the T4 backed clear and headed further up the inlet toward the next mooring, two nested corvettes. They looked like Grisha II types to Lofton; new, rather boxy, slabsided, they bristled with electronics, twin fiftyseven-millimeter mounts, and enormous twin RBU6000 antisubmarine rocket launchers rested just forward of the pilothouse.

"Brad, there." Dobrynyn jabbed a thumb to port.

Lofton peeked around the pilothouse superstructure. A one- hundred-foot barge loaded with large commercial containers lay in midstream held by anchors fore and aft. But, he remembered, *Brutus* was inside, the containers formed a fake structure. An armed oceangoing tug was moored on the side nearest him and--and moored on the other side, he could see its hull number, *831*; a Stenka patrol boat, one that had helped kill the *Kunashiri Maru.*

Something caught his eye three hundred yards forward of the fake container barge. Something he'd missed as they dodged turnips from the icebreaker sailor. Another barge, perhaps 150 feet, was anchored forward of the one that carried *Brutus.* It looked like a floating warehouse, with corrugated walls, roof, and large sliding doors. A single dim light bulb on the shallow pitched roof illuminated a drooping red flag--a bravo flag. This was an ammunition barge.

Vessels were moored to either side of the ammo barge. To starboard was Krivak hull number 059 and to port, a darkened patrol boat. He barely made out the bleak white numbers, rested Stenka number 726, the one that had removed him from *Brutus* at gunpoint. And whose crew had beaten the hell out of him.

The Krivak blazed with lights, her after port side thirty millimeter gatling gun poked straight up into the night; the forward one-hundred-millimeter gun did the same. Ghostly shapes drifted through shadows as men worked near their guns and hatches passing crates and long ammo belts. The hangar doors gaped open on the helo deck where five sailors pushed a KA27 Helix ASW helicopter onto the launching platform. Two sailors pulled at the rotor blades, extending them. The chopper looked as if it was being prepared for flight.

Lofton pounded the stanchion softly as he took in the scene. The Krivak was loading for another kill, filling its belly after having emptied death on the *Kunashiri Maru*.

"Looks like they're about done, Brad. Stupid of them to take on ammo in here. But those guys won't go out to the explosives anchorage, they don't trust anybody now. Let's hope they're in the sack by the time we get to our barge."

"Those bastards!" Lofton growled.

"Easy, *tovarisch*," Dobrynyn said softly. "OK, let's take care of this nest. After that, we'll head back to the barge. All set?"

Lofton took another look aft at the *Krivak*, nodded, and checked forward. They were almost to the end of the basin. Two hundred yards ahead, nestled alongside a wooden pier, lay three Stenkas, their snouts pointed toward Avachinskaya Guba; dark, yet their high, humpbacked superstructures and pilothouse windows made them look hulking, waiting, suspicious of every move in the harbor. Smaller craft were scattered about; work boats, camels, a couple of fuel-oil barges, and two armed tugs, all dark and at rest. He looked back to the container barge. *Brutus* was inside that phony structure, waiting under the guns that had killed the *Kunashiri Maru*.

The T4's diesels clunked into neutral, Dobrynyn backed down and stopped between the two Grishas' fantails. The small ASW ships were dark and snugged down for the night. But still, Lofton could tell the corvettes were alive, sleeping but alive. Their exhaust blowers whined up and down their lengths, almost as if the ships were snoring. "Where have you people been? It's late!"

Lofton looked up. Four men lined the rail of the ship above him, five on the other. All cursed and heaved loads of waste, some in dark plastic bags. More raw garbage gushed and plopped from large metal barrels into the T4's well deck.

"That's it?" Dobrynyn waved to both ships.

"Suck off, man." The KGB sailors disappeared.

"OK." Handles down, he backed the T4 clear, spun her with starboard ahead, straightened out, and threw the port engine ahead. Leaving the T4 in idle he called, "Josef?"

"Right here, Colonel," Ullanov's head popped to the top of the ladder.

"OK, listen you two. I'm going to move in slowly so we don't attract attention.

"Brad, you and Josef head for the bow and jump aboard as soon as we're close enough. I'll be right behind. We take out the guards on the barge first, there should be four. After that, Brad, go directly for your submarine, remove the limpets, and power up as best you can. It probably needs salt water for cooling, doesn't it?"

Lofton nodded. "Yes, I can bring it up partway but we'll have to wait until we hit the water before I get 100 percent output. Let's just hope no one's tampered with it."

"Right."

They looked forward. The barge loomed closer, a hundred yards away. Dobrynyn said, "The tug and the Stenka look like they're secure for the night. Crew's probably ashore but I'm sure each has a cold iron watch aboard, maybe two or three people. Josef and I will take care of them. Brad, make sure you cut away the tarp and get the securing chains off the sub. And try to grab a rifle along the way."

"Got it."

"What time, Colonel?" Ullanov asked.

Dobrynyn checked his watch.

"Yes. We should decide when to set the charges." Lofton bit his thumbnail.

The three exchanged glances.

"It's 10:14," said Dobrynyn.

Lofton said, "The sergeant's job is the most critical. We should work backward from when his are set to go off."

Lofton looked at Ullanov. "How long to set your charges and return? Forty minutes?"

Ullanov shrugged.

Dobrynyn said, "That is a lot of time for us to wait around, but we have to make sure you get clear, Josef." He flicked the T4 in neutral. They were getting close. "Set your limpets for 11:10, Josef. I'll set mine for one minute later, 11:11. Your limpets have real-time clocks, don't they, Brad?"

Lofton said, "Yes."

Thirty feet. Dobrynyn dropped the T4 into reverse.

With a nod to his brother, Lofton followed Ullanov down the ladder and to the bow. The barge loomed ten feet before them. Lofton looked aft as Dobrynyn switched off the navigation lights.

Full reverse, then all stop. The T4's bow nudged between the tug and the barge.

They were almost level with the barge's deck. A figure separated from the shadows, a corporal; he wore an overcoat and fur cap. He held his carbine loosely in his left hand. Towhead, pimples, a young kid. His voice squeaked. "Hey, we don't have garbage for you. Get out of here."

Ullanov jumped aboard lightly with, "We're out of gas, man."

"Get off." The corporal raised his rifle and barked, "You're not authorized."

The heel of Ullanov's hand flashed, a neck chop. Lofton heard the crunch and caught the rifle before it clattered to the deck. The corporal's eyes glazed. Ullanov bear-hugged his victim; the corporal's head lolled on his shoulder. More crunching. Ullanov spun around, raised the corporal by his armpits, and threw him into the T4's well deck, where he landed with a soft squish.

Dobrynyn materialized alongside. Lofton handed over the carbine.

"OK. You get the next one. Let's go this way."

Dobrynyn had started toward the starboard side when another guard, a sixfive giant sergeant, walked around the corner. "What the--?"

Dobrynyn hit him with a nose chop. Bone cracked. The enormous sergeant flailed at his face with a surprised grunt. His arms groped for Dobrynyn. Ullanov tried to get around but there wasn't enough room on the narrow deck.

Dobrynyn's arms spread wide. He splayed his fingers and swung both palms hard against the man's ears. Blood spurted out the guard's nose. He sank to his knees, retching. Dobrynyn grabbed the sergeant's ears and drove a knee into his face. The man fell on his side with a groan. Ullanov reached around, pulled the AK74 off the guard's shoulder, and handed it to Lofton.

Ullanov and Dobrynyn rolled the guard to the deck's edge. They each grabbed a hand. Ullanov kicked the body over the side. It hung there, its boots three feet above the water. Dobrynyn nodded. They let go and the body hit with a soft splash. Lofton looked over the side to see the KGB sergeant floating facedown. His boots gathered water and pulled him under. All that weight, the saturated overcoat--he'd be on the bottom within a minute.

A crude, wooden-framed doorway materialized next to Lofton. It had a canvas cover. He hadn't seen it before. "Pffft." He raised a hand and gestured with a thumb. Dobrynyn nodded, then pointed to port and starboard.

Ullanov went to starboard and peered forward. After a few moments he gave a thumbs up.

Lofton went to port and peeked around the corner. He could see up the length of the barge and, beyond, the lights of the Krivak alongside her barge where men still loaded ammunition.

Water lapped at the tug next door as she waited to tow *Brutus* to Vladivostok. Big, powerful, it looked to be over 150 feet. An enormous reel was mounted on the aft deck with an oily, glistening wire line coiled around. Soft, yellow light glowed from a porthole on the main deck below the pilothouse.

Lofton turned and joined the other two. He whispered, "All clear forward. But at least one guy is awake on the tug."

Ullanov said softly, "Clear to starboard. All lights out on the Stenka. I can't tell if anyone's aboard, but I know where to find them."

Dobrynyn nodded. He turned and nudged the canvas aside with his gun barrel. It was a light lock. Another section hung four feet ahead. He moved inside, followed quickly by Ullanov.

Lofton ducked inside as the forward curtain grazed over Ullanov's back. His mouth fell open when he moved through. Dobrynyn already had the drop on four surprised men as Ullanov quickly stepped around to their left. Their hands rose as Dobrynyn tapped his lips with a forefinger. Their eyes caught Lofton, then jerked back to Ullanov and Dobrynyn.

Two wore coveralls, Lofton checked their shoulder patches: torpedomen. They stepped back to Dobrynyn's soft command. The other two were KGB guards, a sergeant and a corporal without tunics, overcoats, or hats, only rolled-up sleeves. They eyed one another and stepped back, waiting.

"Don't try it," Dobrynyn said softly, waving his rifle barrel. "I'll chop you to pieces. Brad, cover them while Josef and I tie them."

Lofton made a show of cocking and aiming his AK74. He stood before the four at an angle, his feet spread apart, ready.

Dobrynyn ordered, "Down, now. Flat on your stomachs or we start shooting. And no talking."

They sank to their knees and flopped to their bellies. Dobrynyn nodded. Ullanov stepped over, searched them, and came up with nothing more than the guards' AK74s stacked against the wall. He found some rope and knelt to tie and gag them.

While Ullanov worked, Lofton examined the inside of the false structure. Dim hand lanterns provided the only illumination in the cavern. It was supported by wood members, two-by-fours overlaid with plywood.

But there, above him, resting in shadows, was a sleek sixty-five-foot torpedo shape covered with a dark brown tarp. Heavy chains crisscrossed the tarp and were secured to padeyes on the barge's deck, where twelve seized pelican hooks absorbed the tension. Crude but effective: they'd gone to a lot of trouble. *Brutus*! Home! Two days ago he'd given up hope. Yet there was his submarine, waiting.

Lofton eyed the prisoners as Ullanov finished tying the last one.

Dobrynyn muttered, "OK. Let's throw 'em in the T-4." He and Ullanov grabbed their prisoners' collars and started dragging.

"Looks like they're setting up for a combined shipment, Brad," Dobrynyn nodded to the gloom.

Lofton turned to see two large Aframes. A long, cylindrical shape, supported by a differential hoist, hung under each. One, a dull white-twelve-by-two-foot cylinder, hung suspended by a lug. The Mark 60 deep-water CAPTOR mine. "My God!"

Lofton walked to the CAPTOR and ran his hands over it. A special towing padeye was mounted forward, the one Thatcher had used to haul it to the Kuril Straits, where it had detached at Renkin's programmed command.

The torpedomen had removed the mine's end cap. Lofton looked inside, seeing a dark, oily emptiness. Where was it? There, six feet away in the gloom, the other Aframe hoist suspended the CAPTOR's parasite, a gray, glistening Mark 46 mod 4 torpedo. Lofton stepped over and whistled. Eight feet long, a foot in diameter, 560 pounds, the Mark 46 was the U.S. Navy's third generation-lightweight torpedo. Designed as an antisubmarine missile, its warhead was relatively small, packing ninetysix pounds of plastic bonded explosive, PBXN-103. That would have been enough for the *Truman.*

The Mark 46 tilted in the hoist as he touched it, and the chains clanked. A thin umbilical wire ran from behind the torpedo's twin counter-rotating screws back to the CAPTOR cylinder. Probably to its logic section, Lofton surmised.

"Brad, hurry," came a hoarse whisper. Dobrynyn's head poked around the curtain. "Pull the tarp off and get aboard. We're going to check the tug and Stenka now."

"In a minute, Anton. It looks like these people were preparing the capsule body and torpedo for shipment. Here, see all these tools, the torpedo dolly? They must have just pulled the torpedo out of the CAPTOR tube when we surprised 'em."

"Is it safe?"

"I think so."

Lofton stepped back from the Mark 46, examining it. The torpedo was no longer a CAPTOR-enslaved missile but was still subject to its logic because of the umbilical.

"Brad." Dobrynyn crouched at the light lock. "Get going."

"OK," Lofton muttered.

Dobrynyn ducked through the canvas.

Still curious, Lofton walked back to the CAPTOR and checked the operating panel, finding three allen type recessed nut receptacles. The settings read:

AUTO MAG INFL MAN

ARM SAF

BATT: ON/OFF

Do it! Just in case.

He scanned the deck, grabbed an allen wrench, and set the first lug to MAN. He set the second to ARM. He set the allen wrench in the third lug, BATT. It was in the OFF position. He flipped it to ON. Nothing happened. No lights, no indicators. He'd look again later.

He ran to *Brutus* and took long minutes to unseize the starboard side pelican hooks and kick them loose. Chains rattled loudly as their lengths snaked over *Brutus*'s topside and fell to the deck. He untied the tarp sections, pulled them off *Brutus*, and pushed them into a corner as far aft as he could get them.

Brutus lay nested in a wooden cradle. Black, long, the minisub was hard to see with its anechoic skin. Yet Lofton sensed the minisub's power more than he saw the shape in the gloom. He walked around; the hull was all right and the rudder and dive planes looked clear. Someone had done a reasonable job unfouling the *Kunashiri Maru*'s line from the five-bladed propeller, although he saw a few nicks in the shroud.

It took precious seconds to find the ladder he knew would be on board. It turned out to be a fifteen-foot aluminum one. He laid it against *Brutus*, grabbed a hand lantern and climbed up. It was hard to squeeze to the hatch, the fake container roof was three feet above his head, impeding the crawlspace. He got on his knees and lifted his back against the plywood;

nails creaked, then popped. A four-by-eight-foot section worked loose. He carefully lifted it aside on the roof and looked out.

The tug and the Stenka rode comfortably on either side. It looked as if the Krivak was almost finished with her chore; her ammo detail had waned. Her forward and amidships work lights were out.A few men still trudged around the fantail and worked at crates piled on her main and helo decks. Two large drums stood alongside the Helix helicopter. It looked as if they were servicing the helo, maybe refueling it.

Forward of the Krivak and her ammo barge, the red beacon announced the entrance to the KGB naval basin. The black waters of Avachinskaya Guba and the muted lights of Petropavlovsk beckoned beyond.

He eased inside, laid the AK74 on *Brutus*'s deck, knelt to the hatch, and popped it open. Black inside. He found the ladder and dropped below. His first look would tell. He knelt to the deck and shone the lantern about. No open panels, no ripped-out wiring; so far, so good.

He worked himself into the familiar pilot's armchair and relaxed to its contours.

Home. His cramped cylinder comforted him; he had been with *Brutus* in San Diego, he had built *Brutus*. This was a shred of home, or at least as close as he could get to it, and much better than the cell in Petropavlovsk or Sadka's Moscow interrogation chambers. Six days in the Pacific, and he could be home.

First things first. He brought up the interior lights and checked the battery levels. Cells three, four, five, and six were in the green, numbers one and two at the top of yellow. Good enough to start the catalytic beds, although he couldn't bring them up to full power until *Brutus* was immersed where he could kick in the coolant pumps.

He flipped on his CRTs and checking POWER, tapped the keyboard. The CRT read:

$$H_2 O_2\ 67\%$$
$$JP_5\ 62\%$$

All right, enough fuel left for extended cruising.

The Master CRT caught his eye. It flashed:

KRIVAK CLASS FRIGATE 347/0.2 nm
STENKA CLASS PSKR PATROL BOAT 007/0.1 nm
STENKA CLASS PSKR PATROL BOAT 195/0.0 nm
UNK VESSEL* 187/0.4 nm

(* Bottom 377 Ft)

Lofton imagined the computer's belch as the battle management system figured it out. The HP 9028 blinked and reflashed the data. The screen cleared to a soft light green. The cursor winked in the upper lefthand corner, ready for the next problem. Lofton sighed, sat back, and stared at the CRT for a moment. The readout was blank, gone with the *Kunashiri Maru*.

His eye jumped to keel depth; it read 0.0. The catalytic bed temperatures climbed to one hundred degrees and held. He found enough power for a trickle charge to battery cells one and two, plus a Hotel load.

OK. Lofton lurched out of his chair, went aft to the galley, and knelt to the deck plates. Pulling the four securing levers, he squeaked the deck plate up out of the way and reached down to snap open the magazine lid. Six dull black skeetshaped limpet mines rested on edge like plates in a dishwasher. He deftly removed their straps, laid them on deck, closed the magazine lid, and repositioned the deck plate. Lofton grabbed two in each hand and started for the hatch.

He was startled to see a dark face in the oval above him.

"Is it all right?" Dobrynyn whispered.

"All clear, so far. Can't wait to clear the harbor so we can take showers. We'll smell like goats in here." He handed up a pair of limpets. "How'd it go?"

"Fine, we found five people in the tug's duty section and another three on the Stenka. They're tied up and in the barge with the others. Josef is down there now securing them to the well deck bulkhead. Talk about stink." Dobrynyn reached for two more limpets. "They're writhing in garbage where they belong."

Lofton passed up the last two mines and climbed onto the casing. He handed all six down to Dobrynyn, who knelt on the main deck and set their clocks.

Ullanov brushed through the curtain and walked up to them, a scowl on his face. "That idiot Stenka petty officer gave me a bad time. He kept wiggling and almost bit through his gag. I had to hit him hard." He looked up to *Brutus* and whistled. "So that's it, huh?"

Lofton nodded. "Yeah, he's powered up now as far as I can risk. We'll have to wait for the big splash before I go to 100 percent."

Dobrynyn checked his watch. "OK, it's 10:39. What do you say, Josef?"

Ullanov shrugged. "Twenty minutes?"

"Be on the safe side. Make it thirty," Lofton said.

The three looked at one another and nodded.

Dobrynyn sighed. "OK, Josef, like we planned, set yours for 11:10 exactly. I'll set mine for 11:11."

"Don't forget to set your arming levers, Josef," Lofton said.

Dobrynyn chuckled. "Josef, I think he likes to give you as much crap as I do."

Ullanov stuck out his chin. "Officers. All bullshit. Not a brain in their heads. For example, what about the Stenka and the tug? Hadn't you better untie them so they won't keep the barge afloat? Huh?"

The twins exchanged glances; they nodded.

Ullanov slapped their backs with his large paws. "Officers. I spent three quarters of my life just keeping officers alive and their noses clean. Think they'd learn something."

Ullanov picked up his two limpets. "Eleventen, Colonel. I should be back in fifteen to twenty minutes. If you officers have trouble casting off those ships, I'll be back to show you how." He turned and walked toward the light lock.

"Josef," Dobrynyn called.

"Sir." The master sergeant kept walking.

"Have fun with the T4. Don't eat too many turnips."

"Sir." Ullanov disappeared through the light lock. The brothers went out and watched the T-4 back away. Ullanov waved once, spun, and idled toward the fuel dock.

"Let's go." Dobrynyn said.

They went inside, knelt beside the limpets, and set the timers.

"It's your submarine, Brad. Where's the best place?"

Lofton rubbed his chin. "Two either side amidships, the other two either side all the way forward, as deep as you can go. The way I figure it, this thing will sink bow down and pitch us forward so we can launch. If we place the charges at all four corners, it might take forever to sink.

"Makes sense." Dobrynyn nodded. "These barges have a lot of compartmentation. I'll plant the limpets, you cast off the tug and Stenka."

"Yeah, but I'm going to leave their stern lines attached," Lofton said. "Since the tide is going out, they'll stay alongside more or less and nobody will get suspicious."

Dobrynyn nodded, stripped to his skivvies, and walked out with two limpets.

Lofton picked up the others and followed. Dobrynyn grabbed a small line, threw it over, and jumped into the black, oily water. Lofton threw off the mooring lines as he followed Dobrynyn around the barge, handing the mines down. All four charges were set and Dobrynyn climbed aboard, where he stood shivering next to Lofton and patted himself dry with the torpedomen's rags.

Checking his watch, Dobrynyn said, "It's 10:46. Josef should be back. Why don't you wait on top of the submarine? I'll go back and watch for him as soon as I'm dressed."

Lofton went inside, mounted the ladder and knelt on *Brutus*'s casing near the hatch. He peeked out the top of the plywood overhead again. Salt air wafted to his nose, a horn honked, water slapped the barge's side. He glanced toward the fuel tank farm. No sign of the T4. Ullanov must have moored inboard of the fueling pier. Forward again, the Krivak's crew still worked the fantail. A small derrick hoisted torpedoes aboard, where four lay stacked near the KA-27.

Something caught his ear. He ducked his head and looked inside. Anton was bending over and onelegging into his trousers but aft, near the light lock, stood a KGB maritime warrant officer. Lofton crouched; the man wore a parka and his naval garrison cap, but no trousers or shoes. A Makarov pistol drooped at his right hand as he looked for his comrades in the gloomy space. Dobrynyn or Ullanov had missed him. The man had been asleep in a dark, obscure cabin somewhere.

The warrant officer spotted Dobrynyn. "Who are you?" he shouted. "Where is everybody?"

Dobrynyn's head twisted. He dove for his rifle six feet away. The warrant officer raised his pistol in a twohanded stance and fired, hitting the rifle and giving it a threequarter spin. The report echoed as Dobrynyn stood up with his hands in the air.

"What the hell is going on?" yelled the officer. "Raise your hands higher." He walked closer. "Where are my torpedomen?"

Lofton knelt slowly and picked up the AK74. He aimed and squeezed the trigger, sending a two-second burst into the man's chest. The KGB officer's arms splayed straight up, the pistol flew from his hands as the rounds thrust him back eight feet. The blast's echo died while brass cartridges tinkled down *Brutus*'s starboard side.

Lofton started down the ladder as Dobrynyn rose and held up a hand. "No, stay there, Brad. Watch out the top and see what's happening outside. I'll look for Josef."

"How much time?"

"Ten-fifty-one. Another nineteen minutes." Dobrynyn walked through the light lock.

"Damn." Lofton poked his head through the ceiling again and checked the harbor entrance.

His heart sank as red and green navigation lights swept toward him. A siren wailed ashore, barracks lights flicked on. Another siren wound up, then a third. They crescendoed and ripped at the night. Lights beamed up from the perimeter fences. Forward, the Krivak's searchlight snapped on, swung aft, and found the barge. Lofton raised an arm over his face as it blinded him. But his peripheral vision caught three patrol boats converging on the barge.

Shielding himself from the Krivak's searchlight, he saw the T4 was underway, plowing toward him. Ullanov would never make it before the patrol boats charged in.

19

The patrol boat swooped in to port, two hundred yards ahead of Ullanov's T4, and throttled down, its transom raised as the wake caught up. Troops stood next to the rail, their rifles ready.

"Aboard the *Yarev*, is everything all right?" a voice hailed as the patrol boat's spotlight flicked over the tug.

As the boat wallowed, Lofton noticed a perceptible movement from the tug. At first, he thought it was rocking from the patrol boat's wake but, carried by the tide, the tug slid forward and cleared the barge. Lofton turned to starboard. The Stenka also drifted. Anton had cast off their stern lines.

Another patrol boat roared in to starboard, slowed to an idle, and hailed, "Stenka 726, what are your intentions?"

Gunfire aft. Lofton ducked and looked inside. The port side patrol boat had opened up, and plywood chips exploded from the aft bulkhead. Dobrynyn dove through the light lock and fell to the deck as bullets stitched the panel behind him. Lofton jumped down the ladder and ran.

"I'm OK," Dobrynyn said, getting up. "I had to cast those boats off. Otherwise, it would have been easy for them to board us."

He nodded his head to the doorway. "Josef will be here in a few seconds. I've got to help him."

"Let's go."

"No, you stay here."

"Let's go." Lofton grabbed his rifle and ducked out the light lock.

They emerged onto the barge's narrow aft deck to see the T4, now thirty yards away, roaring toward a third patrol boat where it idled under the barge's stern. Someone shouted. The boat's engines bellowed. She dug her screws and cleared the T4's jutting bow ramp by two feet.

"Anton, he's not going to stop. I think he'll jump. We've got to catch him."

Dobrynyn shouted over the noise. "As soon as he's aboard you take port and I'll take starboard. Make sure they don't try to board us. We'll send Ullanov up to the bow." He checked his watch. "Ten-fifty-seven. Thirteen minutes to go."

Ullanov backed the T4's port engine and threw in left rudder, slewing the garbage scow's stern toward the barge. At full speed, the T-4's port engine sputtered, then wound to full rpm astern, belching an enormous cloud of black smoke.

The patrol boat crews caught on. Sparks and bullets ricocheted about the T4's pilothouse as it twisted in. The bow ramp flashed by, then the odorous midships section. Lofton glimpsed wideeyed bound and gagged forms in the well deck, buried to their hips in muck. Lofton fell flat as bullets whanged at the barge's freeboard. He raised his rifle and tossed a burst into the nearest pilothouse. The searchlight shattered, screams and grunts cascaded over the water.

The T4's aft structure swept by. A dark figure rose and jumped. Ullanov landed on the barge, crashing against plywood as bullets punched around him. He crouched, unslung his rifle, and squeezed off a burst, dousing the port side patrol boat's search lamp. Dobrynyn opened up to starboard. A loud, prolonged scream etched the night.

The port side patrol boat maneuvered wildly to clear the skewing T4, which roared in lazy circles toward the east basin docks.

Lofton caught Ullanov's eyes. Each sent another burst into the aft patrol boat.

"OK, Commander Brad." Ullanov checked his watch. "Another nine minutes to go."

"Josef?" Dobrynyn's voice came from the starboard side.

"Yes, Colonel."

"Go forward and watch the bow. We'll board the submarine when your fuel tanks blow."

"Sir." Ullanov rose to a crouch and ran for the light lock.

A burst ranged from the aft patrol boat. Bullets chewed up the barge's freeboard, then found Ullanov and spun him. He fell with an incredulous roar.

"No!" Dobrynyn yelled. They reached him at the same time and, kneeling, emptied their magazines into the patrol boat. Its engine growled and it backed away.

Dobrynyn bent over Ullanov and rolled him over. "Josef!"

Ullanov gritted his teeth, then rasped, "My leg, damn it. My leg, it's on fire."

Ullanov's foot was gone, missing below the ankle. Glistening darkness shot from his squirming calf and smeared the deck.

"Inside, quick," said Lofton.

They grabbed Ullanov's armpits and dragged him toward the light lock. Lofton fully expected to be cut down but, incredibly, there was no gunfire. They pulled him through the double curtain and reached the ladder below *Brutus*. A broad trail gleamed all the way to the light lock. "Tourniquet!" Dobrynyn panted.

Ullanov began to shout, then roared and kicked his legs. Lofton held him as Dobrynyn scrounged for a piece of line. He returned and looped a small rope around Ullanov's calf and tightened it. The spurting blood slowed to an ooze in the dimness.

"Time?" Lofton asked.

Dobrynyn flicked his wrist as he secured the tourniquet. "Elevenohthree. Seven minutes."

"They're not shooting anymore."

Dobrynyn glanced around. "Umm. They're afraid of hitting something inside. Maybe that torpedo, maybe the submarine. Who knows?" He knelt. "Let's get him aboard."

A bullhorn sounded as they bent to grab Ullanov. "Throw out your weapons and give yourselves up. You have five minutes."

Lofton arranged a moaning Ullanov over Dobrynyn's shoulder. "You're right, they're worried about hitting something. They could have opened up with their twentyfive millimeters and chewed us to pieces by now."

"Yes." Dobrynyn grunted under Ullanov's weight. "I'll be surprised if they hold their fire." The ladder creaked heavily as they worked Ullanov's bulk to *Brutus*'s hatch.

"Anton, lay him on the starboard side bunk. You'll find a medical kit aft in a locker next to the galley bulkhead."

"OK." Dobrynyn climbed down.

Lofton handed down Ullanov. The master sergeant's head lolled as he descended, yet he caught Lofton's eye with a thin smile before he disappeared inside.

Lofton shouted down the hatch, "I need to check the hull again. We may have taken some hits." He slid down the ladder and ran around his submarine. No bullet holes, although he did run his fingers over a bright, dollar-sized area where a ricochet had chipped off the anechoic coating. He knelt and looked under the keel.

The bullhorn blared, "You have three minutes!"

For emphasis, a twentyfive millimeter methodically pumped six rounds on single fire into the barge's forward starboard section. Lofton ducked. Cannon shells shrieked and whined, their noise intolerable. He crawled under *Brutus*, lay on his belly, and held his ears. Whole panels blew away. The roof crunched, then sagged over the starboard bow.

Dobrynyn's head popped out the hatch. "Brad," he screamed.

Lofton scrambled out to where he could look up. "I'm OK."

"Well, get in here, damnit. Four more minutes."

Another twenty-five-millimeter round blasted through shredding a panel with a deep, thudding crash. The area was open, and Lofton saw shore lights, the perimeter fence, even the brightly lit Krivak's fantail. He reloaded his AK74 and blasted out the interior lights with four rounds on single fire.

As the echoes died, another sound reached his ears. Strange, immediate, a highpitched winding became a prolonged wail. Smoke, corrosive, noxious, drifted over him. The wailing was near, aboard the barge. A wind gust cleared the smoke enabling him to see the CAPTOR's body had been heavily punctured near the front end.

Lofton ran to it. The whole operating panel was demolished, along with its logic section. A mild sparking from ruptured batteries flashed inside.

To his left the Mark 46 torpedo vibrated in the chain falls as its counter-rotating propellers gained full rpm. The liquid monopropellant engine screamed while the rudder and depth planes jinked back and forth.

Dobrynyn materialized next to him. They nodded. Lofton ran for the torpedo dolly and wheeled it under the shrieking torpedo. As he ripped out umbilicals, Dobrynyn frantically worked the chain fall. The seconds needed to lower it twelve inches were excruciating. Finally, the Mark 46 bedded on the dolly. The brothers worked quickly, their hands shaking. Lofton tore a fingernail on the chain hook while Dobrynyn unscrewed the lifting lug.

It was clear. Lofton kicked wood stringers aside, then nodded to Dobrynyn. With their hands braced on either side of the midbody, they slowly pushed the 560-pound screaming, smoking torpedo onto the barge's weather deck.

Lofton yelled, "Side launch so the dolly doesn't catch the screws."

Dobrynyn nodded and stepped around next to Lofton just as the Krivak's searchlight found them. They tilted the dolly's frame. Their load was almost three hundred spasming pounds apiece. The torpedo tipped and fell free with a splash as they held on to the dolly.

The Mark 46's whine abruptly dropped to a burble as it shot forward and nudged the barge's side. Releasing the dolly, they saw minute bubbles trail into darkness. The Mark 46 probed its computer while working to fortyfive knots.

"Three minutes, Brad, come on."

"Hold on." Lofton caught his brother's elbow.

They dropped to the deck, watching the Krivak's searchlight discover the torpedo's wake. A patrol boat spotlight flicked over, intensifying the path as the Mark 46 ran a tight figure-eight pattern. It broached. Bullets plinked in the wake long after it dove again.

Lofton muttered, "It's still seeking. The depth engine must be screwed up. It should have bottomed before this."

A patrol boat flashed under the barge's stern. Its engines roared in the brightly lit night toward the figure-eight pattern.

"I think they're trying to ram," said Dobrynyn.

The torpedo popped to the surface and tore for the Krivak's fantail. The patrol boat's thirty-knot speed was pathetically slow as the Mark 46 bored in at fortyfive knots. It broached again, then dove.

There was a dull explosion. Water shot up the Krivak's stern. The frigate vibrated momentarily, seeming to shrug off the ninetysix-pound charge. Fifteen seconds passed. Her lights winked out, the gas turbine engines wound down. Then, inexplicably, tongues of flame broke out on the main deck aft and licked upward toward the helicopter platform.

Lofton squinted. The barrel-sized drums next to the helo had been knocked on their sides. "Do you think that's fuel?"

"Either that or napalm mixture."

A whitehot flash seared across their eyes, followed by a loud, cracking whump. The KA27 Helix helicopter exploded. Its counterrotating blades settled to the flaming deck like the wings of a dying bug. A rocket fired from amidst the helicopter inferno and arced high over the hill to the west. Small-caliber shells detonated as the fire engulfed the entire fantail. Another rocket went off, caromed into the helicopter hangar, and exploded. The fire suddenly mushroomed and brightened. Figures on the Krivak's fantail writhed and twisted. Flames engulfed them. Some jumped over the side. Others fell and were immolated on deck.

"Brad. We're cutting it too close."

"Right." As he turned, Lofton saw flames leap from the ammunition barge's roof and eat down the sides. Another rocket flashed into the night while smaller-caliber rounds detonated like firecracker strings.

He ran after Dobrynyn. "That ammo barge is going to blow, maybe the outboard Stenka, too."

"Hurry!" They dashed up the ladder. Dobrynyn checked his watch. "Any time now, if Josef--"

A bright, reddish-yellow flash was followed by an incredibly loud "WHOOM," which roared from their starboard quarter. Then another, even louder explosion. Flames boiled three, then five hundred feet up from the fuel tanks.

"Josef remembered the arming lever." Dobrynyn wiggled into *Brutus's* hatch.

As he waited, Lofton quickly poked his head out the roof. Singeing, bright heat tore at his hair and eyelids. A glance told him the whole western shore of the KGB naval basin was aflame from the burning Krivak to the ruptured tanks. Igniting fuel rolled toward the water, engulfing small craft at their docks.

There was crackling sound aft. "My God!" Lofton dropped inside *Brutus* and secured the hatch.

"What is it?" Dobrynyn knelt by Ullanov, working on the tourniquet.

Lofton slipped; the deck was bloody. Stumbling, he reached for the pilot chair. "We're afire. Back aft. The plywood." His eyes darted over the panels as he punched switches. He checked the Ship CRT; all green, everything closed tight. "The wood must have been dry. It's burning like hell out there."

Two loud detonations shook the barge amidships. Lofton felt as if a horse had kicked him in the buttocks. His brother's face jiggled violently even as two more quick, muted blasts jolted forward.

Lofton checked the CRTs. They blinked and went back to all green. "OK, here we go," he urged softly. The deck tilted. He eyed the pitch inclinometer: five degrees with a slight port list.

A loud thumping came from overhead.

Dobrynyn said, "Must be the infrastructure coming down."

The deck lurched: seven degrees.

"Come on," Lofton urged. Then, "How's Josef?"

"Out. I gave him morphine."

A crunching, tearing sound came from above. The whole fake super structure must have collapsed. Hoping the wreckage hadn't fouled *Brutus's* dive planes or propeller, Lofton fought the urge to raise the scope and take a peek.

With a piercing clatter, the barge lurched to a ten degree list. Lofton shouted, "Looks like we may launch to port. Do you know if that tug's clear?"

"Not sure, I didn't see--"

Moving. They slid forward and to the left. The wooden cradle moaned from below as it slid on steel deckplates. They stopped with a jerk. Another squeak. *Brutus*'s stern swung, Lofton guessed, sixty or seventy degrees clockwise.

Dobrynyn stood, looking over Lofton's shoulder. "The barge's bow is off our port side now, I think."

"Yeah, the cradle may have jammed up against a cleat or a towing bit--"

WHAM! A tremendous concussion hit directly in front instantly followed by an earsplitting crack. *Brutus* shook throughout his entire length. Dust kicked up.

Dobrynyn looked down. "The Krivak?"

"Could be. Last time I looked, her whole stern section was afire. The ammo barge, too. Damn, I want to use the periscope but all that crap up there might break it off."

"Take your time. Those people out there have other problems now."

"Yeah, can't tell, we could be just settling evenly. I think-- whoa!" He pointed to the depth gauge: 1.1. "We're starting to immerse."

"How much do we draw?"

"Um, about eight feet in this condition. The ballast tanks are dry. Trying to get out of here without a trim dive is going to be interesting."

Two almost simultaneous detonations hammered the bow. *Brutus* shook. Then a third, enormous explosion tore at the submarine. A light bulb shattered aft. Bits of insulation floated down.

"Damn, like a depth charge." Lofton eyed his twin. "Those guys don't carry nukes, do they?"

Dobrynyn shook his head and checked the depth gauge: 4.1.

Lofton saw it too. "OK, the salt water intakes are underwater." He pecked his keyboard, bringing the converters to full power.

A low groan reached them from below. Strangely, it started aft with popping sounds, almost like gunfire.

"Barge compartments collapsing, I think," Dobrynyn said.

Suddenly the barge lurched. The deck sank. *Brutus* fell to port with a loud gush of water. Then they were bobbing.

"We're afloat," Lofton checked the keel depth: 8.1. "I'm going to wait a minute so we can drift clear. Can you raise the hatch and check for debris?"

"Right." Dobrynyn moved aft, reached up and spun the hatch wheel. It clunked open and he stepped up the ladder. Lofton heard coughing and hacking as the hatch slammed shut.

"Flames everywhere. All I saw was the barge, it's about twenty feet aft, with the stern sticking up. We're clear of junk. But that damn armed tug and Stenka are fifty feet ahead in a nest. Somebody must have boarded them and dropped their anchors."

Acrid smoke attacked Lofton's nostrils as he reached up and pulled on the periscope housing. He pushed the "up" button: Two feet would be enough.

"Fires all over the place," Dobrynyn muttered as he bent over Lofton, watching the CRTs flutter. "I couldn't see the Krivak, too much smoke."

The Master CRT periscope video picture unwound, then set itself. Lofton trained the scope forward, then to starboard. "Jeez, see that?" he pointed. "The Krivak's bottomed on her starboard side." He flipped to high power, and the glistening bilge keel jumped into view, a lonely bronze propeller gleaming in the flames. "The ammo barge is gone. And the Stenka too. The whole mess blew up."

"Time to go, Brad. It won't take them long to get organized. And the outer harbor will be on full alert."

"OK. How's Josef?" Lofton nodded toward the pilot berth.

"The stump's still bleeding, seeping through like a sponge. I better tie the tourniquet tighter."

"No, hold on for a minute. Let me get going here." Lofton nudged the throttle. *Brutus*'s propeller chopped the water. A red warning light bleeped on Master as a ship's ID scrolled through:

GRISHA II CLASS ASW FRIGATE 112/0.2 nm

Lofton flipped the scope to port. A frigate cleared her nest; water frothed under her transom. "Looks like she's backing straight out of the basin. She's gaining speed." He checked Sensors. "Seven knots sternway."

"Not enough time to turn around."

"Yeah. I'm going to dive now." Lofton checked his Ship CRT. Guessing at neutral buoyancy, he eased the throttle forward and admitted ballast manually. The tanks roared as water rushed in.

"Here goes." He pushed the stick forward. "Hope I don't stick it in the bottom."

They eyed keel depth. It hung at nine point five, then dropped suddenly to twelve, then fifteen, then twenty feet.

"Whoops." Lofton eased back on the stick and squeezed out ballast. *Brutus* hobbyhorsed to ten feet, then back to twentyfive. "Can't go faster than five knots," he muttered, "I've got to follow that Grisha out there."

Depth settled to fifteen feet. As Lofton puttered with his keyboard, fine-tuning the trim, a buzzing sound rose from astern. It ripped past close above to starboard. The CRT announced:

STENKA CLASS PSKR PATROL BOAT

Lofton nudged *Brutus* to twentyfive feet. Two more Stenkas zinged over-head as Dobrynyn wrestled with Ullanov's leg. The master sergeant stirred. A hand went to his eyes and he moaned.

"We'll be out in a few minutes," Lofton said. "I was going to say some-thing about Josef." He checked Sensors, making sure they matched the Grisha's speed. "Kirby," Lofton said softly, "the SEAL buddy I told you about, he's an orthopedic surgeon now. He told me about this type of wound."

Another Stenka zipped overhead, then a smaller patrol boat.

"Sounds like they're clearing the basin." Lofton checked NAV and ener-gized his BQR37. The channel entrance sprung into a gridlike view one hundred yards ahead. Beneath the Grisha's hull were portrayed the deeper waters of Avachinskaya Guba.

"Come on, come on," Lofton muttered. He looked up. "Kirby said corpsmen are told to clamp the bleeders with forceps, as many as you can find. There's maybe three or four major arteries or veins, I forget exactly. But you'll find forceps in the medical bag. Clamp the bleeders, leave the forceps attached. After that, wrap the stump in gauze with an Ace bandage and tape it off."

"You mean, we take off the tourniquet?"

"Yes."

"Commander Brad is right, Colonel." Ullanov's voice was hoarse yet surprisingly distinct. "We had a lecture. The dressing will last for several days if necessary...wound isn't as likely to become septic..."

"Josef, how do you feel?" Dobrynyn demanded.

"Like I was kicked by an elephant...woozy. My mouth is dry..."

"Any pain?"

"No."

"We're at the entrance," said Lofton.

"Can I see?" With a grunt, Ullanov rose on an elbow.

"Just for a second." Lofton rose to seventeen feet, flipped off the BQR37, then raised the scope. Ahead, the Grisha's transom swung to port, killing her sternway. Water kicked behind her as her captain rang up "ahead full" on her port screw.

Lofton trained aft. The breakwater lay fifty yards behind. Its red beacon shot rays onto the screen's right edge. Ullanov whistled as the periscope panned over the KGB naval basin's flaming western section. The Krivak lay immobile on her side. The ammo barge and Stenka 726 had virtually disappeared. Further aft, the container barge's stern protruded amidst burning wreckage.

Boats whizzed about. Another Grisha backed clear of her pier. Headlights darted on shore as three highpressure water streams spewed at the fuel fire.

The three watched the scene, their lips pressed. Ullanov slumped back and lay a forearm on his forehead. "...really in it, now..."

"We'll see home again, Josef," said Dobrynyn.

"We're clear," Lofton said. He retracted the scope and eased *Brutus* down twenty feet. "Time to go fast." He set the throttle, and their speed climbed smoothly to twentyfive knots.

Suddenly, the Sensor CRT jumped with grids and alphanumerics. A red light flashed. The display automatically transferred to Master:

HAZEA DIPPING SONAR 076/0.8 nm
STENKA CLASS PSKR PATROL BOAT 091/1.1 nm
STENKA CLASS PSKR PATROL BOAT 122/1.4 nm
SONOBUOY PATTERN (8)' CENTER 122/0.6 nm
HAZEA DIPPING SONAR 163/1.4 nm

GRISHA II CLASS ASW FRIGATE 190/0.8 nm

"Oh, no! They've mounted a hunterkiller group already. Look, two helos, two Stenkas, the Grisha and, for crying out loud, they've already planted sonobuoys. Look, eight of 'em." He eased in right rudder.

Dobrynyn folded his arms, studying the screen. "See how the Stenkas are lined up with the two helos outboard of the screen? That means they're trying to herd you down to the southwestern part of the bay to an area called Bukhta Tar'ya. It's a culdesac. Once they get us in there they will close the door. We'll never get out. Come left again. Head for the nearest Stenka, the one at zeronineone."

"You sure?" Lofton tweaked the rudder.

"Yes, it's our best chance. How fast can you go?"

"Thirtyfive knots if I'm really burning rubber."

"Rubber?"

"Uh, yeah, like a car peeling out. Why?"

"Chances are the Stenkas aren't fully manned. They're rated for thirtysix knots and it's going to take time for them to build speed.""How about the Grisha?" Lofton ran the throttle to full power. *Brutus*'s screw dug the water; the knotmeter clicked smoothly through thirtyone.

"It's rated at thirty knots, I think. You should outrun her."

"That leaves the helos."

Dobrynyn sighed. "Yes, see? They're scattering." he pointed at Master. "They realize the ruse didn't work. Come right a little, now. The Stenka may roll a depth charge."

Lofton eased in right rudder. With a glance to Dobrynyn, he said, "The KGB carries depth charges?"

"Um. Come further right. Yes. He wants to swing in to parallel your course. Soon now if--"

WHOOM!

"Damnit." Lofton fought the joystick. *Brutus* lazed to port, broached, and resubmerged. The lights went out, flicked, and went on again. Through a vaporous haze, he said, "Jeez, that was close. We broached--think they saw us?"

"Possibly. A little left now and head straight for the entrance."

Brutus cycled up and down as Lofton tried to hold a mean depth of thirty feet. He eyed the knotmeter: 35. "The fuel cells are only delivering 89 percent power. We may be able to squeeze out another knot or two."

"OK. Abeam of the Stenka," Lofton said. He checked NAV. "Petropavlovsk is two miles to port. It should be another five minutes or so to the Izmennyy Narrows."

Dobrynyn pointed to Master:

HAZEA DIPPING SONAR 162/1.2 nm
HAZEA DIPPING SONAR 163/1.9 nm
STENKA CLASS PSKR PATROL BOAT 345/0.4 nm
STENKA CLASS PSKR PATROL BOAT 346/0.9 nm
GRISHA II CLASS ASW FRIGATE346/2.6 nm

"Good, everybody is astern except the helicopters. Is this our best speed? Thirtysix knots?"

"Um. More or less. *Brutus* is rated at thirtyfive. We never exceeded that in trials."

"Who's 'we'?"

"Me, I built this thing."

"You?"

They looked at each other.

"Relax, Anton. I shifted from the SEAL business to the sub business and became a practicing naval architect. I build submarines."

Dobrynyn looked about him. "Sadka told me about the submarines, but I didn't realize you built this little machine."

Lofton nodded.

"We're one and the same. It's as if I built it too." Dobrynyn said to Ullanov. "Josef, did you hear that? We're going to be OK. I built this submarine."

"Officers, my ass."

The twins grinned.

Lofton lowered his voice. "We have to clamp his arteries, soon."

"I know. It's amazing he's not in more pain."

"Shock does it, I think. The nervous system shuts down and the body protects itself, something like that. The morphine helps, but he'll feel it soon enough."

He checked NAV. "OK. Abeam of Izmennyy Peninsula. Babushkin Kamen is coming up on our right. We'll be in the Pacific in three minutes or so." He sat back and arched an eyebrow. "How soon, do you think?"

Dobrynyn bit his thumbnail. "They'll drop when we hit deep water, probably at the one-hundred-meter curve."

"Could we hug the coast and stay in shallow water until the helos run out of gas?"

"Don't think so. The bottom is irregular and treacherous. Reefs, islands, steep peaks reach up through swift currents. And the helicopters can be relieved by others, so their onstation endurance is unlimited. If we stay inshore, they can bring up the Stenkas and depth charge us or hit us with RBU 6000s from the Grishas."

Lofton nodded. "OK, top speed and we'll hug the bottom."

"That's our best chance."

Two minutes later NAV blinked, indicating Mys Mayachnyy lay seventeen hundred yards off their port beam.

Lofton punched a program to hug the bottom. *Brutus* tilted and headed to two hundred feet. "It's cold water here. Think we'll find a temperature gradient to hide under?"

"Maybe, but not for another mile or two." Dobrynyn examined the Sensors CRT. "The helicopters are drifting astern and to starboard."

"Their contact must be getting fuzzy." Lofton came left to course 095.

"We might get clear before--"

TORPEDO 406 MM 46 KT 301/1.1 nm

"They've dropped." Lofton urged, "Come on." He checked the catalytic bed temperatures: four hundred degrees. *Brutus* arrowed at full power, the knotmeter read thirtyseven.

"A nine-knot differential." Dobrynyn did the math. "Seven minutes. We might outlast it."

"What if I change course?"

"It's acoustic -- active/passive. It just follows what you do."

"Proximity fuse?"

"Yes, twenty feet I think."

Their eyes gripped the screen. The torpedo blip crept closer.

"Five and a half minutes to go," The screen flashed. Lofton said, "Hey, it disappeared, something happened." They heard a detonating roar aft.

"Faulty. But look, a helo is dipping ahead and there's yet another to starboard. Come left, we may still be able to break contact."

"Gotcha." Lofton swung *Brutus* to 045.

TORPEDO 406 MM 46 KT 180/0.2 nm

"Hey, that's close. Jeez!"

"Come further left."

"NAV says the bottom starts shoaling to port; if we do that we'll have to go up."

"Do it quickly!"

A whining noise grew behind them.

"What if--"

The explosion hit like a thunderclap. It jiggled their skulls and rolled them sharply to port, almost to beam end. Canned goods, books, tools, spare parts, and packages spilled from cabinets. Lofton's head struck the side panel with a crack. Dobrynyn tumbled over the armchair as Ullanov fell on top of them with a shout, then an elongated roar of pain.

A scream pierced their madness. But it wasn't Ullanov. Vapor clouds filled the kaleidoscopic interior as it gradually faded to black.

"Get off!" Lofton shouted.

Brutus rotated to an even keel and pitched down.

The CRTs jiggled to life and glared as the wailing scream persisted aft.

"We're taking on water," Lofton shouted, jabbing his keyboard in darkness. The Ship CRT flipped wildly through damage control assessments. Master CRT methodically blinked on and off with large letters:

JAM DIVE

"Dive planes are stuck in Full Down position!" Lofton's hands flew over the keyboard. He pulled on the joystick. *Brutus*'s dive planes remained at Full Down. Lofton tore open a panel, flipped the planes' hydraulics to Manual and pulled the toggle--nothing. He chopped the throttle and threw it in reverse--he had to stop the descent.

Sparks flew. Large white bolts of electricity arced from the side panel and grounded through the deck plates. Dobrynyn was outlined in a blue-white glare as volts spasmed through his jinking frame. He fell over Ullanov with a loud, piercing scream.

Lofton fought the controls, but the CRTs winked out one by one. The whole display became lifeless. No power, the propeller had stopped. *Brutus*'s plunge continued as Lofton read the depth gauge spinning through twenty-seven hundred feet.

His hand groped for the emergency power switch on the side panel. He flipped it to Aux. A bright flash zapped back at him. *Brutus* groaned as he sank bow down.

The hull thudded on the bottom. Lofton lost his balance, surprised. The submarine canted to starboard with an obscene angle. He fell from his chair and tumbled atop two other grunting bodies onto the starboard bulkhead.

He blinked and clawed his hands into a sightless void. His mind reeled. Pitch-black water gurgled and splattered at his feet. Aft, the wailing reached him through a cry, his brother's, his own.

It was humid, dripping, the temperature was that of a tramp steamer's boiler room. Lofton raised his head; it fell back. His eyes closed as his own darkness swept through him.

20

At last rid of a miserable, humid summer, Washington, D.C., was reveling in an extraordinary autumn. Joggers and cyclists included Kalorama Circle on their Sunday tour, enjoying the deep reds, yellows, and ambers that bristled over exclusive homes. Strollers turned onto Tracy Place, sniffing the perfect mid-morning air, admiring the architecture, and wondering how much money the houses might cost. As usual, the Georgian brick at 2236, the one with the steep pitched slate roof, passed inspection admirably. Its gardener, an unmatriculated philosophy major with 182 units, took care of four houses in a row: 2236 through 2242.

But next door at 2234 the owner did his own gardening. As he started his leaf blower, the unmuffled gasoline engine ripped the air and Ted Carrington could not hear the football game he had videotaped yesterday, even when he punched the remote to full volume. He had opened the study windows to allow the fall air in. Dr. Renkin was settled out back with his easel after conducting an early morning staff meeting. Now, Carrington tried to watch Notre Dame. It was close, 1715, and Purdue had just passed for a first and ten to the Irish's twentysix yard line.

Carrington kicked at the ottoman and almost spilled his perfectly chilled Steinlager beer. He stood and entertained dark thoughts of shoving the leaf blower's tube down the owner's throat. He walked to the window.

His eyes automatically assessed the neighborhood as he jerked the sash down; street quiet, the same two parked cars--one belonged to the house next door. A man waited patiently at 2238, pooperscooper in hand, while his leashed basset hound arched its spine and spasmed its hindquarters over the philosophy major's wellmanicured lawn. Carrington glowered. The dog had chosen to decorate the wrong yard.

A movement down the street; he evaluated the white van as it approached, slowed, and pulled up in front.

With a sigh, Carrington punched the TV and VCR remotes to Off. Purdue's quarterback faded to a blank screen. Carrington watched the Watkins Air-Conditioning Service driver pause at his steering wheel, make a note on his dispatch board, then descend and approach the house.

The van drew away three minutes later. Two minutes after that Dr. Felix Renkin arranged himself at his desk wearing plaid shorts, a white Burning Tree Country Club polo shirt, tennis shoes, and white athletic socks. Carrington mournfully closed the TV console door, then sat and waited patiently while Renkin's pencil twirled.

Finally Renkin sat back, read the message, and clicked his teeth. Then he handed it to Carrington:

TO: MAXIMUM EBB
FM: SPILLOVER

LOFTON ESCAPED VIA AID OF TWIN LT. COL. ANTON P. DOBRYNYN AND MASTER SGT. JOSEF ULLANOV. BOARDED BARGE IN PETROPAVLOVSK KGB NAVAL BASIN AND REFLOATED X3 VIA LIMPETS TO BARGE. OTHER DIVERSIONARY LIMPETS RESULTED SERIOUS DAMAGE TO SHIPS, FACILITIES, WITH OVER 100 CASUAL-TIES. ASW GROUP PURSUED X3 TO OPEN OCEAN. BELIEVE SUCCESSFUL TORPEDO HIT. SUB RESCUE UNITS EN ROUTE FOR EVALUATION AND POSSIBLE RETRIEVAL WEATHER PERMITTING. BE ADVISED: SMALL CHANCE X3 STILL OPERABLE.

The leaf blower growled outside as Carrington finished the message. He whistled softly.

The back of Felix Renkin's bald head rotated. Facing the window, he steepled his hands. "A limpet, Carrington. That's a mine of some sort, isn't it?"

"Yes, sir."

"And?" Renkin spun around.

Carrington took the cue. "Well, since Mr. Hatch and his friends tend to minimize things, I'd say Lofton and the other two blew the crap out of that KGB naval base. A hundred casualties is a lot. It sounds like they blew up something big, like a, a--" he waved a hand, "--a building or a bridge with a train on it, or a theater full of people, to stage a diversionary panic. Then, it sounds like they blew the barge the *X3* was mounted on, so it would sink and refloat the *X3*."

"Those three men are underwater demolition experts. They could do these things easily?"

"Yes, sir. Surprise was on their side."

"Anything else?"

Carrington held up the message to reread it. What the hell was Renkin driving at? Lofton's twin was acting as predicted.

"Come on, Mr. Carrington, I'm not paying you two hundred thousand a year to stand around and say 'duh,'" Renkin said impatiently.Carrington dropped his hand and focused on the back of Dr. Felix Renkin's bald skull. *The hell with you too, Boss.*

It worked. Renkin spun in his chair and faced the window with a sigh. "Let me know when you're ready." He drummed his fingers lightly.

Carrington extended his ruminations for a full minute. "The Russians sandbag like hell; we both know that. And it sounds like they're doing it in this message. You just don't take down one hundred or more elite military people without something catastrophic happening. As proof, we can check the next satellite pass for damage assessment. We should order it before they have time to camouflage the place."

"Agreed."

"That being true, I'd say they're not sure if *Brutus* has been destroyed. If he was, they're not sure everybody is dead inside. In that regard, I think Mr. Hatch is doing you the kind courtesy of saying there's a real chance, not a 'small' chance as he says, that *Brutus* could still get away and that Lofton and the other two could return to the U.S.A."

"Yes."

Carrington flipped the message on the desk, then sat in the leather armchair. Neither spoke as the leaf blower sputtered and raged down the driveway next door.

"Interesting."

"Sir?"

Renkin leaned back in his chair. "A highly trained elite, professional soldier. Dobrynyn--a Spetsnaz. He's a career officer, a lieutenant colonel with how many years?" The bald head rolled sideways to Carrington, eyebrows arched.

"Ah, a lieutenant colonel has between seventeen and twenty years, I'd say."

"Yes, a citizen of the Soviet Union with eighteen years of professional, dedicated service suddenly blows the place up and runs away, leaving many of his comrades dead or wounded. Why?"

"His brother. Like we talked about."

"There's more to it than that."

"Maybe they dumped on him. Maybe he didn't like the Navy. Maybe he had women problems or money problems. Maybe his brain is sloshed with vodka."

"No."

Carrington gave in. His eyes wandered to the closed TV console while he waited.

"Reciprocal altruism."

"What?"

"Your report. You didn't see it?"

"No, sir."

"Had you studied Chapter Fourteen you would have found it. Reciprocal altruism is a concept or school of thought in psychology circles that attempts to define behavior between close relatives or friends. In essence, it says that one party will ultimately act unselfishly for the other and that the cumulative result accrues to both parties, Carrington. Not one individual, not the 'me' generation, no women, no money or alcohol problems, no military discipline problems. Altruistic acts are oftentimes compulsive and are committed by one so that both parties gain as a unit toward a specific goal."

Renkin propped his chin on his fist and gazed out the window. "In this case the goal is twin survival. It's clear that twins, especially identical twins, watch out for each other, even as adults. You were right. They become very close and commit altruistic acts for each other. Lieutenant Colonel Dobrynyn chose Lofton over his country and the KGB naval basin was severely damaged with over one hundred casualties."

Carrington said. "It must have been easy for them."

"What do you mean?"

"From what I've heard the KGB and Spetsnaz hate one another," he spread his palms, "just like the Company hates the SEALS and vice versa. The twins probably didn't have to think too hard over that one."

"Possibly." Renkin turned and folded his hands on the desk, "Now, is everything set for next weekend?"

"Do you mean your NSC meeting? San Diego?"

"Yes."

"Yes, sir. All the people we invited have accepted."

Renkin rubbed his chin. "What about Dr. Kirby's place? Lofton may go there if he does survive."

"I'll put a team on it. His place in Point Loma, too. Four men in pairs. Round the clock." Carrington looked at the floor. "Uh, do you want them alive if they do show up?"

"Use your discretion, but I would like to question Lofton if it's possible. The other one doesn't matter. And, to play it doubly safe, set up a link to NOSIC in Suitland, too. Use top level priority. I want to see all SOSUS information relative to any unidentified submarines transiting within a hundred miles of the West Coast."

"SOSUS didn't pick up *Brutus* going out."

"Yes, but perhaps there's a chance the system may detect the *X3*'s return trip. And, if so, I want to be aware of it as soon as possible. Make sure any NOSIC data reaches us immediately, whether here or in San Diego."

Renkin went back to his painting while Carrington made sure the instructions were neatly logged on a pad. Laying the pencil down, his ears perked up. The leaf blower was silent and, he hoped, had been put away until next weekend. He raised the window, opened the console doors and flipped on the VCR and TV as he sat, propping his feet. Purdue connected with a pass to Notre Dame's five yard line.

A scream... no...a loud wailing ranged through his mind. It wouldn't go away. His eyes blinked. Darkness. Pitch black. *Where am I?* The noise. *Who's screaming?* He opened his mouth. A croak came out. He tried again. Same thing. He licked his lips. "Anton?"

"Uhhh."

"Anton!" he yelled.

"Yes." Another groan. "Brad? Ahhhhgh. My head hurts. You?"

"Yes, me too. I hit the side panel. Don't move, let me find a battle lantern."

"OK."

Lofton groped for a handhold. Over the wail, his ears caught a rushing of water. *How long have I been out?* A leg lay over his shoulder, the thing smelled. They all smelled like garbage.

Lofton felt around with his hands. Here. The pilot berth. He lay on the pilot berth bulkhead. Cushions and body parts were wedged against him. He patted along the bulkhead to the overhead section. Fumbling, he found the boxy battle lantern, snapped it from the bracket and pushed the rubber switch. White, hoary light penetrated the ozone-laden interior.

He pushed the leg aside and sat up. *Brutus* lay at a fifty-degree angle to starboard. Hot, steaming, the pressure in the boat was oppressive, nearly two atmospheres, he guessed. His head ached where the Stenka sailors had kicked him. He took a breath; his ribs felt OK. Ullanov's tape had helped.

Ullanov! He shone the light, found a leg and traveled the light to Ullanov's face. The sergeant was pale, his eyes half-closed, glazed. His mouth gaped open. The light traveled back down the leg; the stump hung obscenely off the side of the pilot berth. A trail of uncoiled rope dangled into inky water.

"No!" Lofton sat up and put a thumb to Ullanov's neck. No pulse.

"Josef!" Dobrynyn yelled. He struggled up and grabbed Ullanov's shoulders. "Josef! Damnit, Josef!"

Lofton checked the stump again, seeing no spurting blood. It had all drained and now mixed with the seawater that lapped at his feet. The tourniquet had unraveled somehow. Master Sergeant Josef Ullanov was dead.

"Josef!" Dobrynyn hugged Ullanov.

"Anton, I'm sorry." Lofton shouted over the wailing. He found Dobrynyn's shoulder.

Dobrynyn rocked back and forth as he embraced his master sergeant. Softly again, "Josef."

Lofton glanced aft. It had to be a water leak. And they had no power. Were the batteries shot? Their depth must be well over three thousand feet. *Get going!*

He staggered aft with the lantern. An inch-thick stream of high-pressure water shot across the galley. The stream had drilled a hole through a tool cabinet on the port side and expended its energy on the pressure hull. He flicked his light down to starboard, to the source, somewhere, he thought, near the high pressure air compressor unit. He knelt on the starboard bulkhead and steadied himself with a hand on the main hatch ladder.

"Brad, what do you think?" Anton yelled.

"Not sure," Lofton roared back. "I'll know in a minute."

Dobrynyn hacked out a cough. "We're running out of oxygen."

Lofton's throat was scratchy, too. He stuck the lamp into the crevice between the high-pressure air compressor unit and the bulkhead. "Here, a broken valve stem! Jeez! The solenoid blew, the whole unit's destroyed."

He carefully reached behind the first-stage cooling unit and twisted the manual globe valve. The thread seemed endless. He kept turning and looked forward to see his brother's expectant silhouette hovering next to the pilot berth, watching.

Lofton's wrist became tired. He changed hands and kept turning. The wailing changed to a higher pitch, then to a hiss, then--nothing. Ten more turns and the water jet suddenly curled, dropped to his feet, and stopped.

Lofton sat back and mopped his brow in the dripping cylinder. Dobrynyn sloshed up next to him and knelt on his haunches. They looked at each other. "I'm sorry, Anton, really I--"

Dobrynyn held up a hand and coughed. "Don't, just don't. This is some-thing I choose to do. It's just that--Josef--so needless, it shouldn't have happened." His voice trailed off.

Lofton dropped his head. "The damn tourniquet--we must have been out for a long time."

Dobrynyn nodded. "Can't be helped."

"Yeah, look, let's see if we can figure out what happened." Lofton whipped the light up to the depth gauge over the galley table, it was almost over his head. "Damn!" It read, keel depth: 3122.

Dobrynyn said. "Close to a thousand meters." He pointed to an analog eightday clock next to the depth gauge: 0147. "Is that right?"

"We've been out for more than an hour!" Lofton sucked in a deep breath, yearning for oxygen.

"Our friends should still be up there," Dobrynyn sighed. "If I were them, I'd put down a rescue unit first thing in the morning. The weather is good and the rescue ship is only ten miles away in Petropavlovsk. It could be on station in an hour. They could launch a salvage submarine or a remotely piloted drone for visual inspection. They might even lay a mine or a torpedo alongside." He looked at his brother. "Can we regain power?"

"Don't know. We've had a major battery casualty, maybe a ruptured cell." Lofton lurched to his feet and flashed the lantern fore and aft. Surveying the wreckage, he shook his head slowly. "This whole damn boat is screwed. To begin with, I have to restart the catalytic beds to generate power so we can pump bilges and scrub the crap out of this atmosphere."

"Are the fuel cells shut down?"

"They tripped out automatically when everything went haywire. We're going to need main battery power to restart them. Trouble is, the batteries could be covered with salt water. We would have to pump bilges to get at them." Lofton's mind twirled. He looked down. "All that takes power. I don't know, Anton."

"Try."

"Yeah." Lofton hacked out a cough. He reached overhead to a cabinet and pulled out two portable air bottles and masks. "Put this on. I'll see if I can sort out this mess." He unclipped another battle lantern and handed it over.

Lofton sloshed forward to his armchair and checked the battery gauges. All were dead except number six, which fluttered between the red and yellow zones.

"Anton." His voice was muffled behind the mask. "The problem is beneath the deck plates. Grab some rubber gloves out of that locker under the bunk. There's a rubber mat there, too. Lay it on the deck. This can get tricky. Those batteries are rated at fortytwo kilovolts when they're fully charged." Lofton flipped switches at the circuit breaker panel. "I'm killing everything, including the auxiliary load, to completely isolate the batteries."

Dobrynyn drew on the thick, black gloves. He laid the mat down and knelt.

Lofton said quietly, "Lift those deck plates just forward of your knees. I want to see the aftermost battery. It still has some juice." He doublechecked circuit breakers while Dobrynyn worked at the deck plate screws.

"OK." Dobrynyn bent low, saying, "Not too much bilge water and I see the batteries. This one's labeled 'six' and it looks like one of the copper rods is burned in half." Dobrynyn dropped his head below deck level and shone the light aft. "Yes--"

"Watch your head!" Lofton shouted.

Dobrynyn jerked up.

"Your hair almost touched the top of number six. It's still hot. Easy, Anton. We're sweaty and wet as hell. The boat's full of crap and our electrical resistance is really low. Touch something like that battery, even with your hair, and gzzzzzsst." He drew a finger across his throat.

Dobrynyn exhaled slowly. He crabcrawled forward, then bent and shone the light aft. "OK, the rod is severed in two places, near the front of the battery compartment and just aft of number- five battery, which looks like it's cracked."

"Port or starboard rod?"

"Port."

"Hmmm. The plus rod." Lofton sat back, thinking. *What the hell? Try it!* "There's a tool box aft, starboard side, near the tunnel hatch. Disconnect the rod while I check the rest of the batteries. We might be able to jump the load from four to six. If it works, maybe restart the catalytic beds."

"Maybe?"

"It's our best chance."

Dobrynyn went after the tools.

Lofton took a deep breath and worked furiously at the forward deck plates. He wiped sweat out of his eyes. The air mask pinched his face.

Soon the deck plates were up. They lay everywhere: on the toilet, on the starboard bulkhead. Lofton had to rest a deck plate on top of a gaping, dead Ullanov.

"OK, disconnected here," Dobrynyn gasped. "What have you found?"

"Number five *is* dead. The others look OK, but I won't know for sure until we hook up and throw the switch." Lofton stood and squirmed out of his garbage-stained Soviet naval teeshirt. Sweat ran down his chest and arms. The carbon dioxide level was rising. He took another whiff of air from his mask. They'd have to do something about the atmosphere soon, no matter who awaited them topside. "Here, catch this." He tossed one end of a copper rod to Dobrynyn. "Connect that to the plus side. I'll do the same down here. And go easy with your wrench, don't let it touch anything."

As their wrenches twirled, a scratching sound, like bouncing pebbles, rattled outside the hull. "Sonar. They may have found us," Dobrynyn muttered. He kept working.

"We'll know soon. All right, that's the plus side. Now let's do minus." They worked in silence as sound waves scratched at *Brutus*.

"Set here, how about you?"

"Go."

Lofton reset the circuit breaker to number-six battery. "I'm going to try interior lights first." He tapped a switch. The interior lights blinked, some remained on. Junk. Everywhere. Papers, books, cans bobbed in the bilge water.

Lofton threw power to the fuel cells. The lights dimmed as he punched switches. "If I can get a start sequence going in the reformer unit we'll be OK."

A sustained scratching raked *Brutus*'s hull. Lofton tapped the fuel cell gauges and sat back, waiting.

"Nothing." Lofton rose, sloshed his way aft to the tunnel hatch, and disappeared.

Dobrynyn looked around, then his eye caught the clock: 0427. Sunrise soon. He looked to the blank CRT panels and saw the reflection of Josef Ullanov's eyes. Dobrynyn bent and lifted a deck plate off Ullanov's hip, then arranged the body so it rested in the vee formed by the starboard bulkhead and the pilot berth. He looked at Josef one last time, then brushed a hand over the limp, cold face and closed the eyes. A soggy blanket lay in the corner; he straightened it, covered the body, and pulled the blanket to Ullanov's chin.

He hesitated. Pulling the blanket back, he exposed the sergeant's hand and the signet ring with the gold "U" set in onyx. Dobrynyn twisted it off and put it in his pocket.

Lofton hobbled back and stood for a long moment. With a nod, he bent and dropped the blanket over Ullanov's head. He stood looking at the form under the blanket and bit his thumbnail. "Breakers were all tripped back aft. I reset them. We might be able to light off. Maybe without pumping bilges."

Dobrynyn took a deep breath. "Come on, then."

"Right." Lofton stepped to the control panel and punched the start sequence. He tapped his gauges, checked the battery and auxiliary panels. Exhausted, he flopped back and waited. Soviet sonars scratched outside. Now it sounded like two, different frequencies. Come on! Come--

Fuel cell number two jumped to one hundred degrees. One, three, four, five, and six quickly followed. "All right!" Lofton yelled. "They're cooking."

He fed power to the CRTs. "Anton, grab some of that copper bus rod and reconnect batteries one, two, three, four, and six. Hook them in series. Let me know when you're ready and I'll kill the battery switches. We can be out of here in fifteen minutes. Remember your gloves."

He switched in the hydraulic systems, then checked the rudder and dive plane indicators. The planes were still jammed in the full down position.

He tried the joystick.

Nothing.

Lofton's hand flew to the auxiliary hydraulic panel and he tried again. A groan aft. He tried the joystick again. The indicator followed his movement. "We were lucky, the rudder and dive planes reset themselves. I was afraid I was going to have to rig a chainfall and grind 'em to zero manually. How are you doing?"

"Give me time!"

The Soviet sonars clawed at them.

"Do you think we should pump bilges and right ourselves now? We have power."

"Too noisy."

Lofton shook his head in frustration. He tapped at the keyboard, bringing up the battle management system. The CRTs danced with bolts of color, grid and data. Images pulsated and settled on the Master CRT:

iNGUL CLASS SUBMARINE SALVAGE VESSEL 05/0.1 nm
STENKA CLASS PSKR PATROL BOAT 019/1.2 nm
GRISHA II CLASS ASW FRIGATE 092/0.8 nm
UDALOY CLASS BBK DESTROYER 167/0.7 nm
GRISHA II CLASS ASW FRIGATE 185/0.6 nm
STENKA CLASS PSKR PATROL BOAT 211/1.0 nm
STENKA CLASS PSKR PATROL BOAT 272/1.2 nm
STENKA CLASS PSKR PATROL BOAT 341/1.6 nm

Lofton whistled. "Eight ships, seven of them with ASW gear. They're circled around us with the corvettes and destroyer to seaward." He pointed. "Is that Ingul class ship any good?"

"Yes. You can bet that's the *Alatau*, the one that recovered your CAPTOR mine. They're welltrained, professional, with the best equipment." His voice drifted for a moment. "And a Udaloy class destroyer. There's only one in the Pacific Fleet, the *Admiral Shaposhnikov*, almost cruiser size, a monster. She has a variable- depth sonar, that's probably what we're hearing."

"No helos are dipping, though."

"It doesn't look like it, although the *Shaposhnikov* carries two KA27s. They can be launched almost immediately. And they can send others from shore, as we discovered recently."

"We have to break out of here."

"Ummm."

"Anton, are the batteries hooked up?"

"Yes."

"OK. Let's try it. Put the deck plates back on. No use those things flying around if we get hit again.

"I'm going to see if we can creep away. We don't need another pissing contest with a torpedo. Can they go this deep?"

"Yes, but they have a difficult time down here." Dobrynyn knelt over the battery compartment.

Lofton swung up into his armchair with a mutter. "Damn, I wish I had thought of a seat belt." He wedged himself with his feet. "Ready? I've got to pump ballast first."

"Go ahead, I'll finish here."

Lofton's hands hit the Ship CRT. A pump came on the line aft whirring loudly. "Damnit! Listen to that. Might as well crank up a siren." *Brutus* rotated and leveled. "Here we are, you bastards!" he yelled.

Brutus rose. Lofton eased in the throttle. The digital knotmeter clicked to five knots. He carefully nursed the minisub to two thousand feet.

Dobrynyn puttered aft, stowing tools and gear and picking up debris. "Anything yet?"

"No, they might not have heard us. Ohoh, maybe they did. The tin can is moving."

"Hardly a tin can. The *Shaposhnikov* is over eight thousand tons."

"What's her top speed?"

"Around thirtyfour knots, I think."

"We can't do that now, not with a cracked battery. I think we're only good for twentyfive or so. When we get the batteries charged we might get to thirty, but not much more."

"I have a feeling you'll need every turn you can throw to that propeller."

"Ummm."

Master flashed:

SINGLE SALVO RBU 6000 (12)

"Go to seven knots, Brad."

Lofton pushed the throttle up. Fortyfive seconds later explosions ripped the sea floor off their port quarter.

"Crappy aim, four hundred yards aft."

"Five knots again, please." Dobrynyn stood behind his brother and looked over his shoulder.

"OK. Five knots."

DOUBLE SALVO RBU 6000 (24)

"Here they go again," Lofton said.

"Ten knots this time, Brad."

Brutus had just reached nine knots when, behind them, a mightier, closer series of hedgehogtype detonations struck the ocean floor.

Lofton checked Sensor. "Looks like they've moved to a line of bearing above us, but to the right. We can go all day like this. All they'll get are a bunch of bloated fish."

Dobrynyn nodded. "They'll shoot one more round of RBU 6000s, then try torpedoes again. Go back to five knots."

DOUBLE SALVO RBU 6000 (24)

"Another full salvo, Brad. Come to bare steerageway this time and start your bilge pump when they explode. This is going to take a while."

Lofton pulled the throttle to "stop." The contactfused projectiles detonated well ahead this time. They went to five knots again and waited as the pump hammered away.

It sucked dry in the bilge. Lofton flicked off the switch and pumped the water to sea from the sanitary tank. He adjusted trim, then peered at Master again. Minutes passed. The seven warships stayed above in a line of bearing.

"Anton, no torpedoes, and they're drifting far right. Think they're losing contact?"

"Don't know. Come to dead stop, I want to see something."

They watched the screen for several minutes. Suddenly, seven ships gathered speed, reversed course and headed toward Mys Mayachnyy.

One remained.

Lofton bit his thumbnail. "They're heading home. Figures. I think we're under a double gradient, Anton. Even that destroyer can't probe it with its VDS. I think we can--"

"--Brad." Dobrynyn's voice rose. "How is the battery charge going?"

Lofton's brow furrowed. He looked to the overhead battery gauge cluster. "About 30 percent now. Why?"

"What would be our top speed?"

"Around twentysix or twentyseven knots, but that's not sustained. We'll have to drop back to--"

"Go, now, before everyone gets clear!" Dobrynyn urged.

"What?"

"Do it! Now!"

Lofton jammed the throttle to the hilt. *Brutus* dug in, squatting slightly as he accelerated. "What's going on?"

"Keep as deep as you can!" Dobrynyn shouted.

"All right. But tell me."

"The *Shaposhnikov* is the only one that has lingered, everyone else is clearing the area. I've seen this exercise before, it's fleet standard ASW doctrine. Just one ship. What does that tell you?"

"Yeah." Lofton scratched his chin and coaxed speed. *Brutus*'s knot log nudged 27.2, then fell to 26.8.

"That's all we can do for now."

TORPEDO 533 MM 45 KT 273/4.5 nm

Lofton pointed to Master. "Is that it?"

"Yes."

"And you think it's a nuke?"

"Yes. See, even the *Shaposhnikov* has turned for shore at," Dobrynyn leaned closer to the CRT, "thirty knots. She's clearing the area with the rest of the group."

"What's the effective range of the blast?"

"Umm, three to four kilometers at a depth of five hundred meters. Below that, it's less because of the pressure, but I don't know how much."

Seconds ticked. "Why can't we hear it, Anton? We heard the other one."

"It's still too far away, and be thankful. You don't want to hear this one."

Dobrynyn stood back and rubbed a hand over his face. "I don't think it's set up for a homing routine. It looks like they shot at our last datum..." His voice dropped to a mutter.

"What?"

"...I said, it would take too long for the torpedo's sonar to acquire us through this double gradient."

Dobrynyn snapped his fingers. "Yes! We might outrun it. Come left fifteen degrees."

Lofton eased *Brutus* through a gentle left turn.

TORPEDO 533 MM 45 KT 172/3.7 nm

"That's it, Brad, it's on a fixed heading. Come all the way left, course zero-zero-zero. Let it clear us astern."

Lofton whipped *Brutus* to true north. "What sets off the bomb?"

"It's--"

They heard a tremendous whang, like a gigantic underwater tuning fork. A freight train rumbled toward them.

"It's detonated! Hold on!" Dobrynyn yelled.

Roaring, the shock wave lifted *Brutus*'s stern and enveloped them, swinging them violently back and forth as a shark worries its prey. Five seconds, ten. Cabinets burst open, lockers spilled, the divers' trunk hatch clanged forward as Lofton fought the controls. *Brutus*'s aft section rose twenty degrees as Lofton pulled on the joystick. Rushing, gurgling, the submarine shook. Dobrynyn twisted on his knees and wrapped his arms around the ladder. *Brutus*'s nose leveled as Lofton's hand flashed over the keyboard.

The roaring subsided. Then, silence.

Lofton checked his gauge: keel depth 3322.

"Whoa!" he pulled the stick back. "Anton. You OK?" he called over his shoulder.

"OK, Brad." Dobrynyn stood, then sat on the edge of the pilot berth and faced his brother with a shaky smile. "OK."

. . .

Lofton sat back. "We're there." He nudged the throttle to stop, set depth to hover at fifty feet, then heaved himself from the armchair with a glance at NAV:

WAY POINT	CS	DIST	TIME			ETA-Z		
			d	hr	m	m	d	hr
1. Mys Mayachnyy	—	—	—	—	—	—	—	—
2. 50 00'.0 N - 180 00'.0 E	—	—	—	—	—	09	28	1551
3. 33 40'.0 N — 121 00'.0 W	089	3145	6	13	15	10	05	0506
4. San Pedro Ch. Dogleg	092	137	—	6	51	10	05	1157
5. Avalon Harbor	181	15	—	—	45	10	05	1249
		3297	6	20	51			
		SPD	=	00.0				
		DEPTH	=	50				

Master Sergeant Josef Ullanov, born July 16, 1955, in Vinnitsa in the Ukrainian Soviet Socialist Republic, now lay in a weighted canvas sack with his arms crossed over his chest on board the USS *X3*. Lofton had cleaned Ullanov's illfitting, garbage-soaked naval uniform as best he could and put it back on, while Dobrynyn sewed a shroud.

They carried Ullanov forward and gently lay the body in the divers' trunk. Dobrynyn climbed in with him. He wore a mask, scuba tank, and immersion suit. Lofton shut the hatch. After a moment's pause, he yanked the brass handle and listened to roaring water fill the trunk. The ballast tanks automatically compensated for trim as *Brutus* dutifully hovered.

The escape hatch clunked open. A minute later it was shut and dogged tight. Dobrynyn rapped twice on the bulkhead. Lofton threw the lever the other way. Compressed air pushed water from the trunk.

He caught his brother's eyes, his own eyes, through the thick glass peephole. They nodded as water receded below Dobrynyn's shoulders. Ullanov was gone, headed for the bottom of the cold North Pacific Ocean where he would rest on the International Date Line, the imaginary border that separated the twin's nationalities. One Soviet, the other American.

Lofton dropped his head as the trunk voided. Words came to him, not the Russian he'd spoken the past several days, but this time his own language.

> Eternal Father, strong to save
> whose arm hath bound the restless wave,
> Who bidd'st the mighty ocean deep
> its own appointed limits keep:
> O hear us when we cry to thee
> for those in peril on the sea.

PART III

_____

He has placed before you fire and water: stretch out your hand for whichever you wish. Before a man are life and death, and whichever he chooses will be given to him...

Ecclesiasticus 15: 16-17

21

Tired, he wished the harsh noise would go away. Waving a hand, Dobrynyn bumped *Brutus*'s throttle with his fingers. He settled back in the command chair: his head lolled.

BEEP-BEEP

Dobrynyn's eyes snapped open. He focused on the CRT cluster. Sensors read:

SONOBUOY PATTERN - (6 RANDOM) 347/5.6 nm

He heaved from the chair, walked aft to the open tunnel hatch, and looked through the long, shimmering tube. "Brad!"

Lofton's face popped into the motor room hatchway. "Yeah?"

Dobrynyn concentrated on his English. He wanted the practice. "Sonobuoys, once more."

"How many?"

"Six. And much closer this time. Under six miles. How long you will be?"

"Almost done. All I have to do is test the bypass valve and torque the manifold nuts."

"Did it work for you OK?"

"What?" Lofton was lost to view: a wrench clanked.

"Will the fuel system function?"

His face popped back in the hatchway. "Yeah, but that's the last spare valve. No more extended cruising in this sewerpipe until someone does a corrosion analysis work-up." After the International Dateline, Lofton had crawled aft to the motor room every twelve hours for inspections. Seventy-five miles from the San Pedro Channel, he found rust again on the H_2O_2 fuel block, growing like a virulent five o'clock shadow toward the master control solenoid valve. It was worse than the rust he had found on the trip over. He wondered if battle damage had aggravated it.

"Sewerpipe?"

"We're in a stinking tin can, Anton." Lofton's head disappeared, his voice echoed. "...like a death trap...still have to fix that heat exchanger globe valve, too...damnit..."

The console buzzed. Dobrynyn turned, seeing large letters flash. He yelled, "You better come, now. They just laid another pattern."

"OK. Be right there. Steer reciprocal again."

Dobrynyn ran for the console and focused on the display.

SONOBUOY PATTERN (6 RANDOM) 345/7.2
SONOBUOY PATTERN (12)'CENTER 185/3.2

He felt it. Not just the sonobuoys or the P-3 aircraft orbiting overhead that laid them. People were nearby. Americans. "Brad! Sonobuoys in front of us, now."

Lofton's voice grew loud as he scrambled through the stainless steel tube. "On my way. Come left to zero-nine-zero."

Dobrynyn barely had *Brutus* on the new course when Lofton moved next to him. They changed places.

Lofton shoved the joystick. "Let's try two thousand feet. Maybe hide under a thermo layer."

"Six hours now. How do you think they found us?"

"Umm. SOSUS, probably." He looked at Dobrynyn's raised brow. "Underwater listening arrays. Funny thing. They didn't pick me up going out. I wonder if--"

They felt it. *Brutus*'s hull shimmered with a sound like a soft rubber mallet.

"Hey, that's close. Where did?"

His answer popped on SENSORS:

SINGLE PING - BQQ-5 277

"What is BQQ-5?"

"Trouble. Almost dead aft. I think the cops have found us." Lofton pushed the throttle through the detent to "flank". *Brutus*'s screw dug in. They crept to twenty-four knots, their best speed.

Dobrynyn asked again, "How did they find us?"

"Vectored probably by the P-3--whoa! See that?"

Master flashed:

BQQ-5 276 LOS ANGELES (SSN-688) ATTACK CLASS 276 USS Oakland

"Can we outrun her?"

Lofton bit a thumbnail. "Not a prayer. Not even if we had full battery capacity. And they can go as deep as us. This doesn't make sense, all this firepower out here. It's all too pat."

"Your submarine is close by. I can feel it."

"Me too. Look." He pointed to a small panel left of the CRT cluster labeled UQC-17. The underwater telephone ready light blinked with an amber flash. Even as he flipped the switch, *Brutus*'s hull shimmered with another ping from the seven-thousand-ton *Oakland*'s sonar.

The speaker popped and scratched. They heard, "...*unknown Sierra, Sierra. Surface and identify yourself...*"

"Damnit!"

"What do you think?"

"Don't know." Lofton reset their speed to twenty knots. "Might as well conserve power. They can stay with us until the cows come home."

Dobrynyn's eyebrows went up. "Cows--"

The speaker blared like a hi-fi. *"Surface and identify yourself."*

"Close to us. Is there any way to ask how far?"

"Can't ping him. He's masked by our prop."

"Then change course. Nothing loses now."

"Yeah, I--sonofabitch!"

Another ping struck the hull. Immediately, they heard a heavy throbbing just as something nudged their stern. They felt a loud, jarring bump. *Brutus* shook and vibrated throughout its length.

"Hold on!" Lofton yelled. "Damn thing is overrunning us!"

The minisub jolted. Then rolled. A loud grinding sound swept through the hull. Lofton pushed on the joystick.

"No! Go up," Dobrynyn roared. "He's just underneath. His sail will hit us!"

Lofton yanked the stick back and threw in right rudder. Machinery noises wailed through them. Lofton's teeth rattled at another ping.

"You are ordered to surface. Now."

"Bastards did that on purpose. He knew we had slowed down." Lofton flipped off the underwater telephone switch. Master Flashed:

USS OAKLAND 084/0.7 nm

"Fourteen hundred yards away." Lofton snorted. "At least we can spin inside him."

"Yes. But we have to lose him."

"Got an idea. How about his wake?"

"Submarines don't make wakes. But there might be a little turbulence. It might be worth doing."

Lofton eased in left rudder and headed for the attack submarines's track. "Let's hope he has trouble pinging through it for a while."

Dobrynyn gripped the back of the command chair. "We can't hide long."

Brutus buffeted slightly. Lofton pulled the throttle to "all stop." "OK. I'm going to try something. It could be they found us because we're making noise with a bent propeller shroud or a nicked blade. I don't know, something from torpedo damage. That might be how SOSUS picked us up to begin with. Let's just sit tight."

"Possibly. Set your sonar to passive and we find out."

Brutus hovered as the CRT displayed the American attack submarine's course change. Her aspect changed from stern to beam then swung to bow on.

Lofton swore softly, "Right at us again."

"No. Look."

The *Oakland*'s bow came further left and steadied on a starboard beam aspect. "All right," said Lofton. "Let's try it again. He might not be able to pick us up if we stay bow on to him." He kicked the thruster pedals.

He steered for the wake five hundred yards away and stopped.

"Good. Remain stopped and pump a little ballast. And yes, keep your bow toward him."

"Go up?"

"Yes."

Lofton thumbed the button on top of the stick. "Don't want to be too noisy."

"Only a little ballast. We can rise above him. Just do not turn the propeller."

Brutus rose. At fifteen hundred feet, their passive display told them the *Oakland* remained at two thousand feet running an oval pattern. Lofton reached to the pilot berth, grabbed a rag, and ran it over his face.

One thousand feet: the *Oakland* dove to twenty-five hundred feet doing figure-eights at thirty knots.

Fifteen minutes later, Dobrynyn sat on the bunk. The depth gauge read five hundred feet. "How much speed would you need to hold this depth?"

Lofton exhaled loudly. "About five knots. That's interesting."

"What?"

He pointed to Sensor. "The P-3 laid another sonobuoy pattern, but it's eight miles away this time."

"Go to five knots."

Brutus crept away. The *Oakland* stopped pinging and disappeared from their screens.

Lofton said, "She's gone quiet. Whoa! Another sonobuoy pattern. Ten miles away. We're on to something."

"Possibly your anechoic skin."

"Yeah. That and no screw noise."

After a rigid four hours Lofton heaved from the command seat. He sighed and shook Dobrynyn awake. "Nothing around us. It's all yours. Speed is ten knots. I think we're quiet enough."

Dobrynyn blinked and rose. "Are you still thinking of going to San Diego?"

"Don't think so. I've got a strange feeling about our run-in. Let's keep going on to Catalina, pick up Kirby's boat, and head to Newport Beach. I want to talk to him first and see what's happening."

"OK."

Lofton trudged to the aft bulkhead and bent to the second-stage air compressor. He muttered, "Still have to fix this damned heat exchanger globe valve. And sometime before we close the mainland we have to surface and recharge the high-pressure air flasks without being detected." He wiped his bleary eyes, opened the tunnel, hatch and crawled through in search of his tool kit and spare parts.

Repairs made, they arrived at the San Pedro channel dogleg at noon on October fifth, several days later than planned, due to repairs and having to creep past the ASW picket. They lay on the bottom and waited for sunset. When it came, Lofton nudged *Brutus* to periscope depth and set a program to take them to within five hundred yards of Catalina Island and buoy W35.

Dobrynyn took off Bubnov's ill-fitting Soviet naval uniform. They'd both had to wear them; leaking battery acid had destroyed Thatcher's two poopie suits.

Lofton asked, "Again?"

"These things still stink. I want to wash them and take another shower."

"Second time today, Anton."

Dobrynyn walked to the divers' trunk and tossed over his shoulder, "A man should be clean when he goes to war."

Lofton peered through the periscope and maneuvered to clear wildly zinging pleasure boats. "I don't think we'll be going to war yet, Anton. Plenty of time for showers when we get to Kirby's."

Twenty minutes later Descanso loomed two miles away. He flipped to high power and picked out *Them Bones*. "There it is, our ticket to Newport Be--"

Lofton stared at his brother. Dobrynyn settled in the pilot berth, arched a brow, and gave a thin smile. He was clean-shaven, the salt-and-pepper beard of Lieutenant Colonel Anton Pavel Dobrynyn had disappeared.

"Good God. You're like me!" Lofton stammered. Nothing distinguished the two except the rating badges on their Soviet naval uniforms and subtle differences in the indelible stains on their striped teeshirts. Dobrynyn's beard had been the cordon sanitaire establishing their individuality.

"Exactly." Dobrynyn bowed slightly. "The same and one--"

"Uhh, one and the same."

"Yes. You are like me, too. I thought it might be well if situations arise. You know, how can one man be in the similar as many different places?"

One and the same. Lofton's hand felt clammy as he went back to the periscope. Sweat from his brow dampened the rubber eyepiece. "I don't think we'll have to worry about that. I'd just as soon as grow mine--"

"Watch out! Dive the boat, quick!"

**UNK VESSEL 179/0.6 nm SPEED 22 KNOTS
CPA 179/0.0 nm COLLISION COURSE!!!**

Lofton jabbed the joystick. Just before *Brutus* dove, he caught a glimpse of spreading red-and-green side lights. Twin bow waves of a charging catamaranstyle Catalina ferry-boat filled his eyepiece.

Lofton breathed deeply. He calculated the fortytwo-knot rangerate while the boat growled overhead toward Long Beach.

"Close," said Dobrynyn.

Lofton waited until the ferry was gone and rose to periscope depth, concentrating on his approach to Descanso. "Lost track of things. Almost got us killed."

· · ·

Dobrynyn stayed aboard *Brutus* while Lofton exited, swam to W35, and scrambled onto Kirby's skiff.

Lofton looked in all directions. It seemed clear. It was a quiet evening and Descanso was only half-full. Soft rock music drifted from a trawler moored toward the casino. He unsnapped the tarp, folded it, and packed it in the vee-berth.

Them Bones's engine barely cranked. He waited ten minutes hoping the battery would come back. He tried again. On the starter's last crank, *Them Bones* sputtered into life. He untied the moorings, powered back, and picked up Dobrynyn. They sent *Brutus* to nestle once again in 250 feet on a low hotel load.

The channel was calm. "The trip should take thirty minutes," Lofton said.

As they bounced along, Lofton watched his brother's brow furrow while he glanced furtively at the emerging Southern California coastline. The Soviet twin became more quiet and pensive, as they neared Newport Beach.

The coast baked in a Santa Ana condition under a deep, yellow full moon. Even now, about eleven-thirty, the temperature was seventy. Both shrugged off their parkas as Lofton cut the power. *Them Bones* wallowed; her stern wave caught up and shoved the runabout toward the green bell buoy off the Newport Harbor jetty. He set their speed at five knots, saying, "Here's the channel entrance. Welcome to California. You'll love it here."

Dobrynyn nodded to two dark shapes on the buoy as they closed to within five feet. "Are you certain?"

Two seals awoke, barked their protests, and jumped off as Lofton swung left to enter Newport Harbor. "Better than Petropavlovsk."

"No, I mean about coastal patrols. Is it for sure we won't be stopped?"

Lofton said. "There's no KGB maritime patrol here. The only reason for stopping us is if the Coast Guard thinks we're running drugs, and they won't, since they know Kirby's boat. The only way we're going to get boarded is if somebody gets wind of these parkas--whew!"

Dobrynyn leaned back and propped his feet on the gunnel. "Brad?"

"Yeah?"

"What's going to happen? What will we do now? If Dr. Renkin can make a submarine attack upon us--" Dobrynyn snapped his fingers and jabbed a thumb over his shoulder, "is difficult opponent. He could have people at many levels. This is, yes, a country of freedom. But wouldn't he have big influence?"

Lofton rubbed his chin. "I don't know what's been going on here since I left. At first, I thought we would be OK after we escaped the nuke; that they thought we were dead. But that attack submarine could have been put into position by Renkin. They might have warned him if they got a good solution. And a lot happened on your side."

"Exactly."

"My plan is to go to Kirby's. Since we're out of options," he shook his head, "I'll have him line up a lawyer. And we'll probably go to the press."

"Can you trust your press?"

Lofton smiled. "Here? Yes. Don't worry about that. It'll make a big stink. Trouble is, our lives will be screwed up. Maybe for a long time. But I can't see any other way."

Dobrynyn nodded and *Them Bones* muttered into the channel. Looking at the Tuesday evening sky Lofton was relieved for the moment, glad to be out of Kamchatka's daytime chill. He felt relieved at his decision and, as China Cove slipped by to starboard, set his mind on what he had to go over with Kirby.

They cruised by the Coast Guard station, where the brightly illuminated USCG *Point Divide* brooded at her mooring. Dobrynyn cast it a wary eye, then they came left and headed deep into Newport Harbor. Moonlight danced on small wavelets stirred by their wake as Balboa Island slipped astern. *Them Bones* gurgled on and slipped between Bay and Harbor islands. Music, laughter drifted across as a ninety-foot harbor excursion boat rumbled past. Little groups of tuxedoed figures stood on her deck. With drinks in their hands, they joked with their ladies.

"There." Lofton pointed toward the darkened mainland. "See that mast, the tall one? That's *Bandit*, in Kirby's dock."

"You weren't pulling a joke. Dr. Kirby owns a luxury house on the water and a boat."

"Umm, many people do. And the yacht's half mine, but I don't live on the water."

"So, he's a very rich man."

"Not necessarily, just comfortable--whoa. No lights. Looks like Kirby is out."

Lofton eased *Them Bones* into the dock. He muttered, "Must be out with Nancy."

"A girlfriend?" Dobrynyn jumped out and secured the mooring.

Lofton reversed *Them Bones* and killed the switches. They bounced softly on rubber fenders. "His fiancee. Come on. We'll raid his fridge."

His stomach rumbled. Both were hungry. Most of the food had spoiled when *Brutus* took on water after the torpedo hit off Kamchatka's coast. They had rationed the rest, mostly crackers and packaged cold cuts.

They walked across the patio. Lofton stooped and lifted the mat. "Funny. It's not here."

"Key?"

"Yeah. There's one in the garage. He's always forgetting and locks himself out."

Brushing aside hibiscus shrubs, they walked down a side yard and into the garage. Lofton snapped on the light and reached over the doorsill. "Here it is. I--"

"What is it?"

"Both cars are gone. He must be out of town. Guess he loaned one to his Mary, his nurse. He's done that before." He opened the door. They walked through the laundry room into the kitchen, where he punched the security system. Lofton opened the fridge and handed Dobrynyn a bottle. "First things first. Elephant, dark. Right?"

"I have not known about the Elephant, but the dark is correct."

With the tops pulled, they clinked bottles. Lofton flipped on kitchen lights and rummaged in the freezer while Dobrynyn toured Kirby's house.

"Two cars, you said, Brad?"

"What?" Lofton found two frozen enchiladas in the freezer and popped them into the oven.

"Dr. Kirby has two cars, a boat, and a house on the water?"

"Well, yes. You'll get used to it after you're here a while." Lofton flicked his wrist. Damn, he missed his Casio. He checked the oven clock: 12:47.

Dobrynyn moved into the laundry room and peered into the washing machine. He whistled. "All automatic. What's this?"

"A trash compactor." Lofton smiled to himself and checked the oven.

Dobrynyn stepped in shadows. "A clothes dryer?" He whistled. "So many buttons. Digital display. Does one have to go to school to learn how to use it?"

"Yeah. A four year-course. Almost ready."

"What is that? It smells good."

"Enchilada. A Mexican dish. Have a seat. I'll set the table."

Dobrynyn looked at his hands. "Bathroom first. Where is it?"

Lofton waved. "Through there and to your left."

As Dobrynyn disappeared down the hall Lofton pulled the silverware drawer open. A stack of flyers on the counter caught his eye. He hadn't noticed them while making dinner. His hands groped at the silverware as he read the page. It was a picture of Kirby's house. *This house!* Bold letters jumped out at him:

FOR SALE
CHARMING WATERFRONT CAPE COD
ONLY $8,799,000

Wha--what?

A knife dropped from his hand and clanked on the floor.He bent to pick it up, still reading.

Glass shattered over Lofton's back as he seized the knife. Crockery exploded, the kitchen lights blinked. Plaster dust rained and crashed over him. A heavy thudding, bullet holes stitched up the cabinets.

Instinctively he dove to the floor.

"Brad, what is it?"

Lofton heard the bathroom door yank open.

"Stay down, Anton, somebody--"

Another fusillade raked just above his head. Incredible. He couldn't hear the gunshots. Sparks jumped from the oven control panel, smoke gushed out. To Lofton, it sounded like a silenced Ingram as more bullets pounded the counter and cabinets.

"Brad, are we under attack?" Anton shouted from the bathroom.

"Yes. Kill the lights, then roll into the hall." Lofton reached for the wall switches as more glass shattered, a kitchen chair spun around and fell on its side. The switch panel took a hit, blew up, and shot sparks inches above Lofton's clawing fingers, plunging the kitchen into darkness.

Silence. "Brad, are you there?"

"Yes, I'm OK," he whispered loudly, "I'm pinned down. Somebody is out back. Sounds like a silenced Ingram--there are probably others. Kirby has a shotgun in his bedroom closet. That's through the hall to your left."

"Yes."

Lofton heard him scramble on the carpet. "Kill the lights as you go."

"OK." Dobrynyn's voice faded.

Thump! Something heavy cracked through the living room window, rolled to a stop and hissed. Then another rocklike object sailed above his head and crashed through a kitchen cabinet among metal cooking utensils. Then, Thump! Thump! Two rounds penetrated windows on the other side the house.

Tear gas! Sharp tentacles raked in his lungs. He ripped a hand towel off a hook. Dobrynyn's hacking and coughing in the living room told him there was little time to lose.

White smoke enveloped Lofton as he rose, dashed to the sink, and soaked a hand towel.

"Brad!" Dobrynyn's voice gurgled from the living room.

He slapped the wet towel over his face. His eyes seemed to burst from their sockets and his lungs raged with fire while he fumbled for another towel and soaked it.

"Hold on." His voice was muffled.

A loud crash. The front door, he thought. Feet stomped into the living room. It sounded like two, maybe three pair.

Smoke, white, opaque. His brain screamed to get out as he jammed the wet towel over his nose and mouth. He balled the other towel in his fist and started for the living room.

Glass crunched behind him. He stopped. The table scraped. The sounds came from the patio where the window had been blown out.

Get out of here! The hallway to the living room was somewhere to his left. If he went straight he could escape to the garage.

No. Anton! He started for the living room, tripped over the kitchen chair arm and fell heavily on the floor.

"Ughh--Brad."

They were fighting in the living room. Lofton rose to his hands and knees. A short burst erupted above him. Ricochets unleashed trails of sparks. Punctured pots and pans screeched. Silverware crashed on top of him.

"Toby, that's enough. There's too many of us in here." The muffled voice was near the window, Lofton calculated. Yes. A foot mashed glass in the roiling tear gas no more than five feet away.

"Knock off the shooting, you guys," another muffled voice drifted from the living room. "OK, cuff his hands and feet, Vito. Hit the sonofabitch again if he comes to."

Lofton recognized the inflections of Ted Carrington. Rage rose within him as he stifled the growl in his throat. He choked into his towel. Carrington. That bastard! Renkin!

The glass crunched nearer. He dropped to the floor and looked back, barely distinguishing the shape of two approaching shoes.

Lofton's eyes were almost swollen shut. He had to get out. They had gas masks--but where? There, almost at the man's feet--a ten-inch kitchen knife.

"See 'em yet, Toby?" The voice came from behind him.

"Uhuh."

The man's crotch came into view. He wore Levis, dark tennis shoes, and an unzipped leather jacket.

"Check to your left, but I think he went down the hall to the garage. We may have to put some gas in there."

Lofton reached out slowly and grabbed the knife. The man's upraised gun was a silenced Ingram. His belly...

"Time's wasting, Toby. In and out in two minutes."

"I think he's in the garage. He--"

Lofton rose to his knees and lunged up with the knife, throwing as much of his shoulder behind the awkward movement as he could. The blade penetrated the man's abdomen, glanced off a rib, and jammed to the handle.

Toby gurgled horribly behind his mask. Lofton caught the Ingram as it fell from the assassin's hands. The dying man took short, scraping steps as a thick, dark wetness gushed to the floor.

Toby's masked face dropped into view. Lofton raised the Ingram and pumped a quick burst into Toby's chest at pointblank range. The man flew backward with a crash. Lofton followed.

Another canister masked face appeared before him, two feet away. "What the--"

Lofton put a short burst into the man's upper chest and neck. The canister erupted and the left side of his mask and face disappeared in a reddishwhite vapor. He fell with a thump.

"Anton!"

Lofton's cry was answered with a burst from the living room. He kicked open what remained of the French doors, scrambled through the patio, and rolled behind a brick tree planter. His eyes were on fire and he hacked loudly. He held his breath, trying to stifle the noise. Loud, wheezing chokes rasped from his throat and lungs. He rose to all fours. His eyes ran, watching white smoke gush from Kirby's shattered windows.

"Fred! Toby!" Carrington shouted through his mask. "Vito, you and Curt take Lofton to the car. The Russian made it to the patio. Tell Dick and Ed to flank him from the side yard and then you back 'em up."

"What about Fred and Toby?"

"Dunno. Hurry up with Lofton. Make sure the sonofabitch is tied securely. Tell Curt to move out. Come on. We're outta time."

"Back to the sub-pen?"

"Yeah."

In pain, Lofton squeezed his eyes shut. He coughed. Phlegm rose in his throat as he tried to clear his lungs.

"I hear him out there, Ted."

"Move!"

They scrapped and grunted in the house. Moments later, leaves and gravel crunched in the side yard. Lofton sat, debating. He could spray the living room with the silenced Ingram. Carrington was in there still, he was sure. But, where was Anton? The trigger lay against his forefinger, ready. A little pressure, maybe a pound or two, and Carrington would be filled with holes.

Gravel crunched twenty feet to his right.

Adrenaline raced through him. Carrington waited inside, maybe Anton was next to him. And two, possibly three killers approached down either side yard. Five men. He would be flanked soon.

No chance.

Lofton flipped the Ingram to safe and tucked it in the small of his back. Crouching on all fours, he weaved through Kirby's patio furniture. His hip caught a table, the umbrella fell with a crash. He paused where a thirty-foot section of lawn eased down to the quay wall.

The dock was to his left. But, where was?--*Sonofabitch! Them Bones* hung from its bow by a dock line. The rest of Kirby's skiff was underwater--sunk. Lofton grit his teeth.

A twig snapped behind him. They were being cautious. Cold, professional experts assembled by Carrington for a deadly, grisly job. Carrington knew the best, active and retired.

A car started out on the street, shifted into gear, and raced down Bayshore Drive. That would be Vito and maybe Curt, along with Anton.

Three or four men. Poor odds with no surprise or backup. Within seconds they would be ready for their frontal assault. Lofton took a halting, spasmed breath.

Reason now--revenge later.

He jumped to the lawn, landed on all fours and rolled toward the quay wall. Fully expecting to feel bullets slam into him, he gripped the cement quay wall and flopped into the cold, dark water with a splash. He rose once and quickly took as much air as his seared lungs could accept, then dove, deep. His hand squished on the bottom as he frantically counted his strokes. Ten: *How far?* Twelve: He guessed--hoped--eighteen would do it. Sixteen: Lights flashed in his brain. Seventeen: Images went dark. He pushed a hand overhead and kicked.

Eighteen: He rose and broke the surface with a loud gasp. *Where?*

The moon shone overhead. He spat salt water as his head clunked against something solid. He reached out. It was smooth, glassy, highly polished. *Bandit's* bow rose above him. Somehow, he'd made it under the dock and to the other side of the Santa Cruz 70.

Kicking lightly, he pushed himself aft along *Bandit*'s sleek hull and reached the transom.

Two Ingrams sputtered and coughed in the patio. Furniture screeched and bounced across the brick. They would be here soon. Lofton looked across the channel toward a darkened Lido Isle 250 yards away. They'd had no trouble with *Them Bones* and they would have no trouble ripping *Bandit* apart, and him, too, if he remained. He checked the Ingram--it was secure in his waistband--and took a few experimental breaths. Embers still glowed in his lungs but he felt better.

One more deep breath. Lofton submerged and pushed away from Dr. Walter Kirby's dock into the dark, early morning channel. His head was clear now. He counted his strokes and silently surfaced after fifty yards. Two more deep breaths and he dove again.

Sergeant Roger T. Kilpatrick of the Newport Beach Police Department took the call at five-thirtysix A.M. The tape ran, but he dutifully made notes while trying to calm the outraged young man.

"What's the address on Lido Isle, sir?"

The young man gave details while Kilpatrick scribbled. He finished. Kilpatrick sighed, sat back, and twirled the telephone cord.

"Yes, sir, I'm sorry about your sailboard. Was it in the truck, too? What is the vehicle's make?...yessir, an '83 Toyota pickup stolen from in front of 972 Via Lido Nord. Color, sir?... Red, yessir, I..."

He listened patiently as the victim sputtered.

"Can you describe him, sir? I know it was dark." Kilpatrick sat up and took notes again. "Dark hair, Caucasian, striped tee shirt and dark trousers...yessir, that could help...No, sir, it's good you didn't try to stop him...

"Yes, sir, we'll send a patrol unit as soon as possible. We're dealing with an emergency on Bayshore Drive, a shooting... Yessir... If you could come in later today and fill out a report, sir, we'll make sure all units are alerted.

"...You say it was stolen about fivefifteen?... Yessir, I'll put that out also. Sir...me? My name's Kilpatrick--KILPAT RICK. Yessir, badge number 2436. Good day, sir."

22

Ted Carrington pulled the white government pool car up to the Del Coronado Hotel's main portico.

A valet snapped the Chrysler's door open. "Checking in, sir?"

"Waiting. My party will be here in a minute." He gave the black-vested youth a sour look.

"Yes, sir." Closing the door, the valet walked to a cab next to Carrington and struggled with luggage.

Carrington checked his watch: 9:46. He'd barely had three hour's sleep at the Five Palms Hotel on the mainland when he'd been summoned. The trip over the Coronado Bridge in the bright morning light should have perked him up. Usually, one could see Point Loma to the west and, to the south, deep into Mexico. Not today. San Diego's weather matched his attitude. Although there was a warm Santa Ana in Newport Beach, the fringes of a humid tropical storm hovered over San Diego. It had hailed and rained yesterday. The lingering overcast obscured his panorama at the bridge's crest. San Diego Bay lay torpid beneath him, sludgy and full of runoff. Beyond, the Pacific Ocean, spent from the storm, rested flat and oily, reluctant to flush the harbor with its cleansing tide.

Carrington eyed his watch. 9:51. Activity on the portico was brisk, with guests checking in and out. Engines caught and growled, tires squealed on the pavement as cars worked their way around his Chrysler. Carrington blinked. *Where the hell is he? Still languishing in the Presidential Suite with its view of Glorietta Bay.* Rubbing sleep from his eyes, he waved the valet over and pulled a ten dollar bill from his wallet. "Is there any chance I could get a traveler of coffee?"

The passenger door clicked open. Felix Renkin got in, saying, "Good morning, Carrington." He fastened his seat belt.

Carrington replaced the bill in his wallet, started the car, and drove off. Turning left on Orange Avenue he glanced at Dr. Renkin. He wore a gray herringbone suit, red bow tie, and patent leather loafers.

"I imagine you're tired," Renkin said.

"I'm fine, sir."

"You were successful last night?"

"Uhhuh, except Dobrynyn escaped." Carrington told him about the raid. "I could have got both of them but our forces were divided between here and Newport Beach. He won't get far," he quickly added. "We monitored a report from the Newport Beach Police Department. It sounds like Dobrynyn stole a pickup truck. But he doesn't know the area. He has no money or clothes and I have my best men looking for him. I think we'll have him by the end of the day."

"And the Soviet sergeant, what's his name? Ullanov--what about him?"

"He wasn't there, sir. Probably stayed with the submarine. We'll nail him when we catch Lofton's brother."

Renkin propped his elbow on the window sill and stroked his chin. "Too bad about Adams and Perelli. Were you able to recover their bodies?"

"Yes, sir. We stashed narcotics around Kirby's place, just like his car. It will look like a mob problem."

"You're sure that's not too shallow a cover?"

"No, sir. Vito's an expert. He knows how to arrange things. The police are buying it. We even..."

Renkin's mind was elsewhere.

Carrington waited.

"And you are sure it's Lofton?"

"Reasonably so, sir. The one without the beard. We haven't been able to talk to him, though. He's--ah--sort of indisposed." Carrington turned right on Fourth Street to approach the Coronado Bridge. "He hasn't regained, uh, awakened yet."

Renkin's finger toyed with his lip. "There is something else."

"Yes sir?"

"Mr. Hatch."

"Who?"

"The art dealer. He's flying in this evening."

"What? How does he know we're here?"

Renkin leaned back. "It couldn't have been too much of a secret, especially with the president blabbing and grinning in Balboa Park last week. And, Hatch wants to see us badly."

"Do you know why? Is it the Petropavlovsk matter?"

"No, it's something else." Renkin paused. He absently flipped the electric door lock button up and down. "Senator John Phillips called a nationally televised press conference a half hour ago."

"Phillips! What's his problem?"

"Visibility, Carrington, visibility. He's hardly in office and already he's campaigning for votes five years hence."

"I don't understand."

"The V22 Osprey buy for the NSC. Apparently Phillips has decided to blow the whistle to Congress.""But you told him you were going to have the purchase rescinded."

Renkin nodded. "Phillips has learned something. I don't know what yet, but maybe he feels I don't intend to rescind the order. On the other hand, he could be pulling a William Proxmire with me as his target. I just don't know, yet.

"Somehow Mr. Hatch got wind of Senator Phillips's announcement over the weekend. He called this morning and said we have to meet today." Renkin looked out at San Diego Bay. "Tonight, actually."

Silence fell. Carrington picked up on it. "Is there something else?" He slowed at the Coronado Bridge toll booths, accelerated up the bridge, and waited for Renkin to speak.

Renkin took a deep breath. "I think he's going to pressure me."

"To do what?"

"Get out. Retire. They've brought it up before. I think they're nervous about what might happen if I'm drawn into a protracted investigation, especially if it's televised. They'd be embarrassed if my cover was blown."

"What are you going to do?"

"Don't know yet." Renkin looked at Carrington. "And don't worry. You'll be taken care of one way or another."

"I appreciate that, sir." Carrington rubbed his chin. "Where?"

"I think we'll meet in my suite. Hatch is to call back in two hours when his flight is confirmed. I want you to be present at the meeting."

"Yes, sir."

They crested the bridge and dipped toward San Diego. A DC-10 popped from the overcast, almost at their eye level, wallowing toward Lindbergh Field with its gear and flaps extended.

"And now Lofton."

Carrington said, "We may have to waken him. He could be tough to question."

Renkin looked at his watch. "I'm not interested in questioning him now. What do you suggest?"

"I see. Uh, a .44 magnum, hollow point will take care of him. His head will disappear. Would you like to do it?"

Renkin set his mouth; his fingers drummed. "I'll leave that up to you."

Carrington headed south on I-5 then took the offramp to Harbor Drive. Five minutes later, they turned on a narrow, potholed street, bumped over rail sidings, and eased into a small parking lot.

Brutus's pen was a bleached cream three-story clapboard building, perhaps seventy feet on its facade, surrounded by a ten- foot chain-link fence. A sign with peeling black letters read "Trade-Winds Tuna Company." On their left, mothballed Navy ships lay nested to piers. Faded haze gray superstructures, naked masts stripped of their radars, and gun turrets spotted with red lead stretched beyond their view. To their right loomed the Consolidated Industries Shipyard. A large container ship was perched nearly complete on her ways. White letters on her bow announced *Empress Olivia*. Welders, riggers, and painters swarmed her decks. Two overhead cranes reached over the ship. Thick steel panels descended into *Empress Olivia*'s hold. Pneumatic tools ripped at the air as they got out of the car, arc welding lights flashed behind protective covers. A heavy sledge clanged deep within the ship.

Carrington walked around, opened the trunk, and hoisted a lead-lined suitcase. Their feet crunched on gravel as they approached the fence. A man in a dark brown suit walked out of the building and wordlessly unlocked the gate.

The main door had a foot-square chicken wire safety glass panel. They waited until a face flashed behind the panel and they heard a loud, electronic click. They walked in, and the door swung shut behind them, muting the shipyard hammering next door. Two men stood in the lobby and eyed them as they passed. The building was cool, their soles squeaked on the green linoleum floor. Opening a set of double doors, Carrington led Renkin past a row of small offices, each crammed with heavy black file cabinets. Bright red labels marked "secret" were fastened below dial-combination handles. Three of the offices were occupied. Men sat at metal desks in white shirts and ties, talking on telephones. Pistol butts bulged from shoulder holsters.

Renkin's eyebrows went up.

"They'll find him. They're tracing," Carrington explained as they turned up a flight of stairs.

"Maybe you should check with them."

"In a minute, sir. Here, this is it."

A dark, heavy-set man stood before a thick door. Carrington waved a hand at the entrance. "OK, Vito."

The man nodded and unlocked the door. Carrington walked in, then motioned for Renkin to enter.

Felix Renkin stepped into a well-lighted room. Four wooden desks were stacked against one wall. A counter and empty cabinets took up the opposite wall. He sniffed. The room smelled dank and humid. It hadn't been used while the X-3 project was active.

A figure in a striped teeshirt and dark trousers lay tied and manacled to a chair that had been tipped over. Touching his nose bandage, Renkin stepped forward to inspect the man's face. The prisoner was unconscious, yet breathed heavily.

Renkin put his hands on his knees. "You really worked him over."

Carrington lay the suitcase on the counter. "Yeah, he kind of looks like he did in those Petropavlovsk photos."

Renkin nodded. "Sit him up and place him against the wall, please."

"Yes, sir. Hey, Vito, give me a hand."

Carrington and the guard wrestled the chair upright and shoved it against the wall. The captive's head rolled and slammed against the plaster. He groaned.

"That's all, Vito. Close the door on your way out." Carrington's mercenary nodded, walked out, and pulled the door shut with a dull thud.

While Renkin waited, Carrington rummaged in the suitcase and selected a Ruger .44 singleaction magnum. He loaded it with a hollow point round and spun the chamber.

The man in the chair groaned again and tried to raise his head.

"Hello, Brad, you look good without a beard." Carrington stepped before the prisoner. "Ah, Doctor Renkin. You should stand off to the left in case of ricochet."

The prisoner raised his head. His blackened left eye was closed. An ugly gash ran from the corner of the eye down to his cheek. The other eye was partly open but no pupil showed. His face was bloody. The swollen mouth hung open. Pinkish saliva drooled from one corner.

"Interesting uniform for a Spetsnaz."

"No, sir, that's a Soviet Navy uniform, petty officer second class. Must have been a disguise."

Carrington raised the pistol with both hands. "You ready, sir?" The hammer ratcheted back.

"Uhhh," a gurgle from the man in the chair. "*Serzhant. Josef.*"

Renkin said, "I'll wait outside." He headed for the door.

"*Brad. Zady doma ne odin chelovek, a dva.*" The man coughed, then weekly spat phlegm. It dribbled onto his teeshirt.

Carrington's heart jumped. *No!*

Seconds passed.

Renkin's hand lingered on the knob. He turned. "What did he say, Carrington?"

"Uh. Something about a sergeant."

"What else?" Renkin, his hands on his hips, walked back to the prisoner.

"He said, 'There are two men, ah, outside on the patio, not one.'"

"Did he use the word 'Brad'?"

"Yessir." *Make up your mind, damnit!* "Do you still want to do it, Dr. Renkin?"

The prisoner's right eyelid fluttered, "...*ya grzhdanin Sovetskozo Soyuza.*" Renkin rubbed his jaw.

"Sir, do you--"

"Shut up, Carrington. Let me think for a moment."

Carrington uncocked and lowered the magnum.

"Tell me what he said." Renkin sighed.

Carrington said, "Says he's a Soviet citizen."

"You knew?"

"Not until now."

"But how--"

Dobrynyn gurgled loudly.

They jumped.

"*Poshol ty na khuy, Dr. Renkin.*" His head fell to his chest.

"He knows who I am, Carrington. What did he say?"

"Ah, politely, he said, 'Screw you, Dr. Renkin.'"

"Indeed." Renkin sat on the workbench and crossed his feet.

"Sorry, sir." Carrington ran a hand through his hair. "Must have shaved off the beard. They weren't in the same room. One was--"

"Yes, yes. Please be quiet." Renkin put his palms on the bench, swung his feet, and studied the floor. After a moment, Renkin actually smiled, a rare gesture outside the cloakrooms of the U.S. Capitol Building. "Your screwup could be our good fortune." He stared at Carrington.

Carrington shoved the pistol in his belt. Leaning against the opposite wall, he rubbed his eyes and folded his arms. *I don't need this crap now. I need sleep. Let's blow the Ivan's brains out so I can go back to bed.* "I don't understand."

Renkin pointed. "That's Anton Dobrynyn."

"Yes, sir. Uh, I said I'm sorry." Carrington walked to the prisoner and propped the unblemished eyelid open. "Out like a light."

"The advantage is that we have a bargaining chip when Mr. Hatch shows up. A goodwill trade, so to speak, to take the pressure off their concern with the V22 purchase." Renkin looked down and muttered, more to himself than Carrington, "Plus, we can't return their $250,000 since we bought the Houston office building."

Renkin didn't mention the question of ramifications of world opinion if Dobrynyn's story became public. His having an American brother would cause intrigue and ultimate sympathy that would weigh heavily against the Soviets. And Renkin could, if he choose, add a bombshell about being Dobrynyn's father. He could twist the story. Talk about a pathetic German mother who, perhaps, he loved. Yes! And how he had been torn from her arms when he was transferred to the Pacific. He would say he wanted to go back and find her but learned too late that she'd been killed by a bomb blast and that the boys had disappeared. The Soviets couldn't fight that. The press would bury them. And espionage charges in the U.S. might be mitigated if the press took off on the story of Anna and her twins.

The Soviets would want Dobrynyn dead in any case, Renkin figured. His recent escapade in Petropavlovsk and, particularly, his heritage presented difficult problems for them--

"Sir?" Carrington let Dobrynyn's eyelid flop shut and nudged his cheek with his knuckles.

"One moment." What if he had Carrington interview Dobrynyn on videotape and got the full story? After that, he could hand Dobrynyn over as a goodwill gesture and would have the videotape as backup if the Soviets became difficult.

Except that--Renkin's feet swung faster--there was Lofton. His would-be protégée had seen him kill Thatcher. That wouldn't be too hard to refute, but Lofton knew too much about everything else. He needed Lofton dead as much as the Soviets needed Dobrynyn dead.

Felix Renkin looked at Carrington. "The disadvantage, Mr. Carrington, is that Brad Lofton, not that man," he pointed to Dobrynyn, "is on the loose--plus the sergeant they escaped with." His lips pressed together. "Therefore, tighten your net. I want Lofton captured, now."

Carrington unloaded the pistol and walked to the suitcase.

"Do you understand?" Renkin roared.

"Yessir." Carrington stopped. His head jerked in a nod.

"First those brain-dead Russians. And SOSUS couldn't keep up with him. That damned attack submarine flubbed its opportunity. And now you." Renkin pointed a finger and yelled, "Bunglers! Idiots! I want him. Now, damn you!"

Dull thuds and clangs drifted across from the *Empress Olivia*.

Renkin drew a breath. "And make arrangements to leave for Washington tomorrow. I'll try to wind up or postpone my meetings." He jumped off the bench and walked to the door. "Let's go. I have to catch Phillips's press conference."

Carrington packed the magnum and shut the suitcase. "Uh, sir?"

"What!"

He nodded at Dobrynyn. "What do we do with him?"

"Get him cleaned up, fed, and attended to. Mr. Hatch's conversations should be with a subject who doesn't smell of his own excrement. And have some videotaping equipment set up here. I want you to interview this man first thing in the morning." Felix Renkin turned and walked out of the room.

Sunlight. Something jiggled. Lofton heard scraping sounds but pushed them aside. His eyes were open, blinking. A face. Someone bent over him. He fought for consciousness. *Who was it?*

Blond, towheaded, freckles on young cheeks, green eyes; a boy, perhaps ten or eleven, stared openmouthed at him. Lofton sat up suddenly, and the spinnaker slipped off his shoulders.

The kid jumped back and found his voice. "Mommy! Someone's in here!"

Feet rushed the companionway. Tanned thighs, shorts. Bonnie Duffield stepped into *True Blue*'s cabin.

Their eyes locked. Lofton flicked his wrist--no Casio--and pulled *True Blue*'s three-quarter-ounce spinnaker cloth over his bare shoulders.

"Who is it, Mommy?"

"Brad! My God, you're all right!" Bonnie started toward him. The boy pulled at her elbow. "Tim, stop it, please. This man is Brad Lofton. He's a friend of mine."

"Did he know Daddy?"

Past tense. Lofton looked at her.

Bonnie nodded, shrugged, her eyes scanned the deck. "No, he didn't. Look, Tim, there's your math book, take it to the car. I'll be up in a minute."

The boy grabbed the textbook off the starboard shelf and trudged past Lofton. "Mommy," he said, "why can't we stay here today?"

"You know why," Bonnie said. "Go on up. I'll be right there."

"OK." The boy looked at Lofton, then shuffled up the small ladder. *True Blue* rocked as he jumped off.

"I--" they both said.

Lofton looked down.

"You first," Bonnie said. "The papers are full of what happened at Kirby's last night. Was that you?"

"Yes, we'd just arrived. What time is it?"

"Almost eleven o'clock. You said 'we'?"

"Yes, I have a twin brother."

"A what?" She sat next to him and took off her glasses.

"My own twin, Bonnie. An identical twin. He looks exactly like me. He saved my life. And...and... Look, I have to find Walt. Do you--? What's wrong? Bonnie?"

She sat next to him.

"Bonnie...?"

Her eyes glistened. "Brad. Walt's dead. A--"

"No!" Lofton roared.

Bonnie took his hands. "A car accident, the morning you left. It was terrible. I didn't know what to do. I couldn't talk to anybody. Finally I spoke with Daddy about it. He said he would nose around, but they--"

"What happened?"

"They said there were drugs in his car. The autopsy report showed his intoxication level was very high."

"He never did anything like that." Lofton's mind spun. Autopsy. Cutting up Walt. Alcohol. He shook his head, "No!"

"I know. We talked...about you...about him after you left. Two, three hours. We had breakfast, then he went home to clean up for his trip to San Diego. I liked him...and now..."

Her arms went around Lofton. "Oh, God, Brad. It's been awful."

They rocked and swayed.

"Where?"

"Ortega Highway, about halfway to Lake Elsinore. He skidded into a power pole. It fell and electrocuted him."

"He wouldn't have taken Ortega Highway to San Diego."

"I know."

Deep within him, a wail grew. It caught in his throat, he fought to keep it in. He shook, his hands spasmed. "Renkin!" he cried loudly.

Bonnie's arms went tighter. Her tears ran on his shoulder.

"Renkin staged it. Walt didn't make it." He looked at her. "Do you know if he talked to anybody?"

She shook her head.

"So that's why nothing happened on this end. No wonder they got away with throwing me in jail and ...and...killing those poor fishermen..."

"Killing who?"

"Those bastards!" Lofton clenched his teeth. "Those dirty, bastards! And Renkin's goons were there to shoot up Walt's house and kidnap my brother." His head went to the nape of her neck. She drew him close as he shook and wrapped both arms around his head.

"My best friend." Lofton's eyes became liquid. "Walt."

"Brad," she said softly.

"They took my brother away. I didn't even know I had one until two weeks ago. He saved my life."

"Yes."

He buried his head in her neck. "He didn't have to help me. He just did it."

She rocked him for a moment.

Lofton jerked up and looked at her, his eyes red. Tears ran down his cheeks. "Bonnie, this is hard to say, but, subconsciously, I've always felt like something was missing in my life. Then I met Anton..."

They fell silent as she rocked him. After a while, he told her about Petropavlovsk and their return to Kirby's the previous night. He talked faster. His sentences fused. He stuttered.

She held him as he sat in a heap, crying openly, the spinnaker gathered about his nakedness. Bonnie pulled him to her breast while he shook, then kissed him on top of his head, and they swayed.

"Mommy?" from outside.

"Up in a minute, dear." She kissed Lofton's forehead and eyes, then his lips. "Gotta go, Brad," she said softly. "Look, stay here and get some sleep. I'll take Tim to his soccer game, then bring us dinner."

Lofton sniffed and rubbed his nose. "Feel like a damned crybaby. I'm sorry."

They hugged tighter. "It's all right." She nodded at his soaked uniform heaped on the deck. "Do you need clothes, too?"

"Yes, everything. I still have my billfold." He reached down to his trousers, pulled out his wallet and handed over damp currency.

She took the money. "I'll be back as soon as I can." They hugged again, then she put on her glasses, rose, and made for the ladder.

"Bonnie."

"Yes?"

"I'm sorry about Bob, and I'm sorry to throw all this at you on top of it. When did it happen?"

A curtain dropped over her face. "Five days after you left. He died in his sleep. He'd been almost brain-dead for a long time, they said. And," she exhaled loudly, "we knew it."

She'd been through a lot, Lofton realized. First Kirby and then her husband.

They looked at each other. Both tried to smile and failed.

"Back later, Brad. I'll close the hatch. Get some sleep."

Bonnie Duffield went through the companionway. She replaced the hatch-boards and snapped the canvas in place. *True Blue* rocked gently as she stepped off and walked away. Lofton eased back on the settee and pulled the spinnaker around him. His eyes glistened, and tears ran for a long time before he fell into a deep sleep.

While Lofton walked up to the guest dock to shower and shave, Bonnie set the table with cold cuts, potato and bean salads, lettuce, and rolls. She finished and checked the clock. Lofton had only been gone five minutes, he'd be up there a while. She tapped a fingernail on a tooth. *Do it.* Grabbing her purse, she jumped off *True Blue* and headed for her car.

She returned with the Chardonnay ten minutes later, finding Lofton bent over the NAV table. His back was to her as he studied a chart. "Chow time, Brad. Dig in. Look what I got." The sack rattled she pulled the bottle out.

He turned briefly. "OK. That looks good." Lofton's attention returned to the chart. He twirled a pencil on a pad.

Bonnie rummaged for plastic glasses, checking him from the corner of her eye. He stood with locked elbows, his hands gripping the NAV table edges as he stared at the chart.

"Brad? You hungry?"

"Yes. Very." Lofton pushed away from the table, sat stiffly, and heaped a plastic plate while she uncorked the wine. He looked different, and it wasn't, she decided, the clothes she'd brought which he wore now: Levis, pullover dark green sweater, and topsiders. He'd changed. Imperceptibly, Bonnie noticed, something was different. Wrinkles, not those of age or debilitation, had gathered around narrowed eyes; his mouth had a certain resolve under slightly flared nostrils. His stance at the chart table and even now as he sat seemed firm...almost tense.

She poured the wine and started on her own food as Lofton bent close to his plate. His fork moved swiftly. *My God!* "When was the last time you ate?"

"Umph," he slurped. "*Brutus.* Crackers and some canned beans. A lot of our stuff was ruined. And I didn't count on having two mouths to feed on the way back. We had to ration." He looked up at her as he forked in another huge load. Without apology, Lofton wolfed everything on the table while Bonnie managed to salvage half a plateload for herself.

"I'll bet you drank bug juice." She tried a smile.

Lofton leaned back and laced his fingers over his stomach. "Oh, yeah. We had some of that..." His eyes wandered around the salon, then fixed over her shoulder. His brow was knitted.

What is he staring at? "What do the two of you look like together?"

Lofton turned to her, a suggestion of a smile at the corners of his mouth. "I am he and he is me." His gaze wandered back to...

...The NAV table! She casually turned her head, seeing the chart he'd laid out. She knew it well. The legend's large black letters read:

NOAA Chart Number 18740
San Diego to Santa Rosa Island.

No! She searched for his eyes.

He focused on the starboard bulkhead and spun a fork.

"Could I have some more wine, please?"

"What?"

"Damn you, Brad Lofton!" Bonnie slammed her fist on the table. Dinnerware jumped and tinkled.

"What? Bonnie, Jesus you scared--Bonnie, don't cry." He slid over and held her. "I'm sorry, Bonnie, I really am."

She sat up and wiped her eyes. "Me, too. We've both been through a lot. First Walt. I couldn't do anything about Bob. For a year and a half I couldn't do anything about him..."

"I'm sorry." He kissed her ear and stroked her hair.

"And you can't do anything about your brother."

Lofton leaned back and arched an eyebrow.

She looked at him, "He's like you?"

"Exactly. You should see, like I was standing outside my head and watching myself. I got to know him on the way back and--oh, God!" His gaze went back to the NAV table.

Bonnie paused for a moment. "Why don't we just go to the police?"

Lofton shook his head. "Nothing's changed. Renkin has me over a barrel. They'll arrest me for Thatcher's murder. And then--"

"How about a lawyer? Maybe somebody in government service? There has to be somebody..."

Lofton put his palms to his temples. "There's nobody. And if I just sit back, Carrington will find me. It's as simple as that. He probably has people out looking for me now." His eyebrows shot up. "Maybe you, too."

Staring at the NAV table, he slid out.

Bonnie grabbed his hand. "Brad," she said quietly. "You don't even know where he is."

He slumped back. "I do. It came to me in the shower. Last night, someone said 'sub pen.' That has to be the place where I work--worked. It would be a good hideout. A good place to keep a prisoner."

"You're sure?"

"I think so. But they'll have him in Mexico soon. Or stuffed in the hold of some freighter. I have to move, now."

He slammed a fist. "Damnit! If only Walt were alive we could raid the place. Hell, we could set up a diversion somewhere, then drive a truck through the front door and have Anton out in sixty seconds. Walt..."

"That's what I'm trying to say. You can't do it yourself."

"It's my only chance." He stood. "Bonnie, would you like to go to Avalon again?" He spread his arms and looked around. "*True Blue* this time."

He looked at the bulkhead-mounted Seth Thomas: 1622. Sunset would fall in a little over two hours. He went to the NAV table and checked his figures. Twenty or so miles to Avalon. The seas were calm, *True Blue* could power at a little over five knots. That was four hours or so. He could board *Brutus* between ten and tenthirty.

Lofton said in a half-tone. "Without help, a land assault isn't feasible. But I could do it with *Brutus*. In and out. All I have to do is swim under the gate and set up a diversion."

"There will be guards." Bonnie waved a hand. "That--that man's henchmen, his goons."

"Not that many. I know that place well. Hell, I practically lived there for the past eighteen months. I can get in all right. I'll only have to take out one or two people. The rest will be asleep."

She stood and moved next to him, her eyes glistening.

He took her in his arms. "He's my brother. My...my last one. Kirby, gone. Ullanov, gone. I've got to, I've got to try, Bonnie."

They held each other and swayed. Lofton kissed her. They swayed again.

"Brad." Her voice squeaked.

He broke away. "Losing time." With a pair of dividers, he stepped off the distance from Avalon to Point Loma: sixty-eight miles. If he could squeeze twentyfour knots from a wheezing *Brutus*, the trip would take a little less than three hours. The San Diego Harbor transit would take another fortyfive minutes or so. He would be there between twelvethirty and one in the morning. O.K. Except...

"Rust." He bit his thumbnail.

"What rust?" She ran her arm around his waist as he stared at the chart.

"Damn thing almost blew up." He told her about the H_2O_2 master control solenoid valve problems he'd had aboard *Brutus* on the trip to and from Petropavlovsk.

He did not tell her that just before he exited off Catalina to pick up *Them Bones*, he'd seen it growing on the fuel block again. And no more spare parts nor time even if he did have spares. *Brutus* could explode while he was en route to San Diego. He'd have to chance it.

23

The open, brass cage elevator took Yuri Borodine up to the Del Coronado Hotel's fifth floor. He walked down the hall to a blue-and-white paneled door marked "Presidential Suite." Borodine checked both directions and knocked.

Ted Carrington opened the door immediately. "Good evening, Mr. Hatch."

Borodine shuffled in with a nod. His limp was pronounced from fall dampness and further aggravated by the hotel's proximity to the coast.

"Ah, welcome to San Diego, Worthington, good to see you again." Felix Renkin rose from a sofa and greeted his control with both hands. "Come on in, Carrington will fix us something." He waved to a wet bar. "What can we offer you?"

Borodine took in the room. Green and pink pastel walls and mauve carpeting complemented rosewood furniture and heavy Victorian accents. An area to his left contained a pool table. The room felt cold. He stifled an urge to hug his arms to his chest. "Sorry I'm so late, Dr. Renkin. Sherry, please."

Renkin led him to a conversation area situated before a large window. They stood for a moment taking in Coronado's empty streets and Mediterranean-style buildings with tile roofs. Except for two ships and small craft navigation lights, Glorietta Bay and San Diego Harbor stood as a black void to his right. Lights from the San Diego Naval Base winked across the bay. He'd seen parts of the North Island Naval Air Station as he crossed the Coronado Bridge. The brightly illuminated USS *Constellation* was moored there and he'd recognized a pair of S-3A Viking ASW jets practicing night touch-and-goes on North Island's main runway. The submarine base was over at Point Loma. It hit Borodine that he stood in one of the great centers of U.S. naval power.

Renkin waited until Borodine got his bearings, then waved him to a chair. "Marvelous, isn't it?" He took the sofa. "Where are you staying? Close by, I hope."

Carrington handed Borodine his sherry in a crystal goblet, moving tactfully to the pool table.

Borodine sat and peered out. "I haven't made arrangements yet. A motel, perhaps." He looked around. "The Presidential Suite. Where did the president stay?"

Renkin smiled. "With friends in Rancho Santa Fe."

"Ah, security. You were his surrogates?" Borodine sat back and relaxed.

Renkin nodded. "In a manner of speaking. They believed he was quartered here. The president commuted by helicopter to North Island Naval Air Station and did conduct his press conferences here in the hotel."

"I see. And how long will you be staying?" Borodine winced as Carrington broke the triangular cluster of balls with a loud clack.

"We were scheduled for another week. But something has come up. We return tomorrow afternoon."

Carrington drove balls with a vengeance. They slammed into the pockets, rattled underneath, and clacked to the bin at the table's head. Borodine gritted his teeth. He raised an eyebrow to Renkin. "Can we speak?" he asked softly, and waved his glass at Carrington.

"Yes, there are no devices here and, as you know, Carrington is my administrative assistant."

"All right, Dr. Renkin." Borodine crossed a leg and sipped his sherry. "We have a problem. We need assurances about our V22 purchase. Senator Phillips's speech today has us curious about your ability to deliver."

"You doubt me?"

"No. We need assurances."

"Mr. Hatch, please, I would like to know your name."

Borodine sipped again, then nodded. "Please forgive me, but I am compelled to remain Worthington Hatch, art dealer." He watched Renkin. The man almost pouted.

"Very well. Yes, the V22s. Unfortunately your down payment has been invested in some very illiquid real estate. An office building. Otherwise, we'd give it back."

"That was not our--"

Carrington blasted another rack of balls. One skipped off the table.

"Carrington."

"Yes, sir?"

"Perhaps you could find something else to do."

"Yes, sir." Carrington stowed the cue, sat in a club chair and flicked through a magazine.

Borodine said, "That's not our intention, Dr. Renkin."

"What?"

"A refund does not worry us. You promised a V22 and we have closed other channels because you were supposedly the best source. We would lose too much time reopening those channels. Therefore, it has to be you."

Renkin steepled his fingers. His bald head gleamed. "Fine. Is that what this is all about?"

"Of course."

"Ah. Then please explain to your associates that the matter will be taken care of," Renkin said. "Even sooner than I had indicated previously."

"Meaning?"

"Meaning I can deliver a V22 to you sooner than we had agreed."

"How? We had agreed on a 1992 delivery in South America."

Renkin exhaled. "What I can say is that I may have an opportunity to hand you one of the first five."

Carrington stopped flicking pages.

"Indeed. How soon?" Borodine asked.

"Umm, within six months or so. I can arrange a disappearance, over water perhaps..."

"Are you sure?"

"Yes."

Carrington picked up another magazine and stared at the cover.

"We need proof."

"Look, Mr. Hatch. I have not failed you before, in forty years of dedicated service."

Borodine watched a pair of lonely headlights sweep over the Coronado Bridge. "Dr. Renkin, they're very angry about the Petropavlovsk affair. They feel it's your fault. I shouldn't be telling you this. I'm doing you a favor." Borodine waved a hand. "Now we need proof."

Renkin smiled. "How can you accuse me? You had both the man and the *X3* in your custody. The blame lies elsewhere."

"Possibly, Dr. Renkin, but it was your man and your submarine that did the damage and escaped."

"And your man," Renkin reminded him.

Pins and needles shot up Borodine's right leg. He crossed it over his left. "Yes, but--"

"Or was it men? Your message said something about a master sergeant-- Carrington!" Renkin called loudly over his shoulder. "What was that sergeant's name?"

"As I remember it was Ullanov, sir."

Renkin swung back to Borodine and counted on his fingers. "Three defectors, Mr. Hatch. We've exposed three defectors for you: PITCHFORK--
"

"Who?"

"Your man in Petropavlovsk plus Ullanov and Dobrynyn. You should agree that we're doing our job well on this side, so you can begin to control yours." Renkin gave a tight-lipped smile, pleased with himself, pleased to swing the subject away from V-22s.

"Dr. Renkin, we believe they were kidnaped by your man."

"Two highly trained, elite Spetsnaz, kidnaped?"

"Well, yes, coerced by a highly trained SEAL," Borodine shot back.

"Mr. Hatch, your message said Lofton escaped with the *aid* of your two men and that they planted limpet mines."

"That's not what the evidence shows now. Our men were kidnaped."

"If they were kidnaped, why did you try to kill them with a nuclear weapon?"

"We killed them because we thought they deserted. We didn't know until later that Colonel Dobrynyn and Sergeant Ullanov had been coerced." Borodine paused to gain control. "And, incidentally, your Mr. Lofton--"

"My Mr. Lofton? It was you who suggested he work for me."

"I wont go into that now." Borodine drew a breath. "Mr. Lofton is also responsible for the death of one of the Soviet Union's top physicians. Colonel Sadka perished horribly. His hands and legs were tied with piano wire and he was burned alive in the car that was to carry him and Lofton to the airport."

Renkin checked his watch: a little after midnight. He'd taken care of the V22 problem and Hatch's zealous blunders had provided a good night's entertainment. Amazing. He'd given Hatch more credit for intellect and diplomacy. The little man was really upset, he must be under terrible pressure. And he hadn't mentioned retirement. Maybe they had forgotten about it.

Time to get it over with. Be nice to Hatch, make him feel useful. Offer him a nice room, a Lanai suite perhaps. They had spectacular ocean views, one could see the Coronado Islands off the coast of Mexico. Then, after videotaping Dobrynyn, send Hatch home with his prize.

Renkin set a grim expression. "That's terrible, Mr. Hatch. You can rest assured that we are very sorry for Lofton's actions. Did Colonel--Dr. Sadka have a family?"

"I suppose so. Now, Dr. Renkin, about the--"

"Are you certain the blast sank the submarine?"

"Yes, nobody I know of can survive five kilotons." Borodine sat back, satisfied with the strength of his rebuttal. He recrossed his legs. "Perhaps you do?"

It was time. He had to do this right. "Yes, Mr. Hatch, I know of at least one."

Borodine said, "A disfigured freak, perhaps?" For some reason he thought of his foot.

"I'm sorry to tell you the submarine survived the blast--"

"What?"

"--and we have captured one of your defectors."

"Impossible!"

"His name is Lieutenant Colonel Anton Pavel Dobrynyn."

Borodine's eyes flicked right and left. Then he managed to say, "You're joking! He's dead, with the others."

"Not in the least, Mr. Hatch. Colonel Dobrynyn successfully journeyed to Southern California. He arrived last night and we captured him."

Borodine shifted forward in his chair, still stunned. He'd been assured the midget submarine had been sunk. What was Renkin trying to do?

"We have him nearby, Mr. Hatch. He's yours to interrogate and, after a day or two, send home if you wish. We'd be glad to help. I suggest going by way of Mexico. Things aren't too difficult traveling south through Tijuana."

Borodine narrowed his eyes. "He's in San Diego?"

Renkin nodded. "About ten minutes away."

Borodine's mind whirled with the possibilities. Dobrynyn still alive! How? "May I see him?"

"Of course."

Borodine nodded, started to rise and sat back. He rubbed his leg, but it wasn't pins and needles that bothered him. Renkin was trying to divert him from the V-22 problem. And he hadn't touched the main part of his agenda. Belousov had issued the ultimatum. Make Felix Renkin commit to retirement within twelve months--V-22s or not. If he refused, Borodine had permission to imply that Renkin would be killed.

Borodine hoped the Ph.D would choose retirement without further pressure. For in the process of winding up his affairs, Renkin could still provide a V-22 within, as he'd just said, the next six months. Excellent. Borodine could still carry out Belousov's order and have his prize, too. He could even take care of the Dobrynyn matter.

Borodine stroked his cheek. He would have to make sure.

Renkin drummed his fingers on the sofa's arm. "Mr. Hatch. Do you wish to see him now?"

"How can you do this?"

"Simple. We'll arrange for a nice room for you here and drive you over. We can be back within a short period of time and--"

"That's not what I meant, Dr. Renkin."

Renkin's fingers stopped drumming. His eyebrows went up. "Yes?"

Sitting close to Renkin, Borodine lowered his voice. "I said 'How can you do this?'"

"Please explain."

"That man is your own son."

Renkin's mouth opened, then closed just as quickly. His lips pressed together. "You'll never let me forget, will you?"

Borodine's voice was chillingly cold. "You are willing to send Anton Pavel Dobrynyn to a firing squad to deflect our attention from V-22s?"

"Of course not. I'm merely trying to help."

"Can you really deliver a V 22?"

Renkin looked out the window.

"Dr. Renkin?"

Silence.

"Dr. Renkin."

"I don't know. Possibly. It all depends on how this Phillips investigation turns out."

Borodine's heart sank. "When will you find out?"

Renkin shrugged. "A few months."

With a sigh, Borodine said, "Dr. Renkin. I have instructions. We want you to retire."

Renkin's head jerked to Borodine.

"They've given you twelve months."

"I wont be uncovered," Renkin said.

"We can't take that chance."

"All right. If I am discovered, I'll just come over to you."

Borodine steepled his fingers. "No."

"What?" Renkin sat forward.

Carrington rose and walked toward them.

"Sit down, Carrington," Renkin said. He looked back to Borodine. "What do you mean?"

"We can't take that chance, either, Dr. Renkin. We would jeopardize our relationship with the U.S."

"I'll insist." Renkin waved a hand and stammered. "I could fly to Moscow and turn myself over."

"We wouldn't allow that, Dr. Renkin," Borodine said.

"No!"

"What is all this crap?" Carrington said.

Borodine eyed Renkin and Carrington as they stared at him.

Renkin asked softly, "You would use the apparatus?"

Borodine cleared his throat. "I'm sure that won't be necessary."

"Bastards!" Carrington roared.

Renkin waved a hand. "Sit, Carrington. Just sit."

Carrington drew up a chair and sat. The three stared at one another.

"I'm sorry, Dr. Renkin. There is a nice villa for you and," he nodded to Carrington, "in the South of France."

"What if the investigation becomes involved and they don't let me retire?"

Borodine shrugged.

"You bastards," Carrington said in a low voice.

"I suppose we could set you up in a country where there is no extradition. Cuba? Libya? Bulgaria, perhaps. We're not sure, yet."

Renkin squared his shoulders. "I can still deliver a V-22."

Borodine smiled. "I hope so, Dr. Renkin. That would be nice. In any case, they'll do all that is necessary to make you comfortable. After all, we do recognize your long career, your forty years of dedicated service."

"Yes." Renkin nodded slowly.

"I'd like to see Dobrynyn, now. I'll follow in my car."

Renkin looked around the suite. An ancient Tiffany clock was perched on a highly polished side table. Next to it, a Lalique owl glass carving caught his eye. He'd had dinner sent up this evening, his table had been set on the same ornate coffee table that stood before him with china, silver utensils, and linens. The hotel had provided a fine French Burgundy. He'd watched San Diego's lights twinkle as the stereo played a Beethoven piano sonata. His gaze wandered across San Diego Bay to the naval station's mothball fleet. Two amber sodium vapor street lights marked the Trade Winds Tuna Cannery.

I'm not through with these people yet, Renkin thought. Especially after I have the videotape.

Dobrynyn's hands, waist, and upper legs were tied securely to the chair. They'd left his feet undone so he could hobble to the bathroom, where they would untie his lower bindings, shift the chair aside, and yank his pants down. His left eye remained blackened and closed. Ugly red welts ran down his neck, chin, and forehead. A fresh compress was stuck on his cheek, other bandages covered smaller gashes. Under close guard, he'd been allowed a shower and they had given him clean baggy slacks, a dark-brown work shirt and tennis shoes.

A man, the one they called Vito, sat on the counter and swung a foot loosely. "Ready for more chili, Ivan? Good stuff. Huh?"

It was good up to a point. At three, they'd spoon fed half a bowl to him before Vito poured in large dollops of tabasco sauce. Dobrynyn's throat and mouth burned terribly, and without water, he'd choked and wheezed while Vito and two other guards laughed. Dobrynyn gave up after two more fiery mouthfuls. Still, he felt better.

"Hey, Ivan. I'm talkin' to you, man. It's past your dinnertime and Ted gave orders for you to eat." Vito slid off the counter and walked toward him. He stopped when they heard voices in the hall. They eyed each other as the door clicked open.

Carrington walked in leading Felix Renkin and a short, thin, dark-haired man who walked with a limp.

Renkin walked up and waved a hand. "Lieutenant Colonel Anton Pavel Dobrynyn."

Borodine stooped and looked into Dobrynyn's unblemished eye. "That's not Dobrynyn."

"It is. He shaved his beard," said Renkin.

"I see."

Carrington said, "Sorry he's not in mint condition. He put up a fight."

Dobrynyn tracked Borodine with his good eye as he circled the chair.

Borodine said, "How can I be sure this is our Spetsnaz?" The man rubbed his thigh and gazed back to Dobrynyn. "He may be your Mr. Lofton." He sighed. "Forgive me. They'll need assurances that some sort of elaborate counter-switch is not taking place."

"Mr. Hatch. What would I have to gain? You're going to eventually shoot this man whether it's Lofton or Dobrynyn. And if it was Lofton, I would have had him shot by now. As I said, this one is yours. All you have to do is check fingerprints. I assure you, they do vary."

"Yes. I read your report. But I don't have the time or equipment available for verification, do I?" He casually stepped behind Dobrynyn and stooped. Borodine bent closer, running his index finger over a signet ring with a gold "U" on Dobrynyn's right hand.

"I would like to talk to him, alone, please."

Renkin paused and looked out the window. "All right. Carrington. You better check his bindings, too. Just to make sure."

Carrington walked over and yanked on Dobrynyn's bindings. "He's not going anywhere."

"It's getting late, Mr. Hatch. How long do you need?" Renkin asked.

"A half hour, perhaps." He raised an eyebrow to the three men.

"All right. Ah, we'll leave Mr. Calabra here just in case Dobrynyn becomes violent."

Borodine put his hands on his hips.

"Don't worry, Mr. Hatch," said Renkin. "Vito doesn't understand Russian. You'll have complete privacy."

Renkin opened the door and paused. "Oh, and Mr. Hatch?"

"Yes?"

"Carrington tells me you're armed. Is this true?"

Borodine had hidden the nine-millimeter Beretta seven-shot automatic in the small of his back. "Yes."

Vito folded his arms and stared at Borodine.

Renkin nodded to Dobrynyn. "We wouldn't like you to use it here."

Borodine flushed slightly. "I never intended to."

Renkin glanced at Vito. "Fine. You won't mind giving it to Calabra for the time being?"

Vito walked over, his palm outstretched.

Borodine reluctantly drew the pistol and dropped it into the man's hand. He eyed Renkin. "I want it back."

"As soon as we leave." Renkin said.

Just as well, Borodine sighed to himself. Wait a day or two. Confirm the order Belousov was sure to issue to have Dobrynyn killed as soon as possible. The Spetsnaz represented an international stink that would be laid at the Pacific fleet admiral's doorstep.

"We'll get some coffee," Renkin said. "Do you care for any?"

"No, thank you."

Renkin walked out. Carrington followed and shut the door.

Vito sat on the counter, glanced at Borodine, then picked up a magazine.

Borodine waited until the footsteps faded. He pulled up a chair, sat, and spoke in Russian. "Sergeant Ullanov is dead, isn't he?"

Silence.

"I'm sorry to learn of it, Colonel. The file said Ullanov served with you for the past eighteen years. You must have been close."

Dobrynyn lifted his head.

"It's all right." Borodine reached over and patted Dobrynyn on the shoulder. "Please relax. Now, there are rules. I can't tell you my real name. I do know your superiors, some intimately. Also, I know a lot about you, more than even you know, I suspect."

Dobrynyn exhaled. *So I just found out.*

Borodine looked down, wondering how many of the Lofton-connected disasters, from the sinking of the *Kunashiri Maru* to the hideous inferno in the Petropavlovsk KGB naval basin, he would take the blame for. Investigators in Moscow could charge that coaxing Renkin to bring in Lofton had triggered the whole predicament, one with serious international implications.

Momentarily, he squeezed his eyes closed. There must be a way to mitigate the situation. Delivering, or at least liquidating Lieutenant Colonel Dobrynyn, would help. And perhaps Jet StreamCBelousov's disinformation program over the Okhotsk oceanbed cables--was salvageable. That could return things to a status quo.

Borodine rubbed his jaw. "We can help each other."

Dobrynyn looked up. *Damnit.*

"What do you or Lofton know about an operation called Jet Stream?"

Dobrynyn stared at the man's slicked-back hair, sunken cheeks, and full lips. *Look at his eyes.* They darted every half-second with a new thought. It swelled over Dobrynyn. *Hatch knows everything about me and he's agitated, perhaps scared.*

Borodine rubbed his hands together and looked down. "Colonel," he said softly. "Dr. Renkin will have you killed. Tonight probably. Your only chance is with me. I can take you home. You will have a chance there. Things have slackened. There will be a fair trial. They would understand the circumstances with you and your brother. They would be lenient."

Get moving. Buy time. Dobrynyn spat, "How do you plan to do it, *Zamp?*"

"Please don't call me that, Colonel. *Zampolits* wouldn't survive five minutes in the U.S." He paused. "We have a Canadian pipeline. You could be home within, um, three to five days. Leningrad. How would you like that?" He slapped Dobrynyn's shoulder again and checked Vito from the corner of his eye. The man sat all the way against the counter, his magazine folded over as he concentrated.

"What are you? GRU?"

Borodine eyed the door and said softly, "Fifth Division."

"Fleet Intelligence?"

"Yes."

"Where?"

"Pacific. I don't have time to parley with you, Colonel. This is how it must work. You do me a favor and I will save you from Dr. Renkin. In fact," Borodine sat back and pointed a long, bony finger, "I will tell you something very interesting about that man out there who wants you and your brother killed."

"Dr. Renkin? What about him?"

Borodine kneaded his leg. "Cooperate and I'll tell you." They stared at one another. "Now, I must know what either of you learned about Jet Stream. It affects some very serious work we are doing. If Lofton knows too much, we can simply shut the operation down. It will save us a lot of time and expense--"

"And embarrassment."

"Possibly. What happens to Lofton is not our concern. He is here. Fine. He's resourceful and may remain free, or perhaps escape to..." Borodine waved a hand, "...to South America. Possibly, you can someday be reunited." Borodine leaned forward and spread his palms. "It's just the fact that knowledge of Jet Stream may be out. That's what concerns us."

Dobrynyn looked at the man and considered his options. Hatch seemed almost plaintive. He really needed to know. That was it. Give him enough to buy time. *But what did he know about Renkin?* "You're worried about Ivy Bells?"

"Where did you hear that?" Borodine stood.

"They had to brief me for the switch. But--"

A loud "whump" shook the building. Reds and yellows flashed through grated windows.

Dobrynyn shook his head and was surprised to see Hatch rise from his knees.

Vito jumped off the counter, ran to the door, and yanked it open.

"Wait!" Borodine said sharply.

Vito paused and turned.

"My pistol. You can't leave me without it."

Vito's lips worked. "Dr. Renkin said--"

A second, smaller explosion, yet with a pronounced "crack," rattled the building.

"Give it to me, you idiot!" Borodine yelled. "We don't know who is behind the assault. You'll need all the help you can get."

Vito nodded, ran over, and handed the Beretta to Borodine. "You better stay here 'til I find out what's goin' down." He ran out and slammed the door.

Borodine's eyes jerked to the window. A deep amber washed over the heavily smudged glass, something crackled outside, people yelled, footsteps pounded on the stairs. He stepped over and looked out. Flames leaped up the building's side near the front. He saw charred wreckage that looked as if it once had been a fuel truck of some sort.

"Police will come," Borodine muttered. He turned to see Dobrynyn struggle against his bindings. Only one thing to do before he ran. He pulled out the Beretta and worked the action while Dobrynyn thumped in his chair, moving toward him.

Borodine's thumb found the safety and flicked it off. He aimed at a wildly gyrating Dobrynyn and fired.

Dobrynyn spun. The chair seemed to twirl beneath him. It teetered and stayed upright. "Filthy *zamp!*" he roared. His shoulder felt numb. Sweat beaded on his forehead. He drew quick breaths and swallowed back the nausea. Hot wetness ran down his arm.

Borodine held his Beretta with both hands and steadied his aim on Dobrynyn's head.

"Hatch!" A voice shouted from the doorway.

Borodine heard and at the same time felt an enormous explosion. A fist, no, something much bigger slammed him against the window. He looked up, then slid down until he was sitting on the floor. Thick wetness ran over his crotch, his legs. His stomach. It throbbed. Ahhhhh, it burned. Pain...he looked down, his eyes blinked at a darkness oozing between his legs. His legs! He couldn't move them.

He raised his head. Felix Renkin stood in the doorway, a pistol dangling at his side. Borodine looked to his left. The Beretta lay with reach. But he felt tired. His arm wouldn't obey the command. He blinked and looked back at a perplexed Dobrynyn...tired...

Dobrynyn looked from the gasping Borodine to the doorway. Renkin stood with pressed lips. They locked eyes.

Renkin croaked, "What did he tell you?" Was there--"

"Dr. Renkin." Carrington's head popped over Renkin's shoulder. He shouted, "We're out of here. Now. Lofton is pinned down outside. We can get out the back before the fire department shows up, they'll call the police."

Renkin whirled. "The front gate. Is it locked?"

"Yes. Come on."

Renkin looked over his shoulder to Dobrynyn.

Carrington cocked an ear, an Ingram sputtered. Voices shouted toward the front stairway. "Please, sir. I've already lost three men!" He nodded to Borodine. "Don't worry about him. Gut wound. He'll be dead, soon. I'll take care of the other one."

"No," Renkin said. "I need him on videotape."

"Videotape? What are--"

"Protection, Carrington. Come on. He'll keep for a minute. I want to check downstairs."

"Yessir." Their footsteps clumped down the hall.

Dobrynyn rested momentarily and caught his breath. The *zamp* gurgled and looked at him. His mouth worked.

He yanked at his ropes. Go! Only minutes to get out, maybe less. How? Wildly, he looked around. There. Those drawers under the counter. Something to cut with.

Dobrynyn heaved against his ropes. The chair lurched and pain clamped over his shoulder.

Leading with his left shoulder, he bounced forward again. It helped. The pain wasn't as bad. Twenty centimeters a thump: The counter was over two meters away, it would take ten to fifteen thumps. He lurched, sweat ran down his brow. His shoulder thudded and surged as bones ground together. He growled at his ropes. He had to catch himself as he almost pitched forward. Head whirling, he paused and took deep breaths.

Four thumps to go--three. As he reached the cabinet, the windows glowed again, redder this time.

An Ingram sputtered. Closer. Someone screamed, a loud, prolonged sound.

Dobrynyn thumped in a half circle and twisted himself to fumble at a drawer. There had to be something to cut with, maybe a knife. He rose slightly, grasping at the chrome handle; his hands finally found it and he arced forward to pull it out. He couldn't stop his pitch. He fell, but he kept his grip, and the drawer came with him. They crashed on the floor. The drawer's contents spilled about him as he rolled to his side. He gagged with pain as torn nerves sent outraged messages to his brain.

Another Ingram sputtered. It sounded as if it was near the lobby. His vision focused.

The *zamp* watched him with a thin, pale smile. His lips moved. He gurgled, "Renkin..."

Dobrynyn groaned and shook his head. A handful of paper clips spilled down his shirt. He shook them off and looked to his knees. A pencil jabbed him as saw a letter opener. He grabbed the handle and ran its blade over the rope.

Carrington was yelling "Vito" from the machine shop.

He worked the letter opener violently. The blade was dull and the ropes were still shiny and strong.

This would take hours. He rested his head on the floor. Something hard lay under his ear. A pair of scissors.

He picked them up and began to cut.

24

Lofton spotted the heavy-set man a millisecond before he plowed into him at full tilt. Lofton had seen him a millisecond earlier. He spun the man and slammed a forearm against his windpipe. The man jerked and fell but not before his spasming hand fired his pistol, pumping two rounds into the asphalt.

"Dick!" someone yelled from behind.

A bullet whizzed over Lofton's head. He ran around the corner, diving behind a dumpster.

Lofton swore. He needed Ullanov's ghost. Why hadn't the other two cars exploded? The fuel truck, still empty of JP-5, had detonated on fumes, but not violently enough. The car--a white Chrysler--had also gone up. But those fires on the other side of the building had been subdued. And the exterior walls of the Trade Winds Tuna Company were merely scorched. He wanted the building alight so the fire department would have to go inside. He listened. No sirens, yet. Carrington's problem had become manageable.

They knew where he was. At least two other men plus Carrington. And Renkin. He'd heard the man's shrill voice. How many guards? He guessed six or seven. When Lofton had left *Brutus* bottomed just outside he'd swum under the gate, surfaced inside the sub-pen, and silently knocked out and tied one drowsy man who languished near the launching basin. Outside, near the fuel truck, two more fell to rabbit punches, and he'd tied them, too.

That left two or three more. But without those two cars blowing up, he would need--

--*Get inside. Now!* Quickly, he checked both directions and ran across the pavement. He crouched beside a heat pumping unit just under an office widow.

The window would be locked, but it offered his only chance for entrance. Around the corner, the front door was on the latch but someone was in the lobby or at least near it. *No way.*

He knelt, palmed his Ingram, and slowly shook his head. What a hashedup assault--the desperate run in *Brutus* to San Diego had absorbed all his attention. No time to plan, no weapons; Ullanov's AK74 was hopelessly corroded with salt water and the damned Ingram had only half a magazine. And surprise and confusion would soon wear off. Carrington and his soldiers would methodically ease him into a corner.

A shadow flicked over the heat pump's rusty housing and remained stationary. Someone inside peered out the window, examining the side driveway. The two cars that should have exploded sat happily within the man's view. *Damnit!*

The hell with it. Now! Lofton flipped the Ingram to full automatic and stood. A surprised face jerked down toward him.

Realizing he was too late, the guard screamed as his weapon, another Ingram, rose.

Lofton squeezed a quick burst into the man's chest. The window shattered and the guard flew backward.

Lofton reached in, unlocked the window, and jerked it open. He scrambled onto the ledge and was almost through when feet pounded down the driveway. Whoever it was shouted, "Lofton!" A shotgun blast erupted over Lofton's head. The glass blew out as he hit the floor and rolled into a desk, banging his head. The feet thudded closer, a shadow whipped past the window. Footsteps dashed around the corner toward the front door.

"Vito, no!" Carrington's voice drifted from the first floor machine shop on Lofton's right.

"I winged the sonofabitch!" The front door crashed open.

"Wait, I said." Carrington was nearer. Lofton fumbled at his Ingram. Glass shards tore his hands and knees as he crawled on all fours toward the door. There! The staircase to the second floor was just across the hall.

"Vito! Damnit!" Carrington was closing. His voice jiggled.

The double doors burst open and Vito lurched into the hall with a double-barreled sawedoff shotgun. He stopped, and his mouth dropped open. He fired. Lofton wrenched back as an enormous blast shook the room. A six-inch-square area of the door jamb disappeared in white smoke where his head had been.

Lofton lurched to the doorway and raised the Ingram toward Vito's weaving shape. He fired the last of his magazine. Two rounds punched through a double door; one hit Vito in the left shoulder, another blew off his left ear, and the last round penetrated the top of his forehead. Vito's eyes rolled up and he thudded heavily on the floor next to his shotgun.

Lofton looked back for the dead guard's Ingram. It was lost under a desk. *No time!* Tossing the empty machine pistol aside, he jumped across the hall and dashed up the stairs. He had just made the landing when feet skidded to a stop behind him.

"Lofton. You! You--"

Bullets splattered the wall as he twirled around the corner and ran up the stairs.

Carrington pounded behind him.

Panting, Lofton gained the second floor and ran down the hall.

"Brad. Down."

A heavily bruised face, his own, peeked around the corner at the far end. His hand held a small, dark pistol. Anton! Lofton fell flat and slid on his belly.

Dobrynyn fired.

The bullet went over Lofton's head.

"Sonofabitch!" Carrington took refuge on the stairway and clacked a new magazine into his Ingram.

"Anton?"

Dobrynyn yelled. "Through that door. Quick!"

Lofton looked up. A door stood open two feet to his left. The old accounting room. He leaped and made it through the doorway as Carrington fired a short burst. His bullets chewed the hallway wall and door jamb above him. Some ricocheted and spent themselves at the hall's end, near Dobrynyn.

He rose and kicked the door shut. The room was dark, but he found a chair and yanked it over and wedged it under the doorknob.

Another burst ranged down the hall. Carrington let out an incredulous cackle. "I can't believe this. Throw that peashooter out, Ivan. This thing can chop you to pieces."

"Up you, spook."

Lofton stood next to the door and bit a thumbnail. Carrington did have the firepower. And no sirens yet. How could he delay? Who else was--

"Eyagghh." It was an inhuman sound.

Lofton spun. A man lay on the floor. His arms were splayed out. Even in the soft lighting he could tell the glistening about him was an enormous pool of blood.

He pressed an ear to the door. Quiet. Padding over, Lofton knelt beside the man.

Borodine's mouth gaped open, spittle ran down his chin, his breathing was shallow, almost imperceptible. But his eyes moved quickly. They found Lofton and focused on him. He groaned again. Loudly.

Lofton jumped.

"*Dobrynyn*," the man gurgled.

The man's inflection was strange. He'd rolled the "r." Lofton took a chance. "*Da*."

Borodine's arm raised slightly, then fell. "*Ya khachu vam rasskazat' o Renkinye.*" I wanted to tell you about Renkin.

"*Nu, shto o nyom?*" What about him?

"*Renkin.*" Borodine's voice was very low, almost a whisper. He pronounced it "Renkeen." "*Felix Renkin vash otets.*" Felix Renkin is your father.

"No!" Lofton grabbed the man's shoulders. "Who are you?" he yelled in English.

Borodine's eyes blinked rapidly. His breath rattled. "*On brosil vashu mat',*

Annu Lubeck, do tovo, kak vy rodilis'." He deserted your mother, Anna Lubeck, before you were born.

"Pochemu?" Why? Lofton gaped at the figure beneath him. *It can't be.* The man gurgled. Lofton realized he was trying to mutter last convoluted words and not listening.

The corner of Borodine's mouth turned up. His lungs heaved and he breathed. *"U nas yest' fotografii gdye oni byli vmeste. On ubezhal na Dal'nyi Vostok. Kunitsa byl tam, kogda bomba ubila vashu mat'."* We have pictures of them together. He ran to the Far East. Kunitsa was there when the bomb killed your mother.

Borodine sighed; his lips quivered. *"On rabotal dlya nas. Sorok lyet. V nachale on byl Amerikanskim kour'erom. On nam daval meshki."* He worked for us. Forty years. A courier at first. He gave us pouches.

Pictures. Blackmail? Kunitsa! Lofton's mind spun. Kunitsa...who? Where had he heard that name. Anton! He--

"Dobrynyn..."

Lofton could barely hear him. He placed his ear next to the dying man's mouth. *"Da?"*

"...vash otets, Dobrynyn." Your father. Borodine's eyes fixed on the ceiling. He gave a prolonged sigh and his soul escaped with the last of his breath.

Lofton sat back. His eyes darted wildly. Who was this man? Felix Renkin a traitor since his days in the Navy, the early fifties?

Kunitsa! Anton's foster father had been named Kunitsa, an NKVD sergeant who had served in Berlin and adopted Manfried LubeckCAnton. Ernst Lubeck--Lofton. Anna Lubeck--his mother. And this man had just uttered her name. Anna! A prostitute, Anton had told him in Petropavlovsk.

He pressed his palms to his temples. Anna Lubeck *was* their mother. Felix Renkin *had* sired him and then run off.

The door kicked open behind Lofton. The chair shattered. Pieces flew across the floor and light spilled into room, silhouetting Ted Carrington.

Lofton saw the Ingram's muzzle and squeezed his eyes closed. Silence. Nothing happened. *Why am I still alive?* He opened his eyes. Carrington stood, his feet apart, his machine pistol still aimed at him.

Sirens. He heard sirens.

"Carrington! Hurry!" Felix Renkin's voice drifted from the back stairwell.

"Yessir." Carrington looked at Lofton. "Up! Now."

Incredulous, Lofton rose to his knees.

"Move, you sonofabitch. We haven't got any time to screw with you." He fired a short burst. Bullets pumped into the floor three feet from Lofton. "Hands on your head. Now!"

Lofton jumped up, put his hands on his head. Carrington stepped behind and prodded him to the back stairwell. As they descended, the sirens grew louder. Two, three minutes away, Lofton figured.

Carrington moved him through the machine shop to *Brutus*'s chamber. It was dark. Lofton squinted at two shapes next to the launch basin. One shape, Dobrynyn was on his knees at the ramp's edge, his hands over his head. The other, Felix Renkin stood behind him pointing a pistol at Dobrynyn's back.

Adrenaline coursed through Lofton's system as Carrington prodded. He drew himself up, with flared nostrils. The man that stood before him, the one he had seen stab and bludgeon Les Thatcher in this very room, the one who had caused the deaths of innocent fishermen for his own traitorous intent, the one who had consigned him to Dr. Sadka and his death-chambers, the one who now aimed a pistol at his twin brother, this hideously convoluted creature was--his *father*!

"Bastard!" Lofton roared.

"Carrington?" Renkin squeaked.

Carrington stepped close behind Lofton. "Don't try anything, Brad. You'll both die."

Lofton stood three feet from his father, staring.

Renkin's lips moved. He opened his mouth. Nothing came out. At last, he found his voice. "You've caused me a lot of trouble."

"Not enough."

"Down, Brad. Right beside Ivan." Carrington said.

Lofton remained standing while his father stepped back two paces.

"Down, now!" Carrington yelled. His instep slammed the back of Lofton's knee.

It buckled. Lofton dropped to all fours beside Dobrynyn. He rose to his knees seeing dark glistening on his brother's shoulder. As he put his hands on his head he growled, "Are you all right? Did he shoot you?"

Dobrynyn whispered, "I'm OK. That *zamp* upstairs shot me. Then Renkin shot him. He sneaked to me after you--"

"Shut up!" Carrington shouted.

Renkin stepped closer. "Did you get it done?"

Carrington said, "Bodies are out of the driveway. I turned all the lights off and the front door is locked."

"All right. We have enough time." Renkin's toe nudged Lofton's back. "Lofton."

Silence. They listened to sirens pull in front. Radios crackled. Fire extinguisher flasks hissed loudly.

"I don't intend to play with you. Either you talk or your brother gets a bullet in the back of his head. His body will fall in the water right before your eyes," Renkin said.

Tiny reflections sparked off ebony waters three feet below Lofton's knees. "Yes?"

Renkin said. "These bodies around here...bullet holes. There's a dead man upstairs I can't afford to be connected with. The firefighters will demand entrance soon. And I must be gone. So I have a proposition for you."

Lofton said, "make it quick, Felix. Who knows when they'll start chopping down doors?"

"Don't toy with me. And don't delay or I'll kill him. I don't care who he is or who you are."

Renkin had killed the Russian upstairs. And his voice almost cracked. Renkin was serious. Panicked. He would pull the trigger or at least have Carrington do it. "Yes?"

"The *X3*. Is that how you arrived here?"

Buy time. They don't know Ullanov is dead.

Renkin said, "Come on. It should be clear. What I propose is to let you two live as long as Carrington can pilot the *X3* and take me out of here."

Lofton shook his head.

A short burst raked the water next to Lofton. "Now. Damnit!" Carrington yelled.

"All right," Lofton said. "I used *Brutus*, yes."

Carrington asked, "where is it now?"

"Bottomed, right in front of the chamber door."

"And the escape trunk--I've forgotten how it works."

"It's a modified Mann system, set on automatic. A bronze lever is mounted to the trunk overhead. Yank it and the trunk will blow. The interior lights will go on as soon as the deck hatch is closed and dogged."

"Depth?"

"Seventeen feet."

Dobrynyn moaned and grabbed his shoulder.

"Hands on your head, Ivan. I don't give a rat's ass how much it bleeds."

Lofton checked Carrington's Ingram from the corner of his eye. No chance to run. He thought about springing into the water but he and Anton would be instantly sprayed with bullets. Yet they would be killed, anyway. There had to be something. Some way. *Keep stalling.*

"Have to raise the gate, Ted."

"Already done that." Carrington started removing his clothes.

From the corner of his eye, Lofton saw the gate's muddy bottom grazing the water's surface. Carrington could slip *Brutus* in submerged and surface right here.

"Start talking, Brad," Carrington said, tossing his shoes aside. "How much fuel is on board?"

"Twenty eight percent JP5 and 32 percent hydrogen peroxide."

"What kind?"

"Seventy percent solution."

"How far can we go?"

"I used fiftyfifty on the trip to Kamchatka. But I found on the way back there's less fossil fuel residue if you run fiftyfive percent hydrogen peroxide to 45 percent JP5. Then, on the way down here, I increased the mixture to sixtyforty--"

"That's a bunch of crap. You're trying to waste time. Just tell me, what's the remaining fuel range?"

They heard from the side driveway, "Hey Ernie, this window's busted...jeez! Bullet holes!"

"Come on, Brad, you're stalling. Don't screw with me." Carrington's voice was thick, but lower.

"OK," Lofton said. "I would imagine five thousand miles at twenty knots, and more if you lean the JP5 back to 35 percent."

"Come on!" Carrington stood in his skivvies.

"Check the computer if you don't believe me," Lofton said.

They heard, "We need cops."

Carrington said. "Use this, Dr. Renkin. It's on full automatic. Just squeeze the trigger if they give you any trouble."

A spotlight flicked over the frosted bayfront widow.

"Fireboat," Carrington said.

"Or a police boat. Hurry," Renkin urged.

"Back in a minute." Carrington dove cleanly into the water.

A metallic voice crackled from out front, "Hallooo. Is anyone inside?"

"How long will it take, Lofton?" demanded Renkin.

"Two, three minutes if he does it right."

They listened to pounding on the front door. Sirens wailed and drew up.

Renkin whispered, "That man upstairs. Was he alive?"

"He was until you shot him, Dr. Renkin," Dobrynyn said.

Renkin drew a deep breath. "Lofton. He must have been alive when you went in there. Did he say anything to you?"

Lofton watched the water. Bubbles rose to the surface and popped. A minute swirling ruffled the surface. *Brutus* was edging in.

"I asked you a question!" Renkin roared.

"He was dead."

"You're sure?"

Lofton nodded.

"I heard somebody out back--shit! There's a dead guy in the lobby."

"...call a SWAT team..."

"...yeah, keep a close lookout. Make sure nobody leaves....Johnson! Grab your shotgun. You and Pillsbury cover the water side...be careful..."

The water boiled to a creamy foam before them. *Brutus* nudged a piling which groaned heavily. The minisub surfaced kicking spray and hissing air.

Brutus's hatch clanked open. Lofton turned to see Renkin, feet planted, ready to fire.

"Felix?" Lofton said.

"What?"

"Carrington doesn't know about the modified carbon dioxide scrubbing system."

"What?"

"You'd better watch out for chlorine gas, too. And battery cell number five is ruptured, inoperative; Carrington should know about that."

"What is this?"

"What I'm saying is this," Lofton said. "You get aboard and go down below. Give the gun to Ted so he can keep the drop on me and I'll tell him the rest of what he needs to know."

Carrington popped through the hatch. "All set, Dr. Renkin. Come on," he urged.

"And Colonel Dobrynyn starts walking out of here, now." Lofton stood and faced Renkin, his hands still on his head.

Cars roared and screeched to a stop out front. Men shouted and clumped down either side of the building.

Lofton kept his voice level. "The place is loaded with police now. Make up your mind."

Renkin's jaw worked as he moved his head from left to right.

"Go now, Anton," Lofton said quietly.

"Brad, what are you doing?" Dobrynyn whispered.

"Not sure yet. But at least one of us can get out."

"Hurry, please, Dr. Renkin," pleaded a glistening, bare chested Carrington. He looked up. A helicopter thumped overhead. The windows became brightly lighted.

"Go on, Anton," Lofton said, "while Renkin worries about how not to split his fortune with Carrington. Go, now!" He nodded toward the machine shop doors.

"Dr. Renkin!" Carrington almost yelled.

"Carrington," Renkin demanded, "have you been able to determine if one of the battery cells is inoperative?"

"Not yet, sir, I--"

"Please look, now."

Carrington lingered for a moment, then ducked below as soft voices ranged outside the walls. A flashlight played over the window.

"Anton, please, go." Lofton eyed his brother. "I know what I'm doing."

Carrington popped up. "Yes, Doctor, it looks like one, maybe two batteries are trashed. But I can't tell--"

"Hold on, please." Renkin's gold rims flicked back to Lofton. "Tell him."

Lofton nodded. "Also, the second-stage air compressor cooling valve needs replacement because--"

Carrington jumped to the dock and grabbed the Ingram. "That's enough, you bastard. I don't know what you're pulling but if something's wrong, you're going to be there to fix it. Inside! Now!" The Ingram waved to *Brutus*'s hatch. "Both of you."

Lofton's mouth dropped open.

"Police! Hold it right there!" The window had been pried open. Two helmeted heads peeked through. One wore glasses.

"Bastards!" Carrington raised the stubby submachine gun and squeezed off a burst. The window shattered and the policemen ducked. Carrington aimed below the window and fired a second burst through the wall. Ricochets screeched and whined around in the chamber. A deep-throated scream tapered to a whimper. Feet scuffled under the window and withdrew toward the front.

"Now. Everybody inside." Carrington waved the Ingram. "I'm through farting around. You better go first, Doctor."

Renkin stepped onto *Brutus* and scrambled down the hatch. Lofton and Dobrynyn jumped aboard and followed. Carrington grabbed his clothes, threw them inside *Brutus*, and descended carefully with the Ingram. The wheel squeaked as he secured the hatch.

Carrington reached in his jacket, pulled out a pair of handcuffs, and tossed them to Renkin. "Cuff this one to the bunk, Doctor. Use his right hand, that way he won't want to move around too much." He pointed the Ingram at Dobrynyn. "Move, Ivan!"

Slowly shaking his head, Dobrynyn stepped forward and sat at the aft end of the pilot berth. He grimaced as Renkin snapped a cuff around his bloody wrist, then yanked it up and snapped the other end to an overhead bracket.

Renkin studied the key for a moment. He tossed it across the aisle where it bounced against the throttle and came to rest.

Gingerly, Carrington eased forward around Lofton, the Ingram pointed at his belly. He stood next to the armchair. "What's this mean?" He nodded toward the CRT panel.

Lofton followed his gaze. The Master CRT was blank. NAV still blinked with the program he'd set for the trip from Catalina. Then, POWER! *Good God!* It read:

AUTOHEAT

Lofton's heart raced. He swallowed. "Just the automatic airconditioning system, Ted. It's trying to compensate for our body heat and humidity."

The hydrogen peroxide ready service tank gauges had picked it up too late. *How long?* He looked at the clock: 0319. Dobrynyn grimly followed his gaze and nodded.

"You sure? It started blinking the minute I powered up. And the override command didn't work," Carrington said.

"Yes." Lofton swallowed again.

"That's more bull," Carrington said. "But you'll fix it soon." He nodded aft. "In there."

"What?"

"There, jerkface." He pointed to the tunnel hatch.

Lofton stood immobile. Maybe he should tell them. His heart pumped faster.

"Go, or he's dead." Carrington switched the Ingram to single fire and aimed it at Dobrynyn.

Lofton looked at his brother.

Dobrynyn barely shook his head.

He grabbed the wheel, spun it, and opened the hatch. Turning around, Lofton crawled in backward.

Carrington walked aft and slammed the hatch in his face.

Total darkness. Lofton heard squeaking as the hatch sealed. His mind saw the wheel twirling.

Then, within seconds--Carrington was fast--water roared in the ballast tanks. *Brutus* sank on an even keel, and the DC motor wound up. *Brutus's* screw bit the water, the minisub backed out of the pen.

Lofton cocked an ear and waited for Carrington to screw up and snag something. Thirty long, silent seconds passed. Nothing. Carrington remembered how to conn *Brutus*. He'd escaped cleanly.

Lofton squeezed his eyes close, wiped sweat off his forehead, and bit his thumbnail. The last thing he had seen on the Power CRT before Carrington slammed the hatch was:

AUTOHEAT!
H2 O2 TRANSFER PUMP
H2 O2 READY SERVICE TANK
$H_2 O_2$ MANIFOLD

Brutus gathered sternway. Twenty seconds later, the submarine vibrated. Carrington had shifted to an ahead bell. The screw beat the water, slowing the sub's sternway and making it wallow. Soon, Carrington would shift the rudder, gather forward momentum, and head through San Diego Bay. Nothing stood in Renkin's way now. Except all that damned oxidation kicking off the hydrogen peroxide. *How soon?*

The shaking stopped. *Brutus* had headway on now. A hiss. The bow dropped. That damned Carrington was maneuvering the boat with depth commands, having no idea of *Brutus's* trim. *Brutus* might hobbyhorse. Carrington could stick the nose in the mud.

Mud! Stop! Air!

Lofton scuttled to the aft hatch, spun the wheel and jumped into the motor room. Another hiss. Carrington worked the after trim tank. Lofton sensed *Brutus's* plane. Carrington had things under control.

Hurry.

He snapped on the light switch. The DC motor whined softly behind him. Where was it? *Up there!* He reached to an overhead panel labeled "DC motor--main circuit breaker." Frantically, he flipped the door open, found the toggle, and threw it.

The breaker clicked loudly and the DC motor stopped. *Brutus*'s stern squatted as they lost headway.

The damned valve, where is it? I built this turd. Why can't I remember where a simple check valve is? He lifted a deck plate. There! The after trim tank. And there was the check valve between the HP line to the trim tank.

Screwdriver! He crawled to the other side of the motor room, finding the tool box. He pawed the lid open. Hex wrenches, pliers, channel locks, a hammer all clattered on the deck plate. His eye darted to the hydrogen peroxide fuel block as he reached for the screwdriver. "Ahhhh!" Totally brown. Totally rusted, right up to the fuel inlet.

How long before Carrington rips open the hatch and hoses me down with his Ingram?

Lofton thrust the screwdriver at the check valve. The blade bounced over the gagging screw slot. He reached again. It clicked home. He twisted frantically. The screwdriver's blade slipped out after four turns. He fumbled, swore, seated the blade again, and twirled. Twelve turns. Fifteen. Twenty.

Enough.

He tossed the screwdriver aside and reached for the pressure relief valve. *OK, bypass the vent check valve and hold on.* He cracked it slightly. It hissed. *How much?*

Give till it hurts! He twisted the valve all the way. Compressed air blasted into the compartment. The space misted momentarily, then cleared. His ears. He could feel it. He swallowed rapidly as pressure built up.

Give till it hurts. Lofton kept swallowing. He couldn't relieve the pain anymore. His sinuses ached. An old tooth filling pounded at nerve endings.

He closed the valve, then scrambled in the tunnel. *OK, Ted.*

A lurch. *Brutus* had bottomed. He gripped the hatch rim tightly and braced his feet as best as he could against the slippery shaft. He had to stay in position when--

--the forward hatch wheel glinted as it quickly arced around. *Hold on!*

The hatch exploded open. Lofton heard a loud, gurgling scream. The air misted and roared. Surprised, he was torn from his grip.

Compressed air shot him down the twenty-foot tube like a cannon. Lofton ejected with his legs askew. The inside of his left knee caught the galley table leg and spun him sideways. His right shoulder and head slammed against the ladder.

"...Brad..." Dobrynyn's voice drifted through.

Renkin screamed and retched.

The mist cleared. Papers fluttered among dust and debris.

"Brad!" Dobrynyn yelled.

Lofton blinked. "Uhhhhh." Pain. He tried to move. Throbbing. His leg, the left one. It wouldn't move. His right shoulder, too. He rubbed his head, thick stickiness. Blood. Fire raged in his shoulder as his leg throbbed. He tried to roll. Both broken.

"Brad. Damnit!"

"Yeah." Lofton gasped and opened his eyes. Renkin stood before him choking. The focus blurred, then held. He looked up behind him.

Carrington. *My God!* The hatch had blasted open, forcing the wheel through Carrington's chest. With buckled knees, Carrington was pinned to the bulkhead, his chin and arms draped uselessly over the hatch. Blood flowed from his mouth as he gagged. Carrington's tongue and lips quivered. His eyes rolled to Lofton. He blinked once, then was still. The pupils dilated, his gaze became fixed.

Lofton tore his eyes away. "Anton?"

"Check the CRT, Brad," Dobrynyn said urgently.

Lofton raised his head, his shoulder raged. He found the CRT panel. Both Power and the large Master CRTs read:

A U T O H E A T ! ! !
EJECT
EJECT
EJECT

Lofton's eyes grew wide. "Let's go." He rolled to his left shoulder, then fell back. "Uhhhh!"

"What's wrong?" Dobrynyn stood and jerked against the hand cuff. Four feet separated the twins.

"Think my leg and shoulder are broken. Can't move," Lofton sputtered.

Renkin stepped toward Lofton with the Ingram. "What did you do back there? Why did we lose power?"

"Autoheat. Irreversible," Lofton rasped through clenched teeth. "Sub's going to blow up within minutes. Maybe seconds. Uncuff Anton and let's get out of here."

"Nonsense. This is another one of your--"

Renkin's head spun. Dobrynyn had pulled a long screwdriver from a locker and fished at the handcuff key across the aisle.

"No!" Renkin yelled. He jumped back and knocked away Dobrynyn's hand. The screwdriver clattered to the deck.

"I swear. It's going to blow." Lofton coughed.

Renkin walked forward, bent over the armchair, and picked up the handcuff key. "Enough of your tricks. You'll tell me how to regain power."

They watched incredulously as Renkin held the key up, popped it in his mouth, and swallowed.

Felix Renkin's lips glistened in a twisted, triumphant smile. "Nobody's going anywhere, except into the Pacific." He stepped back toward Lofton. "What did you do back there?"

Master gave a low continuous buzz. They turned to look. It rapidly flashed on and off:

<u>**A U T O H E A T ! ! !**</u>
EJECT NOW
EJECT NOW
EJECT NOW

Renkin growled, "How do you turn that thing--yeachh."

Dobrynyn clamped his forearm around Renkin's throat and yanked the wiggling man's back against his chest. "Brad, the drawer above you. Quick!"

"What?" Lofton watched the struggling figures through a haze. Adrenaline should be pumping now. But no. He faded.

Powerful legs were scissored around Renkin's struggling torso. His glasses fell and hung by one ear. He reached behind to claw at Dobrynyn's eyes.

Dobrynyn easily twisted his head away. "Brad, pull that drawer. The kitchen knife. Quick!"

"No! Stop!" bellowed Renkin.

"Our only chance, Brad. Above you. The drawer. Pull it out on top of you."

Lofton blinked. A voice echoed in his mind, *"vash otets,"* your father. He swallowed. His eyes rolled. Les Thatcher stood before him, his mouth open wide. Both hands feebly wiggled the screwdriver sticking out of his chest. He saw the *Kunashiri Maru* roll over, people scrambled up her side as guns roared at them. He saw--

"Brad!"

"...yeah..." Lofton reached up and pulled the handle as hard as he could. The drawer bumped over a catch and crashed down on him. Cheap galley utensils spilled to the deck.

"You can't. No! I'll pay you. Anything. You'll be rich. We--we'll be together," Renkin shrieked.

Lofton rolled his head and spotted the knife on his right, close to his broken shoulder. He reached over with his left hand. Fumbling, pain, his palm found the handle. It spun away and his arm flopped back. The lights faded again.

"Brad. Wake up!" Dobrynyn's voice roared through his haze.

Come on. Do it. He rolled on his right shoulder. Sparks of pain flashed through his shoulder and down his side. He gripped the handle and fell back. Better. He blinked sweat from his eyes. Still conscious, no fadeout this time.

"Stop! Noooo! You can't. I'm your f--"

Dobrynyn's fisted palm smacked into Renkin's nose. Blood spurted, Renkin's splayed hands jinked out before him.

Lofton tossed the knife. It sailed past Renkin's jerking head and fell on the bunk. Dobrynyn grabbed it and secured a grip. Then he plunged the blade into a screaming Felix Renkin's chest.

Lofton faded again. He couldn't hear Renkin but he knew the man still screamed. His mouth was wide open and his eyes were squeezed shut. Veins in his throat and forehead bulged.

Lofton swung his eyes to the galley depth gauge: 42.6. The clock read 0326...

...What was it? His eyes were still on the clock: 0329...

Yelling. A voice, frustrated, filtered through the haze in Russian. "Where's the damn stomach?"

...Ripping, tearing sounds...odors--excrement. Offal gushed and plopped to the deck...

...0332. AUTOHEAT...

...A loud hiss, the deck moved...hands under his back. Pain surged through his shoulder and neck. "What?"

"Easy, Brad. We're on the way up."

Lofton coughed, then retched as Dobrynyn gently pulled him to his feet and propped him against the ladder. "Anton...hatch, unscrew...turn the wheel...now...pressure..."

Dobrynyn nodded and spun the wheel above them. The main hatch blew open when *Brutus* rose to within three feet of the surface. Air roared past them and tore at their clothes and hair. With the pressure equalized, water rushed in just as *Brutus* bobbed to the surface.

Up. Lofton was going up. He forced his eyes open. Felix Renkin was splayed among his viscera in an enormous pool of blood. His torn abdomen was a dark-red, glistening cavern.

Lofton was out and slithering over the casing. Water. Cold, it revived him. A hand tugged at his collar. Shouts in the distance. An impossibly bright light played over him. Something went "thump, thump, thump".

He was gliding on his back, water burbling past his ears. He looked up. Overhead, the weather had cleared; dark sky, plenty of stars, no moon...velvet...beautiful. The Coronado Bridge nearby. A truck blasted toward the top. *Got it made.*

The water lit up. A giant fist hit his back and lifted him. Noise, roaring; fire shot above him as water cascaded and tossed him. The flames spread, crackling, seeking. The water was suddenly hot and steaming. A caldron, it boiled around him, over him as he tumbled. On fire. The water was on fire. JP5? It blazed around Lofton as he surfaced. Oily smoke made him gag and retch. The hand no longer pulled at his collar. Gone.

Paddle. He jabbed water at the flames a couple of times with an open left palm. Three more jabs; he splashed a small clearing in the inferno. He gasped, his mouth barely above the surface. It hurt too much to kick with his right leg. Waterlogged clothing pulled him down. He couldn't hold it. He choked in the smoke. Salt water bit his windpipe.

Let it go...

No! He stroked once more and found another breath.

A bruised face, his own face with a black eye, emerged. Anton. Maybe five feet away.

Hold on. Another stroke. Another breath. The face drew closer. Dobrynyn's hand gripped his collar and tugged again. Lofton's torso rose to the surface as powerful legs kicked beneath him. The light dimmed, they were past the fire.

Alive! Lofton could breathe and blinking his eyes, the night, stars, came into focus. Cool water gurgled past his ears and soothed the gash on his forehead. "Anton..." He spat salt water.

"Hold on, Brad, almost there."

Lofton took a deep breath. "That guy upstairs was still alive..."

Dobrynyn grunted with another stroke. "What?"

"Guess what he said--"

Dobrynyn's scissoring foot jiggled Lofton's broken leg. He groaned loudly as renewed pain consumed him.

"Easy Brad. Here they are."

The water gently swirled as a patrol boat backed toward them and idled in neutral. White, burbling exhaust rose around a stern light. Lofton blinked, seeing two uniformed figures outlined against the sky. They knelt at a transom gate and reached to him.

Dobrynyn's thick accent warned, "Please be careful. I think his shoulder and leg are broken."

Strong gnarled hands cradled Lofton's head; another pair reached under his back. The stern dipped with a wave and they slid him easily into the boat. He looked up and caught his brother's eye as he was hauled over the transom. They winked at one another, just before Lofton passed out.

EPILOGUE

the danger's passed,
the wrong is righted,
the veteran's ignored,
the soldiers's slighted.

Nelson De Mille, *Spencerville*

A fresh breeze stirred San Diego Bay. Zephyrs spiraled up Point Loma and ruffled Lofton's hair as he shook hands with the three men. They got into their car and drove off. When he was sure they were gone, he turned and walked to his apartment, hobbling up the front step.

"They've left?" Bonnie took off her glasses and looked up from the sofa, where a magazine lay open but unread. Tim sat on the floor near the TV.

Lofton nodded and stared into space.

She touched him. "Brad?"

"He takes a plane for London tomorrow. Then, Aeroflot, directly to Leningrad."

Bonnie stood and threw her arms around him. "Tomorrow! Couldn't they wait until the wedding?"

"We'll just have to switch our honeymoon to Russia." Lofton dropped his arm to her waist, a more comfortable position. Both shoulder and leg casts had been off for only a month. "The decision went all the way up to the president. He settled it last night with their president on the hotline."

Bonnie said, "I know he'll be happy but I worry about them not keeping their word."

Lofton nodded toward Tim and walked into the kitchen. "Here's the way the State Department guy explained it to me." He leaned against the counter and ticked off his fingers. "Capitol Hill is angry about all the spies in high positions over the past few years--"

"Can't blame them."

"Yes. They're trying to see if there's a way they can seriously get them to knock it off. And since Renkin was in the NSC, that directly involves the president, which means another layer to contend with. And, in a way, the Oval Office is upset at me for blowing the whistle--"

"You didn't blow any whistle."

"I know. But that's how they look at it. I'm a thorn in their sides is what the guy implied to me."

"Why don't you ask Phillips to reopen the hearings?"

"He's already figured out all there is to know about Renkin's activities and his overseas bank accounts. And if they did reopen the hearings, they'd be closed entirely this time. There isn't much to be gained, anyway."

Bonnie let out a breath. "So it really was settled last night?"

"*Glasnost,* hon. The Soviets are embarrassed--"

"They should be."

"And they have to manage their losses before everything gets out of hand. The State Department said the Japanese are going to demand public apologies and reparations for the *Kunashiri Maru.* Greenpeace is sending two ships to Kamchatka to protest the nuclear torpedo. They'll try to make an international stink out of it."

"Shouldn't be too much trouble."

"Yes and no. It was a low-yield blast, five kilotons. It didn't leave much of an atmospheric trace. But the thought of it is enough to rile Greenpeace."

"I wonder how the Soviets will handle it?"

"They plan to say the torpedo was an attempt to use new technology to recover a deepwater nuclear mine they had lost twenty years ago. The KGB will take the heat for the *Kunashiri Maru.* There's not much they can do about that." Lofton shrugged. "So, they figure if Anton is welcomed back to the USSR with a pardon and restoration to service--hell, they're going to promote him to full colonel--that they will look like good guys and hold on to their *Glasnost* image."

"The KGB will never forget, Brad. It worries me."

"Me, too. But the president was really adamant on that point. He specifically said that if anything happened to Anton, like a convenient "heart attack or auto accident," he would make sure negotiations for their bank lines of credit would break down. And I think Congress would back him on that."

He gave a thin smile. "The good part is their president promised to let Anton emigrate to the U.S. in two years if he wants to."

Which reminds me." He jabbed a thumb toward the street. "The spooks believe me, now." He reached into the fridge and pulled out a can of soda pop. "Want one?"

She shook her head. "Believe what?"

"They finished examining *Brutus*'s wreckage. Their experts agree with the autoheat scenario. Murder charges wont be pressed."

"Kind of them."

"Not really. It's something they would have over my head. 'Don't make a public stink and we won't have you indicted for murder.'"

"You would win, hands down."

"Yeah, but my life would be screwed up for years defending myself. And it would cost me a bundle."

Lofton's leg was tired. He'd been standing too long and walked back to the living room and eased onto the sofa.

Bonnie followed, saying, "I can't help thinking that if Renkin and Carrington were still alive, you wouldn't have to go through all this."

Lofton turned to her. "Bonnie, I..."

"I know it's hard for you to talk about what happened in *Brutus*. But you should, you know." She rubbed his back absently and looked into the distance.

"It blew up...just after Anton and I rose to the surface..."

"I know." She took his hand. "But if the divers' trunk had cycled more quickly Renkin and Carrington would be alive and in jail. The pressure would be off. You wouldn't have been the focal point in the Phillips hearings--"

"I got a call this morning from my old boss at Jenson Industries."

Bonnie shook her head slightly. "All right. What did he say?"

"They want me to head up a submarine program using fuel cells. He said the Navy has ordered twenty modified *X3s*. They just finished building a second *X3* prototype and they want me to begin by supervising the shakedown. They're planning larger ones: seventyfive-footers. Then a big one: three thousand tons."

"What about autoheat problems?"

"Snyder promised full research and development support, especially in materials, chemistry, and corrosion control. Plus, I've got a few ideas of my own."

"So what did you tell him?"

"I said I want to run a program where boats aren't blowing up all the time. I have to be sure of their commitment before I accept."

A commercial popped onto the screen. Tim groaned and rolled to his back.

Lofton reached over and mussed his hair. "You ready to drive the boat today?"

"You bet! Is Anton going too?"

"Yep. He'll grind for you and trim jib. I'll do the mainsheet."

Bonnie shook her head with a chuckle. "Thanks, guys. There's nothing left for me to do except pass sandwiches." Rising, she gathered her sailing gear from the bedroom and walked to the kitchen. She came out with their lunch bags and handed them to Tim. "Here, Rambo. You get to take this out to the car."

"OK." Tim dashed out.

Lofton leaned against the front door, his jacket in his hand.

Walking into the foyer, she saw it in his eyes. "Your leg hurts, doesn't it? Maybe we shouldn't go."

"Are you kidding? My first time sailing in over seven months. The physical therapist said OK."

"Then what is it?"

Lofton jiggled the front door lock and stepped onto the porch, thinking about what the spook had said earlier today. The agent looked up and down the street and answered the question Lofton had been asking for months. The man who died of the stomach wound was authentic. He was Captain Second Rank Yuri Borodine of the Soviet Navy's Pacific Fleet Intelligence--Fifth Division. Most likely, he was Renkin's control.

"Brad?" Bonnie put her hand to his cheek.

Lofton kicked at the doormat. Borodine had gasped "*Felix Renkin vash otets*" before he died.

He looked up. "There's something else Anton has to know. Everything's been so jumbled we haven't had time to really talk in private. Better do it today."

Bonnie said, "I see...if you tell him will it help with your nightmares?"

He let her pass and closed the door. "Maybe, in time." He tried a smile.

Tim shouted at them. "Brad, come on, it's blowin' out there. What a blast! I got the car started."

Lofton followed them outside. Tim was right. A twelve-knot breeze tugged at his shirt, promising a good romp on San Diego Bay. He wondered what classes of one-design sailboat they raced on the Gulf of Finland. The sailing was supposed to be excellent there. Solings? Stars? Anton would show him next month when they got to Leningrad.

He sniffed the wind again, ignoring the throbbing in his leg. It would feel better in the car. As he walked, he was able to put the pain out of his mind by thinking as he had done many times in the past weeks about Bonnie: his luck that she would always be with him, that there was Tim, and that now he even had, gloriously, a brother. They were all three so precious to him, the more so that they had come late into his life. It didn't matter. They were something he had never had, something other people took for granted. Brad Lofton had found a family.

A Call to Colors

General Douglas MacArthur's promise to the Filipinos was "I shall return."

But it will take 165,000 troops and 700 ships in the bloody battle of Leyte Gulf to do it.

Among them is the destroyer USS Matthew and her skipper, Commander Mike Donovan, a veteran haunted by earlier battles. What Donovan doesn't know is that a Japanese admiral has laid an ingenious trap in the Leyte Gulf.

But Donovan faces something even deadlier than Japanese battleships: explosives secretly slipped on board by saboteurs, set to detonate at any time.

Now the ship's survival hinges on the ability of Donovan and his men to dismantle a bomb in the midst of the panic...and the chaos of history's greatest naval battle.

ACKNOWLEDGMENTS

My thanks go to Captain Jerry M. Sullivan and Lieutenant John W. Nelson of the U.S. naval submarine forces (now John W. Nelson, MD) for their assistance. Thanks also to Dr. Nancy L. Segal of California State University Fullerton for her guidance on the subject of twins separated at birth. Dr. William H. Heiser, Distinguished Visiting Professor at the U.S. Air Force Academy and Roger E. Anderson of Aerojet contributed mightily in the fuel cell area. Dr. Russell J. Striff provided advice on medical matters. Susan Kechekian at USC's Department of Slavic Languages was immensely helpful with Russian translations. Steven G. Reed, the Rastello brothers, Doug and the late Mark Rastello, and Gary Jobson are among many who inspired what I have learned about sailing over the years. Any errors describing the settings or technologies represented here belong only to me.

Please don't hesitate to visit my website at www.JohnJGobbell.com for information on all my novels, some articles, and some information on yours truly.

Last, I'm luckiest when it comes to my wife, Janine, who stuck with me over many long hours.

JJG
Newport Beach, California

ABOUT THE AUTHOR

JOHN J. GOBBELL is a former Navy Lieutenant who saw duty as a destroyer weapons officer. His ship served in the South China Sea, granting him membership in the exclusive *Tonkin Gulf Yacht Club*. As an executive recruiter, his clients included military/commercial aerospace companies giving him insight into character development under a historical thriller format. An award-winning author, John has published eight novels. The books in his popular Todd Ingram series are based on the U.S Navy in the Pacific theater of World War II. John and his wife Janine live in Newport Beach, California.

Sign up for John J. Gobbell's newsletter at
severnriverbooks.com/authors/john-gobbell
johnjgobbell@severnriverbooks.com

Printed in the United States
by Baker & Taylor Publisher Services